I, Vampire
Book I: Hiding in the Shadows

Ian O'Brien

Wolverine Press— Elkhart, IN
ISBN: 978-1-7374920-0-9
Library of Congress Control Number: 2021914212
Title: *I, Vampire (Book I: Hiding in the Shadows)*
Author: Ian O'Brien
Digital distribution | 2021
Paperback | 2021

Chapter 1
Night Prowlers

As far as Greg Zook was concerned, it had been a truly exceptional Friday evening. It had started the way all really good Friday nights begin—with a case of beer supplied by Marty's older brother. They'd split it 4-ways, with everyone getting a "six" except Marty, who was drinking Jack Daniels. Greg and Neal were both 17, John was 18 and Dave, the older member of their "gang" was a respectable 19. They were all too young to drink, according to Uncle "big brother" Sam, but they were all old enough to know what was what—Neal had knocked-up a girl last year, John already had his first DUI, and Dave was thinking of joining the navy.

They were insufficiently advanced enough in years, however, according to the "powers that be," to purchase or consume alcohol. At least that's the way Mr. French, their remedial English teacher, might have put it. "A guy named French teaching English," Greg frequently said to anyone who'd listen, "there's something about that that just ain't kosher!" Of course Greg didn't have the first clue what the word 'kosher' meant—and couldn't have been bothered to look it up in a dictionary—but he still enjoyed his little joke.

At any rate, something as trivial as it being illegal wasn't going to stop them from drinking. They'd found Pinewood Park pleasantly deserted—all the kids and soccer moms that had been there during the day had all gone home and were probably camped-out on sofas, watching TV, or playing video games—with the really unlucky ones who had to work in the morning probably already getting ready for bed.

Dave, always the joker of the group, had helped set the tone for the evening with a joke he'd read on his favorite UK joke website—a site he frequented more for the reason their daily jokes featured a completely naked girl telling the joke than because he truly understood British humor. Some jokes, however, were low-brow enough that even Dave could grasp their meaning, such as the one he'd discovered in an old *Playboy* magazine and had memorized that afternoon.

"There was this Scotsman, this Englishman and this Irishman that were talking about their favorite pubs," said Dave between drags on his Winston

Light. Y'know" said the Scotsman, "I still prefer the pubs back home. In Edinburgh there's a little pub called McTavish's. Now the bartender there goes out of his way for the locals so much that after your 4th drink he will buy the 5th drink for you."

"Well," said the Englishman, "at *my* local pub, the Fox and Hounds, the barman will buy you your 3rd drink after you've purchased the first 2!"

"Ahhhhh, that's nothing," said the Irishman. "In Dublin there's McHenry's Bar. From the moment you set foot in the door they'll buy you a drink, and then another, all the drinks you like. Then when you've had enough drinks they'll take you upstairs and get you laid—all on the house."

At that point, Dave had stopped to take a swallow of Busch and stub out his cigarette. After taking a look at his friend's faces, to enjoy himself a little during his pause for effect, he'd continued: "Of course the Englishman and Scotsman immediately called the Irishman's claims absolute rubbish, but he swore over and over that every word was true." "Well," said the Englishman, "are you expecting us to believe this actually happened to you?"

"Well, not to meself, personally, no," said the Irishman, "but it did happen to me sister."

Of course that had broken them up, although they'd kept the laughter muted as they didn't want anyone to notice a group of underage teenagers sitting on a picnic table, drinking beer in the dark, and call the cops. They'd kept the conversation quiet for awhile, talking about which teachers they hated, which girls they liked and what they'd like to do with them, and if the Bears would make it to another Super Bowl with their new head coach and their once-again-great defense, or if the Packers would become contenders again and spoil yet another season as they had done to them so many times in the past.

After about the 3d beer or so, Neal had proposed a game of "bullshit". John instantly claimed, "catshit,". Neal was a second behind him with "dogshit," Marty had picked "ratshit" and Dave had jumped in with "apeshit". Greg was a bit nonplussed, as he always went with "apeshit". After pushing back the instant irritation that came with Dave 'stealing' his handle, he'd tried to claim "elephantshit."

"Can't," said John.

"Why not?" Greg has asked somewhat indignantly, punctuating his objection with a large belch.

"Gotta be a one-syllable animal name," explained Neal, "it's the rules".

"Ok, fuck it," he'd said, "I'll be 'snakeshit'. The queen of whores has dropped her drawers," he started, trying to catch Dave off guard, "and nobody can fuck her but apeshit!"

"Bullshit!" Dave responded instantly, with a chuckle.

"Who shit?" Greg had returned, just as fast, and the game was on.

Greg had actually been one of the last two, but had finally said, "Who shit?" when he should have said, "Bullshit". The near victory, along with the final beer he had to chug as his penalty for losing, helped to put him in the right frame of mind for the rest of the evening.

John had come with Marty (on account of the DUI) in Marty's old Ford pickup. The pickup had a railroad tie lashed to the front bumper and was really great for knocking-down mailboxes... but as it wouldn't hold 5, and Neal had ridden his dirt bike. Neal piled into Greg's 1970 Chevy Nova and they followed the pickup out of American park, over to the bridge and across the river, turning in the direction of the old high school. The Chevy was older than most of their parents and was more gray primer-over-bondo than it was red, but Greg still loved the car—one of the few things that really gave him a sense of accomplishment—he'd slung a lot of hamburgers in order to buy the car and pay his uncle to help him drop a new (well-used) engine into it.

"350 cubic inches with a rocket 2-barrel carb," Greg had grinned at Neal as they'd pulled out of the park, "not too many real muscle cars on the roads anymore!" Neal had said something about, "not too many heaps of shit this old still on the roads, either" That had stung Greg's feelings a bit but he'd laughed along. Of course even Greg sometimes felt the desire for a more modern car—particularly on hot days, like today, when the black interior really warmed up and, even with all 4 windows down, he had to drive fast to keep the interior cool. After all, air conditioning hadn't been standard in 1970 and his car had not come so equipped.

The high school had been their first target. Marty pulled onto the sidewalk and up to the overhang by the door on the river side of the school (and thus also the one least likely to be observed from the road). Dave and Neal climbed onto the cab of the truck and then onto the roof of the school, Greg handed up a crow bar, a couple tire irons and a flashlight, then they'd scampered across the roof of the school while the drivers of their respective vehicles parked them back in the shadows and killed their engines. Marty got in with Greg so they could quietly listen to the radio and smoke Marlboro Reds while they waited.

"Just what the fuck are they doing again?" Marty asked.

Back when this was a full-time high school, instead of just 9th graders, before they merged Central with Memorial High School, the seniors used to have a tradition of doing pranks during the last week of school. Neal's brother and a couple other dudes super-glued all the locks shut. That's how they know about the hatch on the roof they are breaking into right now: that's how the custodians got into the school that day so they could open the doors and let the kids in for class. Of course when his older brother broke in, way back in the day, it was a lot easier because you could open the windows back then, before everyone was all paranoid about school shootings and shit, and apparently all you needed to do was jimmy the lock on the window when the teacher was out of the room and go back at night with a screw driver and some really skinny dude who could squeeze through the window. This is a lot more work, I'm thinking, but they're going to really wonder how anybody got in—I doubt anyone is going to remember about the hatch on the roof, that was like ten years ago!

"How are they supposed to find this hatch or whatever it is?"

According to one of my sister's ex-boyfriends who used to work running lights and doing stage stuff in the theater, the hatch is right above the place in the roof of the theater where they have a... an alcove I think it's called... with lights in it to shine down on the stage. So, all they need to do is go over to the roof above the theater, jimmy the lock and it's easy peasy!

For Dave and Neal, it wasn't going quite so easily. They'd found the hatch after a few minutes, just a 4 inch lid set low on top of the roof. As expected, it was locked, with a hasp and padlock. They'd both watched a video on YouTube where someone had used a pair of pry bars to rip apart a padlock and they figured it would be easy enough for the two of them. To their chagrin, they'd discovered they could only fit 1 tire iron, not two, into the loop of the lock. Also, the Master Lock in the YouTube video had been the type with layers of steel pinned together on either side—this padlock was solid brass. After a number of fruitless attempts to pry the lock, Dave had had an epiphany of sorts and they'd attacked the hasp where it was riveted onto the side of the hatch, which turned out to be relatively thin aluminum. After a few minutes of pushing and prying, accompanied by a lot of cursing and grunting, they'd finally succeeded in prying the hasp loose.

The space beneath them was pitch black, which they had also anticipated. The flashlight showed a narrow catwalk with a bar above if for mounting theatre lights. There was a rectangular opening from side-to-side as far as they could see, like some giant mouth. It opened into a darkness that seemed to go on forever, the beam of the flashlight not giving more than a faint illusion of a bottom to the pit in front of the opening. Painfully aware of what a fall from that height would mean, Neal dropped his old gasmask bag with their cans of spray paint down and to one side, the sound of it's impact swallowed up by the immense vastness of the darkness, without a hint of an echo. Following the bag, they carefully lowered themselves onto the catwalk, the only sounds that of their grunting and groaning as their muscles were forced into unaccustomed exercise. After carefully lowering the cap back into place, they turned left and began crawling to where they had been told a door opened into the top of the theater pin-rail, where ropes that held flats and light bars suspended over the stage were tied off like rigging on an ancient sailing ship.

"Fuck"! The flashlight quit on them just as Dave had started down the ladder to the stage, but a few whacks against Neal's palm had it working again. Their footsteps echoed from the orchestra pit in front of the stage, as they walked across the hardwood surface to the stairs that ran beside the wall down to floor level. Coming to the large, heavy door with it's emergency-release handle (it was impossible to lock the doors from the inside as a safety precaution), Dave paused in the cavernous, spooky auditorium, which was making him increasingly nervous as the full implications of what they were about to do... and what would happen if they were caught...

"Now remember," he cautioned, "there may be motion-sensor alarms, so I'm going to run and run fast and hit the door letting the others in; you trash the front of the building, don't forget to prop the inner doors open with the flashlight so they don't lock behind you, which they will if you forget, 'cause you want to be sure you can get back in here and those inner doors lock from the front so don't forget to prop them open to avoid having to go out the front doors where you're more likely to be seen. Don't forget to grab the flashlight on your way back, then go straight ahead to the cafeteria, right to almost the end of the hall, left and right again at the art rooms, then out the side door. I'll probably be waiting at the turn in the hallway to make sure you don't get turned around, but you need to know which way to go in case I ain't there. Got it? Two minutes, that's all the time you have, then get out of there, you sure you got it? Then let's go!

He counted to three, then hit the door hard, slamming it open, and they set out on their separate missions in opposite directions, a can of spray-paint in each hand. Dave had been chosen to let in the others as he was the only one of the group capable of running reasonably quickly, the rest of them existing in various degrees of couch potato. As soon as he hit the safety-release bar, Marty took off at a sprint to the girl's bathrooms to hang some naked photos of men with really large pricks (he'd bought the magazine for just this purpose—at the additional expense of numerous "gay" jokes from his mates). Greg ran to the student affairs office. By pulling a convenient bench over to the receptionist's window, he was just able to get high enough to take a shit on the counter. "Shit happens," he thought to himself. It was then he realized he hadn't brought anything to wipe with. A banner from some ancient athletic event on a wall opposite the cafeteria solved that problem. He smeared the residue on a nearby trophy case, then hung the bedraggled banner on a pair of the cafeteria doors, by threading it through the oversized door handles. As Greg had stopped back with a smile to admire his handiwork in the dim, emergency lighting, a shadow had moved across the floor. Glancing up at the skylight, Greg had seen, or thought he'd seen, movement—a barely-glimpsed, black shape.

"Shit," he'd said to himself, "time to get the hell out of Dodge!"

At a run, he'd headed back to the side door. He hadn't needed to say anything—once his friends had seem him coming at a run, they'd dropped their paint cans and joined him.

"Stupid fucks," Greg had panted, stooping to pick up the discarded paint cans, "fingerprints, you assholes!" They'd slipped out the same door they'd come through, one of the few doors not visible from the street, with Greg using his shirt to wipe the tired, aluminum frame, his belated realization of the danger of latent fingerprints holding him in good stead (not that he was naturally all that bright, but he'd seen enough episodes of CSI to at least have learned about the science of fingerprinting!)

They'd piled into the truck and peeled out of the parking lot, past the football practice fields and tennis courts.

"Slow down and drive normal now, so we don't attract any attention! What the fuck was that all about?" Neal and John had asked simultaneously.

"I saw someone on the roof watching me through the skylight... all the hairs on my neck were standing up and my heart stopped for a moment—if I hadn't just taken a shit I probably would have crapped my pants for the fright it gave me! Anyway, it seemed like it was time to leave... " Greg had explained.

They'd pulled over next to the cemetery and sat quietly, smoking, for a few minutes to be sure nobody was following them. When it was clear they weren't being tailed, Greg had pulled the cans of spray-paint he'd retrieved from the high school off the floorboards on the Nova (with a few words about "assholes leaving fingerprints on evidence for the fuzz to find"), shook them, and smiled to find there was still a bit of paint left in each can.

Following Greg's lead, they'd hopped over the chain-link fence and on into the cemetery. "Ok," Greg had instructed, "let's find some names we can have some fun with!" It didn't take long. James Johnson was quickly altered to become *I have a big Johnson*. Mack become *Mack my day!* Howard was turned into *Howard's it hanging?* Brown became *Brown Nose*, Strunk *Skunk*, Kay *Gay*, and Dennis Carman became *Erick Cartman*. Marty got points for changing Hola into *Holalotta Rosie* and Beach into *Bitch*. Every Jewish name they could find was decorated with swastikas, *Hitler Rules* and similar obscenities. After they'd defaced and defiled a good 2-dozen headstones, they ran out of paint, piled back into the car, and headed back to the park. The beer was long gone but John had a joint, so they'd gotten high and then kicked back, listening to Greg's car stereo (muted, of course, to not attract attention). Eventually, it got late. Marty had to work in the morning and, as his house was within walking distance, he had headed off first. Soon the others made their goodbyes and headed off as well. Greg walked over to the swings and took a good, long piss on the seats, then walked back to his car and headed off home.

"Damn, I wish I had some more beer," he said to himself while turning onto the country road that would take him home. On the subject of alcohol or, more precisely, the Federally-mandated drinking age of 21, Greg though that this was just "downright unfair"! Greg knew older folks who had lived in a time when the drinking age in surrounding states was only 17 or 18. Many was the time they'd hopped the border to drink, legally, in a bar. It just wasn't fair they'd had their good times and then changed to law to stop the younger folks from emulating them.   He'd have rightly called it "hypocritical," had he known the meaning of the word.

"It ain't fair... it jest ain't fair," said Greg to himself for the thousandth time as he tossed the butt of his Marlboro Red out the open window of his Nova. In his rear-view mirror, Greg could clearly see the lighted 7-11 sign disappearing into the trees behind him. A 7-11, incidentally, that sold beer until 2:00 a.m. (except on Sundays). He had the $50 in his pocket he'd gotten for the golf clubs he'd stolen out of "some dumb bastard's" garage last week. The buzz from the 6-pack was already fading—a couple more would have gone down great. "Gotta get me a fake ID," Greg said to himself (also for the thousandth time). Only problem was, fake ID's had become increasingly difficult and expensive to obtain. "Damn Ragheads and Wetbacks," Greg growled to himself, "making life hard for us REAL Americans—I think next week we oughta go over to the college again and find some camel-jockey exchange students and kick the shit outta 'em— that was a fuckin' hoot!" With a belch, Greg pushed the cassette that was sticking out of the stereo all the way in. The well-worn tape clicked, as the auto-reverse drive changed direction, and then the welcome strains of AC/DC's HIGHWAY TO HELL drowned out the noise of the wind rushing through the open window and the faint chirping of crickets.

For no explicable reason, Greg suddenly felt a chill run up and down his spine. "Cops?" he thought to himself? He glanced into the rearview mirror to be sure he wasn't being followed—and likely would have wet himself if he hadn't just "Drained the lizard".

"Hello asshole!" I said from the back seat.

Chapter 2
Just Asking for it

I didn't often hunt humans these days, but every now and then I felt the need to prey on my erstwhile family of man. I'd been cruising around on my favorite motorcycle, the old 1946 Indian 'Chief'. One of the things that endeared it to me, aside from the great acceleration, was that you could actually turn the headlights off. It was old enough that there was no computer record linking it to the original owner (whom I'd drained of blood before taking his bike), so I'd actually been able to have my lawyer apply for a title and tags for it in my own name (under the pretense it had been restored from a wreck—perfectly believable considering the age and rarity of the vehicle).

I'd long ago learned that the best victims were often those who, themselves, were seeking to avoid attracting attention. So, when I saw a car parked in front of the high school, late, on a weekend, with a nervous-looking youth smoking and pacing up-and-down, I knew something was up. I'd parked back by the loading down, quickly scaled the combination support-pillar and drain-pipe, and run across the roof to the skylight, where I witnessed another youth in the act of defecation. Although the only illumination came from EXIT signs and the light in the fish-tank in the office, my heightened vision had no difficulty viewing the panorama beneath me. I estimated the perp's age at around 18. He was about 30 pounds overweight, and his apparently unwashed, shoulder-length hair and untreated acne let me to conclude he didn't spend much time in the company of the fairer sex. His Levi's looked as though he'd slept in them (even in the semi-darkness I could see the creases) and I could just make out the words on his NICKELBACK t-shirt (apparently the kid had some taste in music). I admit one of my failings is to be a bit cat-like at times...occasionally I enjoy toying with my victims... so I allowed him to see my shadow and had paused long enough to be sure he glanced up in order to see me moving away from the skylight. I could sense the fear this provoked... my intention, of course...and could also sense him moving away, so I returned to my bike and waited.

It didn't take long—soon they were speeding off in a panic and I was following, more leisurely, on my darkened Indian. When they stopped, a few minutes later, I did as well... concealed nicely under the shadow of a spreading elm tree. I watched with disdain as they vandalized the cemetery, congratulating myself on having found my victim for the evening. Later, as the others departed, I stole into the back seat of the decrepit Chevrolet. It's sun-faded paint, torn vinyl and worn carpets (and when was the last time a car was made with ashtrays in the armrests?) all attested to the many miles the car had traveled since it's birth in Detroit. I lay on the foul-smelling floor and allowed him to increase in speed, up to a speed I deemed sufficient... around 55 mph, then I sat up, propped my elbows on the back of the front seat —just the one...not 'bucket' seats like you found in all vehicles these days—and waited. It took a few minutes but, eventually, the head came up, turned to look into the rear-view, and the eyes widened with appropriate shock—and I'd said "Hello," just because I felt like toying with him a little before I killed him.

"So, asshole," I said in my most matter-of-fact-prepare-to-meet-your-end voice, "prepare to say hello to oblivion!" With Bruce Lee-like speed, I lunged forward, grasped the steering wheel with my right hand, and spun the wheel to the right. The blue beech tree in front of us must have been a good 6 inches in diameter... not huge, but more than enough. A moment before the impact, I hurled myself out the driver's window, turning a summersault and sliding to a halt on the gravel at the edge of the road. The Chevy Nova, meanwhile, came to a rather noisy end. The front bumper that had once been gleaming chrome but was now pitted with rust, bent as easily as tinfoil upon impact, caught between the hammer of the rushing half-ton of vintage muscle car and a species tree so dense its nickname was 'iron wood' (tinfoil? another bit of verbal nostalgia—it had been aluminum foil for decades).

The heavy, steel "doghouse" collapsed in on itself like a cake in the oven with a dozen, naughty children all jumping into the air and landing in unison. The pimply-faced former pilot of the vehicle continued forward at the same velocity, even as the vehicle slowed, converting velocity into kinetic energy. Even the antiquated safety-belts in the nearly-antique automobile might have offered some protection, but the delinquent behind the wheel had always made a point of defying even the laws that made sense. As a result, he was still moving forward at 55 mph when his chest struck the steering wheel, cracking ribs, knocking the wind out of him, and sending daggers of pain through his no-longer-partially-numbed brain. As the car continued to wrap itself around the tree which stubbornly refused to give ground, as trees are wont to do, the frame began to bend and the back end lifted off the ground. The remaining occupant continued up and over the steering wheel, his head striking the windshield with enough force to send a whole world of light, fireworks and pain through what was left of his consciousness. The skull yielded, pulping some of the brain underneath, but the decades-old windshield yielded as well, aided by a few pellet-rifle-induced cracks that had never been repaired. Its forward progress finally arrested, the car slammed back downwards, throwing it's dying passenger back into the seat.

Brushing the gravel off my black leather biker jacket and wincing at the scuffs on both it and my boots that would have to be polished out, I rose and advanced on the car. Glancing around, I spied what I was looking for—a bit of metal. I picked up what had once been an arm for a windshield wiper. The old metal snapped in half easily enough and I was left with a 6" bit of metal with a sharp edge to it. Perfect! The dying teenager in the front seat was completely oblivious as I grabbed him by the hair—long, curly, dark and greasy—and dragged him over to the window. I jabbed the jagged bit of metal into his neck, trying not to get blood on my clothes as the familiar, red liquid warmth gushed out. Then I fed.

It had been months since my last taste of human blood. I stopped drinking for a moment as it came rushing over me... life, strength, power... and the primitive thrill of having made a kill. I felt good, strong, alive... or should I say "more vibrantly undead?" The guilt for having taking a human life that still dogged me across two centuries I pushed into the back of my mind. I'd killed as a soldier and sent men to their deaths before I ever tasted human blood—and one learns to push the pain and regret aside—much as the priests and politicians must do after they lie to and steal from those poor bastards who trust and rely upon them, I reflected.

Coming back to myself, I thrust the empty husk of the waste-of-sperm who'd been my meal back into the decrepit Nova. I glanced down and saw there were wet spots, blood, on my leather jacket. "Damn," I thought, "not again!" Hastily, I looked around and spied some wadded papers in the back seat. I reached through the rear window and grabbed them. The "D-" and "F" that were clearly visible, in red ink, left no doubt as to what they were. I put the pages to better use and rubbed the blood from off my jacket as well as possible. Satisfied, I tossed the papers at the stiff's feet. It was then I noticed that the glove compartment lid was hanging askew. Apparently it had come open during the collision and was now barely hanging on to the shattered dashboard. What held my interest was what appeared to be the barrel of a pistol, poking out of the deep, dark recesses of the compartment.

Passing quickly to the other side of the vehicle, I reached through the open window and retrieved the weapon—a .357 Colt Python with a 6" barrel and Pachmayr grips. I hefted the pistol, appreciating its significant weight and smooth, chrome finish. Was this shithead old enough to own a handgun, I thought? Probably not...he'd no doubt stolen it. Another welcome addition to my collection, I reflected.

My examination of my new toy was interrupted by the brilliant glow of approaching headlights. I quickly melted back into the trees. It was time to head back to the park, retrieve my motorcycle, and head home.

Chapter 3
Home Again, Home Again

I pulled the old, trusty Indian into the shed and slid the door closed. Although I didn't need it (my eyes were as good as a cat's at night—or a human with night-vision goggles), I switched on a light... just in case someone was watching. Picking up a rag, I spilled a little water on it and rubbed the dust off the gleaming black paint of the 'Chief.' The cooling radiator made faint tick-tock sounds as I finished wiping the bike off and switched off the light.

I pulled the shed door closed and paused a moment to savor the sounds and smells of the night. Crickets chirping, the smell of dandelions and wet grass, grease and gasoline. I glanced up at the moon. Perhaps... yes... tonight I could see the face... he man in the moon. With a start, I realized tomorrow was the 200 and something[th] anniversary of my being "turned" Of course, I wasn't really sure if that was an event to be celebrated... the instant of my immortality or the damnation of my soul, according to some accounts. Just how should I look at it?

Sighing, I turned the key in the lock, opened the heavy, oak door, and entered the old, brick farmhouse that had been my primary residence for the last century, and knelt to pet the dogs, who were dancing and leaping with joy at my return home. They were a motley crew: Max, an enormous Irish wolfhound; Panzer, a stocky Rottweiler; and Brutus, a timber-shepherd (1/3 wolf, 2/3's German shepherd). All of them were large... intimidatingly so... and potentially ferocious; and damned expensive to keep fed.

"How arc my boys?" I asked them. I was not expecting a verbal response, of course, but I could sense their joy at my return and something more... something I interpreted as recognition of my status as the leader of the pack. I scratched each one about the ears, in turn, then shooed them out the door to do their business. They would run about the property for part of the night, then lounge around the porch until I returned before daybreak. They knew the boundaries and would not pass beyond any of the fencing without my express orders. They also allowed me to sleep through the daylight hours with complete peace of mind—nobody in theirs... a right mind, that is... would try approaching the house or my sleeping place uninvited. Attempting to do so was liable to result in some unfortunate consequences. As a legal necessity, I had "No Trespassing" signs posted at the required intervals, advising any wayfarers of the 4-legged security existent on the premises.

Locking and bolting the door, I headed down to my lair in the basement of the old house. It was still several hours before dawn...time enough to finish my current scenario of World of Warcraft 3. Yes, it was probably considered as archaic as "Pong" by younger gamers, as were Age of Empires II and Starcraft II, two of my other favorites, but I still found all of it to be awe-inspiring. I pulled the chain, illuminating the 60 watt, incandescent light-bulb that was the only lighting I used unless I had visitors, turned on my PC, and bent to scratch my favorite cat behind the ears while he kept himself busy rubbing himself about my ankles and purring loudly enough to awaken the dead...or at least the un-dead. Like Caesar, the black American short-hair who now occupied a place on my lap, and other creatures of the night, vampires cannot see in total darkness. Only a small amount of light, such as that produced by a PC monitor, however, is sufficient for us to see nearly as well as most humans could see in full daylight. I suppose one advantage was that it helped keep my electric bill low.

I'm sure that my life (*unlife?*) would come as a shock to many whose preconceptions of vampires were built upon late-night movies—a vampire playing video games and keeping pets? One constant concerning the majority of nocturnal predators, be they cats, owls, foxes, etc., is that they are solitary hunters; the one notable exception being wolves, who will sometimes hunt by moonlight. They are intelligent enough to work together as a pack—which has been known to happen with vampires but, as with many law firms, dissention within the group tends to lead to members leaving the group with great regularity. Cats are smart enough, of course, but few cats would be content to share their prey. As for my kind, I'd occasionally crossed paths with other vampires back in France—indeed, there was a female I visited with a few times, until we lost track of each other—but most of my years among the so-called "undead" have been spent in isolation. My few contacts with others like myself have led me to believe that they, as well, tend to be solitary creatures.

I don't know if any of them share my malady, but I know that I have a problem: I have difficulty sleeping during the daytime. Partly, it's guilt from my once-human conscience for those people I've killed; especially those I didn't have to, when alternate sources of blood were available. Maybe vampires just require less sleep than mere mortals. Perhaps all of us lie awake, haunted by the question of "what if?" Or, possibly it was the question of "what next?" for those of us who believe in a God and our unavoidable damnation. Whatever the reasons, I'm a *vampiric insomniac*, to coin a phrase...

So, what does one do for almost two centuries when one can only sleep 4 or 5 hours per day? It's not like I could take walks in the woods or go to the market during the other 10 or so hours of daylight. Long, summer days were particularly taxing. For the first 150 years or so, I'd read books... many, many books. I stole books from my victims or "borrowed" them from libraries (in later years, I dared not use a library card, not knowing if the computer might reveal it's owner as deceased—or if the person might be known to the librarian...the drawbacks of having resettled in a small town... but for a long time I'd been quite adept at removing books from university libraries and putting them back when finished... although I did keep a few I wanted to read over and over). In the years predating incandescent lighting I had stolen a good many candles and pots of oil, or purchased such with stolen coin, as even a vampire cannot read in total darkness.

I read all the classics: the writings of the philosophes; the novelists, such as Thomas Hardy; the philosophers (I particularly liked the writings of Jeremy Bentham); and the poetry of Keats, Shelley, Coleridge, Yeats, etc. I became particularly fond of the newer, American writers, particularly Poe and Clemens (why he shied away from his own name in favor of Mark Twain continues to elude me to this day... even though I understand there was a relationship to his riverboat days on the Mississippi). I read Remarque, Crane, Burroughs...avidly and eagerly collecting each new writer.

The past few decades brought an explosion in literature. I particularly liked the new genres: science fiction and fantasy. Tolkein, Heinlein, Asimov...then Zelasney, Niven, Dick, Jordan...I read them all. Then, one night in the 1980's, while glancing through a window of a perspective victim, I saw something unexpected and remarkable. It turned out to be a Commodore 64 personal computer. I watched in fascination for over an hour as the owner played a game called "Raid on Bungling Bay" Over the next few years, I read every book and magazine article I could find on computers—I had finally found something to occupy my daylight hours. The modern age was a wonderful thing... now, my sleepless days were occupied with not only literature, but hours of rapt concentration, learning basic programming and little tricks like Peaks and Pokes which were now as antiquated as the manual typewriter slowly gathering rust in the tool room.

Gaming was the most fun, of course, first with titles such as "Galaga," "Xevious," and "Centipede," then more elaborate games such as "Elite," The Bard's Tale" or "Ultima 4," which later gave way to PC games such as "Civilization" and later improvements on the empire-building-theme such as "Age of Empires," "Warcraft" and "Starcraft" (the Protoss were my favorite, although the Zerg could be fun as well). Basically, I just found the voices for certain of the Terran units to be annoying...as I did the human characters in Warcraft (designed by the same people, of course; I wonder if there was something psychological involved).

I still had the old Commodore 64 with a ton of games on floppy disks. Mold and age had made some of them unreadable, but I still occasionally enjoyed some of the old classics: I had an old vacuum-tube TV I only used for that purpose. It was huge, and I only used it during the winter as it would make a room uncomfortably warm in the summer time—but the clarity and depth of color of the picture was still better than that of my new, plasma TV!

Books, movies, computer games and online shopping were things that provided me with diversion during the daylight hours when I wasn't resting. Nights, of course, were when I was free to roam the land and engage in that most common form of entertainment available to vampires—spying upon the living through the windows of their dwellings. I suppose one might call it "vampiric voyeurism"!

So it was that, a few nights after feasting on the teenager in the pre-fuel-injection Nova, I was crouched in the upper branches of a large maple, drinking in the night air and observing the denizens of a 2-story apartment building. The crickets were in full swing, filling the night with the roaring of their chirping (to ears that can hear the beating of a human heart from a distance of several feet, to say it sounded like roaring was only a slight exaggeration). The light from the streetlights and windows let me see quite clearly. I could see where the cement between the bricks was cracked and crumbling in places. I could see the rust stains where years of water dripping from second-floor air conditioners had stained those on the first floor below. My seventh sense—esper, for lack of a better word—felt the presence of 3 raccoons, 2 adults and a kit, in a neighboring tree. Several cats were hunting—their minds touched mine briefly—fellow travelers in the night—then returned to their pursuit of food or sex or territorial combat...with cats, their minds were never quite clear as to their priorities, but theirs were the easiest to make contact with.

My attention was suddenly drawn to a car pulling into the parking lot. A new-ish Mitsubishi convertible... a Spyder, I thought. Driving was a male, probably mid-30's, dressed in fashionable, casual clothing, whose attention was centered firmly on the female sitting in the passenger's seat. It didn't take long, perhaps 1/1000 of a second, for her to capture my full attention as well. This girl was...exotic! Hair as black as a raven's feathers, superbly smooth skin, rounded face, small nose... features softer and somehow different from the 3 races I commonly encountered, those being Mexican, Afro-American and Caucasian/mixed-European ancestry.

"Thank you for dinner... uh... Alex," she said with a somewhat British-sounding accent, "I had a really nice evening."

I watched with interest as "Alex" took a moment to respond, mental gears clearly grinding away trying to find the words that would get him one step closer to her front door... and the bedroom beyond. "Um... " he hesitated, "how about a good night kiss?"

"Ru Jin Xue Su," she replied... and, to his obvious lack of comprehension, added, 'When in Rome do as the Romans do.' It's not my culture," she added. "In my country, we don't kiss on the first date. But as this is America!"

In one smooth motion, she kissed the driver on the cheek, opened the passenger door, and slipped out. "Let's do this again sometime," she said, closing the door. I smiled to myself as Alex sat there for a moment, clearly at a loss, and then put the car in gear and drove off. The girl walked up the pavement towards the apartments, exuding a sense of satisfaction... perhaps... victory?

Yes, she clearly felt as though she had won some form of competition. "Interesting," I thought to myself.

I watched as the enticing creature, this unknown species of female, passed under a street lamp. I saw then, for the first time, the delicate curve of her eyes, which had been hidden in shadows before. I inhaled her scent as she passed within several meters of my perch, nearly tasting her. Clearly, she was not of any race I had previously encountered. Some Asian race, I supposed, although from which I could not guess.

I watched as she went around the corner of the building and waited patiently for two, then three minutes, until a light came on in a 2d floor apartment. There she was. I dropped lightly from the tree, slipped over to the building, and pulled myself up to the 2d floor balcony. Contrary to popular myth, vampires can't actually turn themselves into bats and fly. However, as we are stronger, with fingernails which grew out much thicker than usual, more like claws, less sensitive to pain and we were much lighter in body weight—has anyone ever seen a fat vampire?—the gaps between the bricks afforded me quite adequate finger-holds.

Once upon the balcony, I pressed myself into the shadows and slowly moved forward until I could see through the sliding-glass door. There she was, with a miniature poodle jumping up and down, launching itself again and again into the air along the length of her very tight designer jeans.

Personally, I never cared for poodles... not even the full-sized ones used as hunting dogs by the French nobility; they just seemed effeminate. Dobermans, Labradors, Dalmatians...the big hounds were real dogs, in my opinion. These miniature poodles didn't even bark like a dog, they yipped like...I don't know, rodents or something. Even so, I had to be more careful so the feeble excuse for a canine wouldn't sense me and give me away. For the moment, however, the dog's attention was focused fully on the girl, who had now knelt on the thick, beige, shag carpeting, and was letting the dog eagerly lick her on the face. "Did you miss mommy?" she said, "Did my wittle baby miss mommy?" As the baby talk continued, I felt somewhat nauseated. Was that how I looked when I greeted my own dogs? I was relieved to be able to answer myself in the negative...a "cutsie" vampire? Surely no!

"Need to go for a walk?" the girl asked the dog (somewhat rhetorically, I supposed, as the animal was spinning circles in a frenzy, clearly impatient to be about its business). She produced a leash from a closet near the front door and went out, taking the dog with her. With nothing better to do, I waited in the shadows, alone with my thoughts.

I thought about the strange language I'd heard, and the exotic shape to her eyes and the unusual fragrance of her skin. Clearly she was from some other place. From my readings, I guessed she was from an oriental country... Japan or perhaps China. I also thought about what I'd seen. It would take more planning, of course, but perhaps I'd found my next victim. The anticipation might not have been that of a child on Christmas Eve, but I could feel a stirring in my loins as I anticipated the thrill of tasting her, both inside and out. As for the inevitable coup de grâce, I would probably have fewer regrets terminating this victim than most—like males of every species, I despised "cock teases" with an unholy passion.

I suppose it bears mentioning that, a century ago, I'd set myself up so that I might never need take another human life. Vampires need blood to survive, as everyone knows. Humans, however, are not the only source of blood available—and not even the best tasting, necessarily. At present, I owned nearly 300 head of cattle. Anyone who's ever had a roast beef sandwich 'Aus Jus' can testify to the fact that beef blood is rather tasty. I had plenty of cattle to feed upon.

Why, therefore, did I still hunt humans, at least upon occasion? I guess, in part, it's the nature of being a predator. As Deep Purple stated in their song 'Knocking at Your Back Door': "It's not the kill, it's the thrill of the chase" Of course, for a vampire, it's a bit of both. Vampires, like their former human selves, have a libido. Like any living creature (and vampires are a form of life despite being known as the "undead"), there is a drive to mate although, as a species (?), I believe we are incapable of producing offspring; I don't even know if there is sperm in vampire semen—but we still feel the desire, the need, to mate...or at least to ravish. In either case, we are driven to hunt humans. This particular vampire, however, decided a long time ago that, if it were necessary for me to hunt humans, I would endeavor to only hunt those whose absence would better the human race. I can't say it was always easy to identify them...much like Santa Claus deciding who had been naughty and who had been nice... but I tried my best to only feed upon those who truly deserved to die.

My reverie was broken by the apartment door opening. The lady with the curvy eyes and jet-black hair unclipped the dog, stored the leash, and went into an internal bathroom. I couldn't see anything. "How like a woman," I thought, "even without knowing I'm here, she's making me wait on her"! Presently, she emerged from the bathroom, clicked off the light in the living room and a light came on from another room. A quick glance along the outer wall showed me another light. Moments later, I was hanging head-down, feet hooked in the overhead eves, eyes gazing in the top of the window as the mark, now dressed only in her underwear, sat brushing her hair and talking to her dog. The window was open just a few inches, at top and bottom, presumably to let in some cool air.

"American men are so stupid," she said to the poodle, as if expecting it to understand, "they wouldn't last an hour in Shanghai!" It's like I would never have to buy my own dinner if I didn't want to"

"And," she added, "with just a little encouragement, they buy me gifts... I can get them to do anything I want just by letting them think they have a chance to get in my pants!" She turned profile-on to the mirror mounted on the wall, hands on her hips, clearly admiring herself. "What a bad way to do business," she added, "anyone knows you should negotiate the terms before making a down payment"!

She scooped her pleated slacks from off her bed, opened a closet door, and carefully hung them on a hangar. Her closet was immaculately organized, impressive in it's neatness. At that moment, however, I didn't give a damn about her closet—I was gazing at something far more impressive. Her long, graceful legs had a lovely cast to them—a rich, smooth color—not too dark, not too pale (stanzas from some children's story concerning 3 bears and a girl about to be eaten came to mind, but I hurriedly pushed them aside). What legs! As she sat at her desk, near the window that was my vantage point, and opened the cover of her computer, I could sense the blood pulsing in her neck, almost hear the beating of her heart... and her smell! Even from a several meters, the smell of her skin... and the warm, musky smell from between her legs... was intoxicating! Most women of my experience, whether European or American, shared particular characteristics of smell, likely determined by racial genetics or perhaps also an effect of diet (you are what you eat, after all). European women generally smelled somewhat sour, no doubt the effect of consuming dairy products with regularity. Blacks and Hispanics typically had a rather heavy, pungent smell. This woman... girl... smelled far more... inviting; perhaps I might even venture to say "tasty". Comparisons to sushi and sashimi came to mind.

"Let's see who's on SKYPE," she said to herself as well as to her dog, "it's not too early to start looking for someone else to buy me dinner—tonight's moron will eventually figure out I'm just taking advantage of him and I'm never going to sleep with him, and he's not a big spender anyway, so let's see about lining up the next mark. Now, pumpkin, let's see if we can find some rich, old man to give me a green card and a Mercedes... or maybe another Japanese businessman to send me money for a plane ticket I'll never buy."

I'd heard enough... this gold-digger would be my next target. Not tonight, however. The element of dealing with the canine required planning. I was sorely tempted to "hang around" a bit longer, hoping to see her disrobe even further, but the gutter I was hanging from seemed to be shifting under my weight, and there was always a chance the breeze which was beginning to pick-up could blow my scent over to the poodle, now resting at the girl's feet. I gathered myself for a moment and pushed up, freeing my feet from contact with the gutter. I pushed out, away from the building and fell silently to the soft, moist turf, turning as I did so in order to land, nearly soundlessly, upon my feet. I straightened up and walked smoothly over to the shadows, melting into the trees. "Soon," I thought to myself.

Chapter 4
The Long Walk

Theresa Hasegawa couldn't believe the day she was having. On any day, leaving her cell phone on the charger would have been a disaster. Doing so on the day of a job interview was an unmitigated disaster. She'd still had the address but, without the phone, she was unable to call when she got confused about the directions. Taking the wrong off-ramp had cost her valuable time and she'd arrived 20 minutes late. This and the resultant embarrassment hadn't helped—she was sure she'd blown the interview... and she had a really small time window within which to find a "practical training" position or her visa would expire right after graduation and she'd have to leave the USA. Things had been easier when she first began applying to study in the USA, students had had a year to find a job, but right after her acceptance and matriculation to Goshen college the rules had changed. The Trump administration hadn't been kind to foreign students, but the Biden administration was even worse, opening the floodgates to illegals and giving them money to settle anywhere in the USA. If she'd entered the country illegally, she'd be getting food stamps, housing assistance and maybe even citizenship, but because she'd wasn't a criminal and had gone through the application process, paid her fees and done everything the right way, now she was going to be kicked-out of the country if she didn't find a job right away. It just wasn't fair!

Not only that, but there was more discrimination against Asian people these days. High-tech employers were afraid of theft of technology, because of all the stories of Chinese spies stealing tech, and people blamed any Asian for the Chinese releasing the Wuhan virus on the world or for stealing the election from Trump. She'd read about an increase in attacks against Asians and even knew a girl—a very pretty girl from a rich family in Singapore—who had been harassed in a shopping mall by a bunch of young kids shouting "Covid" at her; although she wasn't from China and didn't have a think to do with the virus! Again, it just wasn't fair that she'd spent years and tens-of-thousands-of-dollars to study in the USA and now they were going to kick her out if she couldn't find some lousy job and all of this was being made harder because people were mad at China and taking it out on Asians who weren't even Chinese! Of course that didn't stop people from buying cheap Chinese-made crap at Walmart or through Amazon; and no doubt most Americans didn't even realize the hypocrisy of their actions!

It's not as though the USA was that great—they didn't know how to prepare seafood, for one thing—just about everything was deep fried, with almost no exceptions. There weren't any tea houses or spas or sushi bars unless one happened to be in a city of several millions of people, fashion was boring, especially here in Indiana; not to mention very little in the way of music or drama performances, festivals, or any of the other things that made life so interesting and eventful in Taiwan and China. However, she needed some work experience and the job market in Japan was even worse than that of the USA these days. Plus, she wanted to save some money and do some traveling before she went back to Japan: Disney World, Epcot Center, Yosemite, Crater Lake, The Grand Canyon, Monument Valley, Niagara Falls... there were so many places she wanted to visit... and she didn't have the so many dollars required to make it possible.

So, here she was, just a few weeks before she was due to graduate with her master's, with a crapped-out car, a nearly empty bank account, a research paper due in three days that she'd barely started on, a boyfriend she was fairly certain was banging her roommate... it was almost enough to make her scream in frustration! Not only that, but her job-interview shoes weren't exactly the most comfortable. Her feet were starting to hurt and she was sure she would have blisters by the time she got back to her tiny apartment in a shared house. If only she hadn't forgotten to take her phone, she could have called for an Uber... not that she was sure she could have given the driver directions on where to pick her up...

Just at the moment, the crapped-out car was foremost in her mind. The check-engine light had come on during the trip back from the screwed-up job interview. It was already late enough at night that there was no chance of finding an open garage (not for the first time did she regret choosing a college outside of a small town, rather than in a major city). She'd hoped to make it home before the car died but, as previously mentioned, this just wasn't her day. The only good news was that she was only about 4 miles from her apartment. She could probably make it home within the hour, call triple-A, get to sleep before midnight, then get up early and plunge into her research paper.

At least it was a nice night for a walk. Early summer, the smell of clean, country air (one thing she was going to miss when she went back to Kobe), the sound of the crickets—at least she hadn't broken down during one of the horrible winter nights she'd experienced here in the American Midwest.

Of course it was a bit unnerving, walking in the near-dark. The road she was on was only lit with the occasional streetlamp, there wasn't much of a moon and what there was of it was frequently obscured by wisps of cloud drifting across in front of it. She'd debated the wisdom of trying to thumb a ride from a passing motorist. One heard many horror stories about the things that happened to hitch-hikers in the USA, particularly young, attractive co-eds, but it had turned out to be a non-issue. She'd been passed by a only a single car and that had been heading in the wrong direction. It was a strange place, this rural USA. Where she was from, there was a 24-hour convenience store on nearly every corner, all night McDonald's and traditional food stands, KTV's...night life. Even at 3 or 4 in the morning there were occasional pedestrians and vehicles passing by every few minutes. Here, the downtown shops closed at 5 or 6 p.m. and even the strip malls and the solitary shopping mall closed by 9. Wal-Mart was the "maverick" in this town that "rolled-up-the-sidewalks," as her marketing professor said... and even Wal-Mart closed at midnight, ten o'clock on Sundays. Also, until recently, you couldn't purchase alcohol on Sunday anywhere in the entire state unless you were sitting down in a restaurant. There were certain times when you weren't allowed to purchase lottery tickets and automobile dealerships were not allowed to open on Sundays which had long been the case with liquor stores (most of which remained closed on Sundays, allowing the grocery and drug stores a monopoly on the least profitable of sales days for alcohol)—a connection she'd given up trying to figure out.

This particular Monday night at 10 p.m., it seemed everyone was either already asleep (half the houses she'd passed by were already dark) or already in for the night and, where most people were concerned, camped out in front of the TV or PC. Her footsteps sounded oddly flat, as if carried away by the slight breeze.

With a start, she nearly jumped out of her skin as an animal ran across the road about 10 meters in front of her, it's black shape moving silently and purposefully. Fox? Coyote? Raccoon? It hadn't seemed to be a dog and certainly hadn't been a cat. It seemed she'd overheard something about there being coyotes in the area. Did coyotes ever attack humans? Certainly the animal she'd seen was too small—it certainly hadn't been a wolf. Still, it took a few minutes for the momentary panic to subside, for her breathing to slow and her pulse rate to return to normal. The dryness she felt in her mouth was likely to remain until she got home and had a drink of water.

She decided to take her mind off her surroundings by repeating to herself the quote she was trying to memorize: "The first person you were in love with stole your heart; the first person you made love with stole your soul. And if these were the one and same, you were damned." from *Mercy* by Jodi Picoult. This really seemed to fit her mood recently. Of course the first person she'd made love to was a girl. The first person she'd loved had been a boy (and they'd never even kissed), so she supposed she was safe per the 2d clause. Actually, to be completely accurate, she hadn't so much made love to the girl in junior high as that girl had made love to her. Sure, there'd been some mutual attraction, or else things wouldn't have gone as far as they did, but it was the other girl who had pursued her relentlessly, finally catching her at a time when she felt particularly unloved and undesired... and she hadn't "gone down" on the girl to reciprocate. Moreover, after the act she'd felt dirty and nauseated... and had been cruel and abusive to the girl afterwards. Now, of course, she felt an everlasting sense of regret for the way she'd treated the girl—it had been unfair, especially after the girl had only shown her love, kindness and respect. "Why am I such a bitch, sometimes?" she asked herself, confident that no one would overhear her.

Coming out of her reverie, she figured she'd made it about 2/3's of the way to her apartment (on what she was just realizing was really the edge of civilization—such as it was in such a small town), she saw a light on close to the road and heard voices and the sound of metal banging upon metal. Perhaps she could borrow a phone and call for a cab? Her feet were really starting to ache. She was in high-heels still from her interview earlier in the day, having also forgotten to grab a pair of 'comfy shoes' in her haste to leave that morning. Scratch that—it would probably take longer for the cab to get way out here than it would for her to walk the remaining 2 miles home. Maybe she could catch a lift?

As she drew closer, she saw some kid of old car, up on blocks, with a work light hooked onto the open hood. Three rather obese men were doing something in the open engine compartment. There was quite a collection of beer cans on top of the car. The men were uniformly dressed in old, stained-looking blue jeans, dirty, white T-shirts and, even in the shadows cast by the work light, seemed unshaven. Something about their appearance made her feel decidedly uneasy and she decided to quietly pass by on the opposite side of the road, avoiding attracting any attention, and walk the final 20 minutes rather than asking for a ride—with the way things were going today, she could see the driver getting stopped for a DUI... or worse. She walked on, left the rednecks swilling their beer behind her, and her thoughts turned to her cell phone, so inconveniently left off the charger. What else might she have forgotten? As she began running through a mental checklist, their was a sudden noise behind her and she felt herself lifted off the ground, with an arm around her waist—another arm—a hand, actually—clamping hard across her mouth, smashing her lips against her teeth. *"Oh Fuck,"* screamed in her brain as the panic began to rise in her breast and her heartbeat began to thunder in her ears.

25

Chapter 5
Benevolent Evil

Jason Hillenberg, commonly known to his friends as "Jethro," was just finishing his first six-pack of the evening when his younger brother Steve (aka "Stinky" as his farts were literally known to clear rooms) suddenly turned, darted across the grass and onto the road, into the shadows on the far side. He came back into the circle of light holding a struggling woman clamped under his arm like a loaf of bread. "Lookie what I got!" bubbled Stinky. As he drew closer to the work light, it was clear Stinky was holding a slender, Asian woman. She was definitely what Jason would call "high class," dressed in a blue suit jacket, close-fitting knee-length skirt, black nylons, black high-heeled shoes. To Jason, she looked like something he'd only see on TV, a thing from a world far above and beyond the one he lived it. Jason also noticed how her white blouse had been torn partially open and the top of a her brassiere was showing. His penis, which spent most of its time staring at the floor these days, suddenly found new life and was standing to attention.

"Y'all" ready for some fun?" asked Stinky. The girl was vainly beating at Stinky's arms while her legs frantically and futilely kicked air as one of her shoes flipped off, landing near Jason's feet.

"Sure," announced Kenny, setting his beer on top of the car and walking over to the girl, "let's see if she's real." Kenny jerked her blouse the rest of the way open and pushed his hands up under her bra, squeezing her breasts—which instantly resulted in the girl's struggles erupting into a renewed frenzy of kicking and clawing, as she raked Kenny's face. Kenny's response was to punch her in the stomach, hard. The girl slumped, the fight temporarily knocked out of her—a fight which had been pretty ineffective so far, anyway. Apparently this was no girl out of some Kung-Fu movie that was going to kick all their asses. Kenny smiled at the thought—he'd never fucked a girl in the ass before—it looked like tonight would be his lucky night!

While not the brightest cookie in the box (he wouldn't have recognized a mixed-metaphor if it bit him and he would have viewed it as a cause for celebration had he managed to break 500 on the SAT), Jason did have a certain amount of street-smarts, having had several brushes with the law, and middle age had brought about a certain amount of caution yet to be learned by the other two, who were a good decade younger. "Boys," he said, "hold up a minute afore this goes any further, jest one thing—she knows where I live"

"If we're going to do this, we have to kill her after and never tell a soul".

He looked both Stinky and Kenny in the eyes and asked them, "Is that something you can live with?" He grabbed a handful of hair and pushed it away from her face.

"This is a classy babe; she goes missing or shows up messed-up and someone's gonna go to the cops. We fuck her, we're gonna hafta kill her; unless of course you want to spend years in prison for one poke in her pussy. Are you both okay with that? Can you live with that on your conscience?" Kenny, who had not ceased fondling the exotic, partially undressed bundle slumping in Stinky Steve's arms, did not hesitate to chime in: "I ain't never gonna have the chance to fuck a woman like this, not ever, not even if I won the lottery! I don't wanna be the one to do her in, but I'm ready for some slant-eyed pussy!"

Stinky just grinned and said, "are we gonna stand out here all night or are we gonna get this bitch up to the house and do some serious fucking?"

"It's my property," offered Jethro, stating the obvious, "That means I'm first!"

"Jethro" had already had, what was for him, an epiphany—or perhaps a gestalt (words he wouldn't have understood and couldn't have pronounced, much less spelled!). Within moments of seeing Steve dragging the girl up to the '65 Mustang he was restoring, with some help from his friends, Jason had already envisioned what he was going to do. He'd inherited a small farm from his father, proceeds of the same of which was allowing him the luxury of not having to work, for which he was far too lazy. He could have probably handled a job in a gas station or fast-food restaurant, but felt fortunate he was able to follow his dream career of sitting on the sofa all day watching 'reality' TV shows and re-runs.

This girl, however, presented him with a once-in-a-lifetime opportunity. He sure wasn't going to have her just once and then kill her—that would be a terrible waste! If he was going to risk prison and maybe the death penalty for murder—he realized he'd have to do the deed once they were finished with her—once wasn't going to be enough. He could give his younger brothers a couple turns with her tonight then get them to clear off for a few days and then he'd have this little girl as often as he could get it up for a several days, maybe even a week. In between erections he'd amuse himself by inserting various items in her vagina and anus. He had even visualized how he'd kill her... with a plastic bag over her head, her legs tied back behind her neck with a rope around her neck and ankles, slowly strangling while he humped her one last time.

"Go on, take her up to the house," he said, waving in the direction of the old farmhouse. "We'll do her in the basement, so nobody will hear if she screams."

Kenny bent down and grabbed her legs which were now on the ground—she wasn't that heavy but Steve wasn't *that* strong either, being more flab than muscle—and he and Steve began moving towards the house in eager anticipation... probably moving faster than they had since high school PE class. Jethro turned and walked back to the shoe, lying near the old Ford. "No sense leaving any evidence lying around," he said to himself (Jason was a regular viewer of CSI and COPS...shows that were designed, it seemed, to teach people how to be better criminals). Pausing by the Mustang, he collected the remaining beer (they had a real party planned for the rest of the evening), switched off the work light, and shambled along in the wake of his sibling beer buddies. Ten steps took him past an old oak tree that had stood on the property for a good eighty years or more. On his 12th step, I drove my bowie knife deep into the right side of his neck.

The fat, old redneck did not fall silently to the ground. In fact, despite their being full and unopened, the cans of beer he was holding made a considerable clatter as they spilled from his limp arms as he fell to his knees. I grabbed his ear with my left hand, holding him upright, while I took a long look at his friends. No worry—they were distracted, intent upon copping a feel from their struggling victim as they dragged her towards the farmhouse. Knowing they were unlikely to even see me in the darkness, I knelt, pulled the blade from the dying man's neck and waited as the initial spurt of blood ejected itself from his neck. I then fastened my mouth on the wound, drinking deeply. I could taste the alcohol in his blood—I'd have a slight high for awhile... I could live with that—and felt the familiar warmth and strength filling me; his life passing from him to me. I remained that way for a full minute, draining most of his vitality; then I stood, allowing him to fall to the ground. Casually, almost, I licked the blood from the blade I still held in my right hand and rose to follow his partners in crime.

Burdened as they were with an uncooperative cargo, they hadn't moved very far. She'd actually managed to elude their grasp for a moment, only to be recaptured and dragged back towards the house. Having just fed, however, I was in no great hurry. I slowly moved towards them, allowing my body to absorb and distribute the blood I had just ingested, feeling the new life and vitality coursing through me. Again, as I had so many times before, I felt truly powerful.

"Fuck," the redneck on the left (Steve, to those more informed than myself) exclaimed as he dropped the top half of the captive female on the ground. He rubbed his forearm for a moment (clearly indicating he'd been bitten) and then raised his meaty leg and brought it crashing down on her abdomen... hard! Suspended in mid-air, as she was, she flexed with the blow, but I could still hear the gasp as the breath was knocked-out of her and the force of the blow caused the redneck on the right (Kenny) to lose his grip on her legs. The unfortunate girl landed on the ground just in time to receive a follow-up kick to the solar plexus. The men paused then, for a moment, staring down at the limp form at their feet, now curled into a fetal position, audibly sobbing.

Time for action.

I already had my old Bowie in my right hand. With a well-practiced motion, I slipped a butterfly knife out of my back pocket with my left had, flipping it open. The whirring sound made by the knife attracted the attention of the two obese and soon-to-be-deceased men in front of me. They turned slowly, ever so slowly, fatally slowly. In just over a second I'd stabbed each of them over a dozen times—in the vitals but also making sure each received a few in the peripheries—hands and arms—to make it look as though they turned on each other. As they collapsed to the ground, dying, I swiftly drank from each of them (no sense in wasting fresh blood, even though I'd just fed). Next, I wiped my prints off both knives on Kenny's vintage "last great act of defiance" T-shirt (which looked to be at least 20 years old and had certainly seen better days) and put the knives in each of their dying hands (better their prints than mine if the local yokels decided to mount more than a cursory investigation). I hated surrendering the Bowie, it was a good knife, but the local constabulary had to suspect anything but the truth when they discovered the bodies. I tucked her loose shoe into my belt—not quite a replacement for the knife, but I didn't want to leave anything of hers at the scene—I lived not far enough down the road and didn't need the police asking questions from door-to-door...

Bending over the prostrate girl, I stroked her hair, breathing in her lovely fragrance. I wasn't Hannibal Lector, able to identify women's fragrances, but there was something that reminded me of... lavender? So young, so lovely, so...vulnerable...

She rolled over, gasping for breath between sobs, opened her eyes, and looked at me in abject terror. "Don't worry," I lied, "Everything is ok now; it's all going to be all right." I lifted her easily and started walking back to where I'd hidden my motorcycle. Certainly this night had not gone as anticipated. Honestly, I had not felt this alive in years. As an immortal who truly had "too much time on my hands" (per the Styx song), for the first time in decades, I truly wanted to savor the moment: I had laid some wicked men to rest and I had a shiny, new toy to play with. Life—or whatever it was I was experiencing—was good!

My strides quickly began to lengthen as I stole a look down at my new prize. Her white dress shirt, which looked much like what a man might wear with a tuxedo, though with a much smaller and more feminine collar, was mostly open, giving me a nice view of creamy, medium-sized breasts peaking over an expensive-looking brassiere, not one of the ugly, flowery-lace-looking things you saw so often... this had a smooth, satiny surface, and clean lines. She had a trim waist, long slender legs, a small, heart-shaped derriere and long, long dark hair. I could see that, while well groomed, she did indeed have eyebrows—I detested those women who shaved them off and then painted them back on—how phony! (Yes, I realize this is a great amount of detail on a dark night while walking away from light sources and into the darkness...in case nobody ever mentioned it, we vampires see quite well in the dark!)

As I continued to simultaneously walk and admire her, she looked up and me and, in turn, gave me a very long look (or tried to, as we were rapidly passing into the shadows) and then she turned her head and looked past me, back the way we had come. "Are they...dead?" she asked.

"As doornails," I replied, "You just relax...I've got you."

In a matter of moments, I was at the barbed-wire fence that marked one edge of the property. I could easily have jumped it, as I had earlier in the evening—even with the additional burden in my arms—but I didn't want to alarm the young creature... not yet, anyway. "I've got to put you down for a moment," I announced, holding her over the fence and lowering her feet until they touched the ground, "here, put your shoe on." I handed her the shoe from my belt and, as she dutifully bent to put her shoe on, stepped outside of her range of vision and vaulted the fence (no sense in tearing any holes in my clothes).

"My motorcycle is over here," I said, taking her by the hand. I was glad I'd ridden one of the Harley's tonight... not all of my bikes had seats made for passengers. I'd left it in a slight depression, hidden from the road by some scrub brush. It was only the work of a moment to lift the bike from horizontal to vertical and roll it up the 40 degree slope to the road. If she had any idea how much effort this would have required from a human mortal, it was not apparent. "Let me help you," I said. Placing my hands around that deliciously narrow waist, I lifted her gently and placed her on the back of the bike. Without giving her time to comment or object—she was still in shock, unprotesting—I slipped the key in the ignition, mounted the steel steed with one fluid motion, hit the starter, reached back, found her hands and placed them around my waist and gunned the machine down the country road, tires spitting gravel. 200 meters brought me to an intersection with an old stop sign sporting several old bullet holes, no doubt placed there by bored, local youths drinking and driving. The holes were rusty and had been there for quite a long time—online shoot-em-up games had probably replaced the need to shoot at road signs in recent years. I didn't stop—there was no traffic—and this wasn't exactly a part of the country where one had to worry about speed traps and such things.

I rarely kept "guests", except the Mexican girl who'd "entertained" me for a few weeks had been three years ago. Despite my very solitary (and intentionally so) lifestyle, there was always the chance of discovery: the captive might escape, unexpected company might stop by"...and my entire existence was based upon being as invisible as possible. While there were definite benefits to keeping the occasional human captive—a renewable source of blood for one—I usually considered it too risky. After all, my small herd of cattle made keeping humans for sustenance much less of a priority. Having someplace safe to bury my bone (to paraphrase Pink Floyd), however, was always a consideration. At the moment, my thoughts were awhirl with possibilities. If things went according to my newly-hatched plan, this one was going to stay with me for awhile.

How many women had I lain with? How many had I fed upon? Hundreds for certain. Thousands? Germans, Russians, French, Americans...so many I could not even begin to remember. Most of them had been Caucasian, skin nearly as pale as my own. Some had been black or brown, skin like chocolate. This month had been a first, of course; the first two Asian women I'd seen in the flesh... and this was the first I'd touched. She was somehow different than the others. Her scent was sublime; her body so demure, the curve of her legs so subtle...yes, this one was going to stay with me awhile. What made her smell differently, I wondered as I had while peeping in on the girl with the poodle. Was it her diet? I'd read that Asians consume more vegetables, less meat and fewer milk products. Perhaps this resulted in a less sour epidermal bouquet? After all, you are what you eat, to some extent—and one's diet does affect one's body chemistry. Indeed, I was beginning to feel more than a little inebriated, having just consumed several liters of alcohol-laced bodily fluid.

Time to hurry home before my BAC (blood alcohol content) reached the danger level—a DUI arrest would be fatal!

The ride only took ten minutes. She didn't speak; she just clung to me and, after a few minutes, quietly resumed sobbing. I pulled up the drive, parked the bike, secured the gate, and parked the bike in front of the house. I'd park it in the barn later. I opened myself to her feelings to the limited extent to which I was able... it was not as though I could read thoughts but I could sense general feelings, which had alerted me to potential trouble on more than one occasion in the past.

She was still somewhat traumatized but there was no fear of me yet... good! The dogs were overjoyed to see me, as usual. Through a series of mental images I sent them a message—they were to observe and be cautious of this girl; she was not to be allowed to go free. My boys stopped spinning in circles and became quite businesslike. I left them outside and lifted my new treasure, unlocked the door and carried her over the threshold. Pushing the door shut with my heel, I knocked her shoe off in the same motion. The second shoe, still tucked into my belt, heel first, followed a moment later. I usually left my boots at the door, but pulling off motorcycle boots while carrying someone would have been a bit awkward, to say the least...besides, I have things in mind of a higher priority than a clean floor! Flipping the light switch with the back of my hand, I turned and carried her down the hall and into my kitchen—the kitchen I maintained for those rare occasions when I had to welcome the living into my abode.

"Have a seat," I said, "Would you like some tea? Or, considering the evening you've had, maybe something stronger? Tequila? Whiskey?"

For a moment she simply sat at the table, her head in her hands. Then, she raised her head, her eyes meeting mine.

"I appreciate the offer, but not tonight," she explained, apologetically, "I'd really love to, perhaps some other time, but it's getting late and I have a lot to do tomorrow... and aren't you going to call the police?"

"Well, I just killed 3 men who weren't a threat to me at all. Now, if *you'd* killed them, you could claim self-defense. At the very worst, they'd credit you with a whole lot of mitigating circumstances. In my case, they'd be sure to say I should have called the cops and waited for them to deal with the situation and they'd bring charges against me for manslaughter or worse. That's the least they'd do. Most likely, as justice is a game they play these days, they'd probably charge me with 'Murder 1' so they could force me to 'cop to a plea' and save themselves the trouble of actually having to conduct a trial. There's a reason der, how do you say it, um, conviction rate is approaching 8-and-90, that is 98 percent in this country; the police and prosecutors know how to work the game and *little people* cannot afford the very expensive lawyers with which themselves to defend. So, my dear, I think you can understand why I have no intention of going to the police. Besides...those men are no longer in a position to cause you any trouble, ever again, now are they?"

As I watched the conflicting thoughts and emotions chase each other across her face, it occurred to me why I'd brought her home. It wasn't to feed upon her or for sex, although those were both certainly part of the inevitable equation. No, my main drive was for companionship. How long had it been since I'd had someone to talk to? I was going to play that card for all it was worth: enjoy some conversation and a bit of the "human touch"... for as long as possible until I had to kill her. Momentarily, I wondered how long it would take for her to realize she had not been rescued, at least not exactly...

"Are you sure I can't get you a drink? And, if you need help turning in an assignment late ('international student' was my first guess) or something for work (2nd guess, based on the way she was dressed), I'm sure a phone call from me would help straighten things out. I can be very persuasive," I added with a smile, "And I'm sure we could come up with something plausible to avoid having to mention the attack, if you'd rather save yourself the embarrassment. I might even be able to help—I've published papers on history, business, language—I've even written a few textbooks, although I think they're all out-of-print now. Hey, are you hungry? I could call out for a pizza."

"No, thanks," she said, "I am really not hungry." Looking around, her eyes walked across the cabinets, the floors, the tiffany stained-glass lamp and, after a moment she remarked, "This is a really nice kitchen... I love the wood!"

I smiled, remembering the countless hours I'd spent restoring all the antique wood in the old house. "The floors are oak, the cabinets are cherry, and the molding and kitchen table are walnut," I began, "It is all original. When I moved in, the floor was gouged, scratched and water stained; the molding and trim had been whitewashed and the cabinets were falling off their hinges. I spent months stripping, steaming, sanding and staining. I'm glad you like it—wait until you see my Mahogany Victrola cabinet in the parlor sitting!"

"I'm sure it's lovely," she added, "Uh, can I have a glass of water?"

"Certainly," I said, taking a 1970's vintage Snoopy glass from the cabinet and filling it from the spout in the refrigerator door, "That will be one dollar," I added with what I hoped was my most disarming smile.

She took the glass with a ghost of a smile of her own, retaining a bit of humor despite her recent ordeal.

"You're so kind," she said, rising from her seat and walking around the table towards me, "and I really want to thank you... for everything!" At this point she kissed me on the cheek, flowed up against me, warm and soft, and held me in a gentle embrace.

I inhaled the fragrance of her hair, closed my hands around the delicate smallness of her waist, savoring the moment.

"But," she added, gently pushing herself away from me and looking up at me with those beautiful brown eyes... eyes with a delicate, graceful curve to them that to me seemed like an added flourish that even the most lovely eyes I'd beheld in the past had been lacking. "... I really do need to get up early tomorrow, get my car towed... and you don't have to worry, I promise I will never say anything to anyone about what you did for me tonight!"

I bought you a reprieve, I thought to myself. *And still you're impatient to meet your fate of being raped and murdered!* Making one last attempt to delay the inevitable acts of violence I wished to avoid, I said aloud, "It's late and I have several guest rooms upstairs. I could unpack some linens and put you up here for the night; it is probably too late to get your car towed-away tonight, anyway."

"Thanks, really," she demurred, "but I really must get home"

"I'm sorry you feel that way," I sighed, "You see there's something you don't know." I then did something I almost never did—I gave her a big smile... no, a really big smile... the Jimmy Carter of smiles... showing nearly all my teeth—particularly those four that were longer than they should be (for a normal human, at any rate). The tender creature that was still gently held within my deadly grasp just stared. Her eyes slowly widened, taking in the length of my canines, realizing their authenticity, their terrible significance, their deadly potential...

"You... you're a... a vampire?" The temporarily un-victim asked her might-have-been rescuer.

"Yes," I said (understatement if there ever was!) I was prepared for almost any reaction: a futile attempt at flight, screaming, pleading, etc. Nothing could have prepared me for what next passed through those delicate lips.

"That's so...so...*cool!*" the captive bird exclaimed, "I'm rescued by a handsome gentleman on a motorcycle and my knight-in-armor turns out to be a vampire!" All trace of fatigue had vanished from her face and she was beaming. I felt her pulse rate increase, heard her breath catch in her throat and heard her heart beating more loudly in her chest (yes, in case you were unaware, vampires have exceptional hearing as well as scent and night-vision). I could scarcely believe it—from her body language it was clear that this girl was actually excited about being in the grasp of a deadly predator! For the first time in my life, I had a faint idea of what it must have felt like to have been Leonard Nimoy walking into a Star Trek convention.

I moved closer, admiring the incredible, thick blackness of her hair, how smooth and unblemished was her skin... and was drawn to where her pulse beat visibly, in the soft curve of her neck, just above her collar bone. I studied how her earlobes gracefully melded with her neck, noticed with aesthetic pleasure the slight upturn of her smallish nose—and how the top part of her nose was lower than it would have been on a woman of European ancestry. In comparison, it made her look somewhat more like a cat, with western women with their high noses looking more like dogs by comparison (later on, she would reveal to me that Asian women referred to westerners as having 'dog noses' as the upper parts of westerners' noses were, on average, much higher than those belonging to Asians).

Her eyes—what wonderful eyes! Dark they were, pupils and irises nearly the same color, like a deep forest pool. Not ordinary ovals were these eyelids either, but with a long, sloping curve that gave them a really exotic quality. Yes, I was in no hurry to end her life—I found I was enjoying my newfound toy. In more ways that one, she was 'eye candy'. For a moment, I closed my eyes and did my best Hannibal Lector impersonation, exploring her next with my olfactory senses: skin, hair, her womanly scents—yes, she smelled quite delicious as well!

"Now that you know what I am," I queried, as I allowed my inspection to continue down across her white blouse, torn during her recent struggles, giving me the glimpse of a single, narrow, black bra-strap and the hint of small yet well-defined cleavage, "Aren't you afraid?" I brought my gaze back up level with her eyes, to gauge her reaction... playing with my toy, as might a cat with a mouse. I continued my inspection, noticing with approval that her eyebrows, while well-groomed and painted with mascara, were real—few things were more ridiculous, I thought, than those women who shaved off their eyebrows only to paint them back on—and unsightly as well!

"No, well I guess yes, a little." She was becoming flustered. "You saved me... and I always wanted to meet a vampire! I spent years playing 'Live Vampire' while I was living in LA and *Twilight* is one of my favorite books; I just love watching *True Blood* and the other vampire movies!"

I could sense she was nervous yet more from excitement than fear, although there was a fair share of both. She caught the look on my face and paused, apparently not knowing what to say next.

"*Live Vampire*?" I intoned, making a question with my voice while I continued to admire her slim form, the tight, black skirt over slim hips and the apparently expensive stockings she was wearing, with silvery embroidery on the sides-butterflies and roses, it seemed.

Meeting her gaze again, she licked her lips (thin, but with a nicely formed 'dimple' beneath her nose), and explained, "*Live Vampire* is a role-playing game played around the world... at least it was a few years ago, I've been so busy with college I am not sure if it's still popular. Anyway, people take roles as soldiers, monks, villagers, etc., with one or more persons being vampires, only their identity is a secret, and the goal is try to guess who the vampire is."

I raised my right hand, cutting her off in mid-stream. "Do you mean to say you played a *game* where someone pretends to be a vampire?" Incredulous, I looked deep into those dark eyes for confirmation.

"Oh yes," she insisted, adding "It was fun!" I grunted, not knowing what to think of children playing at being the bane of my existence.

"*Twilight*," I went on, "That is the vampire and human love story, yes?" This time it was her turn to appear surprised. "I'm not completely ignorant of what goes on in the world," I explained, "I consider it a matter of survival to keep myself informed... and I spend a lot of my spare time reading."

"Oh," she said, brightening visibly, "Have you read it? It's so romantic! To have a vampire lover would just be so..." She left her statement unfinished, apparently seeing something in my facial expression that gave her pause... or maybe she was only just considering the full ramifications of what she had just said, considering the fact a male vampire stood before her.

"No," I replied, "I haven't read it, nor do I care to. From what I've heard of it, it's supposed to be well-written and I'm sure it's a decent piece of literature—but the concept is so preposterous! A human and a vampire in love, what rubbish!" From the pained expression in those mirror-like eyes, I knew she had painted a romanticized picture for herself. Although I enjoyed reading good fantasy, I was far too old and experienced to empathize. In all the history of vampires, I doubt the adjective 'romantic' had ever been applicable—we were predators, after all, not misty-eyed dreamers.

I turned on *Twilight: New Moon* for a few minutes when it was on TV and it was just silly. This vampire was in a field, alone with a human female, telling her how he was going to kill her...does a cheetah explain to the gazelle why it's about to become dinner? Then, there was this fight between vampires and werewolves, all teeth and claws. From appearances, the werewolves looked much heavier and stronger, with more powerful jaws. So, on one side you had vampires with fangs and fingernails. On the other, you had beasts that could run on 4 legs—meaning they were undoubtedly faster—outweighing the vampires by maybe 150 pounds or more, with claws and powerful, bone-crushing jaws. And, supposedly, it takes silver to kill a werewolf—it wouldn't have been a contest— werewolves win! I just had to turn it off.

"Why?" she queried.

"See these?" I asked, wiggling my thumbs.

Vampires are humanoid. We have opposable thumbs. Not a single vampire in the fight had a gun...or a knife... or a pointed stick! I couldn't watch any more of it at that point, it was just too unbelievable. It was kind of like the film *Commando*, where a heavily-encumbered Arnold lumbers slowly across open ground while being fired at by a dozen, trained soldiers with automatic weapons and nobody hits him! If it becomes too ridiculous I just lose interest!.

Also, I recently watched the beginning of *True Blood, Part 3*. Again, I had to turn it off after about 3 minutes...there was a sheriff at someone's door, asking questions about a missing vampire! The entire concept was absolutely ridiculous: humans *knowing* there were vampires living in their community and allowing them to continue living! When a farmer sees a fox, even when it is no immediate threat to his chickens, he kills it. When someone sees a wolf or a shark or other dangerous beast, they hunt them down and kill them. Have you read Beowulf or see the original *Frankenstein* movie in black and white from the 1930's? If humans knew there were vampires around, they'd form panicked, torch-wielding mobs that wouldn't rest until every single vampire was exterminated—it's human nature!

"Humans keep cats and dogs as pets, and even cherish them more deeply than their family members, in many cases—but they don't take them as lovers, do they?" Her facial expression hadn't changed in the slightest, so I chose another tack. "What are you...Japanese?" I asked. "Yes," she said, "Half Japanese, actually, my mother was Taiwanese, although her father was also Japanese so I guess that makes me more than half..."

I waved her off, continuing: "In Japan, people eat octopodes, do they not?" I got a blank look in response and no change of expression when I next tried 'octopi'. "Do you know what an octopus is?" I asked.

"Of course," she replied.

"Nobody knows their Greek or Latin anymore," I mumbled to myself before continuing. "Octopus comes from the Greek, so the plural form is octopode, although the word was adopted by the Romans, it even coincidentally has a Latin noun suffix, so that many scholars believe that octopi is the plural form of octopus although most Americans are ignorant of this fact and say 'octopuses'. Getting back to my point, I've read that people in Japan eat them, correct?"

She nodded.

"Have you eaten the flesh of an octopus before?"

"Of course," she said smiling, much of her earlier nervousness having been forgotten, "I really love sashimi!"

"Do you realize," I went on, "that octopi are quite intelligent? You can place a shrimp in a jar, screw on the lid, and an octopus will figure out how to open the jar and eat the shrimp" (naturally I had never seen this feat myself, but I had seen it in a documentary on the *Discovery Channel*...or perhaps it had been on one of the old Jacques Cousteau shows, it had been so long since I'd seen it, and I'd seen many such shows, so they had a way of running together in my mind). "Pigs also can be trained much like a dog... I've read that some people in Asia have kept pigs as pets. My point is, do you think it is realistic that a human would ever fall in love with an octopus or a pig? You might admire them, even take care of one, but in the end, they are food." I paused to see if the ramifications had taken hold yet. "Humans...*you*," I added for emphasis, "are *our* food. Vampires kill humans. We suck the life out of them to give us life, much like you eat your, um, sashimi.

Ok, think of it like this: trees and other plants absorb the radiation of sunlight for some of their nutrition, which is non-destructive, but they also suck water and nutrients from the soil, competing over it in fact, and when plants grow tall enough, they block the sunlight from other plants, so while they may be innocent of any motives of greed, they may cause other plants to weaken or die because they are monopolizing the light. The Canadian band RUSH even wrote a song about trees competing for sunlight, I'll have to find and play it for you later. Anyway, the pig or cow or fish eats the plant and some of its vitality passes to it. By killing the plant, it gains energy that sustains its own life, although this is a very inefficient energy transfer and vegetation-eating organisms have to consume great amounts, typically, to steal the energy they need for survival. The human that eats the pig or cow, or the big fish that eats the little fish takes energy from the meal and thus initiates a more efficient energy transfer, which is one reason why it is said they are 'higher on the food chain'. By drinking the living blood of animals, vampires are the most energy-efficient eaters of which I am aware, placing us on the top of the food chain. Humans are one of our food sources. This is the nature of things. Pretty much everything kills something else and takes its life essence or by living denies life to other organisms to prolong their own lives, whether it's krill and brine shrimp or a stalk of celery or a bacon double cheeseburger! Vampires and humans as friends and lovers? To put it in 20th Century parlance: 'get real!'"

I reached up and traced a fingertip from her ear to the nape of her neck, feeling a thrill as I did so, like pulses of electricity racing up my spine to my brain. As much in un-death as I did in life, I enjoyed sex with human females... but generally only as an aperitif! (fucking a corpse might appeal to some, but it really didn't 'do it' for me!) Anyway, Vampires did not have relationships! I was a realist, after all. I was enjoying this, to be sure... perhaps a part of me that had once been human relished the conversation and companionship, and the hardness in my loins was certainly indicative of the sensually erotic quality of what was transpiring and the sex that was to come, but love between a vampire and it's human prey? Utter nonsense!

My point was apparently taken as, with indrawn breath, my slender guest's eyes widened and I felt her pulse-rate increase beneath the gentle touch of my finger. Suddenly, with the speed of a swooping hawk, I placed my hands on her thighs, lifting her (so that I slid her skirt up in t process) and deposited her on my kitchen counter, moving closer as I did so, so that her legs were opened and I was standing between her knees. Of reflex, her hands were on my shoulders and her head tilted back, looking up at me. Fear there was, in her eyes, but also something more: Hope? Determination? Denial?

Had I been a younger (or hungrier) vampire, I would have sunk my teeth into her jugular at that moment and have been done with it. However, I was thoroughly enjoying my little game and, although it came as a shock to myself, enjoying her company (I was, after all, a centuries-old, hardened killer). Truly, I had all the time in the world, which was both a benefit and a curse of being an immortal. Why not play with my food if I chose to do so? I was feeling quite aroused now, like an adolescent fondling a breast for the first time. It was quite a heady sensation, one I hadn't felt in many years. I was in no hurry to end her life—in fact, I was already regretting the need to do so—a quite foreign feeling (how many humans feel regret for the cow after eating their steak dinner?). I was even considering the risk-versus-rewards of keeping her around (i.e. imprisoned) with me for awhile. First things first however...

I placed my hands on her legs, just above the knees. I'd always hated the feel of nylons, the way they seemed to catch at your skin, snagging on rough places you never knew existed. Still, the feel of the warm, vibrant flesh beneath them was more than enough of a thrill to offset the temporarily unpleasant texture of the stockings—temporary because nothing she might say or do was going to keep them from coming completely off. Changing our orientation somewhat, I let my fingers slowly trail upwards from her ankles, gently squeezing her calf muscles, rounding along her thighs and up, under her skirt, to her waist. Of course my mouth hadn't been idle this entire time. I'd nuzzled her neck, nipping her a few times just to feel her pulse quicken, then was rewarded with some convulsions of pleasure as I gently ran my tongue around the cleft of her neck.

Pulling back to give her a sudden look in the eye and a (hopefully) reassuring smile, I then kissed her, thrusting my tongue deep into her mouth with practiced movements. By this time she was practically quivering with pleasure, obviously this was still relatively new to her; I wondered if she was a virgin? In any case, I was about to find out. Hooking my fingers underneath both stockings and panties, I pulled them over her buttocks, then down over her thighs, past knees and calves, over her ankles and then completely off. She didn't resist, but as her stockings came off, her legs closed reflexively. I grasped her ankles, lifting her legs until they pointed straight out, perpendicular to my torso. I rotated my hands, fingers caressing the inside of her ankles, then moved them forward along the inside of her thighs, opening her legs, one to either side of me and took a step back, admiring the view of her pubic region. True to urban legend (and the occasional Asian porn), they really were straight.

Her eyes opened wide as I did this, showing a hint of fear, and her tiny hands gripped my upper arms, but she didn't flinch and he held her gaze steady. I found myself feeling a modicum of respect for my little toy—she was showing more courage in the face of death than many soldiers whom I'd commanded in battle (although, in fairness, most of them had been her age or younger and the booming of cannons and screams of wounded horses and men are unsettling to every man born of woman). With the main target now free from annoying obstructions, I began to unbutton the blouse with the aim of revealing the bonus attractions. "By the way," I asked as I slowly moved my hands around to unsnap her brassiere, "have you had a blood test recently?"

"What?" she asked.

"An AIDS test, syphilis, that sort of thing."

I was now slowly peeling off her blouse and brassiere, peeling them back, off her shoulders, then pulled them halfway down, imprisoning her arms behind her back. I paused for a moment to admire her creamy white breasts, small areolas, erect nipples, then pulled my gaze away to study her face for a moment. "Um...yes," she replied, "last semester... for my visa application. Why?"

I bent forward, sampling the heady fragrance of her hair (was that a pun?), savoring the warm, sweet scent that was somehow more delicious than that of my usual victims, and worked my way lower, blowing a gentle breath into her ear as I moved on to that favorite erogenous zone of all predators—the neck. "What your comic books don't tell you," I explained as I nuzzled and gently kissed her neck, "is that when you consume blood from someone who's intoxicated, you—that is, one of us—feels some effects of the alcohol that's in the blood. I once drank blood from someone who was flying high on something, morphine or heroin, I suppose, and I was nearly incapacitated for days. I don't know if diseases like AIDS can be passed from human to vampire, but I'm not anxious to find out. So, since I had the opportunity, to ask, I thought I would—just to be careful... "

My tongue was busy again, drawing a slow, deliberate line from her collarbone up to just behind her ear. At the same time, my right hand returned to her thigh and my left began, with one finger at first, to caress the bottom of her breast, moving slowly from side to side, being careful not to approach the nipple too soon, building up her excitement in degrees. Very nice breasts, they were—medium sized, perky, with small nipples and areolas (nothing, in my opinion, was more disappointing than a pair of big, floppy, shapeless breasts with huge, ugly, areolas). I started with her left breast, kissing along the lower curve, then back, still avoiding the nipple for the time being. My right hand continued stroking the silky-smooth skin beneath her skirt, with the occasional brush of the welcome coarseness of the thatch where her legs came together.

Her head was back now, eyes closed, her breath coming in short and quick intakes and even faster exhalations. I allowed my tongue to come into contact with her nipple, ever so briefly. She jumped, slightly, and her hands, where they gripped the edge of the counter, tightened, causing her already white knuckles to achieve an even whiter shade of pale.

"Kiss my neck," she moaned, her back arching with another, gentle shudder as my tongue found her nipple a second time. I resumed kissing her, moving higher on her chest, pausing to kiss each rib, her collarbone, then explored each centimeter of her neck, up to her ear. My middle finger, meanwhile, had located an area considerably moister than its surroundings. I pushed until she yielded slightly, then pulled my finger slowly higher until a sudden spasm of pleasure let me know I'd found the spot I was seeking. By now the tip of my tongue was tracing the outer curve of her ear and my left hand, having finished baring her neck of luxurious, jet-black hair and needing something else to do, occupied itself with tracing the curve of her breast.

Leaving her ear with my lips, I moved slowly back down her neck, to the area just above her collarbone, where her pulse was beating the strongest. It was then I did two things simultaneously: I bit her, just a gentle kitten's nip, while I performed a magic trick and my finger disappeared inside of her. Her convulsion was instantaneous and her hands flew from the counter, grasping my chest for a long moment and then, just as suddenly, they plunged to my waist and began timidly wrestling with my belt buckle. She fumbled, futilely, for several moments, brushing against the front of my jeans, while my erection fairly screamed to be released!

I removed my hands from their various tasks, triggering another convulsion as I brushed her clitoris in passing and, in two swift gestures, dropped my pants around my ankles and grasped her skirt, pulling her legs into the air as the skirt went up, over and off. Her legs, however, I held at an upright angle, admiring the view for a moment, then I buried my face between her legs, kissing the ever-so-soft skin of her inner thighs for a moment, just to build the anticipation, then dove in, kissing, licking and tongue-thrusting into the holy of holies. "Oh god, oh god," she moaned (I could have pointed out the obvious error, that in the view of many, particularly theologians and classical horror writers, I was about as far removed from God as possible, but I was otherwise occupied and conversation was an impossibility at the moment).

Her hands were now buried in my hair, pulling as if she were assuring herself it was real and not a toupee! Her legs were propped on my shoulders and my hands grasped both her breasts, not altogether gently, as her body's indications of pleasure increased in proportion to the pressure I exerted. I pushed harder, compressing her breasts into her chest, moving my hands in opposing circles, and her moans and tremors increased in tandem.

Her aroma was warm and musky, her taste sweetly sour, and I could have gone on this way for some time, but the throbbing between my legs refused to be ignored any longer, so I hefted her into the air and fell backwards into the chair. I'd have preferred to have been more graceful, but my pants were around my ankles and I hadn't bothered with removing my heavy, leather biker boots, so I half-sat, half-fell into the chair. The chair was one of those early-American styles, with narrow, vertical wooden rods and horizontal arms, so having her straddle me was out of the question. Placing her feet against my armpits, I helped fold her until her knees came up to my chin and, with my hands beneath that lovely derrière (her butt was small enough it would have fit on a dinner plate!), I lifted her for a moment, then lowered her onto me, carefully centering her. Then, in accordance with vampiric tradition, I impaled her.

Chapter 6
Just one of Those Days...

O n the kitchen counter, behind and to either side of them, were the type of things you'd expect to see in any country kitchen: copper soup pots and stainless steel frying pans hanging on hooks from the walls, spice racks (albeit with a thin layer of dust, obviously unused—why she was noticing dust while in the middle of love-making wasn't quite clear to her) and a wood block with knives of various lengths protruding from it. The surreal superimposed on the mundane—what a day she was having!

"Oh," Theresa's reverie was interrupted by the first rush of an orgasm. A shudder passed completely through her body, leaving a tingling at the base of her spine. She had denied herself sexual pleasure for most of her life and to now let herself go, with a complete stranger in a situation fraught with obvious and scarcely perceived dangers, on a day in which she had experienced frustration and terror like no other, she felt more alive than she had ever felt in her life.

"Bite me," she said, tilting her head a bit to the right and pulling back her long, silky hair with her left hand. Certainly, she thought, it was better to go through with this before she lost her nerve. Alternately tensing and relaxing her thigh muscles, while also pushing against the vampire's shoulders with her hands, she rode him up and down. Although his member no longer felt cold inside of her, it still felt unnatural, somehow, like his skin, which felt too much like an Italian calf-leather jacket she'd once owned. It also felt so right. The hardness pushing into her hurt...but it also felt so good she almost wanted to scream! 'Glorious', she thought, her brain having fumbled around for a few moments, seeking the proper word in English. Shit! She was having the best sex of her life and she was thinking about English vocabulary! That and, of course, the fear that he was going to kill her after drinking her blood when he was done having sex with her. It was the type of thing men typically did with women... use them and cast them aside... only this had a foreboding of finality to it far different from any one-night-stand she had ever regretted afterwards. On the one hand it was terrifying; but it was also exhilarating! She couldn't remember ever having such an exciting moment in her life—of course what he was doing to her was making it hard to think of *anything* at the moment!

She (oh yes!...yes!) submerged herself in the feeling as waves of ecstasy threatened to drive all conscious thought out of her brain and forced herself to focus before she lost her nerve. "Do it," she repeated, "bite me!" This earned her a look in the eye—and from what eyes! At first glance his eyes had appeared to be a very light blue, like sapphires, but not solid in color. Up close, eyes that had before seemed cold, empty and bottomless now seemed like windows into a far galaxy. The orbs gazing into hers were full of myriad gold and silver flecks, appearing for all the world like distant the vastness of space holding a galaxy of miniature stars. She was reminded of the final scene from *Men in Black*, with the marble bag where all the marbles looked like they contained miniature galaxies. Startled, she drew back a bit, bringing her lover's face into full view. Hands that had been beneath her buttocks, helping her up and down motion became still and she was rewarded with a smile...not exactly warm, but not malicious or evil.

"As you wish," he said, as the smile widened enough for her to see past his lips, to see once again those teeth that were usually kept hidden. "Oh my god," she thought to herself, "it's true...fangs!" Then there was pain (a *lot* of pain!) in the soft area of her neck just above her collarbone. For a moment it was all she could do to clench his shoulders, fighting the urge to pull away, feeling a warm wetness welling from the wound that she knew was blood. In her pain, she'd stopped moving, but now *he* was lifting her again, dropping her onto his extended phallus again and again, pushing deeper and deeper into her, as though his penis was growing larger as he fed on her lifeblood.

Shaking herself back into mental focus, Theresa reached out towards the block of knives, just out of reach of her fingertips. Reaching a little further, then a little further still, she managed to grasp the knife on the end and, between one finger and a thumb, pull it from the block. A paring knife— perfect! Getting a better grip on it she quickly slashed it across the vampire's neck making a shallow incision, and then swiftly... before he could stop her... bent her head and began to drink. She tensed, expecting a possibly violent reaction.

Instead, he asked in a rather amused voice, "What *are* you doing?"

"Making sure I come back as a vampire...oh!" she convulsed in an orgasm—but women had never had difficulty talking and fucking at the same time, "Some things I've read say it's not enough to be bitten—that I need to drink the vampire's blood to be sure."

He smiled, "For once, Hollywood might be right—it seems to help—I guess you saw the old *Dracula* movie with Lawrence Olivier—but what's to stop me from ripping your head off before you change?" he said with an evil grin, thrusting even deeper inside her. It felt wonderful, that firm spear exploring parts of her body that held hidden pleasures she'd rarely visited, but that wonderful rush of pleasure was tempered suddenly by fear—would he really kill her? She had to make sure that didn't happen.

A moment ago she'd been about to lose herself in the orgasms that racked her, spasms pulsing through her thighs and arching her back. Now, with self-preservation kicking in, the cunning seductress that dwelt inside most women suddenly materialized. Purring quietly, she slid her lips along the vampire's ear, flicking her tongue along the lobe and down along his neck to the incision she'd made, while slowing her pelvic motions while, at the same time, squeezing more tightly, doing her best to be as seductive as possible. "You drink blood while having sex, don't you?" she whispered. Not receiving a response, she continued, "There's a word for this in English, it's called being 'kinky'...I've always wanted to do something like this!" Gently, she placed her lips around the shallow gash and sucked. This was what she wanted—an end to her pointless life and a new beginning—and being young forever! The hands on her buttocks were gripping her so tightly now it was almost painful, and they began to move her up and down faster and faster, increasing the tempo to new heights. All of a sudden she felt an explosion inside of her as the grip relaxed and she came to rest on his lap, feeling the warmth spreading inside of her for several long, luxurious moments. The vampire leaned his head back, sighing in pleasure, for the moment, at least, sated.

Determined still to show reasons why she should keep her head on her shoulders, drawing one last salty taste of blood, she ran her tongue gently across his neck and then gradually down his chest, letting his body tell her what to do to bring him pleasure. She circled his nipple then bit it gently. This was as low as she could bend down, so she lifted herself again, pulling herself free from his penis, which still stood erect and had a smear of blood... hers... on it. Lowering herself to her knees between his legs, she pushed her head forward and let her tongue dart forth—like an adder tasting a pair of eggs prior to swallowing them. From the sounds in the back of his throat, she could tell her attentions were bearing fruit (she had a brief thought of Eve, Adam and a serpent, from a cartoon she'd seen recently but quickly pushed it out of her mind—the snake she was attending required her full attention; she had never done this before and only had the rare viewing of pornographic videos to rely on for instruction in what she was going to attempt). Did her vaginal blood taste different from the blood she'd sucked from the gash she'd made in the vampire's neck? What would she have thought this morning if she'd known she'd later be asking herself such a question?

Pushing harder now, starting from the base, she began moving her tongue from side to side. She moved up the shaft ever so slowly, feeling his level of excitement increase and hearing his breath (breath?) quicken. As she moved up to the tip she began to make complete circles. She was using her hands now as well, her left hand gently tickling while her right hand grasped him firmly, slowly moving up and down. She felt him place his hands on her head, running them through her hair. For just a moment she thought of the feeling of having her hair shampooed in a salon and again forced the idle thought out of her head, trying to concentrate. Suddenly she felt her hair grabbed in handfuls and she was forced down, taking most of it into her mouth, so far back in her throat she nearly retched.

Again and again she was raised and lowered, each time being penetrated deeper into her throat. She fought the urge to gag, knowing instinctively that this was something she had to learn to master—a primitive reflex that was, at present, a hindrance rather than a protection. She closed her eyes and tried to concentrate, focusing on the favorable aspects of her ministrations; it actually was kind of fun, feeling the warm, firm and yet yielding flesh in her mouth, a toy like those used to silence children, just adult-sized. When the explosion came, it was a strange and bitter taste, but not so much fluid that she had any difficulty swallowing (she guessed the fact that he'd just come inside her moments before meant there was less the 2d time around). She swallowed again and looked up at her captor, anxious for some clue as to what might happen next. She was relieved to see him smiling at her. "That was very nice."

"I'm glad you liked it," she replied with a matching smile, "It was my first time."

"Mine too," he said, "At least it was my first time with an oriental lady... and probably the first time in the last 100 years or so." Seeing the expression that must have crossed her face, he raised an eyebrow, making her think of Spock from Star Trek. She paused a moment, mentally examining her own bodily processes. Nothing.

"You drank my blood and I drank yours... why is nothing happening to me?"

He burst out laughing (so incongruous it seemed when he'd been talking of decapitating her just minutes earlier).

"Fucking Hollywood! It doesn't happen instantaneously!" As near as I've been able to figure it out, it's like a virus. It takes some time for the infection to replicate and spread itself—and it doesn't always seem to take, not that I usually waited around to see what would happen."

"Oh," she said, not being able to think of much to say until another thought hit her. "By the way—what's your name?"

Chapter 7
The Little Corporal

"My name is Dracula, naturlich—of course," I quipped, just to see the look on her face. "No, I'm joking...these days I go by the name of William Miller, William because that is the English equivalent of my father's Christian name...first name...in German. Please don't call me 'Bill,' however. If you feel the need to shorten it, I suppose that "Will" will suffice."

"You don't look like a Will...or a William," she added.

I paused for a moment in deep reflection—I'd learned to 'play it close to the vest' as these Americans sometimes liked to say. Under the circumstances, however, it seemed there would be no harm in adding to what she already knew.

"I was born with the given name of Stanislaus, youngest son of Landgraf Wilhelm IX in the kingdom of Hesse-Kassel which was later to be known, at the time of my 'death', as the Kingdom of Westphalia and is nowadays part of what you know as 'Germany'." With what I hoped was a none-too-condescending smile, I asked her: "How about 'Stanley'? Do I look like a 'Stanley'?"

"Stan?" she asked quizzically, "That has a nice ring to it."

"Right," I said with a tight-lipped smile. "Stan the Vampire," I remarked, wondering how long it had been since anyone had called me by *any* name.

"I'm not much good at history," she continued, "Where is Westphalia... and what is a... land craft?"

Landgraf, actually. Taking your questions in order, Westphalia was a pieced-together territory in the Western part of the Germanic states and its actual territorial composition changed over the centuries, just like Poland, Germany, Yugoslavia and other parts of Europe. In my youth, it was a short-lived creation of Napoleon's in furtherance of his aims to form the German states into the "Confederation of the Rhine" as part of the Continental System to provide economic competition to the Empire of Great Britain.

The name was taken from the historical kingdom of Westphalia that existed at various times in history, going back at least to the time of the Romans and also existing during the time of Charlemagne. The area was much larger in ancient times than it was under Napoleon, and very little of it was actually part of what was traditionally known as Westphalia, with most of it consisting instead of the regions of Hessia and Eastphalia. It was also short-lived in the last incarnation, existing only from 1807 to 1813. Incidentally, "Westphalia" was also the name of the peace treaty that ended the 30 Years War among the Holy Roman Empire and the 80 Years War between Holland and Spain.

Going back to your other question, 'Landgraf' was a title of Germanic nobility. It has no real equivalent in English that I'm aware of... Viscount is probably the closest approximation. So, in terms of position, had I succeeded my father, I'd have been nearly equal to the famous "Count Dracula" of literature.

"Sorry," she said, shaking her head from side to side, "You use too many strange words..."

Not a problem—you're not even from this hemisphere and precious few Americans know anything of European history these days. Schools here seem to only teach US history, usually repeating the same material 3 or 4 times, from what little I know of it, having never attended school here, of course. According to what I've read recently, the damned scheming socialists have even removed "real" American history from the public schools and supplanted it with candy-assed, pussified, leftist whining, sobbing and moping, AKA "Common Core" Commie plots notwithstanding, from what I've observed, Americans know damned little of their own history and practically nothing about the rest of the world. The USA has been the most powerful country in the world for so long that Americans have become arrogant and complacent and don't bother to learn about other nations or cultures.

Anyway, let me give you a little history lesson as a background: when Napoleon Bonaparte came to power as First Consul, France was suffering the enmity—um, she was hated by—all the other nations of Europe because they were all monarchies and the French had murdered their king and queen. Chief among these were Austria and England; Austria because Marie was of the Austrian royal family and England for mostly historical reasons, including the recent rebellion of the American colonies which was inspired to no small degree by the writings of the 'philosophes' as they were called, the authors of the French enlightenment, and to whom victory was achieved courtesy of the timely arrival of the French navy.

That last bit was particularly embarrassing to the British, as England was the preeminent naval power of the age and they were quite enamored with their place on the world stage. In fact, it was only due to the fact the British Parliament had neglected to provide funding for proper maintenance of the fleet during peacetime, that much of the British navy was in port, having rotting timbers replaced, while the French blockaded Cornwallis at Yorktown. French parity on the oceans lasted something like two years or so, after which the British resumed their position as the preeminent naval power of the globe, which they would retain until World War II.

You said you were of mixed Japanese-Taiwanese heritage, with a Chinese grandfather, so I'm sure you know of Commodore Perry and his travels around Asia with British visits to Japan and all that? How three times their tiny island forced the giant of China to cede them territory in and around Hong Kong?

Anyway, England was rich and Napoleon had no hope of competing in global commerce due to the size of the British navy, so he tried to organize the nations of Europe in an economic alliance against Britain. Back then, Germany wasn't a unified state. As France grew stronger, Napoleon conquered the smaller nations of Germany and tried to force them into a trade alliance with France, the Netherlands and other countries on the continent, as a means of competing economically with the British Empire. Hence the term 'Continental System'.

As for Hesse-Kassel, we were allied with the Hanoverian king, George III of England, until our subjugation by Napoleon. He took Hesse and some other lands, combined them, put his asshole brother Jerome on the throne and renamed the region 'Westphalia', alluding to the peace treaty that had ended the thirty-years war in, if I remember my history correctly, 1648.

I was already in the army. Being the 2d son, it was kind of the tradition of those times: the first son, the heir, would learn about life at court, about diplomacy, about pomp and circumstance, double-dealing and back-stabbing, etc. The 2d son would on a military career embark; sorry, make that: embark upon a military career—having all these thoughts from the past is making me think using German grammar! Anyway, if there were a 3d son, he'd usually end up in the clergy or as a merchant. Back in those days, doing business was considered dirty, beneath the station of the nobility. This left only living at the top, off the people's taxes... along with the king and the other nobles... or serving in the military or the church—which was by far the worst of the three.

"Why so?"

Well, to quote Bill Murray in *Ghostbusters*, no, it was in *Stripes*: *"Did you ever see a monk get wildly fucked by some teenage girls?"*

Basically, the clergy doesn't get a lot of sex except for maybe each other and the occasional altar boy and that's definitely NOT what I am into!

Anyway, in my time of my life, the culture was that 'the heir' prepared to become the next lord of the house, 'the spare' tried to add to the prestige of the house through achievements in battle, while any others were hustled out of the way to some monastery or maybe put to work in a trade to add to the family fortune. Of course any females were married off, hopefully adding to either the family standing or its financial well-being. Back then pretty much everyone had their station in life and it was very difficult to move upwards in the social strata.

We rule you, we fool you...sorry, just remembering a famous illustration about the 1st and 2d estates as the royalty and clergy were back then called. I suppose I should also clarify that when I speak of 'Estates' this had nothing to do with land as in 'Real Estate," but it referred to one's position in society. Back then we royalty were classified as the 1st Estate, the Clergy as the 2d Estate, and everybody else as the 3d Estate. Basically upper and lower classes with the church folk lumped into a separate classification. I guess the clergy were ranked second because, like us, they did no actual work, living off the taxes or donations of the commoners, whose toil and sweat provided sustenance for us all. The nobles mostly played at politics or just played around, while the clergy spent their days in dusty libraries, at prayer, molesting nuns and altar boys or whatever they had to do to avoid having to work in the fields or learn a trade. Put it this way: group 1) nobility, what you'd have called samurai; group 2) priests and monks; and group 3) merchants and commoners.

In more modern times you may have heard of the News Media being referred to as 'The Fifth Estate'. I guess this is because they are a relatively new creation that has it's own power over the masses. In fact, I think there was a movie by that name about how Wiki-Leaks revealed to the world what a cold-hearted, corrupt, evil bitch Hillary Clinton was, which contributed greatly to her going down in flames as the least popular presidential candidate in US history! The 2016 election was rigged, like in 2020, although not nearly to the same extent but still there were millions of fraudulent votes cast in her favor, and she was so hated she STILL lost the election in a landslide, winning less than 2% of all the counties in the country or something like that! Anyway, I digress. Hmm, where was I? Oh yes.

Actually, the military would have been my choice anyway—dressing in silks and currying favor or locking myself away from women and engaging in philosophical speculation about how many angels can dance upon the head of a pin really weren't for me. So, when Jerome took command of the Westphalian corps, I rode off at the head of my regiment. I was 20 years old at the time—of course in those days, when the average lifespan was probably 40-something, I was already considered being a man. I can still remember how strange it felt—all the Germanic states, Austria, Prussia, Bavaria, Hanover, Baden, Wurtemburg, unserveiter... um... and so on... considered Bonaparte to be our mortal enemy. However, the smaller nations found themselves forced into his so-called Confederation of the Rhine and I found myself commanding the 1st Regiment of the Line of the Kingdom of Westphalia, Jerome Bonaparte le Corps

Commander, in Napoleon's army, into Russia marching in the summer of 1812.

As I concluded my brief narrative, I noticed that she'd gone slightly paler, her breathing had become shallower and her eyes had gone wider. I knew it was too soon for THE CHANGE to be occurring. I reached out with both hands, one touching her forehead and the other alongside her throat, feeling her pulse. Both her pulse and her skin temperature felt normal. "Are you feeling OK?" I asked.

She continued giving me her wide-eyed stare, like a fawn caught in the headlights. She swallowed, licked her lips, then she gasped out: "YOU KNEW NAPOLEON?"

A moment of reflection and I realized just how fantastic this must seem to my, um, guest.

> Well, I am not entirely certain that I can claim to have really *known* him, I doubt many persons really did," I explained, "but I of course with him on numerous occasions dined, even once alone, the day after he sent Jerome back to France; it was supposed to have been myself and various other officers, but one was ill and the others arrived late due to congestion on the roads. Oh, and there was a ball I attended which he threw in celebration of Jerome's coronation. Mostly I just sat in the back and listened to him at staff meetings, briefings, and so forth, prior to our embarkation. During the campaign the army was split into thirds, with Napoleon at the center and Jerome on one of the flanks, so I didn't often towards the end of my life see him. I was in Paris at the time of his return from his first exile, and his return again from Waterloo, but our paths never crossed, as at that time I was a creature of the night and had no commerce with those from my past.

"You're shitting me!"

"No, my lovely young lady, I shit you not! Napoleon was my boss!"

"What was he like?" she asked, in obvious awe.

"Very smart, very energetic, always in a rush...short," I said, smiling again (although this was my normal smile, not showing the length of my canine teeth, which I did not reveal casually nor had I done so for more years than I could count!), "he was impulsive, supremely self-confident...driven. He would finish dinner while others were just on their aperitifs working—um—still eating their appetizers. Sorry, thinking these thoughts is making me have German grammar again! Anyway, Napoleon was hated by the diplomats and both of his wives but loved by his soldiers. He was a visionary who tried to spread the ideals of the revolution to his people, he was a reformer who made the French legal system less harsh than it had been and an amateur archeologist who had an interest in Roman and Greek history and really started the field of Egyptology at a time when even the Egyptians had little to no interest in their ancient civilization—and he was a thug who stole the treasures of Europe and North Africa at the point of a gun, particularly those of Italy, which he sold to finance his wars. Basically, he was an interesting man to work for."

"Can you tell me about how you became a vampire?" she inquired, "and why you have a spice rack and why there's a mirror in your front hall... and how does a vampire get a Harley...and a driver's license? Also, you were talking about animals on the food chain, but what about humans and dogs, such as the three large ones you have keeping you company here; they can certainly be friends and companions can't they, even if humans are more evolved?"

> My goodness, I am not accustomed to my food asking me this many questions! However, it is a story worth telling, and a tale that I haven't related since World War I, so I will indulge you. As for the spice rack, and the cans of food in the larder and the condiments in the refrigerator—all are there just to maintain the appearance of normalcy; after all, I occasionally have humans in this house and it is necessary to appear as ordinary as possible. As for the mirror, I assume you are referring to the legend that vampires do not cast a reflection?

Receiving her nod in response, I continued.

> Vampires are not ghosts. We are real creatures of flesh and blood (was that a pun?) and we appear in mirrors. What most probably happened is this—many years ago there was an outbreak of rabies... don't ask me where and when because I can't recall... but many people were infected. One of the typical symptoms of rabies, apparently, is that those afflicted cannot bear to see their own reflections. Somehow this became part of the vampire mythos. Either that or ghosts don't

appear in mirrors and someone mixed up ghost stories with tales about vampires.

Anyway, as for how I became a vampire, and how I eventually came to reside in the dull and boring rural backwater of Goshen, Indiana, why don't we move to the parlor? It is more comfortable and you can relax while I relate my history and try to decide what I'm going to do with you. Would you like a beer? I have some Yuengling Black & Tan which is quite excellent, Guiness Stout and also some Michelob Bock which are actually quite good and some English ales and bitters. I'm going to have one, you're welcome to join me.

"Oh yes," I replied to the question in her eyes, "vampires can drink just about any liquid, including wine and beer... it's just solid food that doesn't agree with us...and of course it's really only blood having actually sustenance providing. Sorry again about my German grammar, I am not accustomed to having conversations for so long a time; I am many years out of practice! What I mean is it is only blood that provides the necessary nutrition, although I wouldn't be surprised if we also make use of the protein and carbohydrates in beer. I'm afraid I am not a biologist...maybe I should say 'xenobiologist'. Anyway, apparently most of those who write vampire stories aren't either. As an evolutionary advancement based on the human genome, our physiology is more advanced than most writers take the time to consider.

Anyway, I was offering you a beverage. Sorry, I have no Sake. Whisky? Wine? I have a decent selection. No? How about a Brandy Alexander? You've never had one? Wonderful—this will allow me to use the vanilla ice cream I've been keeping in the freezer. There are things I keep for appearances sake such as eggs and lunchmeat that do not go to waste as I can feed them to the animals, but I don't give them things with sugar as it's bad for their teeth, so let's take a look and see if the ice cream is still good..."

Chapter 8
In the Still of the Night

Little killer paused, tasting the night air. Something was different, a strange smell, something he'd never encountered before. He rolled the taste about on his tongue; oily and flowery, a little sweet...not unpleasant but somehow not normal or natural. Dismissing the thought, he continued his progress across the lawn towards the house. Silent as night, as soundless as death, he flowed across the grass, keeping to the shadows, just a deeper blackness in the dark.

When he reached the shadow of the old oak, he paused again, sensing his surroundings. Crickets chirped, lightning bugs buzzed, moths hummed, mosquitoes whined, the grass breathed—nothing but the normal sounds of the night. With a great leap and ripping of claws he was up the cracked bark of the trunk and onto one of the upper branches. Again, he tarried for a moment, prying loose a few bits of bark from between his claws, as well as a bit of rabbit fur...a leftover from lunch. The rabbit had been a youngling, certainly from this spring's litter, but had still made a satisfying meal. He'd eaten his fill, left the carcass for the big, noisy killers to finish, then enjoyed a leisurely nap on the roof. He tolerated the big, noisy killers, stupid and clumsy as they were, as fellow servants of the god-master.

Little killer's thoughts turned back to the god-master and he smiled to himself. Tonight he was hunting the master, the greatest of all killers—and tonight he would be victorious! Tonight he would best the craftiest killer of them all!

With less sound than the slight breeze through the oak leaves, he leapt to the roof, drifted up the incline like water going backwards, and nosed his way through to his secret passageway—a loose slat in the exterior grille covering an opening into the attic. The smells now were of dust and cobwebs, wood and mouse dung. There were no mice in the attic, he knew—his predations kept them away during the summer, but winter chills often drove them indoors—and what delicious treats they made, as well as some entertainment during the bleak, cold time.

Silently he padded around dusty old boxes, old glass bottles and jars, an ancient child's-size rocking chair and other things that served no purpose he had ever understood nor cared to, over to the rectangle on the floor around which dim light from below shone through and the knotted end of a cord projected through; a cord, he knew, that hung down on the other side but was high enough off the floor to be out of reach as a toy from his days as a kitten when anything that could be chased or batted had fascinated him.

It was at this place a faint light leaked through the floor in straight, intersecting lines. This next bit required the utmost in patience and precision. Carefully, he crept onto the folding ladder. It creaked only slightly as his weight forced it open the width of a paw. Slowly, pushing forward, he was able to get his head and forelegs through the widening opening. He paused again for a moment, listening to the faint sounds coming from somewhere below him... the master was speaking and there were those pleasing, melodic noises The Master often liked to listen to and conjured up with his magic. The Master's magic was very powerful: he could create light when it was dark, make the house warm inside no matter how cold it was outside... and somehow he always seemed to be able to sense Little Killer's presence no matter how careful he was. Even the big, dumb killers who shared his habitat and with whom he a standing non-aggression pact, despite their giant noses and superior sense of smell, didn't have senses as acute as the master; it seemed he didn't have to see, smell or hear things, somehow he just *knew*.

Two leaps took him up, towards the roof, on one of the flat-branches (men used their magic to change the shape of their tree-and-stone houses...a very neat trick, that), then he allowed himself to fall straight down. The surface yielded as he struck and he spun himself around, allowing his tail and hindquarters to go first through the opening that appeared at one end, hung just a moment with his claws to slow the trap-door as it's spring began to return it to its original position (he didn't know why the floor would open and then close again, but he had learned how to make it obey him, at least from the top side). He released, just as the door was about to close, spun around again so he was facing head-down, and whipped his tail to align himself so all 4 paws hit the ground, absorbing the shock of the impact. He paused again. Had he been heard? Both the trap door (heavy, with the folding ladder on top of it) and his impact from his drop to the floor below had made some noise, but very little. He paused, using all of his senses; good, it seemed he had made his entry undetected.

Tonight, however, The Master was distracted and this gave him an opportunity; tonight, he would be victorious! Waiting until there was a increase in sound in the magical noise the Big Killer created out of the air, Little Killer let the rest of his body slip from the trapdoor, spreading his body as much as possible and whipping the air with his tail to slow his descent, then he used first his forelegs and then hind legs to absorb the shock of landing. Again, he paused, trying to sense if his impact on the wood floor, or the squeak of the hinges in the folding-stairs had betrayed him. As the distant conversation continued unabated, he felt confident of his success. Pausing only to brush away some dust and cobwebs that had clung to his whiskers, he proceeded on with his mission. Slinking along the hardwood floor as silently as a ghost, he came to the main staircase.

There were two staircases connecting the upper floor and ground floor. Had he been human, he might have wondered if the smaller, narrow stairs in the back of the house had been designed for servants or for children. Certainly, the back stairs had served him well on other occasions. The wider, main staircase, however, had threadbare carpeting covering the stairs, with only an area slightly wider than his body on either side where the wood was not covered. This night, he used the carpeted area to his advantage, making his silent paw-steps even more so. Slowly, methodically, he made his way down the stairs to the parlor.

The next part was the most difficult: covering the final distance to his quarry without being detected. He hunched down, his head lower than his hindquarters, and began to move forward slowly and methodically, one slow step at a time, wagging his body in barely-controlled anticipation.

Chapter 9
Nappy

“ “Napoleon was born to be a soldier,” I said. The girl had excused herself and spent at least 20 minutes in the bathroom, doing whatever it was they do after having sex. While she was occupied I’d gone outside, put out food and water for the dogs and the half-dozen or so farm cats that roamed the property, then put on some music. I was in a mood for the classics, so I put on one of my old favorites, the Mozart Requiem. Once she was back, seated, with a dessert in her hands (I still loved this miracle of electric ice boxes that allowed one to keep food preserved for months or even years at a time), I continued my life’s saga.

I remember hearing, long before I ever entered service with the French, of one action in which Bonaparte led a charge across a bridge. Leading from the front like that is a good way to get killed, but it also showed the little guy had some “big balls,” as the Americans like to say. It's also one of the reasons his troops were so fiercely loyal. He also ate and slept little better than the common foot soldier and, with us, was always “the general” and not “the emperor,” if you get my meaning. I do not know much about his life at court but, when he was with his troops, he was down-to-earth, approachable, and really cared about the well-being of his soldiers, as is true of all good officers.

Jerome Bonaparte, on the other hand, acted every bit the king he was, even though he was not to it born but was made king by his brother. When we began the march on Russia, he had six wagons and carriages just for his personal baggage and his entourage. He not only had a variety of uniforms, but clothes and shoes suitable for wearing at court, silver plates and place settings, a quartet, two concubines—that means prostitutes—and even a harpsichord! Who on earth goes off to battle with a damned harpsichord! Where Napoleon slept in a simple camp tent, Jerome had this Turkish...what is the word? Anyway, this Turkish tent with a wooden framework which allowed for heavy inner and outer curtains to be hung during the winter to keep out the cold. The damn thing took about an hour to be struck and packed away, along with all the carpets and silk pillows unserveiter...um...and so on. Sorry, (I said with a smile), as I before mentioned I am not accustomed to speaking for such a length of time and about these old memories of history remembering and thinking does seem to be bringing my Germanic way of speaking out. Please forgive me when I forget my English.

> And so...eventually, Napoleon felt much frustration with Jerome for not making the march as quickly as expected and Jerome was relieved of command and ordered to return to Westphalia. At this point I was promoted and placed in charge of the Westphalians as interim Corps commander. It was a position I would not hold for long, for I was wounded shortly thereafter, but for a time I commanded all the forces of my small homeland.

"Got you," I said, spinning on my left foot and snatching the black blur out of the air—the black, furry shape that had been aiming for the back of my head just a moment before. "

Here," I said to my guest, "You've met my dogs. This is my cat, Caesar." I placed the animal beside her on the sofa, stroking his head. He responded by glaring at me, nipped at my fingers, then bounded across the room to his favorite chair, an old William & Mary armchair with a well-worn cushion, where he immediately curled up with his back to us.

"Sorry about that, he's usually more sociable," I said, "I guess he feels he 'lost face' or something.

"What was he doing," she asked. "Does he always come flying across the room like that?

"Yes," I replied, "It is a game he plays, I think, where he tries to sneak up on me, like Kato and Inspector Clouseau (seeing her lack of comprehension, I realized she had probably never seen the Pink Panther movies as they were from the 1960's and '70's, predating her by a generation at least. I made a mental note to explain it to her later on and maybe even show her the movie—the one with Peter Sellers, not the remake I had suddenly remembered existed and might just as well have left forgotten!). He almost got me this time, I did not hear him while I was talking, but I felt his...*Jägerlust*...um...joy of the hunt...just before he leaped."

Her eyes widened slightly. "Do you mean you are psychic?"

> Something like that. I can't really read his or the dogs' thoughts, but I can sense their feelings—and, how to say it...transmit my feelings to them as well, maybe something

similar to how animals can sense fear, etcetera. Incidentally, it was supposedly one of my ancestors who formed an elite unit of 'Jägers' or 'hunters' into what the English called 'skirmishers': soldiers who were excellent marksmen trained with rifles, which were far more accurate than muskets at long range. These men would frequently be deployed to scout the enemy or secure the flanks of columns on the march. In battle, they would often advance individually, in front of the main body of troops, sniping away at officers, sergeants, sappers, artillerymen or other targets of value instead of just standing there shoulder-to-shoulder and blasting away in a group. Anyway, to continue my narrative...

We were assaulting the city of Smolensk. It sat upon an important crossroads and was a major supply depot for the Russians so, for one of the few times during the campaign, they stood up and fought—really fought us. Bonaparte's plan was to capture the town and it's supplies and set up a base in case we needed to establish winter quarters as Moscow was still some ways forward and Poland and France a long ways to our rear.

I was on the flank with my 30,000 Westphalians and the French that had been commanded by Jerome, the divisions of Junot, Poniatowski and Regnier.   Junot technically had overall command. After all, I was a foreigner and commanders above Corps level pretty much had to be French, but as he was suffering from a serious bout of dysentery or diarrhea, I was given operational command of our flank for the battle. I had a total of 80,000 men under my command, facing the Russian 2d army. Bonaparte was in the center and his brother Eugene, the Viceroy of Italy, was on the other flank. Our job was mostly to make sure the Russian cavalry did not try to outflank us while Napoleon pressed the attack in the center, trying to separate the two Russian armies by driving a wedge between them.

On about the 5th or 6th day, I cannot now remember except I recall the battle lasted for 8 days, the order came to move forward, to try to surround the city. We engaged the Russian defenses and I was observing my infantry moving forward when I was struck by a musket-ball. I was wearing a cuirass— a type of metal breastplate, which took most of the impact, and the ball had traveled some considerable distance as I was at least 200 paces removed from the nearest Russian soldiers, but the ball still penetrated and the force of the impact knocked me from my horse. I struck my head and lost consciousness. I 'came to' on an ambulance—a type of narrow wooden, cart or wagon—nothing at all like the ambulances of today.

As an officer from a reasonably wealthy family, I had brought my own surgeon—actually I shared him with several of the other officers in the Corps—which was a common practice in those days. As I recall, it took some time for the runner to find him and bring him to me and quite a bit more time for him to locate and remove all the bits of lead, which involved a lot of probing around in the wound with his fingers—and all I had for an anesthetic was a bottle of brandy—hardly ideal. You see, bullets in those days were not covered in copper or brass jackets as they are now—they were balls of soft lead that would often fragment upon striking something hard—such as bone or, in my case, my cuirass. Many soldiers who survived gunshot wounds in those days would later die of lead poisoning from bullet fragments what hadn't been removed or from infection from bits of uniform that were forced into the wound by the passage of the bullet. Actually, I must recant that last statement: many men died of post-operative infections: I don't know what anyone actually lived long enough to die from lead poisoning: that might just be an urban legend.

In any case, the surgeon had to get every bit which, in my case, turned out to be 2 large pieces and one smaller bit which caused me a great deal of agony while he fumbled around inside of my chest, looking for it. Nothing went deep enough to be immediately fatal, but even with the lead removed, it likely would have resulted in an infection that itself could have been the end of me had the fates not had something else planned for me, something some might call a fate worse than death. At any rate, following the surgery, I was placed on a cot in a temporary, field hospital and that night, while all save myself were sleeping, we had a visitor.

I had passed out for a time but the pain of my recent surgery and the itching of the catgut sutures awakened me in the still hours of the night, when the moon was on the wane, and kept me awake. While lying there, pondering my future, I saw a shadow out of the corner of my eye, indistinct in the dim light cast by the watch-fires. Naturally, I assumed at first that it was an orderly or a surgeon...but there was something odd about the way it moved, almost gliding from cot to cot, sometimes lingering for a long time, bent low over the patient. Finally, the shadow stopped at the cot next to mine and, by what dim light was available, I observed as the shape carefully *unwrapped* the bandages on the patient's leg. Just an orderly changing the dressing, I thought at first. However, it then lowered its head onto the wound and I heard a faint sucking sound...much like what you'd hear from an infant nursing at a bottle. After some moments, just as I had determined that I should call the night's watch, that something was not right, the patient began to convulse, then he attempted to sit up. The creature clamped a hand over the patient's mouth and forced him back down on the cot, hard. As this was done at arm's length, I could see the creature possessed great strength.

I tried to call for the guard, at this point, and discovered my mouth was dry with both a lack of moisture and a hint of fear, my throat shut. In battle, I felt the same fear as any man when going into battle but never before a feeling such as this—I was frozen into immobility and discovered I could not make a sound. I watched in horror as the patient's struggles grew less. Could I find an object with which to make a noise? Surreptitiously, I reached down and began feeling around the side of my cot. My saddle was there, my boots... my personal effects had been placed there so they could be moved with me, if I needed to be moved, without them becoming lost. Thanking my aide or whomever had such foresight, I tried to find my horse pistols, my sword... ... but next I felt my cloak, my hat, my... gloves? Everything I touched was of leather or cloth, nothing that could be used to make a noise. In the meantime, the struggles next to me finally ceased.

With great foreboding I watched as the ghoul *rewrapped* the bandages, obviously in order to disguise the grisly event I had just witnessed. I still quite clearly recall how every hair on my body seemed to stand erect as the creature finally stood up, circled the cot that now most certainly contained a fresh corpse, and came towards me. I lay quite still, my breath stuck in my throat, while my hand beneath the cot moved aside my cloak, searching for a weapon.

The creature must have been drawn by my surreptitious movements, for the next thing I knew it was kneeling over me and for the first time I saw that it was hooded, with a vaguely seen pale face beneath the hood...one that did not look, or smell, quite right. It began running its hands across the bandages on my chest as it bent so low I could smell its fetid breath. Just then, my hands passed back across my hat, touching the metal badge which was my house crest. I pulled it free with the speed and strength of a man about to go mad (which I most certainly was) and plunged the clasp, which was sort of a long, dull pin, deep into the creature's neck.

Blood spurted from the wound, splashing across my face, into my eyes and into my opened mouth. With a howl... or a hiss...or maybe a bit of both, the creature overturned my cot, tossing me quite a distance and causing me to land, on my back, across another patient. It must have fled for, once I was able to roll onto my side (with some assistance from the poor sergeant I'd landed on) and wipe the blood from my eyes, the apparition had vanished.

I had passed out after the attack, still sharing a cot with the sergeant who was either too week or respectful enough of officers that he failed to push me off onto the ground...or at least not until after I'd lost consciousness. By morning, I was back in my own cot and in a fever-induced delirium. If I told anyone what I'd seen the previous night, I have no recollection of doing so. I'm sure anything I mumbled would have been dismissed as feverish ravings, in any case. I did not know it yet, but the small amount of blood I'd swallowed was going to have a profound effect on me.

During my scattered moments of consciousness I had a pounding headache, my chest was alternately on fire or I shook with chills. I'd lost a lot of blood with the surgery, I likely was working on an infection, I was burning up from the fever... my prognosis was poor, to say the least. Oh, I mentioned the change isn't immediate, unlike in the movies? It's not as though my sense of time was that good at the time, but I think it took me about 2 days for the transformation. So, you still have time to think it over. Honestly, I think you might be better off with the alternative.

"The alternative?" she enquired.

"Death, of course...real, true, final death."

"But," she choked, her eyes almost blazing, "I WANT to become a vampire. Or is it vampires?"

I am guessing that the popular media has given you a romanticized notion of what it is to be a vampire, so let me tell you what you can really expect. First of all, vampires don't have friends. They don't go to high school, go on dates, fight with werewolves or plot to take over the world. A vampire's life is one of solitude, of hiding, of repressed loneliness, of the omnipresent fear of discovery and facing great difficulty in accomplishing routine but necessary tasks to maintain your existence and remain hidden from the world. To be a vampire is to be a murderer, a thief, and a rapist. Most of all, a vampire's life is one of planning and being cunning in all your dealings with humans. A careless vampire is a dead vampire—permanently dead as opposed to undead!

"Still," she said, "you are still here...so I gather that means being 'undead' is preferable to being really dead, eh?"

"Eh?" I echoed, "So you are Canadian now? Anyway, you are right, I still find things of interest in my continued existence and, even in the most trying times, I never felt like letting go. I suppose this is true of all life... Say, you must be tired," seeing her yawning, "Would you like to get some sleep?"

"What I'd really like is a shower," she stated, yawning again, "and to hear the rest of your story"

"In the morning," I admonished. "You appear on the verge of collapse and if I'd wanted to put my audiences to sleep I'd have become a priest like my cousin!"

After collecting our scattered clothing, I led her down the hall to the bathroom. It still contained the original claw-foot, enameled, cast-iron bathtub and copper pipes that had been in the house when I'd purchased it almost exactly 100 years ago. However, I'd recently had a modern shower installed, with a glass door and ceramic tiles. While I was at it, I'd had the original sink replaced with a very stylish basin and wooden cabinet combination.

Not that I often used either of them, vampires don't sweat or secrete oils to the extent of mere humans but, after all, what else did a wealthy vampire have to spend money on? It wasn't exactly the palace I'd grown up in, but my old brick farmhouse was much more comfortable than the crypts, coffins, basements, barges, coal cellars, warehouses, hay lofts, caves and other temporary lodging I'd sought out over the centuries. It was comfortable. And it didn't hurt to occasionally have workmen pay witness to the old man in his wheelchair sitting in the darkened parlor and share their observations with the community. No hideous fiend living in the old farmhouse, now encroached on 2 sides by suburban housing and on a third side by a cemetery, just some old man whose son was pursuing graduate studies at Bonn University in Germany. At least that was my story and I was sticking to it!

I showed her how to regulate the temperature of the water then, with the subterfuge that I needed to locate a clean towel for her. I stepped out and closed the glass door, lingering to allow my eyes to take in the full measure of her beauty. Such graceful thighs and calves, slender buttocks, hourglass waist, long straight hair, and other straight hairs (straight!) of a much shorter length in a lovely patch where her legs joined her torso. My close-up view of them, just minutes before, had been my first time to view straight pubic hairs—in person, at any rate.

It had been only a matter of seconds to get past the initial strangeness to decide I preferred them to the normal 'curlies'. I was admiring her nicely upturned breasts when she turned her back to me and...oh my!...bent over to wash her feet and ankles. My instant erection was testament to the fact I'd never before beheld a woman looking so enthralling from that particular angle. A straight line flanked by graceful curves centered in a classic heart shape. Simple enough geometry, but I'd never before seen it look so aesthetically enticing. Forgetting about the towel, I reentered the shower and quietly closed the door. Still with her back to me, I bent slightly and, starting with her knees, slowly drew my hands up the backs of her legs, ending with my hands cupping her firm, elliptical buttocks, my lips brushing against the nape of her neck. As she turned, seeking a kiss, I dropped down and, hooking my elbows behind her knees, lifted her up and pinned her against the tile wall. A brief adjustment using my right hand and I was in position. Simultaneously thrusting with both my tongue and pelvis, I penetrated her again, both high and low. Caught between an irresistible force and am immovable object, she hung there, suspended, while I fucked her...hard! Judging by the noises she was making, she didn't mind at all. In fact, were I to hazard a guess, I'd have said she was quite enjoying herself!

Chapter 10
A New Dawn

The second shagging finally burned off her remaining adrenalin and she was yawning by the time I'd finished toweling her off. "Where would you like to sleep?" I asked. "I sleep in the basement, naturally, but you might want to sleep in one of the upstairs bedrooms and wake up with the sun... you may not have many more opportunities."

"It must be sometime like 3 a.m.," she replied, "I don't want to be up with the sun...in fact, I hope I can sleep until noon. So, someplace dark sounds really good!"

"Bring your clothes," I directed, "and I will show you where this bat 'hangs out' during the daytime."

We returned to the parlor, passing the larger staircase that led upstairs. *Welcome to my parlor, said the spider to the fly,* I thought to myself. Back in the kitchen, I opened the door to the stairs that headed down to the basement, reached around the corner and flipped on the light. "After you," I motioned.

"What's that?" she asked, pointing to the bottom of the old, hardwood door.

That's a cat door," I replied. "You cut a hole in the door and place this piece over the opening. It's flexible plastic, so the cat can push his way through and then it closes again behind him. So, he can come and go as he pleases. Also, because the pieces fit pretty tightly, the amount of light that passes through is insignificant but it does give me a quick reference to know the level of ambient light on the other side... in case I need to unbar the door during the day to let someone into the basement."

Letting her pass in front of me, I turned and closed the door, pressed the stud to lock the knob, while simultaneously dropping the 1 meter-long piece of steel pipe onto the angle irons set into the masonry on either side of the door. "If you want to go outside later, during the daylight, just lift off this bar and place it here, off to the side. This is just one of my security measures in case of a break in or something, just to be sure I'm not disturbed unexpectedly."

At the foot of the stairs I flipped on the triple light switches, two of them controlling the overhead fluorescents and the third, which was another part of my security system. I probably had nothing to fear from my little guest, but the key to not becoming forgetful was to follow the same pattern each time.

"Wow," she exclaimed, "That's one heck of a TV!" Looking around, taking in the oak-paneled walls, the large paintings in heavy, gilded frames, the rest of my rather extensive entertainment system, the work area with its twin computers, the leather sofa, love seats, and the shelves and glass and wood cases holding thousands of hardcover and leather-bound books and some of my memorabilia, she added, "This is a huge basement—I never knew old farmhouses had basements like this!"

"They don't! When I bought the place, all it had was a dank cellar with leaky walls. About 40 years ago I had the area just behind the house excavated, extending the basement, and had it all furnished and turned into what you see here, along with a few other enhancements I might show you later. It took half the summer. I can already anticipate your next question, so I'll save you the trouble. I also own other properties, including a small apartment building in Chicago. A management company takes care of maintenance and rent collection and such things. Naturally, there is a cellar to which only I have the keys. I even have a reserved parking space all to myself. So, while the new basement was being installed here, I was living in Chicago, hanging out in bars and working at my dream job, sweeping up cow shit in the stockyards at night, if only to be where the cattle were kept."

Laughing at her perplexed expression, I told her, "You're tired, I will explain everything in the morning...make that in the afternoon, per your request." Taking her by the hand, I led her to the heavy, maple door with its cast-iron hinges that opened into my bedroom. Upon pushing it open, it was her turn to laugh. "What's so funny," I asked.

"The black bedding I can understand and even expected it," she chortled, "but playboy bunny posters? This looks like a bedroom you'd find in the Playboy Mansion!"

"Very good," I smiled, "that was exactly the effect I was going for. I can afford to, so why not live (live?) in comfort? And these centerfolds, not posters, are art of the most natural form. These date back to a time when *Playboy* was one of the most popular magazines of the day, with excellent editorial quality as well as some of the most beautiful women in existence—and before they turned art into pedophile and truck-driver porn by shaving off the pubic hair!" I nodded in the direction of Nicole Narain and Venice Kong. "And, in case anybody happens to nose around, it makes it look normal... and the fact the ladies on the wall are all from the '70's and '80's helps reinforce my cover story of being a feeble, old man." Turning down the bedspread and sheets and apologizing for the slightly musty smell, I placed our clothes on top of the chest of drawers, crawled in beside her lovely, naked form, and turned out the light. A good twenty minutes after her breath had become slow and steady, I carefully flipped the light back on and pulled off the covers. She continued sleeping. *Good,* I thought to myself. *Why have a phone with photo and video capabilities when I never get to use them?* It was not like I made that many phone calls....

After indulging the photographic muse from a variety of different angles, I pulled the covers over her graceful, naked figure, shut off the light and went back outside to put away the motorcycle. As I began to do so, I was struck by a sudden thought—my guest had mentioned her car had broken down. The police would be all over the crime scene once the bodies were discovered. I'd already decided to keep the girl around awhile longer...and there were various beauty tools, lotions, etc. that women needed to employ to feel good about themselves. I wasn't so concerned with clothing—less is more, as they say—but she might need more than the one change she had, particularly as her blouse was torn, she had a run in her stockings and one shoe had appeared damaged.

I pondered for awhile; would it be better to have the car towed or leave it abandoned to deepen the missing person's mystery? If she turned, it was certain she would not be attending classes any longer! Deciding, I walked to the side of the house, picked up one of the bricks from the stack that had been there for untold years, leftover from construction or repair of some sort, perhaps the chimney, and placed it in one of the saddlebags. It didn't take long to locate her car, just down the road from where 3 corpses lay stiffening in the pre-dawn dew. What had taken her considerable effort in walking took me a mere 2 minutes by motorcycle. Smashing the rear, side window, I then tossed the brick by the side of the road (I'd reasoned that I could easily pay to have the window replaced if it became desirable to keep the car). Then I discovered my error. Instead of the small, overnight bag I was expecting, there was a large suitcase, the type with wheels and an extendable handle. There was also a computer bag, a large purse and a backpack-style book bag. "Smart girl," I said to myself, realizing she'd wisely left it behind and walked off with only her car keys, where most women would have dragged their heavy purses along with them.

So, how to manage all this gear on a motorcycle, with my safety margin before dawn slowly ebbing away? The backpack and PC bag were easy enough to manage, but I ended up having to balance the suitcase on the gas tank, the handle clenched between my teeth. Cursing myself for the lack of foresight, I had an uncomfortable ride home but still managed to get the bike stowed in the barn, pet the dogs for a few minutes and gave them some fresh water, locked the door, and got her bags downstairs with time to spare before the dawn.

The girl was still asleep. Even from the doorway I could smell the lovely fragrance of her hair. I had to admit to myself I was loathe to surrender this source of new, erotic pleasure, yet the risk of keeping her around was so great the slightest miscalculation could lead to the loss of everything I had worked for, perhaps even my death. I mentally repeated the mantra I'd lived by for so many years: Cautious, Secret, Hidden, Safe; Bold, Reckless, Careless, Dead! Deciding to be safe rather than sorry, I removed the Katana and seppuku knife from the stand on the headboard, removed the Colt .45 model 1911 from the nightstand and the HK-91 from behind the door, collected the shotgun and another Colt from the area around my computers, and locked them away in a metal cabinet in my laundry room. There were other weapons in the house, in every room in fact, but none I was worried about her finding without a very thorough search. I then collected all the keys to my vehicles and placed them in the same locker, snapped the combination lock through the hasp-handle, then increased my security by shutting the door and locking the deadbolt. I then placed the key to that room up my ass, where I was certain she wouldn't go looking for it.

Next, without a shred of guilt, I quickly went through her effects. No cell phone: that was good. Her laptop was another potential issue: I didn't want her contacting the outside world, so I turned it on, leaving it open so it would run down the battery (which I noticed was down to 5% already), and removed the hyperlink cable and charging cord. A brief walk outside and they were safely resting at the bottom of one of the three ponds I had on my property.

OK, I felt fairly certain she wasn't going to cause me any grief while I was sleeping, so I got undressed and slid in next to her. She would sleep for awhile yet, but that was fine—I needed time to think. I lay there, smelling the delicate fragrance of her hair while my right hand cupped one firm buttock. What was I to do with her? Running the various scenarios through my mind kept me occupied for at least an hour or so, I finally nodded off.

I awoke to a strange sensation... It was normal to awake with an erection after feeding, especially when I'd drunk so deeply, but what was unusual was awaking to find something stroking me, gently and slowly exploring from the base of the shaft to the tip of my phallus. "Good morning," I spoke to the back of her head, as I still had my nose pressed into her hair.

"Oh shit, is it still morning?" she mumbled.

I levered myself up so I could see the illuminated clock on the nightstand on her side of the bed. "11:27...not quite noon"

"Mmmmmmmuph!"

The fingers that had been just a feather's touch now gravitated to the underside of my swollen member and held position while she slid back against me. I allowed myself the luxury of remaining relatively still while she moved back and forth, sliding me in between her legs. She had apparently been ministering to herself or having a *very* good dream, because she was already wet—and agreeably warm. For several minutes she rubbed me back and forth along her exterior channel and then, just as I was about to lose patience and take control of the proceedings, she placed her fingers under the tip and pushed me up and into her.

Words are inadequate to describe what I felt over the next few minutes as I built to a tremendous, shuddering climax while she repeatedly voiced, "oh shit! oh shit! oh shit!" When I finally came, she took my hand, put it in her mouth and bit down hard to silence her screams. Morning sex—was this something I'd been missing for a very long time. And to be surprised with it upon awakening? Awesome! Obviously I was going to have to keep this little stray kitten—I was just going to have to be careful—DAMN careful!

"Oh god," she sighed, "I need a shower." I reached over to turn on the lamp and then lay on my back while she lay half across me, chin balanced on my sternum, meeting me gaze for gaze. She ran her hand across my chest "don't you sweat?"

Not really...it's one of many changes you maybe be learning about very shortly. Hey, I'd make you breakfast, but it's daylight upstairs, so you're going to have to help yourself. There's some pancake mix in the cabinet to the right of the sink—it's the kind where you only have to add water...just check the expiration date to be sure it hasn't been there too long. If that doesn't do it for you, there are some frozen pizzas, some canned salmon and tuna, a bag of rice...and if you have a hankering for fresh vegetables there's a garden on the south side of the house—you can't miss it!

"A garden?" she queried? "It's all about appearances," I replied, "what farm house doesn't have a vegetable garden? Besides, it's one of the ways I pay my groundskeeper, he gets to take most of the produce home to his family...and I'm sure he sells some as well"

"You have a gardener?"

Yes, this area has a surfeit of Mexican immigrants, many of them illegal. I have an old Mexican cowboy who comes by every weekday, puts fodder out for the cattle, cuts the grass in front of the house when needed, and does odd jobs around the place such as mending fences, cutting and baling hay, etc. Sometimes the wife or one of his kids comes along and they putter around in the garden...or so he says...obviously I don't go out in the sunshine to watch them!

"I never thought about a vampire having a gardener!"

"Just remember Frodo," I suggested, "oh, by the way, I recovered your effects from your car last night, they're on the poker table under the stained glass tiffany lamp in the other room."

"Oh, wow, that was awfully kind of you"

Not at all. After breakfast, if you feel like it, feel free to take a walk around the property. I've got 220 acres in the parcel the house rests upon. There are three ponds with fish, ducks and sometimes Canada geese, a small wooded area with various wildlife and a couple hundred head of cattle. I've got a hummingbird feeder outside the kitchen window and some lovely daffodils down by the mailbox. By the way, don't try to leave the property or the dogs will rip your throat out. Oh, and it's Saturday, so you're unlikely to run into my caretaker, but if you do be sure he sees you puttering around in the vegetable garden or something else outside in the sunlight.

She gave me an odd look, started to say something, then turned and headed out of the room, no doubt feeling the call of nature more strongly than the need to make sure if I was serious or not. I knew I could trust the dogs to awaken me by barking if she tried to leave and then switched the light off—damn—she'd left the lights on in the outside room. A pillow over my head solved the problem. It was nearly mid-day; I needed to get a few hours of sleep, particularly as my guest was likely to require my attention in one form or another after she'd attended to her...what was that Marshal Davoust used to say...something about 'toilette et palate'? Davout (as the spelling appears in American history books) had been one Frenchman I'd really admired—the man had been a tactical genius, perhaps even the equal of Napoleon himself. The little girl's questions had brought back many old memories of my time in the service of the 'little corporal'. Just then, a Caesar of another sort intruded upon my reverie. Even beneath the pillow I heard the padding of tiny paws upon the shag carpet, followed by the soft impact as the cat landed upon the bed. Without fanfare, he curled up against my leg. Within minutes, the two of us were asleep.

Chapter 11
Tuesday Afternoon

Theresa had indeed first made her way to the bathroom on the first floor, feeling quite self-conscious as she was still naked, although of course there was no one around to see. After taking care of certain, pressing needs, she found towels and took a long shower. Once finished, she wrapped a large towel around her and her hair in a hand towel and returned to the basement to get some clothing from her travel bag, congratulating herself for having packed clothes for various occasions. Donning her favorite pink & gray warm-up outfit and her old but still very serviceable aerobics shoes, she was ready to let herself think of what had happened to her the previous evening and start thinking about what to do next.

Looking around, she still was amazed at the size of the basement—the square footage was at least twice that of the ground floor, upstairs, and that wasn't even including the bedroom. She wondered how often her host used the billiard table and if he'd be willing to teach her how to play. Like those upstairs, the cases and shelves were full of old books and what appeared to be all manner of antiques. Being nosy, she decided to open the closed doors along one wall and discovered a full bathroom that could have saved her the trip upstairs au natural, a laundry room with a Maytag washer and dryer that looked like they were probably from the 1970's but appeared to be in serviceable condition, a pantry, just near the base of the stairs (with a thick layer of dust on the cans and jars, some of which were no doubt long past their expiration date), and a workroom.

Unlike the rest of the basement, with its shag carpeting and wood paneling, this had rough concrete walls and a smooth cement floor. A workbench ran along one wall, with tools stacked on it and hanging from a pegboard on the wall. What she guessed was a furnace occupied the middle of the room, while a large water pipe ran the length of the ceiling and several round, metal support columns ran from floor to ceiling. There were the things you'd expect to see...various boxes stacked along one wall, several mattresses covered in plastic and leaning against another wall, some old doors and boards, several long lengths of chain and...were those manacles? The metal, storage closet in the corner seemed bent, so the doors probably couldn't close which is why she could see into the interior. Curiosity got the better of her, so she opened the door a bit wider. Yes, those were indeed manacles...and handcuffs, what appeared to be other restraints made from leather. Like everything else in the house, they were covered with a thin layer of dust, so they didn't seem to have been used in a long time. Still, why would someone keep chains and handcuffs in their basement? A moment ago, her brain had been on autopilot. Now, suddenly, the room seemed far more sinister and the implications made her catch her breath. Closing the door as swiftly and silently as she could, she headed for the kitchen.

Some instant coffee, heated in the microwave, helped her to calm down. She located the pancake mix and, after a brief search, some butter in the freezer. There was also some maple syrup that was partially turned to sugar and refused to open. By tossing the bottle in a soup pan and heating it on the old Sears electric stove, she was eventually able to get the top off.

She was hungry enough she decided to fry an egg after the pancakes and wished for some bacon. Anyway, she could make a run to the store after she had her car towed and..."Oh my God!" She dropped the spatula she'd just used to flip the pancakes as the full implications of last night's rash actions came crashing in on her. Food—was that something she needed to worry about or was she going to have to develop a taste for blood? Was she turning into a vampire? Why didn't she feel any different? What if she didn't turn into a vampire but she was now pregnant with a half-vampire fetus that would chew its way out of her womb? Would she ever see her mother again? Her friends?

As a wave of black panic came crashing down, she dropped to the floor in a crouch, arms hugging her knees, and began rocking back and forth. She felt a rush of tears and tried, unsuccessfully, to hold them back. With the tears came full sinuses. The need to blow her nose brought her back to her senses and she rose up, looking for a tissue. Not finding any, she grabbed a paper towel from the roll hanging on a rod near the sink...and got a face full of dust! Grabbing the next towel from the roll, she blew her nose, then repeated the process.

"Get a grip—crying isn't going to help!" Remembering the pancakes, she retrieved the spatula, rinsed it off and check on her flapjacks...dark on the bottom but not yet burned, she was relieve to see. Still feeling hungry, she finished cooking the rest of the food, sat and began to eat, which also helped to calm her down. She studied the cutlery she was using...a dull-gray metal blade on the knife and identical metal tines on the fork, certainly not the stainless steel to which she was accustomed, but both were free from any rest spots and had handles of some dark wood that appeared hand-made. She guessed they must be old, perhaps as old as the house itself.

Finding some washing-up liquid under the sink...dish soap or whatever it was called here... she cleaned up after herself and went back downstairs to her personal effects. A frantic search revealed the first item she was seeking—a pack of cigarettes with matches stuck into the cellophane. She didn't often smoke but she'd been under so much pressure recently she'd decided to bum a smoke before her interview which had led to her purchasing a pack... then another...

"Wonderful! Damn, do I need a smoke!" Digging through her purse, then through her book bag, she was unable to find her cell phone. "Damn, where the hell is it? Fuck!" She hoped what's-his-name, Stan (?) hadn't left it in her lousy excuse for a car. Maybe he'd put it in the bedroom or left it in his jacket pocket. Well, first things first... she headed outside for a smoke.

Her hands were shaking, so she broke the head off the first match. Taking a deep breath, she forced herself to slow down. She had better success the second time and gladly inhaled a lungful of smoke—and just as quickly coughed it back out. She wasn't used to smoking anymore, she should take it a bit more slowly! The second drag was much more pleasant and she felt herself beginning to relax. Raising her head, she looked around. It was a beautiful day, with the sun about directly overhead. Thoughts of graduation popped into her head and left just as quickly as she noticed the 2 dogs, sitting in the shade of a large maple tree some 30 feet away, tongues lolling out of their mouths as they gently panted in the mid-day warmth. It was the *way* they looked at her that was making her feel uncomfortable. Deciding on a change of scenery, Theresa quickly put the house between her and the dogs and headed down the path she discovered. She felt that she was being observed but refused to bow to the temptation to look over her shoulder—she had enough to be nervous about already!

She walked past carefully tended beds of petunias, pansies, snapdragons and some other flowers she could not put a name to. She also noticed a stack of black, plastic trays, some several dozen of them stacked one inside the other, some large bags of soil and fertilizer and a bucket with gloves, trowels and other gardening tools. Clearly the Mexican man or his wife were cultivating more than just vegetables for sale. In any case, it was quite beautiful. She walked around a pond, past several low-lying whitewashed farm buildings of indeterminate use and found herself at a large, metal gate set in a barbed-wire fence. The gate was secured with an old, chain-link combination bicycle lock looped over a post.

Lifting the chain, she pulled the gate open and fastened it behind her, hoping it would put some space between her and the canines...although the gap between the gate and post looked large enough for them to squeeze through. A few more minutes and she'd crossed uneven, grassy pasture and arrived at the woods. She spent a good hour walking through the woods and smoking until the tobacco began to make her feel nauseous. A sudden crashing caught her attention as a rabbit dashed past her, pursued closely by the third dog, the one that looked like a wolf—Brutus, she thought she remembered. The rabbit disappeared into a...was "thicket" the right word? The dog ran back and forth, barking furiously, unable to follow the rabbit into the dense brush. The dog still made her feel nervous, even with it's attention directed elsewhere, so Theresa turned to make her way back to the house and saw the black dog, the Rottweiler, sitting on the path, looking at her. Seeing her approaching, he turned and trotted away, apparently not sharing his companion's interest in the rabbit. "Curiouser and curiouser," she muttered to herself.

When she reached the pond she continued on in a counter-clockwise direction rather than retracing her steps, which brought her around to the ubiquitous red barn with an old, slightly rusty pickup truck parked alongside. Continuing to indulge her curiosity, she walked completely around the barn and, as the smaller, side door was unlocked, she naturally entered the barn to take a look around, never having been in a barn before. She'd been expecting a tractor, maybe even a horse, but she had not expected the sight that awaited her—a fleet of cars and motorcycles. She counted 8 cars, ranging from a really old one similar to cars she'd seen at the Henry Ford museum, to one she recognized as a 1965 Ford Mustang and another one in the shadows that she thought might be a Honda Accord, but she wasn't sure. She knew nothing about motorcycles, although she'd ridden a scooter much of her adult life, but the ones she saw looked expensive. Damn! This vampire was just full of surprises!

Vampire...shit! The fear came rushing back...just what had she done last night!? She needed to find her phone and check her messages, then check her email and call to have her car towed to a garage and then—did she dare check into a hospital to see if anything was happening to her? No, that was probably not a wise move. Anyway, it was already afternoon—time to get busy.

Chapter 12
If a Body Meet a Body...

Sheriff Gene Miller had seen a lot in his 20-plus years in law enforcement. Until this afternoon, he'd thought nothing would surprise him anymore. He was wrong. When the call had come in, reporting bodies out at the Hillenberg place, he'd expected to find a car full of teenagers wrapped around a tree beside the road or victims of a hit and run. Instead, he found a long line of vehicles pulled up on the shoulder of the road, including an ambulance, a paramedic van, no fewer than three Goshen City police cars, plus one sheriff's department vehicle, to which he added his own. The UPS driver who'd called 9-1-1 was still there, standing on the opposite shoulder of the road looking on, while deputy Ben Williams was unrolling yellow "police line" tape between the telephone poll at the far corner of the yard and the mailbox at the foot of the driveway. "Up by the house," he called to the sheriff, "and it ain't pretty!"

Miller carefully walked up the gravel drive watching each foot of ground before each step to be sure he didn't step on any evidence. When he saw the three corpses, he immediately knew there was something wrong. The brothers might possibly tie one on and beat each other with fists, but to kill each other? No, that is one he wouldn't believe, no matter how stoned they might have been on marijuana or high on something else. He also had a pretty clear view of Jason's body, lying just a few feet into the ragged front lawn.

Miller had done 4 years in the Marines before going into civilian law enforcement. The single neck wound, angled so that the blow had probably come from behind the victim made it look more like an assassination to him than a knife fight. It was also so odd that all 3 bodies were lying within a few feet of each other. Perhaps one person might drop dead on the spot during a knife fight, but THREE? Most knife wounds sent people to the nearest telephone to call for an ambulance but here he didn't see any signs of any of the three of them having crawled so much as a yard towards the house, judging by the blood-stains on the grass.

Also, all three of the brothers were carrying considerable fat protecting their vitals, and that meant that ordinarily, stab wounds should not have been immediately fatal. It was as if some madness had gripped all three of them and inspired them to go for killing blows? He knew at least one of the brothers had played football in high school and probably all three had wrestled, but he was fairly certain none had been in the military or been involved in martial arts. In fact, despite a smattering of alcohol and marijuana-related arrests between them, he didn't think any of them had a violent history other than perhaps a domestic battery or a barroom brawl...and now this? "Get dispatch to put a call in over to Elkhart and ask them to send the coroner and then call the State Police and tell them we need a homicide unit out here; we're going to need some help with this one!"

Chapter 13
The Only Constant

Theresa was not happy. She'd carefully gone through all of her luggage, just in case, and had been unable to find her cell phone (sitting back on her bed stand in the charging cradle, as she'd thought—damn it!) She'd hoped maybe it had gone into a pocket in her luggage in her hurry to leave, but apparently no such luck. Furthermore, the power cord and Ethernet cable to her PC that she was certain had been in the bag were missing. She still had some battery power left, but it was nearly exhausted. Ever worse, there was clearly no Wi-Fi connection. Unlike Taiwan, with free Wi-Fi offered by many businesses, public transportation, public buildings (the most free Wi-Fi per square kilometer of any country on earth, she'd once read somewhere), the USA was decades behind in technology, it seemed, and living America's agricultural heartland was, to her, akin to living in a technological desert (friend at school told her it had been even worse a decade ago, when internet services had been ridiculously slow—not that she thought much about what was available in the USA now!). She'd tried to use one of the Vampire's computers only to discover they were both pass-worded. Maybe....

She reached around behind one of her hosts PC's and unplugged the Ethernet cable and plugged it into her laptop. She had software drivers for connecting to the university network, but would they work with the vampire's DSL line? Success! Not wanting to waste her battery, she replied to her mom's most recent email and then composed a short email to her small group of close friends. She then switched off her laptop to conserve power and replaced the Ethernet cable, being careful to put everything back as it had been.

Her earlier 'celebrity worship' having worn off, she'd gone quickly from a fascination of being in the presence of an actual vampire to apprehension-bordering-upon-terror concerning her future. From his words and the actions of the dogs, she had the feeling she was now a prisoner. To the fear of the physical changes was now added the fear of what might happen if the vampire tired of her. Clearly she was going to have to keep him interested. Suddenly she knew how the girl must have felt while dancing and flipping to entertain King Kong in the version featuring Jack Black.

Remembering another movie, an older version of Dracula dismissing an old-man version of Van Helsing because he'd commanded armies centuries before the vampire-hunter's birth, she had the distinct feeling that this particular vampire would be a lot harder to fool than a giant monkey. For one thing, this vampire had made sure there were no curtains to pull down off the windows, at least where he spent his daylight hours—the basement had no windows at all. He had survived a long time on his own and was obviously quite resourceful. In what book had she read that every woman was born with the tools needed to make a man do her bidding? She was going to have to put that theory to the test!

Wait...maybe he had a gun. Maybe she could shoot her way past the dogs if necessary? Would she want to even if she could? She wasn't sure who else she could turn to if she did turn completely into a vampire, or what she would do if she found she could no longer survive direct sunlight, but being a de-facto prisoner was freaking her out. At least she should keep her options open, just in case she had to make a run for it. It being daytime, she knew she would not be discovered on the ground or second floors, so she made a very thorough search of every drawer and closet, even looking in the antique, upright spinet piano and bench in the parlor. Damn, no guns!

During her search, she couldn't help but admire the beautiful woodwork. None of the houses or apartments she'd lived in had ever had such beautiful wood. The lace curtains appeared to have been handmade—probably in Wicklow or Arklow...she remembered reading in her art history class that one or both of those Irish towns had once been famous for lace curtains like these; back in the days before everything was cheap-junk-made-in-China! Of course there were knives in the kitchen, but she didn't think one of those would make much of an impression on the dogs, particularly the Irish Wolfhound. OK, maybe she could take on ONE dog with a big *Psycho* knife, but certainly not all three!

Fuck! Not knowing what else to do, she had browsed all the artwork and objects d'art decorating the walls. She pulled a random book off a shelf due to some unusual striping on the spine. *Introduction to Principles of Morals and Legislation* by Jeremy Bentham. It looked and felt old. Opening the cover, she has impressed by the micro-thin orange, green and white lines, the colors swirling in eddies and pools on the inside cover. She wondered what type of paper had ever been made this way. It was old, somewhat faded, and yet quite beautiful in it's simple, random—seeming swirls, as if made by nature and not by human design like paisley, for example. The art-historian in her found it terribly fascinating and she wondered if it were simply part of the manufacturing process, some deliberate attempt at decoration, or perhaps some form of lost technology like the varnish on a Stradivarius violin. With a little difficulty reading the script which, although set in type, was more like hand-written cursive that the block letters she was used to, she found a publication date: 1789. That date sounded familiar for some reason. Wasn't that the year the USA became a country?

Of course—how silly of her, the vampire was that old. She was suddenly struck with the realization that, had she been in a library, this and many of the other books around her would have been locked away in a rare book room, only to be viewed with permission and possibly even requiring an appointment made in advance and maybe only while wearing surgical gloves! Of course—she suddenly remembered reading in one of her classes that, centuries ago, books had been rare and valuable items, affordable only by the rich. She recalled that, in cities like London, there were shops that specialized in antique and rare books...had Naggs been the name of the store she had visited during her one trip to Europe and the British Isles? Some of the books in the shop had been really, really expensive!

And there was that Johnny Depp movie, *The Ninth Gate*, which starts off with a con-man swindling a couple out of a very valuable first edition of a Cervantes' work, *Man of La Mancha* if she remembered it correctly. That started her thinking and she browsed, making a mental inventory of the books on the ground and upstairs levels. Every room except the kitchen had at least one bookshelf, as well as paintings on the walls and antique-looking knick-knacks scattered about. Next, she descended the stairs and began to take another look at the basement. Thousands of books, many in leather, in various languages, obviously in a humidity-controlled environment. What might they be worth? Even the newer ones: a complete Tarzan series, Gene Autry, the Lone Ranger, all the Samuel Clemens books, and so on, all obvious first editions, those with dust jackets that were mostly in excellent condition—it was obvious she was looking at a fortune in books!

The paintings on the wall she discovered, upon close-up inspection, were real oil paintings, not just prints as she'd originally thought... she could tell by the brush strokes and, in one or two places, where the paint had cracked due to age or rough handling.

"Oh...my...god," she whispered to herself, "These are both Picasso's, that's a Matisse, Cezanne, two by Degas, Monet or Renoir I am not sure, that's obviously Toulouse-Lautrec, and this one is by...the guy who couldn't paint in three dimensions...Chagall, I think...and this one, um, flat but great use of color...I think his name was Seurat. I am not sure of the others...maybe that one is a Gauguin? Holy fucking shit!"

Her myriad fears and doubts were suddenly momentarily forgotten as she realized she was surrounded by tens of millions... maybe hundreds of millions... of dollars in paintings. No doubt some of the sculptures on the shelves were from the same period. She went back to take another look at the oriental pieces. Sure enough, that bronze was certainly Han dynasty, that was a Sung dynasty bowl with its distinctive yellow glaze and that was certainly Ming with its cobalt over-glaze. She's seen pots like this before as well, brown glaze with the half naked figures in black with armor and spears—obviously Greek. That tall pot in the corner was a wine amphora, Greek or Roman. There were museums, famous museums, that didn't have collections like this! Who the hell was this guy? She'd only half believed his story of being royalty, but this!

Just last night she was saved from probably being gang raped, then had the best sex of her life, may have realized her ultimate fantasy of becoming a vampire, then regretted that decision...and now she was imprisoned in a house filled with one of the best private art collections in the country. She felt week in the knees. What was that old TV show...*The Twilight Zone?* Yeah, that's how she felt.

She never drank in the afternoon, but she decided this day she'd make an exception. She'd noticed a liquor cabinet while unsuccessfully searching for a gun. She decided to go hardcore—Balvenie single malt. Again, this vampire had exquisite taste. Then, she wandered out to sit on the glider on the front porch with a very large glass of whisky (a quadruple?) and smoked one of her remaining cigarettes. This was a hell of a time to get hooked again. What was she going to do when she ran out? As expected, all three dogs were keeping her under close wraps.

After she finished the whiskey (and three more of her dwindling supply of cigarettes), she decided it was time for lunch. She found a can of something that looked interesting, corned beef hash, and picked some vegetables from the garden to make a salad. After lunch she decided to try out the piano and see if it was in tune. It was. After limbering up with "Spinning Song" and "Fur Elise," she decided to try one of her old favorites...Chopin's Polonaise in C. Of course her hands were too small for the 11 and 12 note chords, but she cut corners as so many other pianists around the world had to do. She almost had a heart attack when she realized a space alien was standing behind her.

"Iye," she screamed, sliding off the bench onto the floor. The figure behind her started to quake. It was a long moment or two (or three or four) before she realized it was laughing.

"I'm sorry," said the space-suit-helmeted figure, "I didn't mean to scare you. You played so beautifully I just had to come watch. Please...continue."

"You just about gave me a heart attack! I almost wet my pants," Theresa nearly shouted, "Jesus!"

"I'm sorry, really, but do you take requests?"

"Give me a minute...and what the hell are you wearing, a space suit?"

"Yes," said the muffled voice of the figure behind the mirrored face shield. "A Russian space suit. At least that's what it was advertised as, although it might have also been a test pilots suit, particularly as both the suit and the price of $1500 USD seemed a little light for an actual astronaut's, uh, make that a cosmonaut's suit. Still, it's pretty amazing what you can find on Ebay! Anyway, I've decided on a tune...do you know the 'Brian's Song' theme?"

"Sorry, I don't know that one."

Holding up silvery gloves, the figure stated, "I'll be happy to teach it to you, but obviously not while I'm wearing these. Also, the helmet does a really good job of blocking out UV rays, but it also makes it darned difficult to see anything indoors, plus you have to shout for people to hear you speaking, even as close as we are to each other. Why don't you play something of your choosing."

"Actually," she said, "I need some practice before I have the courage to play to an audience." Remembering her earlier realization that ingratiating herself to her host might be in her long-term interests, she decided upon another tack. "I'd like to go back downstairs and hear more of your story...and about being a vampire"

"Do you know how long it takes to put one of these suits on by yourself," was the response, "but as you wish."

Back downstairs, of course, her first question was, "Are these paintings all real?"

"Of course," was the reply, everything is this house is real?"

"You must have some amazing stories to tell...and you haven't even told me the rest of your story about becoming a vampire." Yes, that was it—keep him talking.

"Stories? Yes, I suppose I have...and it's nice to finally have someone to share them with. I doubt there are many individuals on this planet, human or vampire, who have experienced what I have. If it's stories you want, I can humor you...just help me get this damn tin can off first!"

They slowly made their way down the stairs—wearing the spacesuit, with its oversized boots, he took the stairs very slowly. As they reached the bottom of the stairs, Theresa noticed the door that had been locked before was now open. Past it was another room, about the size of the upstairs kitchen. Instead of carpet, this room had a tile floor. The only furniture was a wooden table and a pair of steel office desks, piled high with weapons and boxes of ammunition. There were racks on the walls full of various guns, which she knew little about, and another rack full of swords, some of which she recognized as being Japanese. In the middle of the room was a cross-shaped rack of wrought iron that had no doubt originally served a different purpose but was now, with the assistance of plastic hooks and bungee cords, a cosmonaut's helmet and fireman's suit rack.

"I only put this on because I thought I was going to be upstairs for awhile. The biggest problem vampires have, as you may soon discover, is the loss of pigmentation in the eyes. If I were to walk outside right now without the helmet, in full sunlight, my eyes would burn in my head like torches, figuratively speaking, and I'd be completely blind. My skin can handle brief periods in the sunlight, despite the discomfort, thanks to my artificial tan and the invention of sun block, but there's nothing that can fix your eyes—you have to wear very, very good UV eye protection that also keeps light from spilling in around the edges and go outside only when it's overcast or precipitating. That's why the space helmet—if I need to go upstairs during the day, I just cover-up and I'm fine as long as I stay inside. "Too long out of doors, of course," he said with a wry smile, "without protection and even with my artificially pigmented skin I'd be dead—of sunburn! Without goggles or my helmet, I'd probably be completely blind in less than five minutes—I haven't tried it and I don't wish to.

I don't know if it's the UV or the Ultra Red or some other band of radiation or a combination thereof, but that is one part of vampire lore that is absolutely true—sunlight kills! Of course it's highly unlikely to be like in the movies where you'd burst into flames after a few seconds—that's just so they can have more dramatic special effects. Anyway, that's why I spent over $10,000 on four of these space suits and bomb-proof crypts that can lock from the inside and put them in various locations no more than a few hours from each other—they are my life-insurance policy. While wearing one of these I'm completely shielded. If necessary, I might be able to walk around all day, outside. Of course I might look a little bit conspicuous doing so, unless of course it happened to be Halloween!"

Theresa helped him hang up the gloves while he carefully mounted the helmet on the stand and then she turned to look around the room.

"What's with all the guns?" Inwardly, she smiled to herself—she'd known there must be guns in the house!.

"As you know, I used to be a soldier. I've always been fascinated with projectile weapons. Sometimes even a vampire needs to deal with threats at long range. Also, you may have noticed I'm a bit of a pack rat...that means a collector. I've been collecting guns, and other things, for a long time. This is an Enfield, used by the British during both world wars. I brought this from France along with this monster—it's called a Lewis gun. I know it looks like a cannon but this is just a barrel shroud...so you don't burn your fingers when the barrel heats up, which it does rather rapidly because it's a machine gun.

This is a Charleville Carbine, a flintlock from my days when I served with Napoleon. It belonged to the first person I killed after I became a vampire. I keep it for...sentimental reasons. This one is a Sharps rifle. It has a double-set trigger and takes percussion caps and was used during the American Civil War. It was one of my first acquisitions in the USA—I took it from a clansman in New York State. Both are over 150 years old and are probably unsafe to fire with modern powders. Now these newer rifles over here I took from people I dined on. Most Americans over the age of 30 have at least one gun in their house or their car. The plastic loses something aesthetically when compared to the wooden hardware, I feel, but these modern guns fire so much faster and are generally much more accurate at longer ranges.

This one is just a toy, but it's an historic toy. This is a Daisy BB gun from 1895, one of the first ones ever made; it's worth a small fortune."

"They had air rifles over 100 years ago?"

"Actually, the Lewis and Clark expedition carried a 22-shot, Italian repeating air rifle on their expedition, the same type in service with the Austrian army in the late 1700's. So, there were air rifles in military service over TWO HUNDRED years ago. I seem to recall that the Japanese had some as well.

And now we come to the swords. The one on the top I carried into Russia with me. This one is a British artilleryman's sword and that one is a Prussian, um German, cavalry saber, both of which I picked up at the front in World War 1. The others I either purchased or relieved their owners of them when they had no further use for them. You're Japanese, so you probably know how rare these Katanas are. As you may know, they folded the steel many times and then just covered most of the blade in clay and fired them in a kiln. Making the cutting edge harder, so it cuts better, while making the rest of it softer, and thus less brittle and likely to break seems so simple, but it took your people to figure it out. The Scottish basket-hilt sword I purchased in a mail-order auction in the pre-internet days through a company called Manion's that specialized in military antiques—probably out of business now with Amazon and Ebay and all the other online businesses these days."

"Fascinating, really, but I have to know...the paintings in the other room...they're real, aren't they?"

"Ah, you have a taste for art," he smiled. "Let me lock up here and we can go take a look." He closed and locked the door and slipped the key into his pocket.

> Personally, I think some of them are overrated...I wish I had a Poussin or a Robert. Sadly, Robert died in 1808 so, when I arrived in Paris in 1813, his works had all disappeared into private collections and I was in no position to purchase any. Not that I really have any walls in this house tall and wide enough to display one of his huge ruins landscapes that are my favorites. Anyway, I am rambling. You have questions; I am being rude. Where do I begin? Are all these paintings real? I assume that by 'real' you mean 'authentic'. Yes, for sure. Of course you have to realize I was living in Paris when these artists were painting. The most I paid for any painting in this room was probably less than $1000 in today's dollars. Several of them probably cost less than $100, relatively speaking.

"You actually bought them from the artists themselves?" Theresa asked in wonder.

Laughing, he explained...

> Mostly I bought them directly from the artists. I'm sure you think of these painters as great men but, to tell you the honest truth, most of them were a bunch of bums who'd drink all night long, sleep until noon, and then go sit in a park and do a little painting because it was easier than having a real job. Yes, I knew some of them and their compatriots. I even shared a few drinks with some of them.
>
> Hemmingway had a depressive disorder and was a real binge drinker. I once saw Picasso walking around one night having pissed on himself and the next night I swear by the smell he was wearing the same trousers! The head of the Paris

ballet was a flaming queer who threw a temper tantrum and fired his best dancer, his former boyfriend, because the guy went straight and married a woman!

The only intelligent one of the entire bunch was a woman named Gertrude Stein who operated the...club, for lack of a better word, where they liked to hang out. She realized that some of these individuals had real, artistic talent, despite their failings as individuals and, like a poor man's Catherine the Great...I guess that should be 'poor woman's Catherine'...she tolerated them filling her salon with vomit and cigarette smoke in order to collect artwork that became worth a fortune after they died. Of course at that time I was feeding on the homeless of the left bank and the drunks and whores of the Paris night scene. I wasn't exactly wealthy, but I also had very modest living expenses and my rent was offset by an invalid's pension I was receiving, courtesy of a stolen identity.

I visited her salon in Montmarte on occasion and I saw what she was doing and felt her excitement every time she acquired an original, new painting, so I followed her lead and, over a period of time, I began to collect, to the point where it became an obsession and I collected as many pieces as I could afford. Anyway, I think we're getting ahead of ourselves, maybe I should continue my story from last night.

"Oh, please do! I want to hear about your turning into a vampire, what it's like, how you tan your skin, how you came to be in the USA in such a boring, backward place as Indiana...and what is going to happen to me."

Theresa hoped she was being casual enough about that last—it was foremost in her mind but she was trying to put on a brave front and also trying to be as ingratiating and charming as she could be. She had not forgotten that, regardless of how fascinating all this was proving to be, she was in survival mode.

"OK, let's see...where was I? August of 1812, Smolensk, Russia. After a couple days they decided I was fit to travel and I was placed on an ambulance for transportation to a hospital in Warsaw. I was getting stronger but not everything was alright. For one thing, I could no longer keep my food down. Every time I ate something, I threw it up soon afterwards. I was frequently dizzy and began having violent headaches, especially in the daytime, but that was nothing at all like the abdominal cramps I began to have. I remember feeling like my stomach was on fire—

and the farts that just kept coming and coming were, well, really foul! The ambulance driver wanted to take me back to Smolensk, but the army had been making ready to resume the march towards Moscow so, after some debate, we continued on towards Warsaw. Poland, you may or may not know, was a French ally and, not many years prior, had been a very powerful country. It was also the closest friendly territory. Anyway, it was a good 400 miles from Smolensk to Warsaw, and that was as the crow flies. It was a good week's journey by horse cart. We never made it that far. I'm guessing it was 2 days later, about 5 days after I was bitten that the transformation overtook me. We were camped at night about halfway to Minsk, at a town called Orsha. It's key geographical feature was a bridge across the Dneiper River.

Anyway, it was nighttime and I guess I blacked out. When I came to, I was kneeling over the bodies of the 2 Polish soldiers who had been guarding the bridge. Their throats were cut and their blood was all over my face and hands...and I had the strong taste of it in my mouth. I felt both like gagging and as if I were drinking the sweetest Chardonnay. I didn't know what was happening to me but I certainly didn't want to be charged with the murder of 2 allied soldiers. I ran back to the ambulance only to discover that I had left a trail of bodies. I remember regurgitating a fountain of blood. Not knowing what else to do, I grabbed my sword and my horse pistols returned to the corpses of the two bridge guards and relieved them of their purses and one of them of his carbine and cartridge belt...the same carbine that is hanging in the other room. I then found a small boat tied to a rickety dock and cast off.

The trip downriver to the Black Sea took about a week. I received strange looks but none of the locals wanted anything to do with a bloodstained deserter and I managed to avoid encountering any gendarmes...French military field police. Daylight was becoming increasingly unpleasant. Apparently one of the transformations one undergoes is that your body ceases producing pigmentation. This is why sunlight is bad for vampires. It takes several weeks for the depigmentation process, incidentally, and months to grow your fangs, just like when you lose your primary teeth around the age of 5 and grow new ones—only this time you keep your eye teeth, they just get longer. There were other, physical changes taking place as well. There were folk legends about Vlad the Dragon...Vladimir the Impaler...or Dracula, as you know him, so I knew what I was becoming.

I was still human enough to have an aversion to killing people, so the 2d night I stole a goat and tethered it to the boat. It sustained me for several days while I made my slow way out of Belarus, what you would call the Ukraine. Incidentally, an adult human body holds between 8 and 12 pints of blood. A vampire can sustain itself on 2 pints a day—and a vampire cannot possibly drain an adult human all at one go. So, why kill the victim? One kills when necessary, to hide one's existence. Because of the weakness with regards to sunlight, the vampire depends on remaining hidden, being unknown and undiscovered, in order to survive."

Sighing, he paused the narrative for a moment. "You know, I never asked to become a vampire," he explained. "I became a soldier because it was my responsibility to my father and my family, but I never wanted to fight for Napoleon—if anything, I'd have expected to fight against him. As an officer, I never thought I'd have to kill anyone in battle—that's what the lower ranks are for. I'm guessing you don't know much about Germany in the 1800's. Are you Christian?"

She appeared somewhat taken-about by the question. "No, I'm a Buddhist."

> Buddhists have the same rule against killing that Christians do, right? Well the Germany of my childhood had essentially two religions: Catholicism and Lutheranism, with the occasional Calvinist church mixed in. As a child, I was taught it was a sin to kill a person—unless, of course, it was in defense of your family or your country or defending the innocent like a Teutonic knight. Unfortunately, the Mosaic code doesn't go into much detail about when exceptions are allowed, if the proscription is absolute or even if it was meant to include animals and God was directing us all to be vegetarians! Judging by references to fatted calves and doves and lists of which animals it is OK to eat and which aren't, obviously I'm joking about that last bit but it illustrates my point. Also, although it's been a couple centuries since I have heard a sermon or read a Bible, I seem to recall the same God who gave the tablets to Moses, a few centuries later, ordered the Israelites to kill 'every man, woman, child, ox and goat' of their enemies or some such thing. I guess there just wasn't enough room on those stone tablets to carry out a really detailed explanation. Maybe a better translation might be 'Thou Shalt not Murder', which would seem to only apply to individual deeds in a criminal context. Certainly a fair and just deity would not damn someone to hell for killing someone for

raping their child or murdering their wife, would he? Anyway, that's a discussion for the priests and rabbis. It does raise an interesting philosophical question for you and I, however. For a vampire, is feeding on humans the same as a human feeding on a cow or a goat? Traditional vampire stories say that we are damned to hell just by our nature, although I'm sure the killing of people figures prominently in that lore. Regardless, because of my Catholic upbringing, I felt guilty every time I had to kill a human being and I have usually lived on the blood of animals whenever possible, especially now that I have a ready supply.

Anyway, I digress. When I reached the black sea I was in a bad way, having lost much of my resistance to the sun's radiation. It was now painful to stand in direct sunlight and I started to feel pain in my eyes during exposure to daylight as well. I hired a boat across to Odessa, a major seaport. I must have looked ridiculous in my broad-brimmed hat, scarf and gloves, with soot all over my face—it was August, after all— and stowed away on a Turkish ship bound for Constantinople. Sadly, there were no goats on board. After 2 days of hiding in a barrel, I couldn't control the thirst anymore and that night, one of the crew went missing. I jumped ship in Constantinople... Istanbul these days...and stowed-aboard a Hungarian ship bound for Marseilles, praying we would not be intercepted by the British navy. Once again, I emptied a barrel full of rum into the bilge, concealed my carbine under some planks in the carpenter's stores and settled in for a long, uncomfortable voyage.

This was a longer voyage but, fortunately, this ship was overrun by rats, so they sustained me for most of the voyage and I was able to avoid raising suspicion by killing anyone except one moonlight night, when a drunken sailor decided to break into the hogshead I was hiding in...um, barrel I was hiding in, no doubt trying to steal a dram of rum from the ship's stores. I drank my fill of the swabbie, dropped him overboard and waited for the hue and cry the next morning but there was none. We were sailing close to the Greek coast, one day out from making port in Athens, so they probably figured he had jumped ship—or gotten so drunk he'd fallen overboard.

At any rate, I arrived in Marseilles without further incident. The barrel I was hiding in remained undisturbed during that afternoon's unloading. They stopped unlading at dusk for supper. Then, once the deck was deserted, I retrieved my sword and carbine and my leather saddlebags containing my meager possessions, slung my horse pistols about my neck and simply walked down the plank and found myself standing on French soil.

Of course it was wartime and my soiled and odoriferous uniform was out of place, so I was soon stopped by a patrol. I had my papers on me but it was rather difficult to explain what a German officer who was supposed to be commanding troops in Russia was doing in the south of France. I was by then quite pallid and of course had my barely-healed chest wound, so I was able to convince them I had just left hospital in Marseilles and was awaiting a ship to take me back to Odessa and then back to the front. After all, it's not like news traveled very quickly in those days. The fact I had my orders appointing me temporary corps commander helped—I probably could have had them shot on the spot for 'attempting to prevent me from returning to my duties at the front' and they knew it.

Come to think of it, with the army in Russia, I was probably the highest ranking army officer in France at that time, not that I was actually in the army anymore, circumstances having forced me to become a deserter. Anyway, I convinced them I was a bit unsure of why whereabouts, which was quite true, and they escorted me to an inn where I claimed I would spend the night and await my ship in the morning—no doubt the Gendarmes were content with knowing my whereabouts while they tried to check on my bona fides; if you've ever read or seen *Les Misérables*, Papillon, etcetera, you know how anal the French authorities and law enforcement were about identity papers! Of course once I was in my room I immediately went out the window in search of a safe place to hide during daylight—and a victim who could supply me with a change of clothing in addition to a few pints of blood.

So, I had successfully made it back to Western Europe but I was without money or horse, had no inconspicuous clothing and was hundreds of miles from my homeland. As you might say, given your proclivity for profanity—I was fucked!

Remember last night when I told you that, to be a vampire meant to be a murderer, a thief and a rapist? Well, that was what I became. I hid in cellars, ruins, crypts and sewers during the daytime.

I also had to find places to stash the carbine, sword and one of the pistols, of course, as it was a bit inconvenient walking around fully armed when I was pretending to be a disabled veteran and I couldn't just leave them in any damp cellar for fear of rust. I admit they were probably superfluous. Nevertheless, I was unwilling to part with them. After all, there was no telling what might happen if Paris were to be occupied by foreign troops! At night I fed; sometimes on animals, but feeding on humans came with the added bonus of being able to pick their pockets and relieve them of any valuables. Even as a vampire, it is difficult to make it in this world without coin.

At this point, France had essentially been at war from 1792 to 1813. Like most countries in Europe, at this point, the streets were teeming with disabled veterans and war widows who had no other means of sustenance but to turn to prostitution. Remember Cosette's mother, Fantine? I recall reading somewhere that, by 1815, there were 10 whores for every able-bodied Frenchman who remained after Napoleon had filled graves across Europe with the bodies of his countrymen. Or, perhaps I was reading about London. In any case, there was an enormous mass of unfortunate humanity to prey upon. The whores were preferable for several reasons: they usually smelled better, often had more coin, and I was able to have sex. You've perhaps seen the movie *Perfume*? It gives a fairly accurate portrayal of life in those days. The streets were truly full of misery. To many, death was a release from endless suffering—at least that is what I told myself. I still had guilt about taking human life, as is normal for a soldier, but no more than that as I did what was necessary to survive. So, over time, I gradually became inured to the taking of human life.

Do you recall the tannery in *Perfume*? You asked about my skin...I decided to see if putting a light tan on my skin with some leather dye, like on a saddle, would allow me to walk around in the daytime. It is helpful, actually, lasting a very long while and providing protecting against whatever band of solar radiation is harmful to my kind, and it made me look like a laborer in that region. Of course nowadays there are other products available that are less harsh on one's skin.

Nothing, however, helped with the blinding pain in my eyes when I tried to go abroad during daylight. After a time I had accumulated some Francs, civilian clothing as well as the uniform of a recently invalided French lieutenant and his identity papers. In addition to his clothing and his life, I also took his crutch and the 2 sous he had in his pocket. His papers turned out to be invaluable as they classified me as a discharged veteran and a resident of Paris, along with travel papers to allow me to travel across the country so, when I was stopped by police patrols at night, I could provide a reason why I was not in active service when every able-bodied veteran had been recalled to help form a new army to fight against the Sixth Coalition as the allies invaded France. After all, it was wartime and they were checking everyone's papers for deserters, possible spies, tax evaders...fortunately there were no such things as photo ID's back then, so it was much easier to assume someone else's identity.

The crutch even helped me feed...a crippled soldier walking down a dark alley at night was an easy mark for gangs of robbers...or at least they thought so. The lieutenant I masqueraded as had been an officer of engineers and had lost all of his toes due to frostbite—no doubt by standing in the river while rebuilding the bridges the Cossacks had burned behind the French army to hinder its retreat. Let me tell you— from what I heard later in the streets of Paris, that is a chapter in Napoleon's Russia campaign that I am very glad I missed!

Anyway, rather than hunt my prey, I began to let them come to me; what easier prey could there be than a shambling invalid who obviously could not walk well and needed a support in order to do so? Of course if that invalid is actually faking it in order to gain the element of surprise, in addition to being highly resistant to most weapon attacks...well, you can guess the result when these cutpurses and highway-men thought I would be easy pickings! I began to develop a real taste—pun intended—for dining on the wicked. Anyway, after a month or two in Marseilles, enough people had gone missing that notices were posted that the police were looking for someone of my description—I had apparently been seen with some of the victims—so I determined it was time to leave.

I headed north for Paris, one town at a time. Travel was simplicity itself. I procured a pair of coffins and fixed them so they could be fastened shut from the inside. I then hired a camionneur...how would one say this? A carter to transport it; ah, I think "teamster" would be the correct word in modern English. This was a common practice back then and what with disease, soldiers dying of their wounds, high infant mortality unserweiter...and so on...coffins on the streets and highroads of Europe were a very common sight in those days. I'd slip out of the coffin late at night and find someone to eat and then locate a new hiding place for the coffins. A day or two later, I would find a new teamster to move them to the next town. Actually, as I just made allusion to, I traveled with not one but 2 coffins...one with my person and the other full of my effects, which also served as a potential spare in case of emergency. No one was likely to disturb an unclaimed coffin...and of course robbers would be much less likely to pillage a poor-looking coffin than a crate, chest, or even a barrel that might contain food or valuables. My Lieutenant's uniform and a few coins were usually enough to obtain temporary housing in a warehouse, stable or even in a church... it was not at all an unusual request to ask to have a casket placed in a crypt or behind the altar so the deceased could 'hear' prayers prior to being entombed, and the clergy were ever greedy for coin, so I managed the long journey without incident.

I arrived in Paris in early December of 1812. Remnants of the Grande Armée had been straggling in for weeks, so I was able to lose myself in the crowd, so to speak. I found an oculist to make a pair of spectacles with darkly tinted lenses and leather "blinders." I suppose I invented the world's first-ever pair of goggles!

In any event, I was then able to wrap myself in bandages and mufflers and go out briefly during the daytime on days in which it was heavily overcast or snowing. If anyone asked, I explained my eyes had been injured and became overly sensitive to light because I was standing beside a cannon when the barrel burst, killing all around it besides myself. Anyway, the glasses...goggles...inspired me to draft a letter to my father, advising him I'd been seriously wounded but was still 'alive' and in need of a long period of treatment and recuperation and asked him to send a bank draft to the Banque Générale in Paris. I'd already decided I couldn't possibly go home as I was, but with the money from my father and my stolen papers, I was able to purchase a small house with a leaky cellar in a poor neighborhood on the left bank of Paris. I was actually entitled to an annual stipend, but I was unable to make any public appearances, of course, and to go home and try to hide my nature would have been impossible, so I made this one request for money and then, as far as my family was concerned, I disappeared.

You might ask how I was able to do all this with the obvious difficulty of going abroad in daylight? Back in those days, solicitors...attorneys...often worked at night—like in Dickens's *David Copperfield*, if you're familiar with the story. Finally, I had a little security. The house came with all it's furnishings— it's previous owner had died in Russia as a captain of lancers and his wife had died in childbirth the same winter, leaving no heirs or lien holders aside from the tax man, to whom I made a payment in settlement of any taxes owed in order to clear the deed from any lien.

I could have bricked up one of the upstairs windows to keep out the daylight but, had I done so, it might have drawn unwanted attention. Glass windows in those days were still a luxury item many could ill afford. For me to have bricked one up and deprived myself of free interior illumination during the daylight would have appeared altogether peculiar.

So, there you have it—I ended up in a coffin in a small coal cellar, with a rotting, stuffed sofa and candelabra for my literary pursuits during daylight hours! I remember how much it galled me to sometimes have to burn a candle or oil lamp in the window at night to maintain the appearance of human habitation, although I did appreciate the added warmth; vampires have a very high tolerance for pain, temperature, etc., but we still feel the cold! If you've read Dickens you know how dear a lump of coal was for the hoi polloi... the poor... of Paris during the winter months. I still recall, on more than one occasion, having given thanks to the gods I was spared the long retreat out of Russia, where more soldiers died of the cold than died in battle against the enemy! Fortunately, Paris was gifted with any number of inns and alehouses that kept late hours and always had logs burning on the hearth—and of course those were establishments that often indirectly provided me with liquid refreshment that didn't come out of a tin or earthenware mug!

Anyway, back in Paris with its large population and particularly a large itinerant population of refugees, the unemployed, wounded veterans, unser..., um, etcetera, I was able to find people to feed upon without being discovered—although I did also remove a number of stray cats and dogs from the Paris streets during that winter. And, having a little money, I also had the option of paying whores for sex and leaving them alive. After all, some of them were so young, sweet and innocent, forced into that life by dire poverty, that they were so pleasurable it would have been a shame to only experience them once, making them 'disposable' so to speak.

Having options, I began to pick and choose. Have you seen *Silence of the Lambs*? I suppose I have a lot in common with the Hannibal Lector character. Those I felt might have a future, I left alive. Those whom were wicked or whose elimination I believed would better the gene pool, those were my food. These days I realize just how overcrowded the world is and that I should not feel so sentimental about taking life—but it does give me a certain pleasure to eat evildoers, so to speak.

"Sorry to interrupt, but how do you know if someone is *evil* or *wicked*?"

"If a gang of men followed me down an alley with the intent of beating and robbing someone who looked like a lame old man, I automatically consider them to be evil, or at least up to no good! Likewise with police or judges who pervert the law. A prostitute who doesn't like anal sex so she pushes off her 5 year old daughter on her clients with that particular interest—and tries to increase the price at the same time, I consider that person to be subhuman and therefore a candidate to become lunch. Come to think of it, I killed her at nighttime, so I guess the proper word would be 'supper'!"

"For real?" she asked.

"Most assuredly," I said, "The same thing happens in the projects in Chicago and other Democrat-administered urban cesspools on a daily basis these days—every so often you read of a woman being arrested for selling sexual congress with her daughter for crack cocaine."

Having a house, now I had places to put things. As I had no occupation, I decided to have a hobby. I became a collector. As I had mentioned earlier, I took money from those I fed upon, for even the undead must needs pay taxes and occasional maintenance when they live in a house like anyone else. In addition to needing an income of sorts, I felt a need to do more than just read books by candlelight or try to lure my next meal. Subsequently, I frequently took items of value or interest from my victims. Necklaces, pocket watches, books, rings, looking glasses—I became a real magpie.

Father had left me a sum of money upon his death, which was deposited to my account in Paris. I begged-off on the funeral, of course, claiming physical infirmity due to my war wounds, and merely wrote a long letter of condolence to my family and put that chapter of my life behind me while silently thanking father for providing me with a roof over my head and a few creature comforts.

And so, I avoided my neighbors, kept up the pretense of being a lame veteran of the Napoleonic wars and went outdoors occasionally on heavily overcast days with my goggles and a wide-brimmed hat to allay suspicion. Later, with a change of uniform and identity papers from another invalid soldier I had made a meal of, I became a veteran of the Franco Prussian War. After all, someone would eventually wonder about my longevity.

With that in mind, in about 1880 I 'willed' the property to a 'relative' using identity papers from someone whose body would never be found. I was then over 90 years old. It was then some twenty-five to thirty years later...you already know I was somewhat of a neighbor of Gertrude Stein and the Parisian artists of the early 1900's. I already told you how observing the flirtatious old madam had influenced me to buy art—that was made possible by my inheritance and the stolen items I pawned—after all, it's not like I had much else to spend it on. Anyway, finally getting to the point of my narrative...one night when I was having a solitary beer in a tavern I met something totally unexpected—another vampire!

"Really?" she asked, was it a man or a woman...and how did you know?" "He was a male, and I easily spotted him from across the room—the pale skin, the white hair, the lack of a prominent pulse in his neck—and I'm sure if I'd been close enough I could have told him by the smell. I'm sure I smell a little differently than other people to you."

"Yes," she replied, "you smell a little...leathery, I guess; in fact it actually reminds me a little of an Italian jacket I have back home in Taiwan. Um, you said something about white hair?"

Worried about the changes if you become a vampire? Yes, I'm sad to say it's true. Your body undergoes certain changes. Your heartbeat really slows down and it pulsates more than beats, your digestive system changes...exactly how, I don't know, but I suspect it becomes another way to use and distribute blood. It must be something like how sea turtles can sit for long times without breathing and move very slowly until aroused—then they can move quite swifly if they need to fight off a shark, for example. You will find that, after the change, you become stronger. Again, I'm not sure how...probably like someone on PCP where you become less sensitive to pain...but there are also physical changes.

Your muscles become more...wiry, I guess, your skin and maybe your whole body becomes more dense, your senses of hearing and smell improve dramatically, as does your night vision. Unfortunately, your body ceases to produce pigment, seemingly of any kind. Your skin, your hair, even in your eyes, I believe the medical term is melanocytes—the things that make pigment—just seem to stop working. This is why I dye my skin and I've been following medical research to see if anyone comes up with a solution, especially for eyes. I've read about some new drugs, but it's rather difficult for me to get a prescription, as you might imagine. Omega 3 oils are supposed it help—I've been taking supplements recently. Anyway, back to your question, if I didn't dye my hair, it would be snow white.

"But your hair keeps growing?" she persisted.

Just like a woman, I couldn't help thinking, she should be worried about not surviving the transformation or the possibility of my killing her and instead she was worried about her appearance!

As you probably know, even after a person dies, their hair and fingernails keep growing. I recall reading how an old tomb was discovered with a man and woman buried together in a hollowed-out tree that many thought were the remains of King Arthur and Guenevere. Their hair had continued to grow for some time after death. Reportedly, the woman's hair was a lovely shade of gold—that melted to dust when some idiot decided to touch it.

It must be much the same for vampires. Technically, by the way, I think we are actually alive, just not in the same way as we were when we were human. Also, your canine or 'eye' teeth grow out and become the famous vampire 'fangs', just like your secondary teeth grow out when you're about 5 years old or your wisdom teeth when you're about 16. I think I might have mentioned this last night. I'm sorry, I don't have many guests for many years, you see, so I sometimes forget my English and my mind wanders sometimes—the curse of being alone for so many years.

Anyway, he happened to have 2 whores with him and apparently he was just as curious about me as I was about him. Soon I was invited to a table to join them. Can you imagine how hard it was to share our histories with two human women at the table? Fortunately, the birds were content to spend most of their time chatting with each other as long as we didn't ignore them completely, so we were able to talk fairly freely. He was from Lyon and had only been turned a few years previously. He'd established a residence in an old warehouse and primarily lived on the homeless and stray dogs. I'm sure my story was a far more entertaining adventure!

In any case, he took us to an establishment of ill repute where we had relations with them. It was too public for us to feed on them so we parted ways, with plans to meet the next night, and then the two of us shared an elderly, homeless woman who was likely grateful to be spared her ongoing poverty and suffering. As the only two of our kind in the city, as far as we knew, anyway, we made a common practice of meeting for a drink, either of beer or something more substantial.

As it happens, it was through my association with him that that I learned how completely wrong one of the main fictions of vampire lore happens to be. The whole stake-through-the-heart thing is completely wrong. I guess the easiest thing to do is just keep telling the story and I'll explain everything eventually.

If you've read your history, you know that Austria declared war on Serbia in 1914 and very quickly after this France and Germany were at war. As two old soldiers, we both understood that war meant a lot of wounded and dying soldiers. If you recall, the vampire who turned me found me in a hospital. For undead predators, this is the best of both worlds. Vampires are able to feed off those who are already dying and, in doing so, avoid the necessity of making fresh kills. After all, dead bodies in wartime are commonplace and create little cause for alarm or investigation upon discovery, particularly if in a hospital.

We also had, how do they say it, some motivation to "get the fuck out of Dodge" for awhile. With many of the men being called up for service, the prostitutes of Paris had fewer customers and therefore there were more of them on the streets of an evening... is that correct grammar?...looking for, um, clients. France being more enlightened than the USA , the police typically allowed these ladies to conduct their business without much reproach or effrontery. One particular member of the police forces, however, took it on himself to become somewhat the "pimp of the left bank" He not only demanded free sexual congress as a price for not arresting them, but he demanded money from them and beat them if the sum was not adequate. Perhaps he just beat them for the enjoyment of it. The man was a real brute.

In my view, "there is nothing worse than a dirty cop" as the Americans are wont to say. So, one night came when this abusive flatfoot happened to be wandering home, drunk on wine purchased with stolen money, and crossed our path. Long story short, we slit his throat, drained him of his life's blood, relieved him of whatever valuables he had in his pockets and dumped the body in the Seine .

One thing police all over the world have in common is that they look after their own, no matter how much of an asshole that individual might happen to be... or have been. After the prick's body was discovered, Paris erupted in a huge manhunt. All the whores were given a "shaking down," if that is the right term, and there were suddenly a lot more police on the streets at night. So, it seemed like a change of scenery was called for. I told a neighbor I had to visit family, paid her a small sum to look after the cats and we left town. Oh, this is completely off the subject, but cats are naturally drawn to companionship with my kind—our kind—much as dogs are with humans, so I had adopted several strays off of the streets.

The front was not that far away and there were now trains, motorcars and lorries—trucks—that made transportation much faster. We forged multiple sets of identification papers, to allow us freedom of movement, and commandeered an entire truck full of coffins on its way to the front. Of course the coffins were for us, and we stashed them in crypts, caves and ruins in several small towns near where the fighting was not far Paris, at that time only about 40 miles away. Of course our greatest fear was that of being caught out after dawn but, with an entire truckload of coffins stashed from Château-Thierry up to almost within sight of the German positions at Blanc Mont, plus nearly every farmhouse in the area having a wine and/or root cellar or sufficient hay to conceal a large, longish box, we had no shortage of bolt-holes. Even if the Germans overran the area, they weren't likely to go poking about in crypts and they were likely to have their own hospitals and of course I spoke German as my native language and we could always change uniforms if necessary. So, as long as the war went on, we could expect a steady supply of dying soldiers...and we wouldn't even have to kill anyone!

Of course no plan is perfect. The Great War, what is now called World War I, was like no other war in history. Previously, men would meet in the open, hack or shoot projectiles at one another, and then one side would lose heart and run away. Sometimes men would hide behind walls and others would have to go over the walls to get at them, but most battles ended when one side's morale would break and they would flee. Very rarely would battle casualties exceed 10 or

15 percent on a side. Trench warfare changed that entirely. Men were not about to leave cover. You see, weaponry had changed. Cannons may have already been the "queen of the battlefield" even before Napoleon's day, but modern artillery was immensely more powerful with greater range and there was a lot more of it. Machine guns and poison gas weren't that much of a threat to us and the early tanks and aircraft didn't operate at night, but the new flamethrowers were dangerous to humans and vampires alike, while the constant artillery barrages of high-explosive rounds, that was something we were really not having anticipated, um, had not anticipated.

In any case, we found it was easy to come out at night, pretending to be stretcher-bearers, carrying wounded to hospitals and aid stations and giving a quick, merciful end to some men that had no chance of recovery...while feeding ourselves, of course. It's probably a constant that could be applied to every army in history—nobody ever pays any attention to stretcher bearers. Occasionally a doctor or other officer would order us to do something, but they were generally busy with their own concerns, particularly the surgeons, who were often worked to the point of exhaustion. You no doubt read about Florence Nightingale in school? Medical care was pretty crude in those times. Actually, conditions in general were so appalling as to be indescribable. Remind me and I'll show you the movies "All Quiet on the Western Front" and "Paschendale" later on to give you some idea of what it was like. Of course there's really no way to imagine the feeling of being always damp in the mud, the stench of burned cordite and rotting corpses and unburied shit in no-man's land, the screams of injured horses...

Anyway, we would creep out into no-man's land during cease-fires, pick up a casualty and carry him back to an aid station or hospital. There were regular truces to gather the wounded and troops avoided shooting at medics and aid workers knowing full well that they might require our/their services at any time. If the soldier was too far gone...we'll, let me just say we fed well most nights. From the deceased, we also amassed a small collection of rings, watches, and cash. Do you think it's wrong to rob the dead? I assume you've seen "Saving Private Ryan?"   Remember how the   American soldiers in the movie searched every dead German they found for booty? Well, you might say this is an ancient tradition among soldiers—looting the valuables of the deceased and, when victorious, raping their women and desecrating their places of worship and cutting the heads off their statues and such behavior.

Anyway, if we hadn't relieved the dead of their valuables, the hospital orderlies or grave diggers would have had them. I know that nowadays valuables and even bodies are usually sent home to loved ones. Back in the day of the great meat-grinder, they were generating corpses faster than they knew what to do with them. They could hardly dig graves fast enough and the war department had greater things to worry about than trying to identify a stiff, or the body parts of what had once been a human being, in order to send its effects home.

In fact, by the time we got to the front, there was already a shortage of coffins and they were reserved for the senior ranks. Privates got waterproof sheets if they were lucky. There were so many dead that many of them went uncollected—they lay in water in the bottom of muddy shell holes in no-man's land until artillery or the treads of tanks buried them. There were occasional slow nights, but we generally kept busy. In hindsight, I guess our presence there saved a great many lives of men who would otherwise have died of their wounds had we not been scavenging the battlefield and pretending to be litter bearers. Of course there were many others whom we treated to a swifter and thus more merciful passing.

I guess you could say the fields of France were littered with MRE's (seeing her perplexed look, I explained); that means 'Meals, Ready to Eat!' (she wasn't impressed by my grim attempt at humor, so I continued). Anyway, as I was saying, nobody paid us much attention, not even the other stretcher bearers. If the nighttime artillery barrages became too intense, we loaded up an ambulance with wounded or even corpses and headed back out of range. Had we wandered away from the front under other circumstances, the Gendarmes, the French military field police, might have tried to arrest or even shoot us for desertion. Nobody, however, ever bothered us when we had a truckload of the wounded—or the dead.

At that point, Theresa shuddered. "It all sounds perfectly ghastly! Why would you choose to stay there?"

"Oh, it *was* perfectly ghastly," I agreed, "But we went there expecting a war like in the time of Napoleon. Any war is horrible—the fear, the suffering of soldiers and civilians alike, the screams of wounded men and horses—particularly the horses—the smells of burned gunpowder and shit and piss and decaying flesh..," I paused a moment as memories unbidden flooded over me, then I took a breath and continued.

When I was shot in Russia, it was terribly painful. I suppose the shock of it raised my consciousness to a higher level for a few moments, prior to my passing out from the pain. Lying on the ground, I was keenly aware of the smells of grass and good earth, the sun was warm, there was color all around me: soldiers in the blue jackets of the French and the Poles; the white of my Westphalians and some of the Russians, though most of the Russians were adorned in green as were the Bavarians and the French lancers and voltigeurs; while the Hanoverians in their red looked quite striking. There were other variations of uniform that abounded at that time, not that I could see them all as I lay on the field, but still, I remember in that moment, with the agonizing pain in my chest and the pounding in my head, just being so aware of the color of the spectacle.

There were brass buttons and buckles, there was gold braid on the officers, there were the tall black boots of the cavalry, the red, white and blue and gold lettering of the French banners, black hats with the red plumes on those of the French grenadiers, blue on those of the fusiliers, the yellow and green of the voltigeurs...and of course the reflection of the sunlight on bayonets and swords and the red of blood in splotches, driblets and sometimes in pools. It was terrible and yet it was wonderful. Perhaps at no other period in history was there so much color on the battlefield. And of course there was the terrible excitement of it all! It was something you hated, feared and loved all at the same time.

Trench warfare was a different animal entirely. The world had never before experienced anything like it before. To make it even worse, the grand colors of the Napoleonic wars were gone, along with the healthy smells of nature. Everything was brown: the uniforms, the wooden wagons and boards lining the trenches and the rifle stocks and everywhere the mud. The artillery and the passage of men's feet back and forth over the same ground, again and again, killed much of the grass and other vegetation and turned it all to dirt and then, when it rained, to mud.

And the smells! In addition to the normal, wartime odors of blood, urine, fecal matter, and festering wounds and chloroform at the hospitals, it seemed everything was rotten. There was truly the stench of death and decay all around, as well of the lingering smells of burnt wood, poison gas, gunpowder and cordite.

Like I said, it had *seemed* like a perfect plan. Once we were there, however, we discovered that, even to a vampire, it was truly a living hell. As a soldier, I'd seen the horrors of war, yet I'd also seen courage, nobility, and what the French called *esprit de corps*. I'd experienced the thrill of victory, felt the personal pride of capturing an objective or of my troops executing a well-timed maneuver and witnessed incredible acts of bravery, such as an unhorsed lancer holding several enemy dragoons at bay to defend his dying horse. In the Great War, it seemed most of that was gone.

Even the roar of the cannon, which had once been as exciting as it had been terrible, was no longer the same. With modern artillery, the sound was quite different and it was...how shall I explain...more mechanical and less personal. And there were the airplanes, that could launch death from above that men on the ground were scarcely able to counter. Watching infantry charge across open ground, raked by machine gun fire and then retreat without ever coming face-to-face with the enemy, being as they were in bunkers and trenches, it was as if one battled machines instead of men. When the tanks began to appear it must have been like watching men do battle against Cylons in *Battlestar Galactica*! Personally, of course, I never witnessed a tank or airplane in action as they did not operate at night back then. I paused then, to gather my thoughts, and my guest piped up,

"What happened to the other vampire?"

"I was just coming to that," I said, "We had been there for months, well over a year, in fact, and we had our routine down pretty well. We'd managed to avoid the occasional question as to what unit we were attached to or why we were never seen during daylight hours or why we didn't know the name of our commanding officer. If necessary, we would just say that he'd been killed that morning and we hadn't been assigned a new one yet. Like I said, we made a point of appearing on the scene when the officers were too busy to more than glance in our direction, or when we were occupied with tasks with which they had no interest in interrupting. As long as we kept busy and appeared to be acting under orders, we were usually ignored."

One winter night, however, after a lull in the fighting due to poor weather left us cold and hungry, we went to the hospital to see if there were any mortally wounded whose passing we could ease. A British captain was there. One of his men had gone on a reconnaissance to scout out some new machine gun positions. He'd been hit by rifle fire but had managed to crawl most of the way back to Allied lines before collapsing. The captain wanted someone to go get him—and any maps he may have drawn of enemy positions—and we just happened to walk in at that moment.

By then I already had learned a great deal of English but, even though I objected, a translator who spoke both fluent French and English was found and was sent with us out into no man's land, just in case the man had information but would not live long enough for the hazardous trip back to our lines. Just as we reached the wounded man, a fierce barrage opened up. They hit the allied positions with everything from the shrill-sounding "daisy cutters" to the big, rumbling 15cm field howitzers. Naturally, the French and British artillery opened up in response, adding to the din. Our translator turned and ran but a German sniper got him before he made it back to our trench.

So, we climbed into the shell hole with the scout, ascertained that he was in a bad way and had lost a lot of blood, and relived him of what remained. We located his notes relative to the enemy positions in his left, breast pocket and settled in to wait. There was no point in trying to have a conversation—the bombardment was far too loud—so we just watched the star shells and illumination flares and shared a drink from the flask that had been in the scout's right, breast pocket. It wasn't our first time caught out in no-man's land during a barrage. Usually, we were safer there than the men in the trenches. All the shells were aimed overhead—nobody wasted ammunition shooting at no-man's land.

I say 'usually' because the Germans must have seen our movements and decided to make sure we recovered no intelligence because, on that particular occasion, we noticed mortar shells falling around our position. Apparently we had our own, personally-dedicated mortar team seeking us out. As the shells crept closer to our hole, we decided it was necessary for us to move. So, we began to run from hole to hole, our stretcher abandoned. Without the stretcher identifying us as non-combatants, of course, we were just 2 men running towards Allied lines in the light of the illumination rounds, so we began to attract the attention of rifle and machine gun fire. Things began to get interesting.

We were nearly back to our lines when an artillery shell landed short, in the barbed wire in front of the nearest trench, and the concussion knocked us flat. The wire, incidentally, was held up in places with wooden stakes. When I raised my head to look around, there was my comrade with a wooden stake through his heart, courtesy of the blast from the shell. I remember he sat up, looked at me and said something along the lines of "well this is interesting" and then he leapt up and began running again, with the stake sticking square out of the middle of him, both front and back.

Earlier I told you about some of the physical changes that occur when one "turns"; I am no scientist, but based on my own experiences, not only does your heart rate slow considerably, giving rise to the myth that vampires have no heartbeat, but apparently your digestive system becomes something of a backup for your heart. Maybe it just acts as a big sponge, absorbing blood and redistributing it around the body. I really don't know. I do know that you can no longer digest solid food...anything you eat comes right back up again. Have you ever seen the movie, *What we do in the Shadows*? There's a scene where a new 'convert' discovered he can no longer eat chips... French Fries in the USA... and he's totally bummed out about it. Oh, and there's also the fact that you no longer defecate. No, really—it's true! I haven't taken a shit since a couple weeks after Borodino!

Anyway, haven't you ever wondered about the great contradiction in vampire lore? Why would a stake-through-the-heart have any affect on a creature with no heartbeat, hence no functioning organ? In fact our hearts do beat—I've proven this to myself with a stethoscope—but our altered digestive systems give us at least a temporary backup system; one of the many reasons vampire are so hard to kill that many legends claim us to be immortal. Sadly, this is also incorrect. While we have much longer life-spans, to be sure, we can indeed die, as I learned moments later.

Seeing he was still alive...or undead or whatever you want to call it, I gave him a hand up and we again started running for the French trench. You know, I once met a Parisian prostitute the locals referred to as the "French Trench"...sorry, I digress. Anyway, I caught my foot in a piece of the shattered wire and went down on my face in the mud. I freed myself of the wire and started to get up to follow after the other vampire when he took a direct hit from one of the big 15cm shells. The blast hurled me backwards, probably a good 10 meters or so, and left me completely stunned for I don't know how long. When I collected my wits, I discovered my mantle and tunic...um...my coat and shirt...had been ripped completely off of me and I was missing one boot. I was also decorated with bits of what had, only moments earlier, been my companion. I remember that one of his arms lay across my chest. I knew it was his because a mitten he'd taken off a dead lieutenant a few days earlier still adorned the hand. I recognized the rip he'd carefully mended by candlelight with a bit of string while we'd passed the day underground in a crypt beneath a ruined church.

So, although a wooden stake had no effect on him, several pounds of high explosive had the same effect it would have on any animal on this planet. He was dead. There wasn't enough left of him to fill a grocery sack."

"Oh, how awful," exclaimed the pretty little Asian girl with the French-sounding name, "What did you do?"

"Do? What else could I do? I got up, staggered over to and then tumbled into the trench, where some soldiers helped me along to an aid station. They gave me a blanket and some hot tea, which was greatly appreciated as I was by then quite cold, and found a boot near enough my size from the pile that had accumulated from that day's amputated limbs. Incidentally, while we can endure extremes of temperature that humans cannot, vampires do feel heat and cold, in case you were wondering."

Just at that moment, an expression flashed across her face that I was certain had nothing to do with my narrative and much to do with the metamorphosis that was soon to be upon her. I had a feeling that, for my little guest and by way of paraphrasing Shakespeare, the worm was beginning to turn.

Chapter 14
Damned if you do

To say she found the Vampire's life story to be interesting would have been a gross understatement. Theresa was riveted! Of course she'd spent so much of her teen years either reading vampire stories or watching movies or playing games...and here was a real-life (unlife?) vampire sharing his experiences with her...and such experiences! The reality sitting in front of her was far more fascinating than any movie she'd ever seen. And, the way he spoke and his kinship with antiquity and the way his eyes seemed to see into her soul—it was like the excitement of being at a live sports event combined with the serenity of wandering through an art gallery—or perhaps a dank and dusty Cathedral, festooned with magnificent and elaborate decorations. She felt like writing a poem, she felt like singing; she was horny and felt like fucking, she...she HURT! With no warning, a racking spasm pulsed through her abdomen, followed quickly by another...and then another...each successively more painful until she found herself on her knees, arms wrapped around her waist. She could feel her pulse racing, her temperature climbing, sweat beginning to bead on her brow and her breath was suddenly labored as well.

"Am I dying?" she thought to herself. After a moment the spasms subsided and she found the vampire's arms around her, helping her to stand.

"It's the beginning of the transformation," he said, "I suggest you go sit on the porch, smoke a cigarette and enjoy the sunshine...while you still can."

"Oh...OK...um, how did you know I smoke? I left the pack in the kitchen and I ate a breath mint and then ate something..."

"I can smell it on your hair and clothes," he explained, "You'll learn very soon that vampires have much better nocturnal senses than humans."

"What if it happens again? The cramps, I mean—what should I do?" she pondered aloud.

"There's nothing you can do...and it **will** happen again and it will be a lot worse," he explained.

It is not like in the movies where it happens in a few seconds...like that old black & white film...I think it was *House of Frankenstein*...where the man running the carnival pulls the stake out of Dracula's heart and he comes back to life with flesh appearing on his bones in a few moments. No, you're in for a rough afternoon and an even rougher night of it. You can't go to a hospital, for obvious reasons. I'm not a doctor and, even if I were, I doubt there's anything I could do for you. You're just going to have to let nature take it's course. Now run along and play like a good little girl.

Theresa did as she was bid, climbing up the stairs to the kitchen while a pall of fear and desperation descended upon her. She picked up the pack of cigarettes from the counter where she'd left them, helped herself to a bottle of Pinot Blanco from the fridge (she really needed a drink right about now) and lifted a corkscrew off its hook on the wall near the sink. She couldn't help thinking that this was the neatest kitchen belonging to a non-gay man she'd ever met. Of course the fact he didn't cook probably made it a lot easier to keep things organized!

The black dog was sitting on the porch, head on his paws, just looking at her. She made a conscious effort to ignore the dog while she sat on the wooden slats of the glider. Setting down the cigarettes for the moment, she peeled the plastic from the top of the bottle with the pointy end of the corkscrew and, with a little difficulty, pulled the cork. Rather than go back into the house for a glass, she took a long pull straight from the bottle. Setting it down, she fired up one of her last cigarettes and took a deep drag, savoring the calming effect, despite the knowledge it was mostly psychological.

She was afraid. She didn't mind admitting it to herself. It was hard to believe what had happened to her during the past 24 hours...her mind whirled with thoughts, memories, fears and other feelings. For probably the tenth time she mentally reviewed how she'd nearly been raped and murdered, then was saved by a murdering, art-collecting vampire with whom she'd had wild sex despite the lingering terror of the assault, and now she was sitting here about to die (?) and become a vampire (vampiress?), never to see her mother again, probably never to finish school (night classes, maybe?), never to have a career, never to eat sashimi again. And yet...to live maybe forever, to not grow old and lose her beauty—wasn't this what she'd always wanted? Theresa took another deep swallow of wine and hit on the cigarette again. She felt like she was going to go crazy. In any event, it wasn't like she had any choice now—even if this was something that could be 'cured', she was certain that the time she had remaining would not be enough for doctors or scientists to do their thing.

When she had first visited the USA as a high school student interviewing at universities, it had been in the final year of the Obama administration—the economy had been in a shambles and about 50 million Americans were living on food stamps, so she had felt it wasn't likely she'd have been able to get a practical training position after graduation, and she'd simply planned on returning to Taiwan or Japan. Under Trump, the economy had been revived, but the previous open-door policy towards immigrants had changed, it was increasingly difficult for even legal foreigners to find employment in the USA, and she'd most likely have had to leave after graduation, anyway.

Things weren't much better in Japan, in terms of employment openings, and Tokyo was probably still a dangerous place in which to live, with uranium and plutonium polluting the environment after the big tsunami—probably the reason her mom had cancer. She could go back to Taiwan and get a job—not difficult with her language skills—but she didn't really know the relatives she had there, now that her grandmother had passed, and the traffic was always so infuriating with all the rude drivers and the houses were so ugly. Or China...hell no! They might have powerful economy that employed a lot of 'foreign experts', but it was still a filthy, polluted sewer full of cheats and people so selfish they made the Taiwanese look positively munificent!

No, becoming one of the undead, if that's what was what was actually happening to her, actually sounded better than the future that had been waiting for her. Hmm, maybe she could send her mom the money for a plane ticket somehow and have her come for a visit. It might be a little difficult to explain her situation, however—not to mention taking her mom traveling. After all, it wasn't as though she could take her around and serve as her translator.

Another spasm suddenly racked through her and she nearly dropped the bottle of wine. This time she felt it gripping her chest like a vise. "Fuck," she exclaimed, "the damn Twilight novels never explained how much this hurts!" No sooner than she was able to breathe again normally, another cramp gripped her abdomen. She pulled her feet up onto the glider and wrapped her arms around her knees in a fetal position—it seemed to help.

After awhile the spasms faded again. Returning to a sitting position, she started taking deep pulls on the bottle—she wanted to get drunk and fast! She also started to study the sky. She remembered seeing a vampire movie, maybe the 1980's Dracula movie, maybe also the one with Brad Pitt, where the vampire goes to the movies and sees the sun again for the first time in years. At least she knew it might be possible to move around outside in the future, albeit perhaps only on overcast days wearing a space helmet. Perhaps she too could get some special eyewear. In any case, she set herself to her task. When was the last time she'd just sat and looked at clouds? She had vague memories of searching the clouds for identifiable shapes, particularly bunnies and other animals. How old had she been? Seven or perhaps eight years old? When had she last looked at the sky or the stars? Surely it was a long time ago!

Piano lessons, the swim team, after-school English lessons...modern life had intruded and all but erased the childish interest in anthills, bugs, trees and the like. She could still remember one particular obsession...she wanted to go hunting, kill a deer or other animal, and hold its heart in her hand while it slowly stopped beating. She wasn't sure what her attraction to death was, but this was something she'd always wanted to do. Another thing that she was sure was not exactly "PC" or "politically correct," she wanted to taste every kind of meat there was in the world—including human and endangered species. Apparently, she was about to become an ex-carnivore, so that particular fantasy was about to end.

The death-experience with an animal's heart in her hand, perhaps that was still possible. As a vampire, who knows, perhaps she could hold a human's heart in her hand while the life expired. She could certainly think of a few people she would enjoy sharing this experience with, from her sexist and perverted art teacher in junior high school to the older, neighbor boy who had tried to forcibly molest her that same year. Wouldn't she love to have her hand around his heart and look into his eyes while the spark of life faded!

"Oh Shit!" With very little warning she was running for the bathroom. She just barely managed to get her clothes down around her ankles as a fountain erupted from inside her. "Fuck," she said, over and over, as geyser after geyser of fetid liquid spewed forth. "What a miserable day," she thought to herself. "Explosive diarrhea, how can that possibly get any worse?" A moment later she answered her own question as she spun around dropped to her knees, and regurgitated loudly into the bowl, splashing some of the foul liquid onto her face and hair. Realizing what she'd just done, and with the assault on her nostrils magnified by the close proximity, she barely managed to pull down on the handle to flush the commode as she convulsed and hurled again and again.

Subsequent to flushing the noxious mass down, she slipped off her shoes, exercise pants and undies, then carefully maneuvered over to the sink, where she rinsed as much as she could from her face before carefully pulling off the rest of her clothes. She was glad the shower was only 3 steps away—she needed a shower like never before in her life!

Twenty minutes later, after a long and very hot shower, she felt a lot better. She wished showers in the USA had a hand-wand like in Asian countries...she'd have really liked to direct the spray directly up inside her to give herself a really thorough cleaning. By lying on her back with her legs in the air, she was able to accomplish this in a small way, but she still felt a little dirty inside and guessed there was still more to come.

Inspecting her clothes, she discovered a few, stray splatters of vomitus. She hand-washed the offending areas and, finding some coat hangers in the closet in the master bedroom, hung them up on the shower rod to dry. Well, she had other clothes in the bag in the basement. She decided to leave off the underwear and just wear the towel, wrapped tight and tucked in so it would stay up.   If she had to repeat the experience, at least she wouldn't mess her underwear. After all, she didn't have that many changes with her; she was going to have to talk with her...host...about getting some of her clothes and other things... and if she could use his computer to check her email. Her mom was waiting for news and would start getting worried if she didn't hear from her soon.

The vampire was sitting at his computer when she reentered the basement, a sight she still had trouble reconciling with her traditional views of vampires. Looking up at her over the monitor, he looked her over, noticing the towel, and raised his eyebrows in a silent question. "I... don't feel good," Theresa said, "I had a... bad stomach and I've been having cramps and... I don't know the word... when my body does things I can't control"

"I remember," he replied, "they're called convulsions—you'll be experiencing a lot more of them soon." Suddenly his eyes brightened and he smiled a not-entirely-pleasant smile. "The epileptic whore," he exclaimed.

"What?"

"It's from a novel," he explained, *MASH*, by Richard Hooker, if I remember correctly. There was this Japanese girl who went into hysterical convulsions during sex...it was supposed to be a wild ride. I was just thinking..." Just then the doorbell rang.

That must be Miguel. Quick, put on your jogging outfit. Go upstairs and introduce yourself as my new nurse. Take a walk around the vegetable garden and have a chat with him. Let him see you walking around in the daylight... that will help allay his suspicions later on. Hurry now, go and say hello. His English isn't very good so don't worry if you don't communicate well, this is all about appearances. When you come back I'll be in my wheelchair and I'll look different. Just act as if it's natural and I'm old and decrepit.

Theresa dressed quickly as the vampire watched in appreciation for a few moments, then pressed the intercom button on the wall next to his desk. "Miguel?" he asked in a voice that suddenly sounded as old as he really was.

"Si Señor," came the response.

"Uno momento, por favor, mes... I mean 'mi'... enfermera abrirá la porte... um... puerta."

"Damn," he swore half to Theresa and half to himself. "After all this time you think I'd be able to keep my French and Spanish separate and distinct! Anyway, remember—you're a nurse—that's your cover story from now on!"

Miguel turned out to be a short, heavily-tanned, weather-beaten Mexican of an indeterminate age, somewhere between 40 and 60. He wore dungarees of some thick, heavy, earth-toned fabric and he wore a somewhat shapeless, cowboy-ish hat, which he swept off to hold in both hands as she stepped out onto the porch. Ad-libbing, she explained (what name did he go by again?) her employer had hired her as a live-in nursemaid and would Miguel be so kind as to show her the vegetable garden? He merely nodded and turned to lead the way, with Theresa hoping her digestive system would remain settled for the time being. The garden was just alongside the house (she'd seen it earlier, during her walk), and they walked around it, with Miguel identifying each type of vegetable in heavily-accented English. When she asked if it would be okay for her to plant some Japanese greens, he pointed out some lettuces that were going to seed and indicated it would be OK for her to pull them out and reseed the ground.

The tour concluded, they returned to the house and descended into the basement, where she received a mild surprise. Her 'employer' was indeed sitting in a wheelchair, with a blanket across his knees with skinny, white legs protruding and ending in a pair of plush, Winnie-the-Pooh slippers, of all things. He seemed to be much paler than before and his hunched posture did indeed give him the appearance of an infirm 'senior'.

"She painted," said Miguel differentially, "troughs and feed filled, rotten wood in chicken house out, new wood in and painted, need part for to fix water pump, truck need gas"

"Thank you," said the old man in the wheelchair. "Mañana puedes tomar el camión para obtener la pieza que tu necesitas. Oh, and on your way back, fill up the truck. Don't forget the receipts... recibos!"

Miguel nodded, then turned and bowed to Theresa, "Many pleased to meet you," he added and then shyly turned and exited the room. They listened as he clumped up the stairs and let himself out.

Miguel is an illegal, been here about 20 years now. I let him and his family live in a trailer I have on a small parcel of land I own on the other side of the road, maybe half-a-mile from here. He does all my odd jobs around the place, watches over the livestock, keeps the place running, and, most importantly, goes to town during the daytime whenever something has to be purchased, such as feed, seeds, fertilizer and so on. I let him have all the eggs and vegetables he wants, a side of beef a couple times a year, $100 a week, plus I pay all his utility bills at the trailer. His wife cuts hair for cash downtown for a second income and their kids sell the vegetables their family doesn't eat at a highway roadside stand on weekends, during the growing season. It works out very well for both of us—he lives off the grid, with no address, free room and board, a land-line for his phone and internet, utilities all in my name and a tax-free income—while doing all the things I can't do during daylight and I don't have to hire someone who might start asking questions and who wouldn't be afraid to go to the authorities if he or she suspected anything."

Smiling, he added, "I don't think he knows I know about the vegetable stand, but I'm not going to eat them and if he thinks he's found a loophole in our agreement that allows him to make some extra money, I'm all in favor of it—with Americans I'd have to worry more about them stealing things. I know Miguel has filled up his personal truck from my gas storage tank a few times as well. His truck's tires are a different size than my farm truck, so if there's mud or snow on the ground it's obvious. Like I said, I don't mind if my 'Renfield' takes a few liberties, as long as they're small ones—he provides a very valuable service."

Theresa had noticed that, while he was speaking, the color had come back to his face and hands. "How did you do that," she enquired, "make yourself look pallid and then bring the color back to your skin?" He stood up, tossing aside his towel to reveal something that certainly was not the shriveled up member of an old man. "Vampires have more conscious control over how blood moves inside of them due to our altered physiology. By concentrating on it, I'm able to shift blood away from the surface and into my internal organs. I know *what* I'm doing, just don't ask me to explain *how* I do it as I'm no scientist. I suppose it's similar to the Indian fakirs who can allegedly drink water up their anuses.

At any rate, it can be very useful camouflage—if the police are looking for a young man, or an older man—you change your appearance and body language and viola! Suddenly you are not the droid they are looking for! That was a Star Wars reference," he added in order to forestall her unvoiced query. "So, how are you feeling?"

"I feel better," she said. "At least at the moment, but I could really use a cigarette."

"You're going to have to break the habit," her host explained. "Human lungs use blood and mucous to clean out, how shall I say it, foreign particulates? Blood inside a vampire is more stagnant, if that is the right expression. You don't have blood being continuously pumped through your lungs at high pressure, so the cleaning process is slower. We are much stronger in many ways than our human ancestors, yet we also have certain weaknesses—with the loss of pigmentation of course being the most serious."

A sudden spasm ripped through her again.

"Ohh," she gasped aloud, bending over to catch the edge of the desk with her left hand which she clasped her right arm over her abdomen, "here it comes again."

Chapter 15
Enter the Dragon

"Cumming again...yes, that's what I was talking about before," I said, taking her by the hand, "Come with me." I led her to the basement bathroom. The shower stall was too small for us to lie down in, so I commanded her to disrobe and sit on the floor. She started to object, then shrugged and began to undress, carefully folding each item and laying it on the counter beside the washbasin. I began to get another hard-on almost immediately as her wonders again came into view. Those creamy, small yet perky breasts, with their small areolas and erect nipples and barely a hint of any sag; her long, shapely legs, smooth and hairless; hairless of course except for the wonderful little patch of straight hairs just where her legs came together, and that tiny yet firm and rounded derrière—she truly was a beauty.

I couldn't help but admire her for a few moments... full-frontal nudity was a real delight with this one... then ordered her to sit on the closed toilet lid. "It is cold," she complained. "Not to worry," I offered as I removed my shirt and my briefs over my now very-erect member, "I'm about to cup your buttocks with my hands and keep them warm for you." I knelt between her legs, parting them slightly, and took a long look at the wonderfully almond-shaped little hole, stroking her thighs as I did so, and then I forced myself inside of her. "I don't feel well," she explained, "I don't really think I'm in the mood for this"

"Just relax," I intoned in my most soothing voice. "This might actually make you feel better, it certainly won't make it any worse for you and I'm hoping it make ME feel a lot better!"

Glad she couldn't see the leering grin I was certain flashed across my face, I carefully positioned myself against her and slid my shaft gradually inside of her, thrust into her a few times to make sure I was well positioned, then I pushed my hands beneath her and gently cupped her little butt. Rocking her gently back and forth, I make sure I was all the way inside her and then I paused. I didn't have long to wait before a small spasm hit her. With my weight on top of her, she arched slightly, rocking my penis back-and-forth within her and giving it a good, strong squeeze for good measure. She gasped in pain—I gasped in pleasure. "Kudos' to the author of *MASH* and his anecdote about the 'epileptic whore'," I thought, "that felt damn good!"

I stood there, patiently waiting, and after a few seconds delay she was hit with another, stronger spasm. This time her legs pushed down against my elbows as her pelvis rocked upwards, driving me deeper inside of her. I doubt her fist could have gripped me as hard as her twat did just then, causing an explosion of pleasure to run through my brain, almost paralyzing me with its intensity. I barely had time to reflect on what had just happened when a series of contractions pulsed one after another. I rode her like a surfer on a wave of bliss as each convulsion clamped on my now rock-hard pile-driver. I discovered nerve endings I'd never really noticed before at the base of the arrow-head where it met the shaft——I'd never had it squeezed so hard before that the area just behind the head had a tight grip and real resistance as her forward and upward motions momentarily threw me into reverse.

As my girl-toy cried out in feral agony, I allowed myself to join her in guttural utterances of ecstasy (I had never really been one for noisy sex, but it seemed to excite her, so I was willing to 'go along for the ride', so to speak). She pulled her hands against my torso in what seemed to be an effort to push me off of her. There was no way I was going to stop now, so I relocated my hands to the front of her hipbones and clamped on tight—I was here for the duration!

"I'm going to throw up," she grunted.

"Try to hold it down," I requested, "but if you have to let it go, just do it on the floor." The spasms had stopped for a moment, so had a change of heart and orchestrated a change of position, so she was kneeling in front of the toilet, lid open, as I took her doggy-style and she was free to regurgitate to her heart's, or rather her stomach's, contentment.

I began slowly sliding myself in and out, enjoying the warm wetness. Very warm, in fact, as apparently the change was making her feverish. The warmth felt good, her hair smelled wonderful, I enjoyed the springy, pneumatic feeling as I pushed my stomach against her tiny, firm butt, driving my dagger deep into her sheath; for the moment, at least, I was one happy vampire!

Another surge of convulsions struck without warning, clamping down on Mr. Happy and tugging on him with each successive seizure. A rush of such intense pleasure pounded through my brain that I couldn't move or think, I could only enjoy the moment. And what a moment! Throughout both of my lives, human and undead, I'd never felt such ecstatic euphoria. I felt a total loss of myself as I built towards the climax. Had I been religious, I'd have had to call it a spiritual experience. Religious, of course, I was not.

Instead I held on in pure, animal lust while the ecstasy poured through me like a main circuit cable plugged straight into god, remembering a line from *Apocalypse Now*. When I came, it was an explosion; the climax just kept on and on as she bucked and churned beneath me. I was completely powerless to move—the pleasure was so intense it was painful at the same time and I would have been unable to go on if it were completely a matter of my own volition. Nature was in control, however, and as the girl continued to scream out as convulsions racked her with pain as her sheath seized and twisted my blade in ways it had never been handled before. It was probably a matter of mere seconds, but it felt like the orgasm just went on and on and on. When it finally passed, I just lay across her back, gasping, my weight crushing her against the vitreous porcelain of the 'petit throne' as Louis the XIV used to refer to his toilet.

The thick layer of sweat between our bodies must have been all hers, I thought, as I suddenly realized a fact of my own existence—apparently, vampires don't sweat—or at least this was the first time in 2 centuries, if in fact any of it belonged to me. No, she was feverish and undergoing a great deal of physical activity, and it had a reasonably pleasant smell to boot. No, it was undoubtedly hers.

She began choking beneath me and I pulled out of and rolled off of her as she threw up in great, heaving retching gasps. From the sound of it, not much came up. Apparently she'd already emptied her stomach, but nature was making sure of it as it began to alter her internal structure. She knelt there for several long moments, then turned and looked at me.

"You know, the sex actually did help take my mind off the cramping and, when you came inside me, it felt really good. I don't know how to describe it; um, every time you pulsated, it just sent shivers up and down my spine."

I noticed now she was staring fixatedly at my penis. I felt completely spent, but my 'little soldier' was still standing fully at attention.

"More?" I inquired.

She nodded, took the cup of water I offered, swished and spit, wiped off her mouth with the hand-towel, and took me in her mouth. While I would have been content to allow her to continue her ministrations, after much too short a time she returned to her former position and indicated a desire for me to resume my activities.

Again, I entered her and just rode the tide, waiting patiently for each round of spasmodic activity. It took some time, blissfully enjoyable time, I might add, before I began to approach a second climax. Unfortunately, by that time her contractions were becoming less frequent, so I rolled us over onto the tile floor, on our sides, and began sharing the workload, pushing into her while grasping her hipbones for greater leverage.

"Harder!" she begged. Panting with the effort, I began thrusting as hard as possible, when another cramp forced her to double-up, which had two undesirable results: one, she pulled herself most of the way off of me and, two, she bent my penis at a most undesirable and somewhat painful angle. Holding myself for a moment while the pain subsided, I pushed her back over onto her stomach and began to re-enter her, enjoying a brief view of her wonderful, youthful gams. I was still quite slick and there was a smaller, rounder hole I had not yet violated and an unexpected thought took me.

"Are you ready to try something different?" I asked. With so many 'firsts' going on with this one, I decided to add one more to the agenda. Without waiting for a response, I centered my member against her anus and began to enter her. From her surprised reaction, I could tell she was an 'anal virgin' like myself. Under other circumstances, she might well have refused these particular attentions. Given the amount of severe discomfort the change was bringing upon her, apparently she decided not to even protest. I pushed deeper into her, noticing how it wasn't as warm or as wet, but the feeling was still agreeable: like the "hand in a velvet glove" that AC-DC had sang about. I decided to try to make it more pleasant for her and slid the middle two fingers of my right hand into her twat, while the middle finger of my left hand traced a line upwards through the narrow channel until she lurched upwards. I'd found the clitoris.

I began to massage it in a rotating motion, while using my fingers to press against my cock, pinning that thin bit of her insides between the two of them. I was rewarded with a convulsive arch of her back and a gasp of pleasure, not pain, having nothing at all to do with the change she was undergoing. When she clenched again with the next spasms, she gripped me even tighter than before and quickly brought me to a long, shuddering orgasm. At some point I'd bit the back of her neck and a small trickle of blood made its way slowly down her neck until I roused myself long enough to lick at it. While not so long this time, I still felt thoroughly exhausted and slowly pulled out of her, rolling over to lie beside her on the welcoming chill of the tile.

Still bathing in the afterglow, I realized just then that I'd made my decision. I wasn't going to kill this one. How could I? She was just too damn much fun, too nice looking, and too good of a fuck to waste! "Good job, little girl," I thought to myself, "you get to live... or is that 'un-live'? Whatever, I'm going to keep you around a while longer."

Still face-down on the floor, my little guest was silent for awhile. When she did speak, it was to say, "Thanks... that really did take my mind off the pain for awhile. I feel a little embarrassed. That thing we just did, um, I feel a little ashamed and dirty, um, but I wouldn't mind doing that again. It felt really good to have you, um, in both places at the same time"

"I suppose that can be arranged," I conceded, "although I find I actually quite prefer it the 'normal' way, in fact this was the first time I committed the sin of Sodom, as our parish priest would have referred to it. After all, just because I'm un-dead doesn't make me a deviant," I declared with a chuckle, "and anyway I don't think we're going to have to worry about avoiding pregnancy; come to think of it, I suspect you will stop having your menstruation"

"I won't miss it," she laughed. After a short silence, she asked, "Have you ever heard of ben-wa balls?"

"Anal beads on a string, aren't they?"

"Yes, they have them in sex shops in Japan. For the first time I think I understand why people use them. Maybe we could get some and try them out?"

I smiled in acquiescence. Honestly, I would have agreed to just about anything at that point. If it excited her to have things shoved up her ass, I was willing to assist. After all, if her change to undead was anything like mine, it was about to become functionless.

After another (!) shower (vampires don't sweat, so I rarely showered more than once a month, unless I had had a particularly messy dinner so washing my face just didn't cut it, but my little house guest had been leaving various bodily fluids all over me ever since her arrival), I picked up the prostrate maiden and held her under the spray, then sat her on the washbasin and gently toweled her off.

Picking her up like a child, I carried her to my bedroom/underground bunker and lay on the oversized bed with her head pillowed on my lap. I wonder what she thought of my sleeping chambers: 4 stone walls, steel ceiling, heavy steel fire door—I had endeavored to make my warren as secure as inhumanly possible. Her facial expression told it all: she was in great, physical distress.

"Tell me about where you come from," I commanded, "not the things I can see on the Discovery Channel," I added, "but some things like cultural oddities, things you've noticed that are different from the USA."

Opening her eyes briefly, she looking up at me, then closed them again. After a few moments thought, she began to speak.

"Chinese people love their walls...you know, like the really big one just north of Beijing? In Japan, most things are really open like parks and so on. In Taiwan and China almost everything seems to be surrounded by walls, even parking lots at supermarkets. Most separate houses in Taiwan have bars on the windows and these big metal shutters like a garage door in front of their front doors that pull down and lock at night. Back doors are basically only fire escapes, they are hardly ever used and often there is no external knob or lock. Also, most of the buildings are square, made of concrete and with metal bars on the windows. My first trip back to Taiwan after living in California, driving away from the airport, I felt like..like..the houses looking like a series of small prisons. Even the junior high school down the road had a huge wall around it and a gate with a security guard. At least the wall was painted by the students with lots of interesting pictures but, again, it was a little like walking past a prison.

Last time I was in Japan was right after the nuclear plant meltdown at Fukushima. A lot of streetlights were off to save electricity. The power was out on the...escalators...in the subways, so everyone had to walk up and down like long stairs. Everyone wore masks and went home fast after work and stayed indoors with all the windows and doors taped shut to keep the outside air out. It was really scary. That's how I ended up in the USA. My mom wanted me to get out, so I started applying to universities here and Goshen College had a summer intensive-English program that didn't require a really high TOEIC score, and they offered me a 'diversity scholarship', so here I am!

Anyway, what things would not be on the Discovery channel? Let me think... Toilets are different. We have western-style toilets now as well, both Japan and Taiwan. In Japan, a lot of people have bidets, not so much in Taiwan, but the older flush toilets are still more common in Taiwan and they are, um... OK, pretend you could shrink a urinal from a men's bathroom down to about 20% of it's size and lie it down on the ground. People then squat down over it. Think of it like a tiny trench with a porcelain lining that you can flush when you're done.

"That sounds messy," I observed.

"It can be," she admitted, "But a lot of people think they're more hygienic, despite research to the contrary. A smile touched her lips, "Can you imagine these really, really obese American women trying to squat down to poop?" Chuckling, "they'd probably fall down in their own shit!"

Also, a lot of Taiwanese have this irrational fear of toilet stoppages, so they have little trashcans and you're supposed to put the toilet paper in the trash cans after wiping instead of flushing it down... so of course a lot of public bathrooms there really fucking stink! Maybe this is one reason Japanese people usually consider people of Chinese ethnicity to be uncultured barbarians... they'd rather live in their own stink than risk the very remote chance of having to call a plumber!

Oh, and toilet paper... A lot of places in Taiwan don't provide toilet paper—you have to take your own! Big department stores, hospitals and most restaurants do, but schools don't, many gas stations don't; you have to carry tissues with you all the time or you might end up in trouble. Of course my mom took me on a trip to the UK one time, the public tissues in some toilets were like waxed paper...they just slid stuff around and really didn't do a very good job of cleaning.

For a moment, as another thought occurred to her, obviously humorous in nature, her face was a delight to behold, then the angelic-effect vanished as she winced again in pain, clutching her abdomen. As the latest agony faded somewhat, she continued her narrative.

Also, showers are different. Usually there's a hose with the head on the end. You can hang it in a mounting on the wall when you need your hands free, but you can also aim in anywhere you want. Americans use messy creams for hemorrhoids, because your doctors don't explain that, anytime your skin itches, it's because there's usually foreign matter irritating the epidermis, just like mosquito bites itch because the insect injects you with a non-sterile anesthetic and with waste matter. Asian people know that, when their asses itch, there's usually a small pebble of dried feces in the descending

colon or anus. A little warm-water spray and it comes out and
10 minutes later the itch is gone, so instead of buying gooey
creams that don't work, we just get rid of the problem."

"I really miss those flexible shower hoses," she said, smiling up at me with
her pretty little mouth and those exotically-curved, inky-black eyes.

"Fascinating," I said, "But of course I haven't had a bowel movement in
over 200 years, so I'm afraid that's one bit of medical advice that is lost on
me. Anyway, this is really quite fascinating, kind of like taking a virtual
vacation, like one a guy named Al Franken did on *Saturday Night Live*
once, back many years ago when the show was still funny, rather than a
lame purveyor of left-wing rants and propaganda. Anyway, it was a really
funny skit, at least in my opinion: he offered to take vacations for people
who couldn't afford them and suggested they send him money and he'd
send them photos from the vacation he took for them."

I grabbed a pen and post-it note and jotted a note to see if I could find
that skit online—there was a pretty good chance that someone had posted it
somewhere on the internet—heck, you could even find old W.C. Fields
videos, so why not SNL from the Golden Years?

Done, I continued with my monologue:

"Pity he didn't stay a comedian instead of embarking on a career as a
politician: he was a lot funnier making jokes than being a joke as a not-so-
in-the-closet communist. It was a relief to see his political career come to a
disgraceful end. I detest Americans who grew up free and yet would favor
a political system that oppresses dissent and typically murders the
dissenters, not to mention turning their citizens into slave labor while the
leaders enjoy all the economic benefits. So, what else can you share with
me?"

"Of course a lot of holidays and festivals are different. For
Valentine's Day in Japan, men have to buy chocolates for
every girl in the office and girls have to do the same for all the
men. The government has been trying to change this practice
as it can be quite expensive if you work for a large company.
In Taiwan, for New Year's, people give children or relatives
without jobs red envelopes containing cash, instead of presents
like Americans do on Christmas. It's not so exciting as not
knowing what's in the box, but it is practical and it eliminates
the pressure of not knowing what to get for someone.

On one island in Japan they have an annual even where they net and kill dolphins; I think this is even worse than the bullfighting in Spain because dolphins are intelligent and have even been known to help swimmers in trouble, chase off sharks, etc. Oh yeah, in the city of Tainan, they celebrate Lantern Festival by getting shot at by fireworks. Really! People will stand in the street in a crowd, wearing motorcycle helmets, gloves and raincoats, and dance over strings of firecrackers. Special displays will shoot thousands and thousands of bottle rockets at them...how do you say it...um...horizontally! There will be curtains of sparklers raining down and people will run through the spark shower. It's actually pretty exciting.

Have you ever had Chinese food? No, I guess not. Well it's a lot different from Japanese food. How do I explain it? For starters, most Japanese food is less oily while Chinese food is usually cooked in oil. In Japan, the appearance is also important, so a lot of food is more simple yet more elegant. Chinese food tends to have stronger flavors but appearance is maybe not that nice. Sweet & Sour Soup for example—very tasty but it looks like half-digested vomit! Taiwanese also love something appropriately called Stinky Tofu. It's very popular, but most foreigners can't stand the smell. To be honest, it kind of smells like dog shit! Both cultures eat a lot of rice and noodles. Americans eat bread; Asians eat rice and noodles.

How do they make stinky tofu? I guess it's made through fermentation. Anyway, it tastes good but it really does smell like warmed-over dog shit...really! You know how people here almost always eat pasta noodles hot? Well in Japan, people eat noodles either hot or cold. Udon noodles served cold which probably takes some getting used to for lao wai, um foreigners...sorry, I am having trouble concentrating: I am feeling kinda sick and dizzy.

Anyway, there's a dish known as Bukkake Udon. Udon noodles are a popular dish with sauce poured on the noodles and things like a soft-boiled egg, sesame seeds, scallions, dried fish flakes... The same word, incidentally, refers to the type of porn movies where a bunch of guys ejaculate onto a girl's face—usually after a gang-bang. Maybe that's what John Lennon was singing about when he sang 'cum together, right now, over me!' After all, he was the same guy who talked about 'rather small holes' filling the Royal Albert Hall and calling his audience a bunch of assholes!

Believe it or not, this word comes from a USA sports legend. I think his name was Dick Butkus. I recall he was like this really ferocious football player for the Chicago Bears and apparently he was famous for eating a plate of cheese-fries before football games and this is where the name comes from. American football isn't very popular in Japan...I also remember reading that about the only time people were really excited about it was when there was this really fat guy called the 'refrigerator' who was like a Sumo wrestler in Japan. Sumo isn't as popular as it used to be—it's mostly baseball and basketball these days, but there are still a lot of girls in Japan who want to lose their virginity to their favorite Sumo wrestler.

So, Butkus allegedly gave us the term Bukkake...like president Bush throwing up at an official dinner in Japan, in front of or maybe even *on* the prime minister, gave us the term 'Bushuru', which means like to totally embarrass yourself in public in a very humiliating way.

Anyhow, while I'm on the subject: sex is different. In Japan, girls and guys both are allowed to "play the field" when they are young and single. After marriage, the girl is expected to be faithful to her husband, while he probably has at least 1 lover and typically visits hookers as often as he can afford them. Also, the amount of sex in Japanese media dwarfs even that of the USA. You can see nudity on normal TV after midnight. When I was younger, back in the 1990's there was even more of it than there is now. There are at least a dozen sex-chat TV stations that have sexy bikini and underwear girls 24 hours a day just to get people to call a phone number and pay to talk dirty to someone and, of course, late at night you see a lot of nudity. There are so many cable TV stations with sex shows and things like naked girls playing sports, working in restaurants and so on. There's even a nude orchestra, stewardesses that give blowjobs on charter flights; there was even a record-setting orgy in a gymnasium that was filmed in front of a live audience; I've seen the video!

I even heard about an old American guy who taught English classes naked because he got over $100 an hour to do it! There are also clubs where you can watch people have sex on stage or girls strip naked while dozens of men make videos. Of course even traditionally there was an...emphasis...on sex. There are ancient temples with huge stone penises where men would go to pray for more...um...stamina or bigger size or women would pray to get pregnant. I once thought it would make a good research paper to compare different cultures to see which is the most oversexed...and it's probably the Japanese!

Strangely, it's been reported in the news recently that fewer college-age Japanese are having sex, more of them are virgins than ten or twenty years ago, while in Taiwan it's quite the opposite where there's been a huge increase in teenage pregnancies and there are more gays than before. I guess it's because there's so much sex in comic books, movies, the internet, strip clubs and so on that it's just easier and more convenient than trying to find a real sex partner.

Anyways, it's not the nudity everywhere that bothers me—in fact I would rather look at a naked woman than a naked man; women are graceful and...how should I put it...'artistically aesthetic' whereas men are hairy and bony and the ugly parts aren't hidden like on a woman. Anyway, it's the way women are degraded that bothers me. Um, how can I explain?

Japan is traditionally a male-dominated culture—until recently, women were restricted to low-paid jobs like nursing, waiting tables, greeting people at the doors to stores, being secretaries and receptionists. Now that women are starting to find jobs in management and are having their own careers and finding more independence, men feel threatened and angered, I guess. So, this is being reflected in our culture by a lot of violence against women in movies. Even in the subway you see posters advertising movies where women are tied up, raped, tortured...and there is a LOT of it.

There are a lot of movies, comic books, and TV shows in which women are beaten by their boyfriends or humiliated in some way. We have game shows where girls in bikinis are made to hang from exercise bars or sit in ice-cold swimming pools and engage in similar kinds of 'contests' where the girls are degraded in some way. There are videos where some young girl supposedly goes in for a massage and ends up seduced by the masseur, girls are filmed...is 'streaking' the right word? Walking around naked in public, giving blow-jobs, urinating, masturbating themselves or even having sex in restaurants or on the subway, sometimes with other passengers present. And, sometimes they are left in public, with no clothes or money—or anyway that's how the video ends; you don't know if there's someone there to rescue them or not. Then there are the violent ones. Girls supposedly raped at the beach or in a classroom or tied up and tortured. It seems most of the time the girls are wearing high school uniforms, so it's like believing you're watching some really young, teenage virgin being kidnapped and raped or made to do strange sex acts. In some of them you can tell it's not just acting, that the girl is really NOT willing; according to stories the Yakuza, the Japanese mafia, like to blackmail actresses into doing porn films and they recruit teenage girls willing to do anything for money. I even read of a case where a man kidnapped a young girl and kept her tied up and raped her every day and the way they caught him was he sold the bondage photos to some website and someone who knew her saw them on the internet and recognized her! If I am repeating myself, please tell me as I am getting a bit light-headed.

Where was I? Of course you know about how the Japanese army raped and murdered their way across China during World War Two. It isn't taught in schools in Japan, but of course I'm half Taiwanese and I also visited the museum in Nanjing on my one trip to China. I cried I felt so ashamed of what the Japanese did there. I heard there was a porn movie showing Japanese soldiers raping Chinese girls and they even hired girls from China to act in the movie to add realism—so I guess a lot of Japanese men today would love the chance to do the same thing!"

"Do you watch a lot of these videos?" I asked.

Smiling through her pain, she replied, "I have to admit I liked some of the sports shows, like nude girls basketball, for example."

"Some of them were so ridiculous they were funny. I remember one where a girl masturbated a man standing on a tower and a really pretty girl ran around down on the ground and tried to catch his cum in her mouth. I am embarrassed to admit I found that one kind of funny. One of them showed girls climbing a mountain in winter time, going skiing and lying naked in the snow; the scenery was really beautiful! It's a pity they digitally 'fuzz out' the ugly spot between a woman's legs—you know what I mean—it's not that I actually want to see anyone's labia, but I find it very distracting when they do that, but it's a law if they are going to show nudity on TV.

Oh, another very different thing is the Hentai...the pornographic cartoons. They are everywhere: in comic books, on TV, in movies...online. Some of them are really ridiculous: girls having sex with robots, being raped by monsters, just about anything you can think of. "My college roommate's boyfriend used to watch them on her computer—especially the ones that featured high school girls in their tartan skirts and white knee socks—he had a real thing for those. Sometimes he'd masturbate to them and he didn't care if I was in the room. He was weird—I think he hoped to turn me on so I'd want to have a threesome with them or something. Um, what was I talking about? (thinking). If you stay in a hotel in Japan, there are just about always sex channels on the TV. The cheaper the hotel, the dirtier the sex shows usually were. As a poor student, I could never afford the expensive hotels. Um, let me see, about Taiwan...

Beetle nut girls! There's a nut that's native to Taiwan that grows on these tall, skinny palm trees that look like something from a Dr. Seuss book. People chew them like some people chew tobacco in western countries. They make you feel a little warm and they taste really disgusting. I tried some once and accidentally swallowed the juice and it made me really sick to my stomach. People who use them a lot have really ugly stains on their teeth (moaning). Um, oh, I had started to explain about the Bin Lan Si Shr—the beetle nut girls. Taiwan is a much more conservative culture than Japan.

Most college students are still virgins, girls wear Hello Kitty and Snoopy T-shirts when they're 20 years old, there's no nudity on TV—even though Japan controlled Taiwan for something like 47 years...a LOT longer than China did in the past century...the culture is very different. There are a lot of Rabuho...sorry, that's Japanese...um, 'love hotels' for clandestine sexual encounters, but no go-go bars, at least no legal ones (groaning). Sorry, I am having trouble thinking straight. What...oh, um, the girls who sell beetle nuts usually wear lingerie or really sexy clothes and they work in little glass booths right alongside major roads. Imagine a 6-cubic foot container made of glass with a door and an air-conditioner and a refrigerator for cold drinks for sale and you'll have the idea.

So, in this mostly conservative country they are really outlandish! As you might imagine, there are also a lot of traffic accidents where men are driving by and looking at...ogling?...the girls instead of keeping their eyes on the road! And that reminds me—the character of people is different. Maybe it's the Buddhist/Taoist influence or something, but people in Taiwan are very passive. Like with driving. Traffic in Taiwan is terrible! It's like there are no rules—people turn right from the left lane, drive scooters on the left side of the road—in Taiwan you're supposed to drive on the right side like in the USA, not on the left like in Japan—cut in front of people, pull out in front of traffic without looking to see if it's clear, sometimes you see whole families of 4 or 5 people riding on a scooter or a child sitting on a wooden stool between it's mother's legs on a scooter, not to mention you can't walk down the sidewalks because people park on them—just rude, stupid, selfish behavior that would get you beaten-up or shot in this country except that, in Taiwan, people just shrug it off and go on about their business.

So instead of the old people going ballistic about the Beetle nut girls in their underwear causing traffic hazards, um, think about Janet Jackson at the Super Bowl and the way anally-traditional Americans overreacted, well people in Taiwan DON'T react. The ones who object to it just turn a blind eye. Maybe it's because it's a culture where people don't have guns, the government has all the power, there's a lot of corruption and so people are too afraid to assert themselves. Maybe it's because people are too busy making money to care. It's like the family is supposed to be the most important thing and to some people it is, but to a lot of people all they care about is making money. Um, what was the point I was trying to make? (pausing to gather her thoughts as her head felt like exploding and her stomach was on fire)."

"Garbage trucks," she moaned, that's another thing that's really different! I remember in California, the garbage trucks are big things with built-in fork-lifts that just grab garbage cans and lift them up and empty them into the truck"

"We have those around here now as well," I remarked, impressed with how well she was holding herself together, knowing the agony that was currently ripping through her in waves.

Well, in Taiwan, people don't use garbage cans alongside the street—a fear of rats, I guess, or maybe just because the streets are too small. So, the trucks pass through each neighborhood at a certain time, every day or on certain days of the week, except some holidays, and everyone stands there with their bags of trash and waits for the trucks. When the trucks come by, people throw their trash in. And, the trucks all play music. In California, when you hear a truck playing music, it's because they are selling ice cream. In Taiwan, that's the signal to come outside and throw out your trash!

"So, they inconvenience every person in the country by making them have to go meet the truck to throw out their trash?"

"Most people, although large buildings like schools and some large, apartment buildings have dumpsters, just like here."

I pondered this for a moment. "The loss in productivity in terms of man-hours must be staggering!"

She smiled for a moment, despite her ongoing, internal torment. "Most of the trucks go by at night when people are watching TV, so it's just a few minutes away from the idiot box; of course if they miss an important part of their show, I imagine a lot of people are unhappy about it."

"It still seems like an incredible waste of time when you multiply a few minutes times almost every day of the year times at least one family member from each household"

"So," I added, "anything else of interest?"

"Uhm," she uttered...in contemplation or in pain or maybe both. People in Taiwan ride motorcycles and motor scooters in very congested traffic while wearing flip-flops; you know, the kind you might wear at the beach. It's not just a few people, either, but a lot of people. Even in wintertime, you see people in really heavy ski jackets with only flip-flops on their feet...I mean it's weird! So, of course, you also see a lot of people with bandages on their feet and ankles. That's one way...Americans... are smarter. In Japan, most people just wear their, um, normal business or sports shoes but, here, a lot of people wear heavy, leather mo-tor-cycle boots which give a lot more pro-tec-shun.

She spoke the last sentence haltingly. It was obvious she was losing focus. "And in Japan?" I asked.

Not so many scooters—that and people in Japan are smarter. Or, maybe I should say they are more cosmopolitan and Taiwan has more 'Tu Bao Tse', people that, um, are more like countryside people. Sorry, I am having trouble to thinking. Oh, something I remembered, some Japanese guy offered some really big money, maybe $10,000 US dollars, to buy someone's cock after he had a sex change so they guy could cook and eat it! Yes, some people in Japan are really sick! Of course Americans had one president who was a rapist and the next one was gay, so I guess it's not only the Japanese that are perverts, eh?

I slid out from beneath her, balling up a towel to place beneath her head. I ran my hand affectionately atop her raven-black hair for it's full length while again admiring the curve of her collarbone, her narrow waist, her long, creamy thighs, those sweet, tiny buttocks that would fit on a dinner plate and I felt myself getting hard again. "Later," I told myself. To her, I said, "rest here awhile, I'll be back"

I didn't need to look at the clock on the wall to know it was now dark outside...it was something I could just sense. As I emerged from the basement into the kitchen, the cat clawed me on the ankle and dashed across the parquet floor, disappearing into the sitting room. "Well done you little bastard," I silently congratulated him.

Turning 90 degrees, I proceeded through the living room to the back hallway and the rear door, opened it, and stepped onto the back porch. All three dogs were awaiting me, sitting in a row like animal miniatures in a wall-mounted movable-type drawer. I'd forgotten about their dinner. "Sorry boys," I apologized while moving to the plastic trashcan in the corner to my left. A strong odor of dried meat and grain emanated as I removed the lid and I felt the dog's excitement rise like it did every time no matter how often I served them the same food. Grasping the scoop that protruded from the 40 lb bag of dog food that resided within, I quickly filled all 3 bowls while the dogs set to work on their dinner, waving their tails in hearty appreciation. I gave each one a quick pat, pulled a few burrs off Panzer's coat, then set off towards the barn on my self-appointed errand. The crickets were already chirping, the moon was about 75% full, what I think is called a waxing Gibbous moon, and the smells of straw, mildew and leather were strong as I entered the barn. Going to the wall where the saddles and tack were hung, I selected a lead—one of the newer ones that had a steel chain attached to a leather collar. Satisfied with my selection, I headed across the farm towards were the cattle were pastured.

When I had first decided to keep my new toy, I'd realized what I would have to do. I was not looking forward to this part. My cows had only birthed four calves this spring and each represented a significant potential return on my investment (which to this point consisted primarily of grass and water and a little corn). I walked quickly, so that after 5 minutes and several gates, I came to the North pasture and located the calf I was seeking. I'd been present at his birth (it was at night and I'd used my walker and played the role of old farmer, joining the vet and Miguel as he came into the world. A little sickly at first, the calf had been growing stronger and more robust. Still, he was the smallest of the three and that is how he had been selected. For what I had in mind, he was the most suitable of all my livestock.

Slipping the lead around his neck, I led him to the barn—a much longer trip this time as I had to open and close each gate instead of simply swinging myself over them as I'd done the first time. Once there I clipped the lead around one of the central support columns. I then looked around and found a pair of sideline hobbles and securely fastened the calf's legs, front to back. The calf took an instant dislike to the restraints and began thrashing-about and bawling. I momentarily considered trying to comfort the animal, realized just how pointless that would be, and turned and headed back to the house.

The girl lay as I'd left her, recumbent upon the linoleum tile of the basement bathroom. Her eyes were rolled back into her head, showing the whites, sweat beading her forehead, and her chest was heaving up and down, rapidly, like Sigourney Weaver in *Ghostbusters*. I picked her up, briefly considered dressing her, and decided that would also be a waste of my time.

The dogs, having finished dinner, danced in circles around us as he carried the limp form of the nymph out to the barn. "Max, Panzer, Brutus," I commanded as the dogs tried to follow us into the barn, "stay outside" The dogs stopped moving, Panzer tilting his head to the side, questioning, and Brutus looked absolutely crestfallen, if that were possible for a dog. "Watch...protect..," I ordered, to try to provide some justification the canines might understand. Closing the door behind me, I glanced over at the calf, which had apparently tripped and fallen over and was now lying on its side, attempting to rise. I laid the girl down on top of a couple of bags of feed I'd laid out on my earlier visit. Her condition hadn't changed. She was still comatose, feverish, panting...and lovely, despite her condition. The virus, if that is indeed what causes the change, was burning through her like wildfire.

The calf farted loudly and then started bawling again for its mother. Along the opposite wall was a workbench and, above it, a sheet of pegboard, on which hung a variety of tools, measuring devices, rolls and tubes of adhesives—barn stuff. Crossing over to the bench, I removed a roll of duct tape from a peg on the wall and, crossing over to the calf, clamped it's jaws shut, tightly wrapped the tape around three times and then looped it around its neck. Not only did this stop the noise which had been starting to get on my nerves (yes, vampires have nerves!), it would prevent the calf from biting the girl when it was time for her to feed. Of course this is why I had selected the calf in the first place.

When she came out of her trance, she was likely to have an uncontrollable urge to feed (I certainly had, when I'd first awakened to my new life...make that 'unlife', I suppose). The calf might die, although it certainly held more blood than she would need, but her actions would be unpredictable. An 800 pound bull would be far more likely to survive any depredations she might inflict, but it might also damage my new play toy— I had no idea if a vampire-in-transition would be more vulnerable than a vampire after the transition were complete, but I suspected that would be the case (like the "trebuchets are vulnerable while setting up" message I used to see when playing *Age of Empires 2*). So, in order to prevent her from turning on me, or perhaps escaping and wreaking havoc on my neighbors, I had decided to risk the life of one calf. For now, however, she slept a very troubled sleep.

Realizing it could be quite awhile before she roused, if indeed she survived the transformation, I locked the barn and gave the dogs mental orders to wait on station outside the barn and alert me if anything happened. Brutus nuzzled my hand, seeking reassurance, then joined his comrades in executing their orders. Being able to communicate telepathically, even in a limited capacity, certainly had its advantages! I went back to the house, leaving Theresa in the care of my canines' heightened senses. I checked to make sure everything was in readiness for the next time I had to play the "little old man in the wheelchair," then I turned on my PC, logged in with my password, and opened my email. After the bogus news coverage following the 9-11 "airliner attacks," I'd realized the major news networks were merely propaganda machines for whatever administration was currently in power. Honestly, did they expect people to believe anything they broadcast after claiming an airplane hit the Pentagon, despite the complete lack of debris (no engines, wings, dead bodies, suitcases, cans of beer and soda—not even the tail section which would have stood taller than the building itself) and of course there was building 7, obviously a controlled-demolition as it hadn't even been hit by an airplane (or cruise missile) like the big towers, yet the mainstream news continued to insist that it also had collapsed as a result of fire per the official story—despite over 3000 engineers issuing a public statement that the fires couldn't possibly have destroyed ANY of those skyscrapers.

As other fictitious news stories followed in quick succession, fake shootings and bombings and highly dubious terror plots, I decided to leave the news networks to the gullible portion of the public and subscribed to several online news services. I didn't get out much, it's true, but part of survival was to stay alert and, in the technology age, that meant to stay informed. I didn't believe everything I read on the independent's sites, either, but they were highly critical of the government, particularly the socialists that were attempting to subvert the American system of government and, on that basis alone, I found them to be much more believable.

After reading the usual gloom-and-doom economic news, checking to see how far my stocks had slipped and how much beef prices and gold and silver and corn futures had increased, I decided it was time to go back to the barn to check on my charge. There were still a few hours until dawn...I was hoping something would happen before then. The lighting in the barn was not all that great—it was a barn, after all—so I ended up in the rafters, straddling a beam with my back against a pillar, in order to get decent illumination from one of the old light fixtures in the ceiling as I read an old David Drake novel I'd recently purchased online but had not yet experienced. Speaking as someone who could not go abroad easily during daylight, the internet was truly a godsend...not that God was thought to look favorably upon the undead!

Chapter 16
Darkness

A sudden convulsion threw her into full consciousness. Theresa couldn't move. She was paralyzed, lying in a fetal position with her arms clasped across her chest. Her head was throbbing, she had a stabbing pain in her arm and her stomach felt like it was on fire. A fleeting thought danced through her mind—if she farted now she might fart flames as a dragon breathes fire. As her eyes focused, she realized he was naked, lying across a large bag of some sort, face just inches away from hard-packed dirt. The smells of straw, grains and urine were strong—very strong. A shooting pain in her chest added itself to the fireworks in her brain and her assorted collection of physical distresses. She was having a heart attack! Waves of pain racked her as a giant fist squeezed her chest. She couldn't breathe! She sensed her new, vampiric friend was nearby. She tried to call out for help but couldn't made a sound.

"Please," she thought, "I don't want to die!" She mentally screamed this to herself, again and again, as the world shrank in upon her like the picture on an old black and white TV that would shrink to a small, white dot while shutting down. After a couple of minutes that seemed to stretch into hours, she blacked out.

Theresa wandered in dark dreams, down endlessly branching corridors of memories, both real and imagined, some half-remembered, some that were surely fantasies or colored by time. Wait...color...weren't dreams supposed to be in black and white? In her half-delirious state, Theresa was amazed that she was...conscious enough to be amazed! There was her grade-school teacher, a man she'd been truly afraid of—the kind of teacher who'd enjoyed smacking students on the back of the hand with a ruler. He'd even made her stay after class once and had spanked her...for whatever offense or imagined slight she couldn't remember. She could see again the threadbare, frayed edge of his trousers and his socks that weren't quite the same color of brown, while he held her across his lap with her skirt pulled up and the tears running down her cheeks. In retrospect, she was sure it was just so he could put his hands on her legs and bottom and feel-her-up underneath her skirt with no-one around to watch and a convenient excuse to justify his behavior—not that she'd ever told her mother or anyone else:

her embarrassment at having been punished was enough to guarantee her silence, in accordance with the culture of the time, anyway. With the clarity found sometimes only in dreams, combined with a decade of maturity, she suddenly realized something that she hadn't at the time—small though it was, he'd had an erection!

Was this really a dream? Had she ever been this...awake...while dreaming? It must be a dream, she couldn't control the direction of her thoughts, but she was so AWARE of what she was dreaming it was almost scary! Next up was when she'd wet herself in her favorite teacher's class. For whatever reason, the teacher had been in a terrible mood that day. She's screamed at them, cowed them into silence (not difficult, as Japanese classrooms were far more controlled than those in the USA). Maybe it was PMS, maybe some problem with her boyfriend, but something had changed the generally easy-going teacher into a surly matron, at least for that morning. The students had been ordered to sit at attention at their desks. When Theresa had tried to ask permission to go to the bathroom, which she'd just been about to do, her teacher had yelled her into silence, not once but three times, until the tears ran down her cheeks and her bladder let go, soaking her panties and puddling on the wooden seat.

In her dream-state, she saw again her teacher's face while she sponged up the pee, realizing that, as humiliating as it had been to her, this had also shamed her teacher into realizing how foolish had been her outburst of temper. At the time, however, Theresa had only had thoughts for her own shame and the ridicule she'd faced from her classmates. As the wisps of memory turned about her consciousness like a smoky vortex, she realized just how much her early education had been influenced by fear and intimidation. When her classmates had occasionally tormented her, she'd borne it in silence, almost never telling her mother or a teacher, for fear of future retaliation; also, perhaps, she was just as humiliated by her cowardice in not pushing back against the bullies. Likewise, she'd never told anyone about the neighbor boy who'd invited her in to play video games...and had then tried to get her to touch his penis. How old had she been? Eleven or twelve? She remembered her first pets, a pair of mice, and how hard she'd cried when they died after her mother had put their cage outside on a summer's day and forgotten about them as the sun had changed position in the sky and shade had turned into blinding sunlight, turning their glass terrarium into an oven. That memory wavered and faded, although the sadness remained.

As she wavered on the ethereal edge between sleeping and waking, in more of a trance than a dream, she was vaguely aware of the changes that continued ravaging her body, although blissfully unaware of any physical stimuli...losing consciousness had finally shielded her from the agonies she'd been suffering for hours. It was just something dimly lurking in the background, feelings that had gone unnoticed until, like a trap triggering or a lock clicking shut, IT WAS DONE! She sat bolt-upright, going from dream world to full-awake in an instant. The agony was ended, the change was complete, she had turned—and before she could think, she was sick. She fell forward, catching herself on the hard floor of the barn, and greeted her new existence by vomiting all over her hands and the surrounding area. She started to lean back and, with no warning, again violently dry-heaved as her body attempted to clear away any remaining matter that was foreign to her new existence.

Theresa stayed that way for long moments. Her innards, which felt STRANGE, convulsing, her head spinning...and her heart beat out a rapid staccato and then lapsed into a slow, muted, background rhythm. She shook her head, trying to clear her thoughts. She must have been completely INSANE when she was a teenager, dreaming of becoming a vampire!

Among the other changes she'd begun to notice was a stronger sense of smell...not only could she smell the obvious smells of the barn: the wood, leather, feed, straw, hay and mold smells, not to mention the smell of the animal lying but a few feet from her and the strong odor of urine where it had relieved itself upon it and its surroundings at least once; yet there were other, more subtle smells she had never in her life been able to smell before...could that be mouse hair? Was that rust on an old, bent nail lying nearby? She felt like she'd been born again as the tanner's apprentice in the movie *Perfume* that the vampire had mentioned previously and that she'd come back into the world with an acute sense of smell like that of the murderer in the story. The murderer...was that what she was becoming? Unbeknownst to herself, for a few heartbeats longer at any rate, this stray thought was far more accurate than she realized...

Continued self-reflection gave rise to yet another surprise: as the pounding in her head gradually subsided, she realized her hearing had improved as well: she could not only detect the scrabbling of a mouse or some other rodent in the hay loft above, she could HEAR the beating of the calf's heart from nearly 2 feet away—a sound that had increased in tempo as she'd awakened and started moving around! The animal had also begun frantically struggling—apparently its legs were restrained and it was trying to rise. Clearly, the animal was afraid; no, it was terrified!

She couldn't believe the speed at which the changes were coming over her. She hadn't expected anything to happen this quickly. Something the vampire had said came back to her, some analogy of how a foal could stand just moments after birth, whereas a human infant is helpless for months after birth. So, she was wasting no time adapting to her new life. She supposed that was a good thing—whatever was happening to her, she might as well get it over with!

Gradually, as she wrestled with her new sensations, she became aware of a growing yearning. Her body had spent the last several hours emptying itself of all manner of substances of various degrees of solidity and liquidity. It was awhile now since she'd had anything to eat, all of which had been expelled forcefully through one orifice or another. Suddenly, she realized—she was hungry! No, that wasn't right, she was thirsty! Yet, that wasn't really it either. Theresa realized that she was both HUNGRY and THIRSTY and that this new feeling was somehow a combination of both and, naturally, was a far more powerful craving than either hunger or thirst alone. This must have been what they referred to as "The Thirst" in the *Blade* movies. It was not, however, some overpowering urge that would have her run into a crowded shopping mall and bite someone with a crowd of onlookers...at least not yet. Somehow, however, she didn't think it would be that bad, at least not for a long while. Humans could only go a couple of days without water. She had not been a vampire for long, not much more than time enough for a few non-random thoughts, but she could already feel that she was...different. The pain and nausea in her abdomen had subsided, she somehow felt her strength and endurance were greater, her senses of smell and hearing were sharpened and, despite the scant lighting in the barn, she knew of a certain her night-vision was far, far greater than ever before.

Turning to the pathetic creature lying bound before her, Theresa crawled across to its whimpering form. What would it be like to drink its blood... At the moment she was more curious than driven. After all, she'd imagined going on safari, killing an animal and holding its heart in her hand as the life drained from it. Now, she had that chance. How to begin? That was the question. She doubted her fingernails, long though they were, could possibly pierce the animal's thick hide. She had no vampire fangs, at least not yet, and chewing her way into it's neck promised to be an arduous task at best. She reached out and placed her hands on the creature's neck, feeling the coarse hair, the warm, thick skin underneath, and the pulsing current of life-sustaining blood within the flesh. The animal looked at her with it's large eye, a huge pupil, indistinguishable from the iris, and a bloodshot cornea. In obvious terror at her touch, the animal pumped it's hobbled legs frantically...once, twice, thrice...and then lay still, panting, driven to exhaustion by the anticipated terror of having witnessed her transformation and the perception that some manner of predator stood over it, accompanied by the knowledge that it was helpless—absolutely powerless to save itself.

Rising to her feet, she took her first look at her surroundings. It did not take her long to spy the workbench to her right, along with the pegboard beside and behind it, festooned with ironmongery and tools of all descriptions. She knew what she had to do. Selecting a long, broad, standard-head screwdriver, she stood for a long moment, facing the wall. She was ready now. If she waited, however, she was afraid she'd lose her nerve. Not wanting to have to look the animal in its innocent, accusing eye as she struck, she steeled her nerves and then, in a single motion, turned and threw herself through the air, screwdriver held aloft in both hands. "WAIT" cried a voice, as she brought the implement down, driving it through the calf's throat and out the other side.

Chapter 17
Tea for Two

I couldn't help wondering what her mother would think if she could see her flesh-and-blood at this moment, standing naked and unashamed in a somewhat dimly-lit barn, blood dripping from her right hand onto her thigh while a dying animal, screwdriver protruding from its neck, kicked-out its death throes at her feet.

"What the hell are you doing up there?" she demanded. "Why are you spying on me?"

"I'll explain in a moment," I insisted, jumping down from the beam to land on the poured-cement floor of the barn, just in front of her, "but let's not waste this." Walking over to the poor animal, it's large, round eye pleading with me. I berated myself for not having acted sooner. Even now, its life could possibly be saved—but that would give rise to too many questions. Fate had spoken.

Hastily pulling off my shirt and tossing it on the workbench, I knelt, grasping the handle of the screwdriver with my right hand, placing my left beneath the animal's neck where the blade protruded, feeling the stream of warm life dripping rapidly from the blade. "Kneel down and get ready to drink," I ordered. "But I'm not sure I..."

"KNEEL," I commanded.

She knelt.

"OK, I'm going to pull out the screwdriver. When I do so, it's going to spurt out. You need to cover the hole with the mouth and just swallow. You won't have to worry about sucking. Pretend it's like you've got a cock coming in your mouth—no need to do anything except swallow. OK, are you ready?" She nodded in agreement.

"On three," I said. I couldn't help thinking of the *Lethal Weapon* movies...'go on three? Or three and then go?' but I decided not to complicate matters by making a movie reference or a joke. I counted, then pulled out the tool from the top while plugging the hole in the bottom of the neck with my index finger. Theresa did as she was told, despite the fact she received a face-full of blood before she was able to get into position to drink. As I'd expected, she took one, big swallow and then pulled away, coughing and choking. At that point I dove in, drinking deeply, enjoying the warm, sweet taste passing down my throat the way an office worker enjoys their first cup of coffee on a Monday morning. When the flow began to slacken, I pulled up, applying pressure to the upper wound try to conserve as much as possible.

The calf had ceased struggling—no doubt it was in shock—and Theresa wasn't doing much better. She was noisily regurgitating onto the sack that had erstwhile been her pillow. Sheepishly she turned towards me, wiping her mouth with the back of her hand.

"Try again," I encouraged, in a softer tone of voice this time. Again, she did as beckoned, with greater success now that the blood pressure had abated somewhat and the blood wasn't spurting out so forcefully.

Looking up at me, she stated, "This isn't as bad as I suspected it might be." She then immediately gagged, but recovered quickly and gave me a sweet smile...or what might have been a sweet smile if not for the blood filling the spaces between her teeth and running down her chin, streaking her chest and naked breasts.

"If you're finished, you can help me—do you see those Ball jars...the glass jars on the shelf over there? Bring me some of them, quickly!"

As she did as she was told, I couldn't help admiring once again the long, slender curves of her legs, the small, rounded ass, the graceful way she walked like a gazelle. I began to get a hard-on again just watching her. "First things first," I said to myself. "OK, I'm going to lift his head. When I do so, put a jar under his neck and fill it, then the next jar and so on. Go ahead and open them all first. You push up on that curved piece of metal...there, you've got it!" I continued plugging both neck wounds as she got the jars open and lined up. Working together, we managed to fill all the jars. I then proceeded to fill half of a small pail while holding the poor creature off the ground with my arms around its waist. "Close those up and put them in the fridge in the basement," I told her, "and rinse yourself off with the hose before you go in the house!" I dropped the body on the floor and removed the restraints, hanging them back on the wall. Grabbing a pair of wire cutters and a screwdriver from the workbench, I threw the corpse over my right shoulder, picked up the bucket with my left hand, and headed out into the night.

It took me a good 20 minutes to carry the calf over to the pasture where the other cattle were bedded down for the night, pry loose some barbed wire on a fence that bordered the wooded lot that was also my property, wrap the wire around its neck so the barbs caught deep into the neck, as if the animal had done it to itself while attempting to escape, then splash the blood in the bucket around to give it an air of authenticity. I'd selected that particular section of fence as the wire was old, and the wooded lot on the other side was also fenced, so that if another animal took it upon itself to leap over the body and cross the fence, it would not go far or end up on one of the county roads, nearby. The smell of blood made the other animals nervous, so I kept close tabs on the alpha-male bull and worked quickly. Perhaps it was also fortunate that the calf's mother was away on loan. I raised beef cattle. It wasn't the mating season and the yearlings had matured enough to eat solid food, so only a couple of weeks ago, I'd rented my females out to a local dairy. It was a good arrangement. I had the females on hand during the rut, when I occasionally got some new livestock as nature took its course. The rest of the year someone else took care of the feeding and housing of them, I received some additional income, plus occasional gifts of milk and cream that I either poured down the drain or fed to the dogs or, as I often did, sent home with my Mexican caretaker for his wife and children.

Another 20 minutes and I'd hosed down the barn, eliminated the visible evidence as well as I could and went back to the house in search of my newest pet. I found her sitting on the glider on the front porch, a bottle of 17-year-old Balvenie single-malt Scotch next to her and a tumbler with three nearly-extinct ice cubes in her hand. "Here," I said, handing her a partial pack of Marlboro Reds, "they are a little old, but I'm guessing you could use one right about now." Her hands trembled as she reached out to take the pack.

"I didn't think you smoked," she observed.

"I don't," I agreed, "and by tomorrow you shouldn't either!" I just happened to have them lying around."

I decided it was best not to mention that, upon rare occasion, I would go to the 'big city' in search of a little entertainment. If I did something that might attract the interest of local law enforcement, such as leaving the body of a teenage girl in a public park or a dead prostitute in a sleazy hotel room, I liked to leave one or more items belonging to one of my recent, male victims just to confuse the issue. The cigarettes had been in the pocket of a leather jacket I'd taken from the owner of the Nova, my last such victim. The jacket was now safely ensconced in the trunk of my 1965 Mustang, along with a few other such items I had put away for 'future reference'. The .357 magnum I'd taken at the same time was resting behind my 1st edition *Tarzan* collection on one of the bookshelves.

"This is good whiskey," she proclaimed while studying the glass in close examination, as if by looking at it she could unravel the mysteries of taste as well as color, "not that I've tried that many, but this is much nicer than the Suntory and Jack Daniels my ex-roommate used to drink."

Ugh, Jack Daniels is paint thinner! I've never tried Suntory—but if it's anything like Japanese beer, I'll pass! Single-malt is the only way to fly! I actually prefer the 15-year old Balvenie to the 17. In fact I like it nearly as much as the Johnny Walker Blue and it's about 1/4 the price. I rarely drink Scotch, however, and you're going to find that the effects of alcohol are different than before. Your liver undergoes changes along with the rest of your body, especially your digestive system. For one thing, I've found it almost impossible to get drunk. I really tried a few times-it required enormous amounts of alcohol and I sobered up depressingly quickly-especially considering the unending headache that beset me for about a week, each time.

> Vampires are cursed with a loss of pigmentation, making sunlight kind of like our Kryptonite. In most other ways, however, we are stronger. It seems that we require much less oxygen, much like sea turtles, I suppose. I guess that's a good thing for when one of us actually does spend the day in a coffin—a normal human would suffocate in a coffin without air holes. Hearing and night vision are radically improved as is the sense of smell—at least for me—I know human females have much better smelling ability than males and, oh it's starting to improve for you too? That's interesting to know. So, how does it feel to be one of the undead? Is it everything you thought it would be when you were playing vampire with your friends?

She took a long pull from the cigarette, tossed down a good sized swallow of whiskey, closed her eyes, leaned back, and marshaled her thoughts and feelings.

"It's hard to say. I feel...dirty...guilty...sad, about the animal. After all, it was little more than a baby. At the same time, I have to admit I felt a little excited; I had a—what is it called—an adrenaline rush when I was...drinking its blood? That was really disgusting. Yet, at the same time, it was kind of...warm and wonderful, I suppose. My feelings are really complicated, confused, I really don't know what I feel. I guess I need some time to sort it all out.

Also, I guess now I can live forever and never die and never grow old, never lose my beauty, never get fat or ugly. But, I will never see my mother or my friends again, never have my own family, never play with my babies or see my children growing up. Is it worth it? Now that I think about it, when I was a teenager playing at being a vampire, as you mentioned, I didn't really think of all the...ramifications. In retrospect, it is really a terribly, terribly selfish thing to want—to become a vampire! To give up family and friends, love and sunlight and birds and butterflies and clouds... Of course every woman wants to be beautiful, it's part of our basic programming, and we all want to stay beautiful. That's why the cosmetics industry is something like a $6 billion-a-year business. But, is it worth the cost?"

She heaved a sigh, nearly a shudder, and gazed at the mostly-molten ice cubes at the bottom of her glass while I poured another 2-fingers for her. "I just don't know," she finally added after a long moment's thought.

"In any case," I chimed in—most unhelpfully, I knew, "it's too late to change your mind." This time she actually did shudder as she tossed back a hearty swallow of the whisky (I was quite impressed! Most women I'd known couldn't drink nearly-straight whisky like this...although drinking sake was probably on a par, now that I thought about it).

Looking at the cigarette in her hand, obviously relaxed enough now that her mind was wondering they way women often did, flitting from one thought to another like a flock of sparrows, hopping from tree to tree, she wondered: "Why are cigarettes so expensive here? All they are is dried leaves, paper and cotton. These things should be the cheapest product on the market...why so expensive?"

Greed. Governments love their taxes only there's a limit to how high they can raise them where it's obvious—after all, this country was founded as the result of a war with England over excessive taxes; taxes which were a *much* smaller percentage, I think, then the taxes we pay these days. When you add in the income taxes, sales taxes, excise and property and inheritance and FICA—that's social security—the average person is paying about 40% of their income in taxes! It's gotten to the point they have to try to hide them. If people knew they were paying half of their income in taxes, they might just stop paying and then the governments would be totally screwed! So, they raise taxes on things that don't affect everyone—such as cigarettes and alcohol, or hide them where people don't see them, like in gasoline taxes. There's even a tax on your telephone! Years ago someone decided poor people needed to have free phones, just in case they might have a need to call 9-11 someday, so they passed a tax to make the rest of us pay for phones for people who supposedly couldn't afford phone service—not that there's likely to be a single household in the USA these days without at least one cell phone! And, there are taxes like workman's comp which are paid for by employers, so people don't see that they're paying those taxes because they pay them *before* the money is in their paychecks, not afterwards like with income and social security taxes. Anyway, let's change the subject. Is there anything else you'd like to discuss?

"So," she said, looking up and spearing me with a glance from those lovely, concave-convex-curved eyes of hers, "something I've always wondered: just what do vampires DO all day long? Do you spend all your time sleeping or are you awake part of the time? When you sleep are you 'dead to the world' so to speak, like in some of those old movies where they open the coffin and find the vampire and drive a stake though his heart and he never wakes up until they are hammering it in?"

"That's more than one question. I can see I'm going to enjoy tearing into stupid movie plots with you! In any case, this may take awhile, so let me make myself more comfortable." A moment later I was lying on my back, my head pillowed on her lap, knees bent over one arm of the glider, staring up at her lovely face and enjoying the gentle fragrance of her hair.

I can't speak for other vampires, having only really known one other, but I only sleep about 4-6 hours a day. Anyway, back to your first question: you have undoubtedly surmised that sitting around waiting for the sun to set, unable to go out and about unless it is heavily overcast, is quite tedious. Of course nowadays I spend some time online, mostly reading international news and sometimes playing a video game. Still, it's been largely the same for 2 centuries—I read. No doubt you saw all the books I have in this house, in every room aside from the kitchen, as a matter of fact. Well, I have been collecting books for over two centuries. In addition to the ones in my collection, mostly hardback and some of them quite old, like my set of Jeremy Bentham treatises on philosophy that pre-date the United States, I have also read paperbacks by the thousands, particularly science fiction and fantasy, everything from Asimov to Zelazny.

Of course my daily routine has changed over the years. The invention of electricity and artificial lighting and later the internet changed everything! For certain there was a time when I spent the day sleeping in a coffin, or a barrel or a packing crate, when my entertainment consisted of reading a moldy book by candlelight in a dank cellar or crypt. For the first century, literally for 100 years or so, reading was about my only daytime activity. I would steal books from my victims or buy them with stolen coin. Of course there weren't so many books back then. In the days of my youth, books were rare and valuable items. Printing presses were few, setting-type was laborious, binding was done by hand...so most people could not afford books.

Also, the truth of it was that most people could not read more than a few words. Have you ever seen traditional British pubs or German Rathskellers? Have you ever noticed how, even to this day, many of them have a sign in front showing a depiction of the pub's name? For example, the 'Fox and Hounds' will have a picture of a pack of hounds chasing a fox. The reason for this was that most commoners were unable to read. Merchants did the same thing—a sign with a picture of a barrel hung in front of the cooper, a picture of a shoe in front of the cobbler, a needle and thread in front of the tailor's shop... This is also why so many roads were named for the place they took you to. In London, there is an "Oxford St" that takes you to Oxford. From Oxford, the "Abingdon Road" takes you to Abingdon. People in olden times also could not read maps, so instead of names like 'Maple Street', they were given practical names, such as 'Market Street', 'The High Street', or 'Forest Lane'. We even have this around here. Go up to Elkhart and you'll find Mishawaka, Goshen and Edwardsburg roads, all named to let you know where you'll end up if you head off down that particular roadway.

Anyway, I digress. Reading was about my only pastime for the first century or so. Fiction and most especially science fiction were my favorites. I started with Shakespeare and Molière, as they were known by their pen-names, and the few fictions of my time, such as Mary Shelley's Frankenstein. As they came into print, I devoured the writings of H.G. Wells, Jules Verne, Edgar Rice Burroughs and also the writings of the Philosophes, men who were the writers who influenced the American and French Revolutions, such as Voltaire and Rousseau.

You are probably familiar with some of what are now known as 'the classics,' such as *Les Misérables*, *Robinson Crusoe*, etc. Later, there were the works of Conan Doyle, Agatha Christie, Dostoyevsky, Thomas Hardy, E.A. Poe, Samuel Clemens...but in the early years I read many books ten or even twenty times while waiting to acquire something new. It wasn't like nowadays when books come out in print faster than you can keep track of them. In more recent times, Tolkein, Harry Harrison, Philip K. Dick, Robert Jordan and many others have helped me while-away the hours. I have even read a few Japanese authors—translated into English, of course, Natsume Soseki being my favorite.

"Really?" she commented more than questioned, "*Kokoro* was one of the books that made a lasting impression on me in junior high school." I smiled, remembering it as a morbidly depressing story ending in that most-Japanese of teenage past-times, a suicide.

"Have you ever read *Atlas Shrugged*?" I inquired, "That was my profound bit of literature at that age. Have you read it?"

When she nodded in the negative, I smiled, "Not to worry, I have a copy I can lend you...actually, I will give it to you: as Admiral Adama espoused in *Battlestar Galactica*, books should be given, not loaned."

Don't bother with the movie. *Atlas Shrugged* I mean; the Communists in Hollywood intentionally made a truly dreadful movie out of it because it has such a powerful message of the correct way to look at government and economics and the Marxists always do their best to bury the truth when it conflicts with the crap they try to brainwash people with. Today's cellphone generation are more likely to watch a movie than read a book, so anyone they hook into watching such a piece-of-shit movie is unlikely to ever read the book, thereby missing-out on valuable life lessons that, among other things, point out the failings of Socialism and how it's all a con-job to take money away from productive people and line the pockets of the dictators and give 'free stuff' to the mob to keep them pacified. It's the same way with their negative portrayals of great leaders such as Churchill, Thatcher and Reagan. The movie *Dunkirk* completely ignored the evil that German Socialism represented and the dedication and oratory skill with which old Winston imbued the British with the resolve to persevere... and don't even get me on what a piece of crap *The Bible* mini-series was. Okay, I admit I watched very little of it, having been warned off by the scathing reviews, but I did watch bits of it, particularly the Sodom and Gomorrah sequence, which hardly resembled God smiting the homosexuals for their deviant, unrepentant passions; if anything, it looked more like a Kung Fu movie with a bunch of ninjas running around slicing and dicing people with their swords. Someone with no knowledge of Biblical history would have had no clue what the hell they were watching!

I was sitting up in bed, my back supported by a pillow between my spine and the carved, Mahogany headboard. My new plaything lay stretched out across the bed, her head in my lap, raven-hair spread everywhere in a delicious cascade, her perky little nipples staring at the ceiling, while I was treated to a top-angle view of her long, lovely legs and enchanting, straight pubes. Yes, for the moment, life was good (or unlife or whatever—I was tired of debating the issue with myself and certainly was no closer to a resolution).

I assume you've seen *The Matrix* trilogy? I really enjoyed those and thought they were particularly well done, aside from the 20-minute dance scene in part 3 and Keanu Reeves in the first one when he is in an old dentist's chair being programmed and he turns his head at a 30-degree angle when he supposedly had a 4-inch spike inserted deep into his skull...that was a little bit of bad acting they should have caught in the cutting room. Anyway, there is a scene in the first Matrix movie where they go into a building full of soldiers to free Morpheus—good, you know the scene I'm referring to—where, in a space of just a couple minutes they have 3 horrendously-glaring technical fuck-ups! First, Neo is shown firing a pair of Scorpion 9mm pistols, but the empty brass bouncing around his feet is .223 rifle brass. Moments later, he's shown firing a mini-gun from a helicopter with appropriately-sized brass pouring out of the weapon. The only problem is this: you could tell the rounds hitting the floor were too long to be empties. They were either loaded ammo or dummy cartridges—either way that was two scenes of total bullshit within a few seconds of each other! Furthermore, they weren't done yet! In the same scene with the mini-gun, Morpheus jumps out of his chair and runs towards the helicopter. The agent is shown firing a .357 caliber Desert Eagle into a wall of solid masonry that's between him and Morpheus. Somehow, a bullet magically penetrates the wall and hits Morpheus in the leg. Now, with the way Neo was spraying down the room, I'd have easily believed it if NEO had hit Morpheus in the leg, but for a lead bullet fired from a .357 caliber pistol to penetrate 6 inches of cement, marble and/or steel...horseshit! Can't they afford a $100 consulting fee to have some ex-military type stop them from doing stupid stuff? It was almost as bad as the way they ruined *Saving Private Ryan* for me. I'm sure you've seen movies like that over in Asia...things that are so stupid they insult your intelligence?"

"All the time," my little pet smiled sweetly.

I get so tired of these stupid Kung Fu movies where some little teenage girl with no training beats the shit out of five or six big, veteran warriors wearing armor. Or these stupid sex-assault films in Japan where some stranger comes up to a girl on a train or in a park or even after forcing his way into her apartment and after just 30-seconds of forcible kissing or putting his hands up her skirt suddenly she changes her mind about screaming and calling for help and lets him fuck her? Or he sticks his dick in her mouth without her biting it off? Of course these are male fantasy situations as Japan is still very much a male-dominated culture and violence towards women and even rape is commonplace on TV and social media. That reminds me: in Game of Thrones, you remember Yara Greyjoy of the Iron Islands? She's this strong, female leader because all her brothers are dead except Theon, who's a hostage of the Starks? When her father dies, she hopes to become the first-ever queen in their male-dominated culture. In the last season, I think it was, the writers suddenly decided to make her a full-on-bull-dyke-lesbian. Don't they realize lesbians have like zero respect in male-dominated cultures? There's no way she would have had that much support as an open and obvious carpet-muncher! In Japan, lesbians are reviled the way late-night TV in the USA ridicules Trump supporters!

Oh, and another thing, you are somewhat of a 'trekkie', right? How is it that the ship is going into combat in *Star Trek Nemesis*, yet the Captain takes the 1st Officer, Science Officer, and tactical officers off the ship with him? Would they really take all of their most experienced officers off the ship when going into battle?

"Good one!" I gave credit where credit is due. "I guess you didn't have a lot of experience with firearms in Japan and Taiwan, but in *The Good, the Bad and the Ugly*, one of my all-time favorites, there's a classic gunfight at the end of the movie. Two out of three of the men are using cap-and-ball pistols but wearing cartridge belts. Why? You can't put a metallic cartridge in a black-powder pistol! True, some rifles back then took the same, short cartridges as handguns, so you could carry one type of ammunition for both, but not one of the three was shown walking around with a rifle—or a second pistol—and they didn't have a powder flask or a box containing lead balls and percussion caps which you would have needed to load that type of pistol. Idiots! As often as the Hollywood types feature firearms in their movies, you'd think they'd take the time to learn a little about them!"

"You're right", she agreed. "We aren't allowed to have guns in Japan. In fact, you can't even go around carrying a sword or even a big knife—pretty much anything that's considered a weapon is illegal to walk around with in Japan. That's why the movie Wolverine is such stupid bullshit but Americans don't know it. There's this funeral scene where all these bodyguards are standing around with machine guns and then this huge gun-battle happens. Yeah, maybe a few Yakuza have guns but there are almost no guns in Japan except for the army and police, so that is just so stupid to any Japanese person!

Even knowing nothing about guns, I too notice stupid stuff sometimes, like at the end of *I Robot* where the guy drops a gun and somehow the gun passes through a solid, metal pipe and is then caught by the strap. It's as though the pipe somehow becomes ethereal—is that the right word?—as the gun passes through it and then becomes solid again, catching the strap. It was so...so...weird-looking that I rewound it and watched it again about 3 times trying to figure out how it happened that the gun got caught on a solid pipe by the strap without the gun magically bouncing off the pipe. It's as though the gun passes through the pipe or the pipe somehow opens and closes as it went through and then I realized it was all done with CGI and what happened was, of course, totally bullshit! The fucks in Hollywood were just too lazy to create a situation that actually could happen so they expect us to just accept a breaking of the laws of physics that is impossible in reality! It was a trick of computer graphics because it was easier to manufacture a lie than to create a situation where the gun could, in reality, actually get hung up! It's like one of those Escher prints where people are walking up and down different sides of a staircase and it looks real but it's totally impossible! I also remember one of the *ALIEN* movies where the monster survives a bath in molten metal, but when it's then subjected to a cold shower it explodes!"

Yes, I remember that one, too", I agreed. "Hot then cold temperatures breaking the exoskeleton, which makes sense, but then Hollywood had to make it more dramatic by making the alien explode like it was under an internal pressure of 3000 PSI! Yeah, that was total bullshit, but they topped that in the next movie where the queen adopts a human reproductive system...for some unknown reason as it produced a quite inferior monster more slowly and one-at-a-time and the egg thing was obviously working quite well. In any case, they had a window out in the spaceship as it hit reentry and Ripley plugs the hole with the human-alien hybrid and it gets sucked out into space. Again, it's total bullshit! If you've read anything about the Challenger and Columbia shuttle disasters, all it takes is a small hole at those altitudes and temperatures and all the oxygen in the ship is instantly sucked-out or burned-up and everyone's lungs are seared and cauterized. Death is nearly instantaneous. Yet Hollywood expects us to believe the alien creates a tight seal on that window during the entire period of reentry? It's an assault on our collective intelligence. Just how stupid do they think we are? For example, Iron Man 3 was on recently and I was considering the absurdity of bits of his armor flying around and assembling themselves on his body...particularly the scene when they are charged with electricity from a 110 volt outlet and then go flying from Tennessee down to Florida. OK, consider Iron Man wearing the suit for a moment. He doesn't have large tanks for fuel, so it probably explains somewhere his suit is nuclear powered or some such thing. We see he has jets in the hands and feet. OK, assuming the hands and feet have their own CPUs and can fly on their own for a couple hundred miles using GPS or some such thing to locate Tony Stark; what about the other pieces of the suit? I don't recall seeing jets and a fuel tank in the mask, knee and elbow joints, breastplate, etc. Are we supposed to believe they fly all that way on magnets!? With what power source to provide forward thrust!? Don't these idiots know there is a difference between science and magic!? Good grief! Even though I am from a time when balloons were the only form of aircraft and even those had only just been invented, in 1783 or '84, as I recall. Obviously I never actually watched the wood-and-canvas aircraft battling over the skies of France during The Great War as they didn't fly at night or with heavy cloud cover, but I knew all about them as the technology was a big topic of conversation in those days. Also, a little casual reading of a few Popular Science magazines has seemingly given me a better understanding of flying than some of these Hollywood idiots who grew up in this century and supposedly studied science for years in high school and college...at least it seems that way! Sure, there is incredible technology these days I can't even begin to understand, but I'm no idiot! I really get upset when they feed us a bunch of bullshit like that; it's as if they really think I'm stupid enough not to notice when they do things that defy logic, common sense and laws of physics!

"You were talking about stupid things in vampire movies earlier," recollected Theresa, "That makes me remember something I always thought was ridiculous. In the movie *Van Helsing* he has some kind of machine-gun that shoots arrows."

Oh yes! The famous fully-automatic crossbow with the rotary magazine! Yeah, that almost ruined the movie for me—that and the terrible overacting by some of the cast, of course, particularly the redhead with the atrocious, pseudo-Russian accent! Parts of it were good, however, unlike that horrible *Abraham Lincoln, Vampire Hunter* or whatever it was called. That was probably the worst piece of crap in the vampire genre

I've ever seen! In fact, I'll gladly put that in my top ten all-time list of terrible movies, along with *Barbarella,* Mandy, *Santa Claus Conquers the Martians, Five Maidens From Outer Space, Bubba Hotep, Cobra, Commando,* where a heavily encumbered Arnold slowly jogs across an open courtyard while professional soldiers shoot at him with fully automatic weapons and can't score a single hit! I guess we can't leave off other atrocious films such as *Striptease, Nine to Five* and *The Last Airbender.* Of course as honorable mentions there are the 'naked gun' and so-called 'scary' movies, the *Nightmare on Elm Street* collection and almost everything starring Jean-Claude Van Damme.

And, let's not forget *Waterworld.* It had a good premise and some really good scenes, I admit, but once again, the stupidity overshadowed the genius of other parts of the film. Supposedly the deluge had happened so long ago that "dry land was just a myth," as they said several times throughout the film, yet they still had canned food that hadn't gone bad, weapons and other ferric-based equipment that still worked despite decades in a saltwater environment, they were somehow able to refine crude oil into gasoline and presumably manufacture new spark plus, batteries and whatever else wore out and needed replacing while adrift on small boats and the big one—they still had plenty of filter-tipped cigarettes! It was an enjoyable movie, as long as you turned off your brain and didn't think too much.

"Die Hard 4," Theresa chimed-in. "There's a scene where McLean has a sexy, kick-ass Asian girl—like me (smiling impishly)— hanging off the front of the hood of an SUV that he smashes through elevator doors and into the elevator shaft and yet her legs aren't broken, she's apparently not even hurt, which of course is impossible as her legs would have been crushed between the steel doors and the steel front grill of a speeding vehicle. Oh, I remember another one, where the girl in the cake takes some seasickness pills and sleeps with people shooting guns right in the same room. I studied nursing for a year and I've taken Dramamine enough times to know they might make you drowsy, especially if you take a small handful, but you're not going to continue to sleep with guns going off a few feet away!"

"Ah", I verbally reposted, *"Under Siege*...another one of those could-have-been-great-if-not-for-all-the-stupid-shit movies!"

Films like that make you wonder if the writers are really that bad or they just think people watching action movies are really that stupid! In that movie, which takes place on a battleship, they show the size of the real anchor chain at the beginning of the movie...but later on, so Segal can climb it, they show a different anchor that must have belonged to a much smaller ship as somehow the links have shrunk to 1/3 of their normal size. Iowa class battleships in World War 2 had 4 cranes, one at each corner, yet in this movie they are seen cutting up an I-beam and welding sections of it together to make a 'railing system' to offload the missiles just to give them the excuse for 'Chief Ryback' to shove a couple of bad guys through a band saw. How ridiculous can you get?

I even viewed the movie a second time to be sure and you can quite clearly see cranes on both sides of the ship during the opening scenes. Maybe the navy needed a trolley or something to run the tomahawk cruise missiles over to the cranes, but if they got them ON the ship in the first place, you figure they would also have the equipment necessary to get them OFF. Plus, we're supposed to believe it would be easier to maneuver long missiles *below decks*, through hatchways and up and down narrow stairways rather than just roll them down the big, wide-open, main deck on a trolley? Certainly if they needed a trolley and there weren't any to be had on the battleship they could have brought one in the helicopter and used it for unloading their band and catering equipment!

Also, they claim all the 5 inch ordinance had been offloaded in Hawaii, understandable as the ship was going to become a museum, but they still had both shells and explosive propellant for the 16 inch guns as well as nuclear tomahawk cruise missiles? Possible, but unlikely...just as unlikely as the ship's 1st officer being in league with a bunch of folks seeking to steal nuclear weapons from a warship with hundreds of military personnel on board. Even if he were so inclined, the US navy ostensibly monitors communications like no other military agency on the planet. HOW would the would-be weapons thieves have even known about a malcontent officer or contacted him in the first place? Again, it was entertaining and some bits of it are almost believable, but when you add in the other ridiculous nonsense, it turned it into a really pathetic movie.

"I guess I'm stupid," she said smiling, "I never noticed the things you mentioned about the anchor chain or the...other things. One question: is there really a rule in the navy that keeps a person from having a job other than a cook or other low-level job? I remember he was working as a cook because he had done something wrong, but it seemed like a really strange rule."

My time in the military was a long time ago...but one thing that has always been true is that there are three ways to do things: the right way, the wrong way, and the army way! However, I agree with you—it seems awfully arbitrary. I'd have to guess you're right—it was probably some bullshit the writers dreamed up to explain how the 1st officer could be ignorant of the fact one of their cooks was a former SEAL. I'm impressed—you seem to have a more analytical mind than most people nowadays. Of course I don't have that much contact with humans, but I read their postings on the internet, hear the comments they post in their videos, sometimes I'll read the diaries or schoolwork of some of my victims...it seems most high school graduates nowadays are morons.

Looking at textbooks, it seems these days that what the schools teach in the first two years in college is about equal to what they taught in the first two years of high school when I first came to this country, so it's just as much the fault of the teachers and schools and the 'no child left behind' bullshit as it is the students preferring to play with their toys rather than learn anything. Most of the ones I've observed recently can't use English properly, have no grasp of mathematics or the sciences, know nothing even of their own history, which is even worse when you consider that the USA is a country that has been around a mere 200 or so years—it's no wonder they have begun passing laws that allow spying on their citizens, restrict political speech, control the types of guns and magazines people can own, allow imprisonment indefinitely—all the things they condemned Hitler for and which resulted in them having to fight a long, bloody war to defeat the National Socialists in Germany they are now doing in this country, despite the fact there are still people alive here who remember those times.

Heck, the new NDAA law allegedly gives the government ownership of all the water in the country including the rain! Clearly this could never happen if people were educated properly, as they were when I first came to this country. Of course popular culture probably encourages people to emulate rappers, rock stars, athletes, movie actors...individuals that are frequently intellectually inferior and poorly educated themselves. Just because someone can sing well or toss a ball through a hoop does not necessarily make them informed or intelligent, right? As for the Hollywood types, my observations of comments made by actors and actresses, rock stars and even news reporters has convinced me that the vast majority of them are total idiots!

And these new 'smart' phones—it seems kids these days spend all their time texting and sending icons to each other and forget about studying and learning things they need in order to succeed in life. As the phones have gotten smarter, people have become less intelligent. It's almost as though the cell phones are sucking the brains out of young people. Maybe they should be called vampire phones!"

"Vampire Phones," she giggled, "I never thought of it that way but you're so right!"

"Hey," she said, changing the subject, "I was watching one of your recordings on your cable TV hard drive earlier and saw a old commercial that started me thinking...what is 'pay it forward?' Laughing, I replied: "That's a really good question! It's one of the most ridiculous concepts I've ever heard of!"

"But really, what does it mean? It looked like people just standing in line to buy something and then paying for the people in front of them...total strangers?"

"Yes, that's about it"

"But why would anyone do that?"

"Indeed! The implication is that the person standing behind you will pay your bill and so on. Of course this is ridiculous as not everyone's amount will be the same, not everyone will be that generous, you won't be able to use your tax deductions, if you had any, because you won't have a record of your purchase because someone else paid for you...the entire concept to total bullshit! Of course if you are rich enough or you have more dollars than sense, maybe you can get a feel-good moment out of it. After all, after years of the Clintons' ripping-off the taxpayers, soliciting bribes, selling influence, attempting to steal national treasures from the White House, even going so far as renting out the Lincoln Bedroom to wealthy donors, maybe advertisers felt people had a psychological need to see people doing something nice for others for a change! As a practical matter, of course, it's total nonsense!"

"So why put it on TV? Advertisements cost millions of dollars, don't they? What's the point?"

"Ads don't usually cost millions unless they are during the Super Bowl or something, but yes, they cost thousands, even tens of thousands of dollars, so if you ran the add often enough you might eventually spend a million dollars. You raise a very good point: why bother? All I can think of is it must be part of the socialist brainwashing that is going on in the USA these days, mostly in the schools and in movies. I guess you're being told you don't have to be responsible for your own finances because someone else will pick up the bill for you... It's the same reason that, instead of issuing food stamps to jobless people nowadays, they get something that resembles a credit card. So, instead of feeling self-conscious and guilty when paying for their groceries while the persons standing in line behind them are glaring at them, knowing the taxes that are taken from their pay before they see their paychecks are paying for that first person's groceries...instead they feel less guilty about not having a job, freeloading off other people's money, and love the socialist state that gives them free stuff instead of being angry that they have a much lower standard of living because all the jobs have moved to third world countries so the really rich can get even richer while 'Joe America' doesn't have a job and has to depend on the government for basic necessities like food.

This sounds so much like the way New York liberals think I'm sure that's the whole rationale behind the ads... After all, real unemployment prior to Trump's election was in the millions; during the last year of the Obamination, something like 26% of working-age Americans didn't have full-time jobs. Angry, hungry people cause revolutions. So, it seems to me that this was all designed to tell people, 'relax, be happy, enjoy your free stuff, you don't have to worry, someone else will take care of you, don't be angry that you can't find a job because NAFTA and Congress sent your job to China or Mexico! Only two years later, after Trump's election, unemployment was down to around 3.5% or so and suddenly you didn't see those commercials anymore!

"Why do you call it the 'Obamination' and why would Americans agree to something like this NAFTA thing?"

Barak Obama was Barry Soretoro's pseudonym, his assumed name, probably to keep people from learning too much about his past until it was too late. An abomination is basically something loathsome, hateful, wicked or vile. So, Obama plus abomination gives us Obamination. It's quite clever really, but I can't take credit for inventing the term, I saw it on the internet somewhere. I'm sure someone will think of something clever for Sleepy-Joe Biden one of these days, especially as his administration is doing even worse things for the US economy than Bath-House Barry ever did!

As for NAFTA, they enacted for it because they were told this would keep the illegal Mexicans at home by creating jobs in Mexico, that it would create jobs in the USA by increasing exports...hah!...and that it would make things cheaper. That last part is true, but it doesn't help if your Made-in-China TV is 30% cheaper if you don't have a job because the company you used to work for moved their factory to China and someone else is making them for 10% of what you used to get paid!

"This is so different than Japan and Taiwan!", Theresa exclaimed! "If you don't have a job, your family is expected to take care of you. There's some help available for mothers with young children and things like this. In Japan, there's a national pension system to take care of old people, and you can get some help if you're sick or physically unable to work. I don't think there's any kind of free help for young people able to work, however. Really, I think most people in Japan would rather kill themselves than have to rely on the government to live!"

> "When I was young, the church gave food to the poor, not the government...which back then was usually kings and other nobility. If you couldn't work, typically you died. So, there are some obvious advantages to the current system. There's Social Security, which is another tax, just under a different name, which people are told is a "retirement system" but it's actually a tax: you get some of the money back, if you live long enough. The rest of the money is used for the same things you just mentioned, people unable to work, kids without support, housing for illegal aliens, etc. It's another way the government steals money from people to pay for things they would not willingly pay for.

"So, people don't get money back for retirement?"

"Yes, they do, but nothing like if they'd put it in a bank account and earned compound interest for 50-60 years." I paused, in recollection, then continued.

> "I remember after World War I, veterans from the war who had been promised a bonus from the government, and were unemployed during the Great Depression, marched on Washington to ask for help. They'd been promised bonuses for their military service and came to ask if the government would be kind enough to let them have their bonuses early. At the time, however, the government had its own financial problems.
>
> The 'Bonus Marchers' were driven away at bayonet point by soldiers like Patton and MacArthur who would become heroes during the next war. Back then you were truly on your own. Nowadays, citizens are taxed so their money can be used to give food and housing to the disabled and even the

millions of illegals from south of the border. Things have really gone much too far.

People used to get cheese, rice and powdered milk from the government—basic commodities. Now they can purchase luxuries on someone else's dime. I was out shopping one night, back in the 1980's, and overheard a conversation between a young couple of newlyweds. He was a full-time student with no income, I seem to recall she was a waitress, no doubt not declaring most of her tip income, so they'd qualified for food stamps, even without children. It was their first time shopping with food stamps. They were given so much free money they couldn't figure out how to spend it! I don't know why I remember this, but I recall them getting a DIY gyros meal and clam dip, excited because those were things they couldn't ordinarily afford. I remember they were even buying canned tuna for their cat because they couldn't purchase cat food with their food stamps, so their cat was getting canned tuna meant for human consumption!

Nowadays, you can watch people using their cards to buy $10 meals at unhealthy, fast-food places, or steak and lobster at the grocery store, I shit you not! At least it's better now after the Trump administration. I seem to recall reading that close to half the country was receiving food or some other government assistance prior to Trump. Then, after Biden was elected, the government handed out $600 in cash... then another $600...then $1400, plus 'reparations' to black farmers, 'resettlement' cash to illegal immigrants, etc. It is just madness! Of course it's madness with a purpose—they are milking the US taxpayers to re-distribute wealth to unproductive members of society who have one redeeming quality: they can vote! Thus the puppeteers pulling Biden's strings—the real power in his government—are basically using the US treasury to BUY future votes for the Democrats!

"Incredible! In Japan only about 1% of people get welfare from the government, and most of those are old or sick people...and of course it's the law that people in the country illegally cannot receive welfare payments. Are people in America really this stupid? How long do they think this can continue before the country goes broke?"

"Those are the questions Americans keep asking their government, especially with the Biden administration pissing-away BILLIONS of dollars in special-interest spending, free handouts to illegals and extra unemployment cash to keep people from wanting to return to work, bailouts for poorly-managed cities and states run into-the-ground by Democrat politicians, foreign aid for ridiculous stuff like 'gender studies' in Muslim countries, and payoffs and kickbacks for the 'Green New Deal' all while killing US jobs! The taxpayers are getting raped!"

"Didn't something like this happen in Greece a few years ago? I remember reading something about it?"

> Yes, and in Venezuela, and I believe also in Argentina, maybe a few decades apart. In fact, both make excellent analogies. Argentina used to have a strong economy, a trade surplus due to their exports, a large military—then came Perron. They cut ties with England, raised taxes, instituted socialist policies and in less than 20 years, if I remember correctly, the country was broke. In Venezuela the socialists really got busy and not only transformed the country into a banana republic like the rest of the continent, but in less than a decade they'd turned the wealthiest country on the continent into a social disaster where white collar, professional women were selling sex for food. If you're really that interested I have a magazine article on it around here somewhere.

"Yes, I would like that. After all, it seems vampires have nothing much to do during the day except fuck and watch movies: both of which I enjoy, but it's good to have some variety and my brain needs exercise, too!"
I stood there for a moment, ruminating over how much more this girl had to offer than the mindless cretins I'd seen on the news, protesting over imagined slights at campuses like Missouri University (aka Mizzoo) or shouting down conservatives trying to make speeches, not understanding that the right to dissent required the other side to be allowed to make their case: how can one properly dissent without also hearing the opponent's position? From the available evidence, American universities were only turning out spoiled cry-babies unable to cope with the real world. It was good to see that there were still some who valued intellectual pursuits— even if she had come from overseas to enroll in a college in my adopted country.

Then, she did something incredible—she stretched. Arching her back, she rolled backwards so that she was balanced on her head and her toes, the rest of her body making a glorious curve of naked flesh. I ravished her with my eyes, running them across her long, shapely legs, her small yet perky breasts, the sculpted area where her neck met her shoulders. Without needing to get any closer, I inhaled her smells, the delicate scent of her hair, the still wholesome and not yet faded emanation of her skin, the musky scent of her cunt. For a moment, I realized I was like the prisoner in the cell near Hannibal Lector in *Silence of the Lambs*, assuming of course that his olfactories were really that accomplished and he was not merely being crude.

Perhaps I couldn't identify all the worlds smells like the killer in the novel, but I could smell pussy from across the room—a gift I hadn't truly appreciated before now. As any connoisseur of female flesh knows, pussy comes in an astonishing variety of scents and flavors, from those that stink like rank cesspools to those that smell more heavenly than freshly-baked bread. My little nymph's gash was, to my continual delight, one of the latter. Also, hers was nice and compact—none of those unsightly protrusions some women had (I guessed that explained the "female genital mutilation" practiced throughout Africa and the Middle East that one read about sometimes, particularly after having once seen *Debbie Does Dallas*; the pussy lips on that babe had been a nasty-looking grayish-green! The rest of her had looked nice, but her labia had looked like one of the carnivorous plants in the version of *King Kong* starring Jack Black!).

Thinking back on that video, I felt rather grateful that my little friend had a delightful little hole shaped like an almond and just as sweet smelling. Perhaps it was a little less so than when she'd been "alive" a few hours earlier; I suddenly had cause for alarm: would her body chemistry change after extended unlife? Would she begin to smell necrotic? Would her vagina dry out and shrivel? I determined to enjoy her as frequently as possible in the immediate future, not knowing what changes lay in wait.

"What are you thinking about?" she asked, becoming supine once again, trailing her fingers lightly along her thighs, across her abdomen and finally her torso, where she slowly drew semicircles beneath her breasts. "Going down on you and then fucking you again," I answered truthfully. "Hmm, sounds good to me," she replied, pulling one leg up to where her left foot was even with her right knee, forming an isosceles triangle of earthly delights, with the door to heaven couched in the left corner. She waved one hand in a fan, like a Kabuki dancer, then balled it into a fist with only her index finger extended. With a smile on her face she 'flipped me the bird' then drew her finger along her inner thigh, beginning at her raised knee and ending at the small tuft of short, straight hairs. Then she closed her eyes and performed a magic trick, making her finger disappear. I needed no further invitation. I had fed recently enough to make an erection possible (indeed, I was standing at attention already!), but right now I was intent upon dessert.

Soon my nostrils were breathing in her sweet fragrance from a much closer distance and my tongue had followed the path of her finger. Cupping her buttocks with my hands, I thoroughly enjoyed both the view and the feeling of making her squirm. I could have gone on for an hour, but after only a few minutes she was pulling on my ears. "I want you inside me!"

I happily obliged.

"Oh yes, fuck me, fuck me!"

It wasn't as though she needed to ask—I wouldn't have stopped now even if she'd changed her mind. Fortunately, for the moment, we were of one accord and both happily 'did it' 'till dawn.

Chapter 18
Mi Casa Su Casa

Miguel Sanchez (not his real name—he'd left that behind the night he crossed the Rio Grande and entered the country illegally) considered himself lucky. He had an easy life compared to most other 'wetbacks'. Instead of cutting grass or waiting tables or picking fruits or vegetables or working on an assembly line for 10 or 12 hours a day, he just walked the old man's farm, doing occasional maintenance and feeding the livestock. Half the day he sat watching television in the small trailer his employer let him and his family live in rent-free. He tended his garden as well as the old man's. He didn't mind—the old man didn't seem to eat much, so must of his employer's produce ended up feeding his family or sold for extra cash, and there was the plot beside the trailer as well, on land he used rent-free.

At Christmas, he was allowed to take home one of the birds (there were chickens, ducks, geese and turkeys and some talk about getting a pair of ostriches). Half a dozen eggs went to the farmhouse every morning along with a quart of milk, while the remaining eggs went home with him as well as plenty of milk when there were cows present during the breeding season, during which time milking them and cleaning and maintaining the milking machine occupied most of his mornings.

Occasionally, one of the older cows would be sent off to be butchered, which usually resulted in a gift of beef, which the master always shared with him. His pay wasn't fantastic—wages for illegal aliens never were— but he had free housing (including utilities), a sizeable percentage of his family's groceries were free, they received and grew extra they sold for cash, he made his own hours, took long siestas...he even had free cable TV (he'd spliced into the line going across the property to the house) and he sometimes filled up his truck on his boss's credit card that he used to gas up the farm equipment. He had things pretty good and he knew it!

Subconsciously, however, he knew that things were not right. He had little more than a grade school education but he was far from stupid. His employer was supposedly an old man with a walker who needed a live-in nurse. Yet SOMEONE sometimes drove the sports cars and rode the motorcycles that were stored in the big barn. His trailer was close enough that he'd occasionally been outside having a cigarette and had heard the sounds of the vehicles leaving, always at night. He'd even, out of curiosity, written down the mileage on the odometers and confirmed, to his satisfaction, that they didn't just shift position on their own, that someone in fact drove them at times. Also, he was fairly certain that things in the barn, tools and occasionally even heavy bags of feed, got moved from time-to-time.

He knew for certain that 30lb bags of dog food sometimes made their way from the barn to the house without his having any involvement in imparting locomotion to them. He knew his boss was not as old and infirm as he pretended to be. Miguel guessed that maybe he was an ex-Nazi like George Soros, hiding out rather than face a war-crimes trial. That would explain the books in German and French and the piano with the European name he'd seen in the parlor on some of his infrequent visits into the interior of the house and why his employer rarely left the house and hardly ever during the daytime. He knew the old man was rich. It wasn't only the hundreds of thousands of dollars worth of cattle and the value of the land, Miguel could sense from the old man's demeanor that he came from money, *old* money, like some of the rancheros down in Mexico who'd been landowners when Spain had ruled.

Still, he was living in hiding in the USA...although fear of arrest and deportation wasn't as great a concern as it had been before a foreigner illegally became president and used (abused) his power to open the border to tens of millions more illegals from south of the border, not to mention tens of thousands of Muslims from the middle east. Years of illegal immigrants pouring across the border had made the risk of being caught and deported somewhat remote. Remote, but no nonexistent; it made sense to keep a low profile and create no waves. So, if the old man had secrets, Miguel was willing to keep them.

Today, however, was something different. He'd found a calf that appeared to have gotten caught on and killed itself trying to escape from a barbed-wire fence. The wire appeared to have been recently cut as the cut was bright and shiny while the wire strand was slightly rusted...and the fence had been in good repair just a few days earlier. Also, when he'd gone to the barn to get a tarpaulin to toss in the back of the pickup truck to use recover the body and inform his employer, he'd noticed traces of what looked like blood in the cracks in the rough cement floor...a floor still damp from having been sprayed with the hose that was also still wet.

He was no detective, but it seemed to him the calf had been killed in the barn and then moved—but why? Part of some arcane ritual? Satanism? Voodoo? Miguel didn't know, but he felt a little creeped-out and determined that he'd attend mass on Sunday. The fact his boss had reacted so calmly to the news of the calf's death only served to confirm his suspicions. Still, he wasn't going to worry himself overly...especially as he had the body loaded in his old pickup and was hurrying off to the butcher. With any luck the meat was still fresh enough to eat and Miguel had been made a present of the meat as long as he brought back the hide—a deal he could certainly live with. As for the strange goings-on at the farm, he was going to keep his eyes open...and his mouth shut!

Chapter 19
I Drink Alone, no More

We'd slept most of the day, with Caesar napping between us for much of it, then roused ourselves and had sex 4 times...or was it 5? I don't know why, but it put me in the mood for some Tom Petty, and I had tossed a CD in my old but trusty (and powerful) quadraphonic music system. "Last Dance with Mary Jane" was playing away while I wondered if Theresa had ever seen the video? Probably not...and it was one of the best ever made, along with "Don't Come Around Here no More" Most likely all she'd ever seen were these choreographed, lip-synched pieces of crap they churned out nowadays where the dancing was more important than the music—half of which was simply rhythm and percussion. I decided I had to show her some of the real classics, along with some of the better modern ones, starting with Green Day and Nickelback. As I mused, Theresa rolled over from the position I'd left her in (we'd finished with her face down with me on top), sat up in a sitting position, held her hands in front of her, wrists curled in a somewhat feline position, opened her eyes as wide as she could and growled in her husky voice, "Feed me, if you dare!"

"Get Dressed," I said smiling. I was in need of some new blood as well. That last time around my dick had been a little limper than usual...and now the thirst was starting to take me as well. "Oh, that reminds me... we need to be sure to leave Miguel a note to ask him to leave an extra quart of milk on the porch each morning for my 'live-in-nurse'. Remember—it's all about appearances and attention to detail." I found some pants and shoes, smiled in appreciation at her cute little exercise outfit, and led her upstairs to the kitchen. Opening the refrigerator, I pulled out the crisper drawer and removed two lengths of plastic tubing with hypodermic needles shoved into one end. In the small pantry I removed 2 cotton balls and a bottle of rubbing alcohol. I swished alcohol on one ball, handed it and one length of tubing to Theresa who said nothing, just looked at me with a quizzical expression, repeated the process and replaced the bottle in the pantry. I then stuffed the tube into a pocket, stashed the cotton ball over an ear, grabbed a handful of doggie treats, handing several of them to Theresa, and opened the door, stepping onto the front porch.

As I'd already known, the dogs were sitting in a line, waiting, tails wagging. If there was any reproach for my having neglected them so much recently, it was certainly not apparent. In fact, they practically danced in excitement and Panzer turned several circles to show his joy. I delayed for several minutes, petting and scratching the dogs and feeding them a few treats, making a mental note that they were low on both food and water, then led Theresa across the front drive, over a fence and over to the south field, where several dozen cattle were sleeping. It was a very pleasant evening. The moon had risen and was partially obscured with clouds. Crickets were chirping and the dew was up, dampening our shoes.

"The cattle are used to me; I'm not sure how they'll react to you. Just move slowly and quietly. They are stupid, but they are large and strong and capable of doing you harm, even the cows."

As it happened, the cattle were sound asleep and didn't budge at all as I showed her how to select a vein, clean the skin with alcohol, insert the needle and suck blood through the tube. "Never take too much from one animal—it can make them weak and sick. I usually feed from two to three different animals each night. Notice their ears? They have numbers. Remember the numbers—I write them down so I can keep track of them. I also rotate pastures. We'll leave the bulls alone. I have two of them. Those are the big guys who have a small field all to themselves.

I then had to give a lecture on the difference between steers and bulls and how much of a difference castration, or lack thereof, made in their general disposition and behavior. Then we got on with dinner. Theresa was surprisingly accepting and didn't speak until after the feeding was finished. "So this is how you live? Drinking cow's blood?"

"Yes, rather clever, don't you think? It's rather difficult to get permission from a human to drink a few pints of their blood. If you kill them, you don't need to ask permission, but it tends to attract attention if and when the bodies are discovered...and law enforcement and pathology is so much better these days! I actually had this plan even before coming to this country. So, I came over here with a pile of wealth, had a solicitor...lawyer...help me to locate some land far away from the cities where I could also hire agents to purchase cattle for me."

"And you were able to do all of this at night?"

"It was a different world back then. Lawyers didn't have the social status they do now—they were workers in a trade like any other. There was no bar association or bar exams or mega law firms. Doctor's used to make house calls, day or night. Actually, even today, you can find lawyers who are hungry enough they'll come to your house on weekends or evenings if the money is there."

We were making our way back to the house, passing the milking shed and the rows of old milk cans rusting in the weeds.

"You have all these cows...what do you do with all of the milk?"

"You're not going to believe this, but most of it is used as fertilizer or just poured down the drain."

"What?"

"Yes, it's the sad truth...and we have the government to thank. I used to donate it to an orphanage and a school for the handicapped and took a tax deduction. Then the government passed laws that everything had to be Pasteurized even milk being donated to charity. For awhile the Burger Dairy bought my milk. They were a small, local outfit. But, they were driven out of business by the big, corporate farms and they can't be bothered to send someone out here to transport the relatively small amount of milk that we produce. So, Miguel takes as much as he wants for his family and he takes so much I'm sure he's also selling it to other Mexican families, quite a bit gets dried out to be used as fertilizer and the rest is poured down the drain. Of course most of the animals you see here are males: the females are on loan until breeding season, at which point the younger ones are brought back in the hope of having more calves."

"So why bother with milking them?"

> "The cows need to be milked. I'm not sure why, but nature
> created an animal that creates more milk than its offspring can
> consume and it's necessary for their health that they be
> milked, particularly during the time of year when there are no
> young calves to suckle them. If you stop milking them, they
> produce less milk, but they can also suffer complications and
> it's better for them just to be milked on a daily basis. So,
> what's bad for the cows is good for humans, particularly dairy
> farmers! Anyway, this was your second experience drinking
> beef blood; is life as a vampire everything you thought it
> would be?"

"It was a little...salty...but not as bad as the first time," Theresa shuddered a little at the memory of the terrified calf she had murdered.

"Glad to hear it. I guess it's time to explain to you what happens when a male vampire gets his fill of fresh blood." I reached out, grasped one of her hands and guided it down to the erection that was attempting to break through the fabric of my old, faded blue jeans. "Are you ready to go again?"

Chapter 20
The Plot Thickens

"Sheriff Miller, there is a FAX for you on your desk."

Mary Williams was all smiles. In Gene's opinion she looked far too chipper for a Monday morning. Maybe there had been a revival service at her church over the weekend. Perhaps she'd found a new, online boyfriend...those always cheered her up until said suitor discovered she was both a cop [in reality a dispatcher for the sheriff's department] and pushing 300 pounds! Gene suspected the truth to her beaming smile and upbeat attitude had more to do with her extra-large, double-latte and the box of a dozen donuts that patrolman Yoder had brought in to work again. Kevin was dating a gal who worked squeezing jelly into donuts at the local bakery. Somehow Kevin found time to squeeze some filling into her between the time she got off work at 6:30 a.m. and the time he reported to work at 8:00. He also had an inside track for day-old pastries and frequently showed up at work with a box of sugary, artery-clogging confectionaries. Sheriff Miller grabbed a chocolate-covered Bismarck from the box, asked Mary to bring him some coffee—black with honey and cinnamon was how he took it these days—and sat down to read his evidence report.

The crime lab in Indianapolis had some surprising things to say about the Bowie knife he had sent them via Fed Ex (which was an excellent way to get things around in a hurry while maintaining proper 'chain of custody' documentation). First of all, it was a hand-made original, as Gene had deduced at the crime scene. Not original in the sense it had been made by Jim Bowie, the makers initials on the tang were T.M., but that it was civil war era or earlier. What was jaw-dropping about it was that blood from at least 30 different individuals had been found embedded in its carbon-steel molecules. Blood that, in many instances, was not nearly as old as the knife. Aside from that of the Hillenburgs, there were at least two dozen traces and indications were they had occurred at different times, some several decades in the past.

Tests were still being run as there were so many individual samples it was hard to separate them. Also, the blade had been cleaned with a solvent on multiple occasions, so it was possible there were other samples that had been destroyed/rendered undetectable. How many more was anyone's guess at this point. Gene gave a low whistle, blew on his still-too-hot coffee, shifted his heavy holster so he could sit more comfortably, and leaned back, his office chair creaking. It seems they might be dealing with a serial killer...or maybe a series of them. After all, it was rather unlikely the same person had been using the knife to kill people for 150 years or so and still had the strength to kill all 3 of the Hillenburg brothers.

The second report was even more interesting. The strap and buckle he'd found had been forwarded to the FBI crime lab. It was indeed from a woman's shoe...a rare and mildly expensive brand of woman's shoe; rare in the sense that it had been made in a factory in Changhua, Taiwan, for export to Japan. At no time in history had that brand been exported to the USA, according to the FBI.

Gene called across the small office to Mary, "Any word on the owner of that abandoned car we found near the Hillenburg place?"

"Yeah, the registration came back. It's owned by an international student...I've got the name here somewhere..."

"Let me guess—she's Japanese, right?"

"Here it is, Theresa Hasegawa from...Japan...hey, chief, how'd you know?"

"I need you to contact her department head and professors, find out who her landlord is, see if she has a roommate or roommates and see if anyone's seen her. I have a feeling we're about to add a missing person's case. In fact, if she doesn't turn up by 5 p.m. let's put out an APB on her as a possible suspect in a homicide." Sheriff Miller didn't think a female college student from Japan was the likely owner of an antique bowie knife, or that she would be physically capable of disarming the Hillenburg brothers and killing the three of them, unless maybe she had a black belt in martial arts. Gene was just doing his due diligence—after all, she was a potential witness and the proximity of her abandoned car connected her to the crime scene and he would be very interested in hearing anything she might have to say about the events of that evening and putting out a 'wanted' alert for her was more likely to bring her in than just waiting for her to wander in on her own.

There was also a FAX from the mayor, complaining for the umpteenth time that his officers were behind in their traffic ticket quotas along with a lengthy dissertation on how much the county depended on fines and court fees. Gene sighed. The mayor was one of these empty suits that seemed to have infiltrated every level of government in recent years. At a previous meeting the man had actually suggested that the sheriff's department needed to make more arrests for the additional revenue it would bring in! Of course any fool should know that you can't just go around arresting people unless they have committed a crime. Unlike the 'super cops' on TV, real sheriffs and their deputies were more like the Tommy Lee Jones character in *No Country for Old Men*...laid back, friendly, respective of individual rights and liberties and far more interested in diffusing situations than in kicking down doors or harassing individuals. The mayor also had difficulty recognizing the fact that, unlike the captain of the city police (who was an appointee the mayor could fire at any time) the sheriff was an elected official in his own right who enjoyed a great deal of autonomy.

It all started with legislatures slowly turning practically everything you could imagine into an offense. For example, if nature happened to cause a single cannabis plant to grow on your property (and hemp was farmed in Indiana for rope as recently as World War II and maybe later—in fact much of the grounds of Valparaiso University had once been a hemp farm), or a jack-in-a-pulpit flower chose to bloom in your backyard and you accidentally hit it with your weed wacker, or your Brownie Scout daughter cut some dogwood branches in a public park and brought them home, you could go to jail!

Take traffic laws, for example. Gene was not only very familiar with Title 9 of the Indiana Code (i.e. the laws pertaining to motor vehicles), he had helped to draft some of the language pertaining to certain traffic offenses (in order to clarify them), so he was well aware that it was actually quite difficult for the average person to drive in excess of 15 minutes without committing at least one moving violation.

Some of the laws were just downright stupid as well. OK, maybe there had been some form of moral rationale in not allowing package liquor sales on Sunday, but then why allow it to be served in restaurants? The recent repeal of the so-called 'blue laws' was a rare example of legislative common sense. Gambling, on the other hand was still illegal, except for the state and multi-state lotteries—unless of course you went to one of the casinos. Of course there were hours during which you couldn't buy a lottery ticket, and the one time Gene had gone to one of the Casino boats out of curiosity, they'd made a big deal about the ship 'sailing': which really meant it moved a couple feet away from shore on fixed rails on a cement pad below the surface of the lake so as to not be touching the Indiana shoreline so they could claim that were no longer 'in Indiana'—hypocrisy at its most disingenuous!

The Federal government, years ago, had intruded into the state's rights to set their own minimum limits for alcohol consumption, so all states age minimums were now 21 years of age. Indiana had already had an age 21 restriction, so that hadn't changed, but there were other ridiculous laws on the books now, such as those preventing liquor stores from selling milk or cola beverages. For goodness sake, why couldn't an establishment selling drinks laced with alcohol sell some caffeinated soda pop!? For that matter, why was it you could vote, serve in the military and potentially die for your country, operate a motor vehicle, get married, get an abortion, basically do anything you wanted as an adult other than have a drink.

And, if the legislatures had screwed the pooch, the damned administrative agencies went on to make things 100 times worse. Catch a fish that is too big or too small or catch too many fish or use too many fishing poles or even catch the fish using your bare hands(!) and you were breaking the law! Likewise, kill the wrong animal or the wrong gender of said animal or use the wrong weapon or ammunition or do so on the wrong day and you were a criminal and maybe even a felon. For that matter, 2d offenses for some (usually) victimless crimes such as prostitution and drunk driving earned you a possible felony. Heck, in Indiana just grabbing someone on the ass could earn you a felony conviction (Sexual Battery, a class D felony), although there was a mental intent element that Gene thought would be impossible to prove if the defendant's attorney was even remotely competent, unless of course the incident was caught on video, and there were more and more of those things popping up in every public space.

Of course having a felony conviction, or these days even a conviction for a misdemeanor domestic battery, and one lost one's constitutional rights to bear arms (apparently the legislators responsible for creating new laws never bothered to acquaint themselves with the older ones—the ones they were sworn up uphold and enforce, such as the very clear "shall not be infringed" language in the primary and sacrosanct law of the land). Also significant is that, depending on one's career, a felony conviction could completely derail your career. You couldn't hold a license in law or even bartending. Say goodbye to your career in banking, law enforcement— heck, you couldn't even get a job as a card dealer at a casino with a felony conviction. In some states, your career in medicine was probably done as well—and maybe even your job in garbage collection! So, taking and ingesting a prescription antihistamine from your wife's pill bottle, even if you were on the same prescription, was technically a felony and, like any other felony, could essentially be a life sentence—your entire life and career ruined due to some technicality.

Unless, of course, you had friends in a Democrat-led administration. Their employees were routinely discovered to have felony convictions and still somehow managed to retain their jobs. Just like the illegals receiving welfare benefits that US citizens could not qualify for, it just didn't make any sense!

Things had become even worse with the development of deferred prosecution and pre-trial diversion. Instead of dropping a lot of bad cases as they would have done in the past, prosecutors started offering to 'make things go away' for a couple hundred dollars. Rather than take the risk of going to trial, many innocent individuals as well as those guilty of minor offenses took the easy road and essentially allowed themselves to be blackmailed into ponying-up some cash to retain their liberty. In Gene's opinion, if the government doesn't have sufficient evidence, they should drop the charges instead of pressuring the accused to come up with some cash in order to walk away.

In many respects it was like the Catholic church selling plenary indulgences back in the Middle Ages: everyone sins and, naturally, the church found a way to profit from it! Then there were civil forfeitures...essentially stealing the property of criminals even where not related to the crime. In theory, it was intended to compensate victims of crimes. In reality, most of the money goes to the trustee's law firms, the auctioneers and the government; very little actually goes to the victims. It was a scam only mildly less onerous than the myriad prison factories in China that pumped out hand-made junk that ended up in the shopping carts of obese, middle-aged housewives at Wal-Mart's and Costco's.

More recently, with the invention of electronic monitoring systems, they invented home detention as a way to make a profit instead of paying to keep people in jail...and all the profits go to their buddies who own the private companies that monitor the detainees, with a kickback to the state, of course...just like bankruptcy trustees who siphon off money that should go to creditors...making a commission by selling stuff off at pennies on the dollar...the creditors get screwed and the lawyers with the political connections are the only ones making any money. Kings, communist dictators, military warlords, democratic legislators—governments of all types lived off the productive classes, stealing the fruits of their labors. The only difference was that some were more blatant about it!

A tune from a YouTube video, done to the tune of "Price Tag," complete with images of everything from Hitler to 9-11 to guillotines, popped unbidden into his conscious thought:
Ok America
It's time to wake up
Listen

Hear me
These days the government's not so nice
They oppress us and they tell us lies
It was bad with Billy and Barry
But Sleepy Joe's even worse
He tells you to just bend over and
Smile
While he spends the country into bankruptcy
Along with crooks like Schumer and Pelosi
All they know how to do is tax and spend
This bullshit must really come to an—end
As the country moves to the left
And the media attacks only the right
Can't you see that now
The end of our freedom's in sight?
It's all about the money, money, money
And we don't think it's funny, funny, funny
These private sector rejects
Are looting all our paychecks
There's no—oversight for agencies
They're spying on—both you and me
And Obama's health care plan
Ain't nothing but a big scam
OKAY!
China wrecked the economy with a virus
Put everyone in masks and closed the stores
Mail-in ballots and hacked voting machines
Stole the election from you and me
Well you can keep the change
We're taking the country back
We're sick of the lies
Stimulus, QE and
We can keep our doctors (ha!)
Global Warming scamming
Fags getting married but they can't make babies
And if you believe in God, you must be a racist!
This PC shit has gone on for far too long
Look out you gun-grabbers
We're 100 million strong
So we ain't gonna stumble and fall never

The USA ain't going down in defeat, oh no!
Not to progressive-liberal-commie-Nazis!
That spread-the-wealth socialist crap they're selling
Ain't worth a plastic penny
They keep stealing our money, money, money
And we don't think it's funny, funny, funny
They say Stalin came from the left
And Hitler came from the right
The end was the same
I'm not going down without a fight!
It's all about the money, money, money
And we don't think it's funny, funny, funny
This tyranny we're seeing
Leaving our country bleeding
Corrupt career politicians
Shredding our Constitution
They want to take our guns next
Well they can just suck our _______
(rapped)
They want to control everyone
And own everything
Think they can always fool you
That you're just lemmings
They lied about 9-11
Sandy Hook and Colorado
They persecute Christians, but it's cool to be a Homo!
They want to take your guns
enslave your daughters
Send you to FEMA camps
Agenda 21—UN code for " slaughter"
We've seen this all before and we know what happens next
First take away the guns, then send millions to their deaths!
Hey Socialist Dims and RINOs
These are OUR guns, healthcare, education
You'd best get back out of our faces
Unless you want a revolution!
It's all about the money, money, money
And we don't think it's funny, funny, funny
CNN, MSNBC and the New York Times
Keep lying all of the time

The IRS just—keeps on spying
And Biden—keeps on lying
Illegals getting stacks of cash
Looters set free to burn and smash
It's all about the money, money, money
And it ain't even funny, funny, funny
We don't want to repeat history
Watch soldiers rape our families
We're locking and loading
Cha-ching cha-ching
You crooks better start running
Or you'll get what you've got coming
In the end there will be justice
And there might be a price tag
Yeah don't forget about the price tag
God Bless America

Within a week of it first appearing on YouTube, it had received over 10 million views! Of course the liberals went ape-shit and it was very quickly disappeared from YouTube and Google, Facebook, Twitter and other sites made a determined effort to remove it from their platforms, the same way they censored other content that didn't conform to their rather narrow ideologies. Gene had been prescient enough to download it, so he still had a copy. Of course the video WAS rather inflammatory—but, there was a LOT of anger simmering in the country. It had yet to boil over, largely because most Americans were generally law-abiding, but nobody could predict what the future might bring, with Americans increasingly divided into diametrically-opposed political camps.

Gene recalled a time when the folks who had steam-rolled Donald Trump into the White House (winning more individual counties across the country than even Ronald Reagan!) would have been referred to as 'True Blue' or 'Blue-Blooded' Americans, while the Socialist/ Communist / Progressives would have been 'Reds'. Of course at some point in time the liberal media had pulled an Orwellian double-take and switched the colors around to try to confuse people.   Now the states where people overwhelmingly voted for socialist policies, gay rights, government handouts, gun control, lax drug laws, unrestricted abortion, environmental Nazism and forced unionism were 'blue' while states where voters still believed in God, guns, The Constitution, the right to work, limited government and straight sex became 'red'.

In a way, it seemed appropriate. The world these days was a backwards, upside-down twisted version of itself. Crack whores, gang-bangers, illegal aliens, meth labs...who'd have ever believed such things would make their way to Indiana, the nation's heartland? Back when he'd first become a deputy sheriff, something he thought would be a temporary arrangement until the RV factory called him back to work, most of his work involved delivering summonses, escorting prisoners to court and back to jail, and the occasional DUI or domestic disturbance. Things had changed, especially young kids. Half of them nowadays were uneducated, tattooed, jobless, and devoid of any sense, turned to mental vegetables by a constant bombardment of crap from Oprah, Jerry Springer clones, 'reality' TV (now there was an oxymoron!), Gangster-Rappers, and raving liberal-lunatics like Bill Maher (at least Maher occasionally got things right, like when he denounced the Cancel-Culture movement or when he warned Americans about China).

Gene sighed, feeling very old. He tried putting the tune out of his head. He got a certain guilty pleasure out of watching the video every now and then, to the point where he'd actually memorized the lyrics, along with others from the afterglow of the Trump election, such as "The Most Wonderful Time in 8 Years", but inflammatory, rebellious songs weren't what he should be thinking about. He had a missing girl, three mysterious deaths and questions that needed answers.

He didn't have a lot on his schedule for the day, so he decided to get out of the office and do some old-fashioned legwork. After all, he'd been at the murder scene in person so, like it or not, he was already personally involved. "Give me the address, I'm going to pay a visit to the girl's residence and see if there's a roommate, then I'm going to try and have a chat with her professors. See if you can get a phone number for the landlord and text my cell. Don't wait on me for lunch, I'll got something on the road. Anything you can't handle or that requires my personal attention, get me on the radio. Hold down the fort!"

Chapter 21
Hollywood vs. the USA

Day had dawned. In the vampire world, this meant finding something to do that didn't involve going out. We had slept a good 6 hours, had sex for 2 more, but there was still a lot of daylight left. I had decided to look over the TV listings and wasn't happy with what I found.

They did a remake of *Straw Dogs*? And another of *Arthur*? Who are they kidding? They couldn't possibly improve on either of those—they were classics! I can't believe they have so few new ideas that they have to keep remaking old movies. What's next, I wonder: The Brady Bunch, the Movie?"

"*Straw Dogs*?" yawned a stretching mop of black hair and a long leg that were the only parts protruding from beneath the sheet. "It's a classic. In some ways it's a so-so movie but it has some awesome insights into people, culture, sex, religion, psychology and human nature, all topped off with a fantastic performance by Dustin Hoffman. It's hard to explain. I have a copy on VHS if it will still play; my tapes are so old some of them are beginning to deteriorate. While I'm looking for it, do you have any requests?" Have you seen Game of Thrones? They really did a good job of it, aside from some unnecessarily explicit gay scenes, right up until they screwed up the ending.

"Yes, I saw it and I loved it until the end, then I was really unhappy when John killed Daenerys and gets sent to the wall for the rest of his life."

"That wasn't the screw-up I was referring to, although I agree with you. What pissed me off was the final battle scene against the Army of the Dead. I know they had some military, technical advisors on staff, yet they obviously let some Hollywood libertards write the scene. It was appallingly stupid: nobody in a real army would ever have deployed like that. Light cavalry is best for harassing the enemy's flanks. They should have been held back. Instead, the Red Woman lights up their blades and they charge off to get killed. Great, more soldiers—and horses—for the Night

King's army! Then, they put their catapults out in front to be overrun! How stupid can you get?!

They had some defenses prepared, I remember seeing what in the French army we called a Cheval de Frise. You made them by cutting down skinny trees, drilling holes in them, then pushing 6-foot stakes through the holes close enough together so nobody could climb through. If you had extra time you sharpened the stakes. The White Walkers would have had a hard time getting over them. So what did they do? They put them in a trench and then fired the trench. In and of itself that was a good move, but they put the barricades INSIDE the trench, so they were set on fire! It's not a good move to destroy your own fortifications! They had nice, high walls...why not stand behind the walls and drop fire down on the dead? I guess it's because they wanted to make it exciting and didn't want something that looked like the Battle of Helm's Deep in *Lord of the Rings*, but what they got was something that looked like a total cock-up. Then, at the siege of King's Landing, suddenly Daenerys suddenly has an army of Unsullied and Dothraki again. Where did they come from? Had she been hiding away reserves somewhere? It seems doubtful, considering their efforts against the Night King. The Dothraki in particular seem unlikely; they don't seem to be the kind of folks to have run away from the initial charge and hide somewhere and then show up later. Where did all these fresh troops come from?"

"Wow", she exclaimed, "I never really thought of it but yes, after the Night King was defeated it seemed like almost everyone was dead, at the banquet afterwards I remember only seeing Northmen, then suddenly there's this huge army of Unsullied and Dorthraki at King's Landing. You're right— where did they come from? Anyway, you just said something about *Lord of the Rings* and that reminds me, you said something earlier about not liking *Lord of the Rings*?"

"So, you want me to go on another rant about the idiots in Hollywood, eh? OK, I'm obviously not going anywhere until the sun goes down unless I want to draw a whole lot of attention to myself walking around in my hazmat suit! Sure, why not? First, however, I loved the books, I just objected to how they screwed-it-up on film and it was *The Hobbit*, rather than the trilogy, that really pissed me off.

Unquestionably, Peter Jackson did a great job with the *Lord of the Rings* trilogy. The music, cast, acting, costuming, locations they used for filming...all excellent! Like I said, I have loved the 4 books for some 60 to 70 years and was really quite pleased when the technology finally caught up with the story in order to really do it justice. That being said, there were problems even with the first three movies.

Tom Bombadil was cut out entirely...no great loss, really, as Bombadil was like a magic-resistant 1960's hippy, permanently stoned, suddenly tossed into the story. He was likely cut to make the film shorter and his character wasn't really missed as far as I am concerned. However, his deletion impacted the story in several key aspects: it was he who rescues the hobbits when they are engulfed by the willow tree and again when they are captured by a barrow wight...a kind of ghoul that imprisons them in a tomb. This is where the hobbits acquire the magical daggers that later allow Meriadoc to deliver a fatal blow to the king of the Nazgûl. This is completely missing from the movie version, so you miss the very important part that the daggers recovered from the ancient crypt were forged by the smiths of Númenor with some form of anti-evil spells so that, when Merry stabs him, the spells that brought him back from the world of the dead are undone even though Merry only manages to stab him in the back of the knee. So, it really isn't Éowyn who kills the Lord of the Nine, she just delivers the coup de grâce as the French would put it. Without Merry's magical blade, her blow would have had as much effect as striking him with a lash made from wet spaghetti!

Also, when she offers Merry a ride to battle, in the book he doesn't recognize her and thinks she's a warrior and she tells him to call her 'Durnhelm'. In the theatre (yes, I used to go to the movies at times before everything was so politicized I stopped going) when he calls her "my lady" with this idiotic grin on his face I wanted to leap to my feet crying 'bullshit!' because I knew that was not how the story went. Merry finds out her true identity only during the battle, after the Nazgûl has shattered her shield and broken her arm.

I also recall a scene with orcs rushing headlong down a flight of stairs...except some of the cast were apparently not so athletic and it's almost comical when they are seen hopping rather gingerly to keep from falling flat on their faces. You'd have thought they could have done a better job of editing that bit. Oh yeah, the deaths of Saruman and Grima were also bogus. It shortened the story, but in the books they lived long enough to travel off to Frodo's shire and make a mess of things and Saruman is stabbed in the back by Grima, not exactly the way it went in the film.

Anyway, as I mentioned, these were rather minor details, other than the magic blade—that was a fairly crucial plot point to be omitted. Now, fast-forwarding back in time to the prequel, *The Hobbit*, Jackson transitions himself to the man I now refer to as Peter 'Jackass'. Adherence to the story line, accuracy and artistry took a huge nose-dive. Maybe success went to his head, maybe he had so many ladies, or lads, lining-up to suck his dick he was too busy to care about the films, or maybe he never got around to reading the damn book!

Whatever the reason, the 3 hobbit movies were good in a great many ways, but not as good as they should have been. For one thing, the word orc is never mentioned in *The Hobbit* as far as I can remember. Those don't appear until the trilogy. In *The Hobbit,* they are fighting and fleeing from goblins. The great, white orc that supposedly killed Thorin's father, battles them in Lake-town then somehow teleports himself to the ancient fortress in the mountains where the Nine had previously been entombed to do some jazz dancing with Gandalf and the ring wraiths at Dol Guldur, if I recall the name correctly, was never in the original story. It's been a long time since I read the actual book, but as I recall, Legolas isn't in the first book, either. No doubt Orlando Bloom's sex-appeal with the ladies and the kung-fu crowd is why they felt they had to work him into the story, but I didn't find that it added anything.

Tauriel and her inter-racial love affair with Kili? It never happened and she wasn't a character in the book, either! The fight scene with the orcs chasing the dwarves in the barrels? It was entertaining but yet again, it never happened. Bard's sneaking them into town camouflaged as barrels of fish was actually quite clever, but it didn't happen that way either and there's no scene with the mayor's assistant and the toll gate...obviously contrived to introduce a character who doesn't feature into the original story just so they can add a scene with a greedy servant who dresses like a woman to try to steal a sack of gold stuffed into his dress...more Hollywood gay shit! There seems to be some sort of unofficial rule these days that everything on TV or in the movies has to have some gender-inappropriate content or pro-homosexual propaganda!

In the book, Bilbo put lids on the barrels as well and he opens then under cover of darkness after they been collected and towed to Lake-town. Even Bilbo's release of the barrels was incorrect—the elves toss them into the river when they send the empties down the river and back to Laketown; I recall some of them commenting that the barrels were heavy and must have been full rather than empty and ready for 'recycling' as it were.

And, it gets worse. Thorin never gets his sword back until after his death at the Battle of the Five Armies, when the king of the elves presents it as a gift 'après morte', the thing with the huge golden statue they drop on Smaug is visually stunning but is also absolute rubbish! In the actual story, the dwarves don't have to worry about entering the mountain from the front as the dragon traps them inside after they've entered through the secret door because one of the group had a premonition of danger and they rush inside right as the dragon shows up outside the mountain and destroys the secret door.

What else? The dragon is shown bursting through an unbroken front gate as he leaves—as if the dragon has skill in masonry to build a wall to block the gate he'd destroyed decades earlier! Then there's the thing about Bard making an impromptu bow from the broken pieces of his longbow—horseshit! In all likelihood, the bowstring would have been too short to be nocked to the remnants of the windlass. Or, in the alternative, it likely would have been limp and unable to impart significant velocity to the arrow. That scene was obviously written by someone who'd never held a bow in his life, that and probably got an 'f' in his/her high school physics classes! In order for it to function properly, a bowstring is under a considerable amount of tension even before it is drawn back—that scene is as ridiculous as the full-auto crossbow with the rotary magazine from Van Helsing you mentioned before!

Um, what else...? Bilbo finds the Arkenstone after the dragon departs, not during a conversation with him—a minor point, but they are indeed cumulative! Bard isn't the 'trouble-making bargeman' as shown in the movie—I'm reasonably certain he doesn't even enter the story until the dragon is attacking the town. The dwarves don't enter Bard's house through the privy and they never try to steal weapons in the town. I think they are weaponless until they arm themselves in the armory under the mountain. I don't remember giant worms drilling holes in the mountain at the start of the Battle of the Five Armies, the people of Laketown don't do battle with orcs and trolls and I don't recall flocks of attacking bats, either.

Actually, I take back something I said earlier—Bombadil wasn't cut to make the story shorter—maybe Jackson did us a favor by doing a little editing and removing the one character that was somewhat out-of-character for the story...sort of like how "Ravishing Ronald, the gay nature boy" is out-of-place in the wresting ring with "The Crusher" (to her obvious lack of comprehension, so I went on to explain:)...it was in a classic Bugs Bunny cartoon in which Bugs Bunny goes from mascot to a studio wrestler and mere observer to masking-up, wrestling tag-team style and winning the match.

Anyway, Jackson did anything BUT make the story shortcr...in fact, he added a scene with Galadriel, who also doesn't appear in the first book, as well as extended scenes with Radagast the Brown. Honestly, I rather enjoyed the Radagast scenes involving the hedgehog and the wild rabbit-sleigh ride, but those also weren't in the book! Not as bad as all the nonsense with Orlando Bloom fighting Azog...who is mentioned as having killed Thorin's father or grandfather in a battle between dwarves and *GOBLINS*, i.e. *NOT ORCS*, but isn't a character *ANYWHERE* in the books that I can recall but is just a historical footnote, so of course he doesn't kill Fili or battle Thorin on the ice, while Legolas isn't introduced until Boromir, Frodo and the others meet to become the nine companions in *The Fellowship of the Ring*.

Oh, and I missed some! The eagles investigate on their own and discover and rescue the company after they are treed by the goblins rather than being summoned by Gandalf through the assistance of a moth, although that was one of the more agreeable additions: one of the few I feel that could be justified through the concept of 'artistic license'. Come to think of it, I don't think the Nazgûl are mentioned in the book, either, nor is there any mention of Galdalf being held captive until Saruman traps him in Orthanc in the trilogy. The scene where the elves interrogate an orc or goblin wasn't in the book, and whichever it was, Fili or Kili, wasn't shot with a Morgul arrow that required treatment with Kingsfoil, neither of which are mentioned until Frodo is stabbed with a Morgul Blade in *The Fellowship of the Ring*. Also, when they get lost in Mirkwood, it's because it gets dark, they are out of food and water and see some campfires off in the woods and go to see if they can get a bite to eat. Also, in the movie version, when the spiders attack, Bilbo ends up fighting some beetle-thing that must have escaped from the most recent King Kong movie and then the elves show up and help them fight the spiders? As I recall, in the book, Bilbo uses his magic ring to release the dwarves and they don't run into the elves again until after escaping from the spiders and I don't remember him doing ANY fighting, such as when he is shown defending a fallen Thorin just before the eagles rescue them. Bilbo uses his wits, his gift of gab...and his hairy feet running from danger rather than becoming a great swordfighter! I'm sure there are probably a dozen other points I'm forgetting at the moment. Maybe the plan is to release a 'director's cut' in the future, fixing the myriad errors, so people will have to go out and buy the boxed set of all six movies...again. One can only hope. In the meantime, all we can do is appreciate something that was good, yet flawed, and regret that it was not as great as it should have been because Jack-asses' idea of 'artistic license' is to do a fucking re-write of the entire book!"

"Wow, that was an incredible analysis. I think you'd make a good movie director!"

"Hmm...I can see it now as a tabloid headline: 'Vampire Movie Director Wins Academy Award'! I appreciate the compliment, but obviously it's a physical impossibility. Also, I'd have little tolerance for prima donnas, idiotic dialogue, scenes that defy science and logic or all the gay crap that is being force-fed to the public nowadays, like the Supreme Court decision that they made up out of thin air—after the probable murder of Justice Scalise and possible blackmail of Justice Roberts—it as really strange how he suddenly did a 180 on Obamacare and gay 'marriage'. I doubt we'll never know, but things went really strange while the Court created the legal fiction of gay marriage. Anyone who grew up when I did would have told you the obvious which, incidentally, was canonized in common law for hundreds of years: the sole and express purpose of marriage is to provide a legal contract to legitimize your offspring and establish their inheritance rights. Since gays cannot biologically reproduce, what need do they have to 'get married' rather than just cohabit? Hold that thought for a second while I digress.

Nowadays, 'bastard' is just one of many derogatory epithets. In olden days, it was far more damning as an insult. Bastards could not legally inherit title or property. Basically, they were an underclass of sorts. As I see it, 'gay marriage' is a perversion of these marital rights with a sinister purpose. If gay couples are seen as legitimate, which seems to have been forced upon the American public, one legal result is this allows them to adopt children. What fate do you think befalls children adopted by a couple of sexual perverts? Now to be clear, I don't really give a damn what people do to each other, consensually, in private, but shouldn't the law and the courts protect children from adults who want to commit sex crimes with them?

We had a number of cases locally, before you arrived in the area. A man in Indianapolis working for some child services group was sentenced for something like 90 years for sodomizing a young disable boy in a wheelchair. A few years later, the priest of Little Flowers Catholic Church in South Bend went to prison for molesting a male minor. These are just a couple of the cases and these involved people whose basic instincts were to *help* children in need. I fear that allowing gay—LGBT to be more precise, I suppose—couples to adopt, people who by the very definition are sexual deviants, I fear that all you're doing is allowing them to purchase captive child sex toys!

The US Constitution is a very simple document and, as I was born only a few years later so I was a contemporary of the times, I can assure you that the men who wrote it had absolutely ZERO intent that marriage meant anything other than a contract between a mating pair, consisting of male and female and capable of reproduction. That decision was just an insult to the intelligence of the American people, passed by a corrupt and politically-motivated court having surrendered its independence to become the tool of the first gay president and trans-sexual first-ladyboy or whatever of the USA!

"You really don't care for gays, do you?"

"It's not really that I dislike them...I mentioned before that I had a good working relationship with a few of them in the French army and I am without a doubt a creation of the French Revolution—I have always felt it's every individual's right to do pretty much whatever they please in the sanctity of their own homes. What I object to is the current media-driven assault on what I can best refer to as 'normalcy'. The gays are no longer satisfied with seeking freedom from discrimination, they are trying to force acceptance of their values and lifestyles on the majority, straight population much the same way the Muslims are forcing their religion on Jews and Christians. In the Middle East it is done at the point of a gun—and if you say "no" you're likely to have your head cut off with a dull, rusty knife!

Mao Tse Dong had that right: 'Power comes from the muzzle of a gun.' Curiously enough, the way the pro-gay camp is advancing their agenda is very much like the mass-brainwashing techniques used by Mao in China. You might conclude they're following a translated version of the same playbook!

In the USA, if you dare to have your own opinion, or try to practice your religious beliefs that teach that homosexuality is evil—beliefs that, unlike gay marriage, ARE expressly enumerated as protected by the Constitution, you're likely to be sued out of business or driven into hiding by hate-reporting in the mainstream media, the same media-Gestapo who are trying to take guns away from the American public and turn them into slaves like Hitler did in Germany in 1933. These lice are pouring their anti-freedom, anti-excellence, pro-gay and 'the world owes me a living' propaganda out at a sickening pace!

Not long ago, there was a lot of humor directed at gays—the Monty Python British comedy troupe was famous for it. Then you had things like *Kiss of the Spiderwoman* which kind of let you examine their lifestyle from a more neutral and sympathetic perspective. More recently, there have been films like the remake of *The Longest Yard*, which had gay-bashing that wasn't nearly as negative as it's predecessor. Then there are things like that absolutely horrid Sandra Bullock Las Vegas showgirl movie that was so nauseating I couldn't finish it, or *Brokeback Mountain* that I've never seen and never intend to. Recently, superhero movies like *Kickass 2* and *The Green Lantern* have gays treated almost as though they are 'normal' persons, intentionally so, I might add, which is quite a difference from how gays were treated by Hollywood a decade or two ago. Just look at Deadpool... the first one has lots of gay humor but was still more-or-less socially-acceptable; the 2d one was so overboard I couldn't even finish the damn movie!

Even children's cartoons are full of this crap. In one of them, I can't recall if it was one of the *Finding Nemo* or one of the *Happy Feet* cartoons, two male shrimp are separated from 'the swarm' and the 'gayish' one of the two suggests they can adopt! Not that most kids are going to understand, but it's these little seeds being planted, like one of the *Ice Age* cartoons in which Sid the sloth is babysitting eggs and an obviously queer dinosaur has his 'little miracle' of an egg he adopted. I recall there is even a line in a song in *Frozen* suggesting one character had an unnatural relationship with his reindeer, ostensibly akin to sheep-shagging! It's no secret that many of these people are also attempting to remove laws against statutory rape so they can be allowed to legally have sex with children. Clearly these people have fallen off the deep end if they're trying to promote bestiality!

Shoot, I remember being mildly amused a couple decades ago when Bruce Willis did a cameo in an episode of Seinfeld and asks Jerry if he wants to 'make out'. He'd taken a blow to the head and the question, or so I thought at the time, was a very off-color-humor twist to show that he obviously wasn't thinking right, although it was still somewhat disturbing on a very rudimentary level. Fast-forward to today and this shit is everywhere!

And the hypocrisy is incredible! Are you familiar with the 'wardrobe malfunction' at the Super Bowl a few years back when Janet Jackson revealed a partial breast? No? She is a singer who decided to 'flash' the audience— but she had a large star covering her nipple and areola, so you saw nothing more than what you might see at the beach, but the networks went nuts, even though these are the same people who have been trying to gender-confuse children who might be watching by having grown men wearing pink, as if men have anything to do with breast cancer! Do they use pink and blue to help teach children gender identification where you come from as well? Here there's even some singer with a clothing line for kids that's all white, black and gray, like she was making clothes for the Amish, just because they are now pushing this crap that supposedly you can *choose* your gender. What horseshit! And the blatant hypocrisy, as I was saying... I recall a football game a couple years ago where a young, black lineman kissed an old, white team owner on the mouth on the sidelines! On camera! Talk about revolting! If this had happened back in the 1960's this would have caused a national uproar! Anyway, this isn't 'homophobia' or whatever *they* would call it, it's science: women are born with two X chromosomes, men have one X and one Y and that's the end of it! You can surgically change your 'hardware', but you can't change your genetic makeup!

Incidentally, I don't think there is any way that was 'accidental' that they just happened to have a camera on the football player and the coach. Plus, not much is actually 'live' these days...there's a tape delay so they can edit out things they don't want the public to see, like when assholes go streaking across the field, etc. Clearly, this was intentional, or at least most likely it was so. It was preplanned, the participants were recruited and the whole thing was staged and then broadcast before the censors could say 'boo'...not that anything is censored anymore... all as part of their campaign to try to convince people that this sort of thing is somehow 'normal'.

Perhaps the feeling is that if people are shocked so often that it is no longer shocking then gradually you achieve acceptance. Well, I may lean favorably towards individual rights, but there is nothing they are going to be able to show me that will convince me that there's anything at all 'cool' about one man having his dick in another man's ass! Well, what about you? Does anything about 2 guys being queer with each other interest you? Well? Hmm, your hesitation suggests I must have hit a chord. So, that actually has interest to you? No?"

"OH! I SEE! You've done it with a woman, haven't you? Hah! You HAVE haven't you!? And here I've been ranting on and on about how the gays are out to destroy US society and all that. I hope I haven't given offense!? So, my new lady-friend is secretly a carpet licker!? I have to hear all about this! First, however, I'm going to grab a beer. Can I get you anything? Sure, coming up! I can see I'm going to have to restock my single-malt!"

I returned shortly with our drinks and a couple of frosted glasses, plus 2 cubes of ice in the tumbler for Theresa. I poured her a good 3-fingers of Balvenie and gave her a long, deep French kiss. Then I settled down where I had a nice view of her legs and everything that lay in-between and said, "OK, now it's your turn to tell me a story. Lay it on me!"

Theresa took a sip of the whiskey, then another, then stared into her glass for a long moment before replying.

"It happened in my first year in college. There were these two guys who both liked me. I liked both of them as well, so it was kind of difficult deciding which of them I wanted for my boyfriend. I was also bothered by the fact that, if I chose one over the other, it might destroy their friendship. Anyway, about the time I'd finally decided which one I wanted to lose my virginity to, they both died in a motorcycle accident. They were waiting to turn left at a traffic light and a huge truck just rolled right over them. I guess I should say 'scooter' instead of motorcycle; they were both riding it and of course not wearing helmets, even though that probably wouldn't have saved them.

> "Anyway, this girl I knew at school was always hanging around me, trying to be my friend, giving me gifts joining me for meals in the cafeteria. Somehow she always seemed to run into me in the library and she joined my aerobics class when she found out I was taking one. So, after the funeral, she suggested we get a drink together. I was really distraught, of course, and she took me home and fed me several cups of warm sake and of course I had no alcohol tolerance so I got drunk really fast. Then she led me to her bed and had me lie down and gave me a massage. It felt really nice and she pulled out all the stops...hot, lavender scented towels and my clothes came off so slowly I hardly noticed. Then she oiled her hands and rubbed all over, including my legs and of course she sometimes slipped and a fingertip would slide across my vulva or my clitoris. Lying there with my eyes closed, I lost myself in the feeling for a while. When I felt her put her finger inside me I tried to roll over and make her stop, but then she started kissing me and I got dizzy and I wanted her to stop but at the same time I didn't, so I let her go down on me."

At this point a single tear ran down her cheek. I didn't know vampires were capable of tears. Of course she wasn't completely vampire, not yet. Interesting—this was proving to be educational in so many ways!"

"So, what happened next? Did you do oral on her as well?"

"No, I guess she took care of herself while she was going down on me. Anyway, she put my hand on her breast and her thigh, but I guess she could tell I wasn't interested. I guess while she was kissing me I was thinking of those two guys, imagining I was kissing them instead".

"So, how long did the two of you date?"

That was the only time: one and done. Afterwards I felt... dirty... ashamed. In fact, I was really cruel to her afterwards. I know she really cared for me and maybe even loved me, but I just couldn't accept that. I felt violated. In truth, the experience was nowadays what they would call a 'date rape'. She got me too drunk to say no and had me against my will. If I hadn't been drunk and depressed and heartsick, it never would have happened. To be honest, looking back, I wish I hadn't been so mean to her afterwards. She was actually quite kind to me...kinder than most of the boys were whom I dated later."

"Did you ever 'take a walk on the wild side' again after that experience?"

"No," she said, smiling and moved towards me until we were face-to-face, then she kissed me with her intoxicating whisky breath. As she kissed me, her fingers slowly traveled up my leg to my 'special purpose' as Steve Martin once referred to it and she then 'latched onto my honker', to borrow a line from *Kentucky Fried Movie*, squeezing it tight.

Backing away and smiling at me, she explained: "I like oral sex, but what I like most is a nice, hard dick inside me and that is something no woman can ever do for me!"

"What about toys and dildos and such things?" Her fingers were now sliding up and down in a slow, steady rhythm and I felt myself responding quickly to her touch.

"Toys are no substitute for the real thing!"

Sex with her wasn't quite what it had been before she 'turned'; her body temperature was lower, close to room-temperature, so the sensation was not at all what it used to be, but sex with her was still preferable to 'DIY'. With that in mind, I allowed her to push me on my back. She toyed with me for a few moments, dragging her long hair across my face, chest, nipples, then her mouth engulfed me, sucking hard...one hand gently cupping my genitals and the other moving up and down in a real rock-and-roll rhythm. It felt so good I considered begging her not to stop as she climbed onto me and thrust me inside of her. After all, she was clearly enjoying calling the shots this time so I decided to just let her go...and go she did! I vaguely wondered if her aerobics classes had included these particular motions and then I surrendered myself in the moment and shoved conscious thought to the background and let the waves of feeling wash over me, again and again.

Chapter 22
Growing Pains

Theresa wasn't happy. Even worse, each day she found herself becoming increasingly frustrated and there was no end in sight. She was unhappy about being unhappy! Actually, it was rather ironic. For years she'd dreamed about becoming a vampire. Now that it was a reality, she wondered how she'd ever though it might be 'fun' or 'romantic'. She missed her mom, she missed her little sister and she missed her things. Her friends were mostly shit, but she missed them too. Maybe she missed texting them and swapping icons and forwarding cute videos more than actually spending time together with them. She had a feeling she knew what the vampire would say if she admitted that to him. The *other* vampire, to be more exact. She was still having some difficulty accepting the reality that now *she* was also a vampire—vampiress? Or was the correct term a succubus, a creature she remembered from her days playing Dungeons and Dragons? She had certainly been using sex to keep her captor's favor—for that's certainly what he was, a captive—to stay alive.
Oddly, she felt a growing confidence that she was quite capable of using her feminine wiles to satisfy her 'host'... or even to snare a victim. No, she reflected after a long moment, she was not destined to become a succubus: those were demons and she was no demon. She *was* cursed however, of that much she was certain. Now that she thought of it, it was obvious life had always been against her.

For starters, she'd been born female in a male-dominated society where women were treated like servants and sex objects. Sure, it would have been much worse to have been born in some Muslim, rape-crazed war zone, but the fact that others were less fortunate didn't change her own luck. She'd been just attractive enough to find herself groped by uncles and classmates from elementary school on up, been smart enough to end up being bullied all through school, lacked any real skills (she had a little musical talent, it was true, but there were 100 million other girls in Asia that were far more talented), her dad hadn't been around to teach, protect or support her, she'd had to put in 15-16 hour days of studying and working in order to get decent enough grades to get a scholarship to some dinky little school in a scarcely-civilized part of the USA (not a single sushi or noodle restaurant to be found, only a few Japanese steak houses that were far too expensive for her budget).   She'd been disappointed in all her relationships; she had always been poor, often to the point of living solely on instant noodles and fruit juice, and owned scarcely any possessions—and those she had were either half-a-world away or might as well be unless she wanted to be hunted as a possible murder suspect—not to mention risking being discovered—and to what end—if she indeed turned into a vampiress. Finally, she'd been just about to finish her education, receive her degree and, with a bit of luck, get a job and finally have some money and material possessions and security and be able to provide for her mother, which of course was the final and worst curse of all: she'd never be able to go home and see her mother again!

Living forever...or at least a lot longer...was certainly the most-attractive positive to the thought of being a vampiress, but not being able to ever go home again, or to go out in the daytime, being unable to travel more than a short distance and then only at nighttime, not having friends, never eating sashimi or pizza again...and it had even been suggested she would have to quit smoking...was it worth all the things she now had to give up?

Shifting position, she tried to get more comfortable. The chair she was draped across must have been made in the 1960's. It was shaped somewhat like a large, shallow basket. Rather than legs, it had hoops of what she guessed was rattan. She'd seen photos of the bean-bag chairs that had been all the rage back then and guessed this was supposed to give a little more support while still allowing one to slouch rather than sitting upright. The overstuffed pillows and Amish quilt that covered the vinyl surface made it somewhat more comfortable, but it still just seemed weird to someone used to hard beds, hard wooden chairs and futons.

And what was up with her body? The heightened hearing and increased sense of smell was interesting to be sure, but her skin felt increasingly dry and leathery and she was certain no amount of lanolin or other skin-care products were going to have any effect. And then there was the matter of her vaginal lubrication: her 'love juices' as one magazine had called them. They seemed to be drying up. The last couple times she'd had sex she'd been excited but felt less wet than usual. Then there was her hair. She couldn't exactly say why, but she knew her hair had changed somehow as well. Maybe it was the smell, possibly the thickness, perhaps the texture, but whatever it was, something just didn't seem right.

There were other, perhaps more significant changes, such as her perceptibly diminished heartbeat. What about her period? She had a very clear feeling that she'd had her last menstrual cycle. She wouldn't miss those of course; cramping and bloating and being moody, emotional and unreasonable for several days at a time wasn't something *any* woman looked forward to. However, it also meant she'd never have children, never create life.

It wasn't that this was something she had been looking forward to. As a student, having children was about the last thing from her mind. Getting a degree and getting a job had been about all she'd really cared about recently. Still, it was hard-wired into her genetic makeup as a woman and, deep down, she felt that this was yet one more thing that had been stolen from her. She supposed she'd really feel that fate had totally fucked her...except that, if her savior hadn't come along when he did, three fat, smelly, disgusting rednecks would have likely spent several days fucking her every way possible and then they'd have killed her and dumped her body somewhere. Or, maybe they'd have just cut her up and had a barbeque. In any case, she was better off than she would have been dead...repeatedly raped first and then dead.

At least she was still alive...sort of. 'Undead', that was the term they used in the stories. She supposed it was fitting: she wasn't dead, she could still think, move about, do all the things typically associated with having life, but she was going to have to exist without many of the things that made life worth living. She'd never hold a baby in her arms, never enjoy the smell of freshly-baked bread (OK, she could actually bake bread if she wanted to, but since she couldn't eat it that would be kind of like self-inflicted suffering, wouldn't it?).

She'd begged to be allowed to get some of her things, some clothes and her photos, but was told it would look 'too suspicious'. She understood the logic. After all, it was preferable to let the police think some other person had killed the three hillbilly-rapists and then abducted her, thereby helping her to hide her new identity—which she would be completely unable to do so if she went back to her apartment and her nosy roommate. After all, she wasn't exactly able to continue taking her classes. Even if she were to transfer to the night program, most classes began when it was still daylight outside. Her host had land out in the countryside with a large house with a basement and a food source that allowed him to avoid feeding on humans that he'd made available to her.

What did she have? She had a lease on 1 room in a shared, above-ground apartment with 2 windows with curtains that let far too much light through. She was realistic enough to know she couldn't go back to her old life. Still, she didn't like feeling like a prisoner, which is essentially what she was—a prisoner of her new condition, compounded by being a penniless student in a foreign country. She was also totally isolated: the battery in her notebook PC was dead (she *always* kept the charger in her computer bag, so she suspected he was hiding it from her somewhere) the vampire's computer was pass-worded and he'd forbidden her to use it anyway, and he didn't appear to have a cell-phone and his landline didn't have a long-distance carrier! (She'd tried making a quick call once while he was feeding the dogs). She hadn't even known it was *possible* to have a telephone without long-distance service! For probably the thousandth time she mentally browbeat herself for leaving her cell-phone in her bedroom when she went rushing off to her interview. Some mornings she just didn't have it together until after her 2d or 3d cup of coffee!

Of course she'd asked him to go back to look for her charger for her PC and he'd said it was too dangerous as her car had been left near a crime scene and her disappearance and the certain discovery of her vehicle just down the road had likely resulted in her disappearance being linked to the murders and there was also a good chance the vehicle had already been towed. He had said he'd go back in a couple of days when there was likely to be less activity at the murder scene, after the police had concluded their investigation, but that had stretched to over a week and, when he finally did go to check, he'd returned saying the car had been towed. So, all she had of her personal possessions, limited though they were in this country, was an un-powered computer (so she couldn't even access her photos) and an overnight bag of clothes and cosmetics and *one* pair of shoes! This whole 'vampire thing' wasn't going at all like she'd dreamed about. It wasn't even what she'd expected after the first week of 'undeath' as the reality of what was happening had made itself known.

Talk about irony! After years of wishing to be a vampire, her wish had some true. Not only that, she was shacked-up with a very good-looking and somewhat charming host/captor (which one he was she wasn't altogether certain). As for the 'shack', it was not only a much nicer house than any she'd ever lived in, she was surrounding by millions of dollars worth of artwork, books and other antiquities. She should feel incredibly lucky. The fact she didn't just made her feel even worse.

The vampire had just finished dusting the picture frames and bookshelves (would it ever have occurred to her previous self that vampires did housework? Probably not!). Now he came over and sat on the arm of the loveseat facing her. "So dear," he inquired, "What would you like to do tonight?"

Without hesitation, Theresa answered: "I want to fucking kill something!"

Chapter 23
The First Misstep

I looked down at the slender, raven-haired creature staring defiantly up at me with those luxuriously curved eyes of hers, hands on her hips, feet placed shoulder-with apart, body-language signaling a heretofore unrevealed stubbornness and I knew she was serious. Putting voice to my thoughts, I inquired: "you're serious, aren't you?"

"Yes! For a whole lot of reasons, most of which I can't really explain, I just really want to kill something, drink it's blood, put my hand around it's heart and feel it slowly weaken and then stop, knowing I had killed it and feeling the thrill of having the power of life and death over another, living thing. Maybe it's a natural feeling of being a, how to say it, a newly-minted vampire...vampiress? Anyway, I'd like you to teach me. You've done it successfully for so long—teach me how to survive, teach me how to do it and not get caught. Please—share your wealth of experience with me!"

Then she turned on the charm, her body language became decidedly more feminine with a quick change of posture from demanding to demure, she gave me a sweet smile and, it seemed to me, only just stopped short of batting her eyelashes at me. So, the little wench was schmoozing me! Instantly I knew the first part of her statement was the truth and the latter was mostly bullshit and she wasn't above flattery in order to try to get what she wanted. This was hardly the first time a woman had tried the approach of using feminine wiles with me—after all, I hadn't been born yesterday! Nevertheless, I could see that this was an issue that wasn't going to just go away with a simple 'no'; this was something I was going to have to deal with, sooner or later.

You do realize that, at present, because your car was discovered abandoned near the scene of a triple-homicide, you are most probably listed as a missing person connected with three homicides and therefore a possible murder suspect. No matter how unlikely it would be for a little Asian girl to kill three large, beefy men—and total strangers to boot—your disappearance coincides with their deaths, making you a possible suspect. Most likely there's an APB—that means

ALL POINTS BULLETIN—out for you as a PERSON OF INTEREST in their deaths. That means if you're found, police would immediately take you 'into custody'...that means arrest you...for questioning in their deaths. If suddenly your fingerprints or your DNA shows up at another murder scene, that would suddenly create a lot of interest in the person of one Theresa Hasegawa, don't you think?

"Why would that matter?" she countered, "It's not like I'm going to be returning to my old life, attending classes, going shopping or talking walks in the park in the morning!"

"Because if they put your face on TV, there are people who've seen you here: my ranch hand and the mailman, anyway. Remember, we made a *point* of letting them see you hanging laundry and poking around in the garden while you still had full resistance to sunlight. Even now, while you still have moderate resistance, we're making sure they see you in the kitchen during the day or on the porch later in the day, when the sun is going down behind the house. Do you think there's any chance they *wouldn't* recognize you? While there are some Asian students here and small communities of Cambodians and Philippinos in the area, this is still a mostly white community, with a few blacks and Mexicans mixed in. How many gorgeous, slender, mixed-race Japanese girls do you think live around here? Probably no more than the fingers on one hand! I don't exactly want the police snooping around looking for you and peeking into *my* life."

"I know," she said. "We could kill my roommate! She's always sleeping around and bringing home guys she meets at bars or wherever. They'd think some jealous lover did it. My fingerprints are already all over the place, so they wouldn't think it was me...and I'd be able to get my passport, my backup drive for my computer with all my photos and some of my clothes—not so much they'd notice them missing, but you wouldn't let me go clothes shopping so I would really like to get some changes of clothes." Smiling slyly, she added, "You really think I'm gorgeous? Just wait: I have some really sexy underwear from Japan...stuff that makes Frederick's of Hollywood look like what the Amish girls wear!"

Funny what she chose to pick up on, I thought to myself. Women are all the same, even to the Terminatrix robot checking-herself-out in the bathroom mirror while beating the snot out of the older-model Terminator. Some things know no boundaries, whether ethnic, racial or even species-related!

"Actually," I countered, "I did let you go clothes shopping, in a manner of speaking. We used my computer and ordered your nurses' outfit along with nylons and shoes, plus some underwear and a Hard Rock T-shirt. Oh, that's another person who could recognize you—the UPS guy! Not to mention the fact that I'd rather you wear nothing, other than those times you need to play nurse for the ranch hand or the occasional visitor!"

"Just because you like gallivanting around naked most of the time," she smiled, placing one hand on my chest and allowing the other to trace a line, slowly, from my navel down to the thatch of pubic hair, then lower, just a fingertip...sliding all the way down, then encircling, slowly...just the faintest of touches but enough to cause an instantaneous reaction. Looking down, seeing the effect she was having on me, her smile broadened and a mischievous glint appeared in her eye.

"Just a moment; have a seat and I'll be back." With that, she dashed away up the stairs, leaving me a trifle perplexed and, at the same time, in anticipation of what the little minx might be up to. For lack of anything better to do, I did as bid and had a seat. Hearing the BEEP BEEP of the microwave oven a scant minute later only increased my curiosity. A few moments later and she reappeared, hair falling across her face, with a coffee cup in each hand. As she knelt at my feet, I could see that one cup held water, the other—ice cubes.

"I saw this in a movie once," she failed in explanation. Then her actions provided all the information necessary as she poured water from the first cup, swished it around in her mouth, spat the water back into the cup, then took me into her mouth. Mystery solved! She'd used the microwave to heat the water and now was proceeding to move her mouth up and down, engulfing me in a very pleasant and wet warmth. I was quite hard and enlarged now and quite enjoying the sensation when she stopped, tipped ice cubes from the second cup into her mouth, spat them back into the cup, then continued her ministrations. The shock of the sudden cold, along with some residual warmth in her mouth, was electric! From long habit I was usually "as silent as the grave" during sex, but I heard an audible gasp pass my lips as she took me all the way in and partly down her throat. At this point she gagged a little, but made a splendid recovery, switching back to the cup of hot water, then the ice, then the hot water... The sensations were so powerful I sat with hands clamped under the arms of the chair, lip firmly held betwixt my teeth. When I finally came I practically exploded, coming and coming for what seemed like an impossible duration of time—it was all the poor girl could do to swallow fast enough to keep up with me.

Still with the evil glint in her eye, she leaned back, hands to the sides and back, parting her legs slightly to reveal those lovely, short, straight hairs and the paradise they sheltered. "Well?" she asked, "how was that?"

Still basking in the afterglow of an immensely powerful orgasm, I eyed the creature at my feet, knees thrust forward, leaning back away from me, supporting her weight with her hands back and to the sides, legs spread more than shoulder-width apart, giving me an excellent view of her delicious little bush, her back arched, pushing her small but firm breasts up, pinkish nipples standing erect, her long, raven-black hair spilling off her shoulders and behind her, mischief glinting in her long, curved, brown eyes, a dribble of cum sliding down her chin as she ran her tongue in a long oval around her lips and I found myself getting aroused again!

Any remaining doubts over my plans for this lovely, white-shinned, dark-haired creature vanished like morning mist when the sun slips from behind a cloud. How could I not keep my new source of entertainment around? Certainly I couldn't kill her—I was enjoying her far too much. Over the years, I'd had plenty of "guests" to satisfy my sexual needs. Sure, I had had sex with every reasonably-attractive female victim I had fed upon, but those were far less frequent these days now that I had myself set up with cattle and a low-profile, giving me far more security than if I were leaving a trail of corpses in my wake as I had back in France. Over the years I'd snatched a few girls walking home at night or grabbed them as they were focused on unlocking their cars or their front doors and kept them chained-up and regularly fucked until I tired of them.

One in particular, a high school swimmer and soccer player who'd had a flat tire on her bicycle on her way home from her night-time, restaurant job, I'd kept fed and healthy for over a month. Missing girls didn't generate the same amount of investigative interest as murder victims, but her disappearance had been big news (she had been well-liked in the community). She'd been a good girl too—a genuine virgin! Even at the age of 16, those were fewer-and-farther-between these days, what with a constant bombardment of promiscuity on TV and in social media, nowadays there were girls getting pregnant at 13, something that was practically unknown a mere 50 years ago. When I allowed myself to think on it, I felt bad for having taken something out of the world that hadn't yet been tainted with the corruption of selfishness, greed and lust (what in my days had been called "sin"). However, I'd snatched her in an opportune moment and, once taken, there was no letting her go!

Perhaps that is why it was only when the urge to have sex was practically driving me blind that I began hunting for human victims, the fair sex in particular. I still took a risk of discovery each time I kidnapped one, especially as there were now so many cameras all over the place: in parking lots, traffic intersections, on individual cell phones and even on automobile dashboards. And there was the fact that sex is so much more enjoyable when it was given willingly, with both parties seeking to please the other; this was something I'd nearly forgotten until Theresa came into my life.

The final piece of my reverie (perhaps "reverie" is the wrong word as it implies a lengthy thought process and I reached this conclusion quite quickly, although not so swiftly as to call it an "epiphany" Was there a word in English or Germany that was more appropriate? I would have to think on it sometime when I didn't have a gorgeous, naked Asian girl spreading her legs at my feet and a continuing erection that begged for additional attention), concerned the guilt I felt each time I killed an innocent victim. I had no problems at all killing those who deserved it—I figured I was making the world a better place—and there were so many these days who contributed nothing.

Was this why the slender, blonde swimmer came to mind? I'd kept her around so long that I'd started to develop feelings for her. After all, she was intelligent, attractive, sensitive and talented, at least once she was no longer terrified and when she wasn't being desperate or depressed due to her captivity. To be honest with myself, killing her was probably the most difficult thing I ever had to do. In truth, that's why I'd sucked her dry when I did—had I waited any longer, I would have been unable to do so. Being a blood-sucking vampire and having an intense fondness for attractive females in addition to feelings approaching a conscience can be a real bitch! So, I did the only thing I could do to avoid feelings of guilt over what I'd done—I simply didn't think about it!

Bringing my thoughts back to the present, I ogled Theresa's pert, creamy breasts as one single bead of cum fell from her chin to land on her chest, just at the inner curve of her left breast. Lowering myself to my knees in front of her, I slid my hands between her thighs and calves, lifting her, until her knees unfolded and I straightened her legs, which I then held to my chest, hands just below her knees, holding her suspended so the only part of her body resting against the carpet was her forearms. Easing myself back into her, I renewed my actions, pistoning with renewed vigor.

As I stiffened, increasing in hardness, I began pushing harder, then faster. Theresa gasped with pleasure, then began moaning as she squeezed me tighter inside her, fingers turning white as she drove her fingertips into the carpeting as her pleasure mounted. I let my eyes wander over her breasts, her slender waist and thighs, the short, straight black hairs comprising her wonderful little bush, then couldn't help but close them as I concentrated on the feeling as I came inside of her one more time.

The sex was over much more quickly this time, even though it was less intense than when she'd used the hot water. Maybe we could find a way to warm her inside and make her feel more like I was fucking a live woman...a steel dildo heated in hot water and inserted for a few minutes prior to love-making? Perhaps just a protracted bath first; with water as hot as she could take it? That was probably something I could talk her into without too much difficulty, considering Japanese and their tradition of taking hot baths in a communal setting. Panting slightly after my recent expenditure of energy, I replied, "So, you want to kill someone?...I guess that can be arranged."

I stood then, looking down at her in her recumbent pose, slightly propped up on her elbows, one leg to either side of mine, an expectant look on her face. I paused to admire the small, almond-shaped opening just below the little thatch of straight, black hair I'd grown so fond on. Where most people's genitals looked like something out of a horror movie, hers were almost attractive. I don't know how I'd ever considered killing her as I had all my other victims. To put it in common parlance, she was certainly a 'keeper.'

> I always have a few potential candidates in case I decide to go hunting; not that I do that very often, anymore—the night I rescued you was only the third time I'd hunted humans this year. When I get bored I read the arrest reports, sometimes I will sit in a bar and listen to gossip or just spy in people's windows and see what they're doing. After all, just sitting in the house watching movies and reading books with only the cat for company gets a little boring, so even though I don't often kill humans anymore, I guess I still 'hunt' them as a mental exercise. I am a predator, after all... I guess now that's a 'we' as you're the one anxious to go looking for prey. Anyway, I've got three at the top of my list these days. One's a brute who beats his wife and kids, another is a corrupt judge and the other is a crooked cop.

"How do you know about them?"

> "Well, I read about the wife-beater's arrest. The wife and step-daughter didn't press charges, but as the address was reported

in the paper, I went around to their house a few times and spied on them from a tree in their backyard—after several such visitations I managed to observe him throwing things about in a drunken rage, so I find it very believable that he is a one of those individuals who beats his wife and kids, although I honestly didn't stick around long enough—I am very good at moving around silently in the dark, but I try not to take unnecessary risks as being arrested for trespassing would be a stupid way to ruin everything I have created here. Anyways, the newspaper article listed a number of other crimes this person served time for, so he is what one would say, I think, in English as a habitual criminal:, so someone the world would be better off without. Sure, he might bring home a paycheck, but these days there's no shortage of government assistance.

Hell, under the Obama administration they even sent out emails advertising scholarships, housing assistance and other "free stuff" at the expense of the taxpayers. Basically it was 'let us buy your vote and we'll give you a free phone' and of course nowadays they want to promise free college and universal health insurance without a clue how anyone is going to pay for it all! Biden's opened the border for illegals who are getting hotel rooms and 'resettlement' payments, courtesy of those of us who pay taxes, all with the intention of turning them into voting citizens who will be so grateful for all the 'free' handouts that they've vote for corrupt Democrats the rest of their lives! It's terrible for the economy and society and nearly as bad as the mass immigration that's been destroying the cultures of Germany, Sweden and other western countries but they don't care—it's all about power! Say what you want about Trump, he worked hard to improve the economic fortunes of Americans and brought a lot of jobs and prosperity back to this country before the Wuhan virus shut everything down. The people running the country these days don't give a shit what happens to the economy or the environment or a strong military or personal freedoms or safety and stability, all they care about is power—and if they ever get what they're working towards they'll then use it to take everyone's guns away and turn them into slaves. Anyway, I'm ranting again, so getting back to the potential widow of this criminal scumbag:

she's young enough she can probably find another man and she and the kids will be better off for it.

"And the cop?"

I was engaging in a little voyeurism in a park, watching a couple teenagers making-out, when the cop came along. He found a small bag of marijuana on them and threatened to take them to jail unless the girl let him see her breasts. After some hesitation, she agreed. He wasn't satisfied with just looking, however and copped a good, long feel, did a little finger-fucking and then stole their weed!

The piece of shit boyfriend... if that's what he was... just stood there and watched. I guess he was powerless to do anything, but he didn't even protest! Anyway, I followed the cop for the next hour until his shift ended and he went home...and watched while he sat on his back porch and smoked a joint of the kid's pot!

As for the judge, he sentenced a man to SIX MONTHS in jail for allegedly making harassing telephone calls! With all the crime we have in this country and real criminals often getting very little punishment—something Americans call 'turn-style justice'. I thought this was pretty peculiar, so I did some research. It turns out the convict wasn't happy with his public defender so he represented himself, which is probably what got him convicted in the first place. Anyway, the victim was a teenage girl with problems, mental or psychiatric or both, who had been staying at his house. With the man and his wife, I might add. Apparently the guy was some sort of lay-preacher whose house was always open to people. There was another, younger guy staying there as well. There may have been some hanky-panky with him and the girl, I don't know, but I think she was old enough and the younger guy was about the same age as the girl.

Anyway, the story is that she went back home and started getting phone calls from the man's house. The interesting thing is he supposedly had proof he was in class at IUSB when some of the calls were made, so he couldn't have made ALL of the phone calls. Logically, it seems to me, that harassing someone is usually an individual thing and not a group effort.

In any case, he was found guilty of making at least some of the calls; possible, to be sure, but the 'benefit of the doubt' is supposed to work in the defendant's favor and as he was able to show he was in class when some of the calls were made, I'd have thought that would be sufficient doubt, wouldn't you? Someone, maybe Jefferson, once wrote, 'it is better than ten guilty men go free than for one innocent man to be wrongfully imprisoned' or something like that.

Interestingly enough, it seems the girl's foster parents were good friends of the judge. According to the rules of ethics he should have recused himself... meaning he should have disqualified himself and sent the case on to another judge because of his personal involvement with the family. Even worse, rumor has it he actually ASKED for the case to be assigned to his court! Six months in jail for *telephone harassment*!? Actual criminals frequently get off with much less! Heck, in places like Portland, Seattle, Chicago, New York City, etc., you can burn down a Starbucks or kick the shit out of some elderly Asian person on the sidewalk and you're not likely to get 6 months in jail...for a crime that does actual, serious harm! I think it's fair to say the sentence wouldn't have been so harsh if the judge hadn't been a friend of the girl's foster family. If the judge did this in one case, I'm sure he's committed other breaches of ethics; in fact, I've heard rumors when sharing beers with old vets down at the VFW upon occasion.

There are few things I detest more than corrupt cops, judges and politicians! They are worse than whores. Whores provide a service for a fee; one might call them self-employed businesswomen. Many of them are a lot more honest than those who claim to be public servants! If the truth were told, I'm sure the main reason sex-for-cash is illegal is that they don't declare their income, as they'd incriminate themselves by doing so, and the politicians absolutely hate it when people don't pay their taxes!

Oh, and there's one more on my list: an Asian college girl. Until you came along, she was probably going to be my next victim. On four separate occasions I've watched as guys dropped her off after a date. She gives them a quick hug and a kiss and then bolts for the door. It was always a different guy, never the same one twice. I decided to peek in on her from the tree outside her window... very quietly, as she has a dog. I saw her answering messages on several dating sites, simultaneously. Apparently she gets guys to take her out to dinner, thinking she's looking for a relationship. I have a feeling they wouldn't be so interested if they could see the photo over her bed—it's like a 2-foot square WEDDING PHOTO! I can't imagine anyone having a photo like that above their bed unless they were actually married, and I'm sure it's there so she can angle the camera on her laptop and let her husband or mother or whomever see it when she's chatting online—or turn away from it if she's chatting with someone she met on a singles site and yes, I've spied on her through her window and noticed her working on her computer while sitting facing in different directions, so it's not difficult to figure out what she's doing. Getting free dinners under false pretenses; I consider that THEFT! Again, I might be wrong, but I am thinking this is another completely immoral person that the world would be a better place without having her in it. I was thinking a good long fucking prior to drinking her dry would be fun for me and 'just desserts' for her, as they say here in the US of A.

"Oh, I think I know her!", exclaimed Theresa, stretching lazily and demonstrating a flexibility I am sure I never possessed, not even as a child.

If it's the same girl, and it could be, she's from Shanghai. The city is famous for all kinds of scams! Anyway, this girl, she dresses sexy and sits in some really visible place in the library or other parts of campus where there are a lot of people around and just waits for guys to hit on her and invite her to have a coffee or dinner, which of course they pay for and she is with a different guy almost all the time. Some of the other students from the Chinese Student Association call her 'the spider' because she just baits her web and waits for horny guys to snare themselves.
I saw her over at Notre Dame University once, walking with a guy when I went there to see a basketball game and saw her again at IUSB when I was visiting a friend there, so she really gets around! Anyway, apparently she doesn't take guys

home; she leaves that to her roommate, who's from India. The gossip on campus is that she's a real slut and literally 'sleeps around', meaning she usually sleeps at the other guy's places so she doesn't have to worry about two of them running into each other at her apartment, which apparently has happened more than once and one time the police had to be called because the guys started fighting over her. I guess they are really the modern-day 'odd couple': you have one girl who fucks any guy who'll smile at her and another girl who never has sex with anybody but goes out on just as many dates with just as many guys, maybe even some of the same ones! Hmm... thinking about it, I think I agree with you, the Shanghai girl is the worse one of the two because she's getting guys to buy her stuff under false pretenses.

"Apparently Shanghai has a long history of having a bad reputation for cheating and tricking people, even back in my day," I observed. "I know the term 'Shanghai'd' comes from sailors being impressed into service with the British navy. They were given a 'Micky Finn' which was a drink spiked with chloral hydrate, a knock-out drug... an 18th century roofie, I guess you'd call it... in a bar and when they woke up they were at sea. I seem to recall this was one of the causes of the War of 1812 because the British had the habit of doing this to American sailors and then hanged them for desertion if they jumped ship later and were caught again. I didn't know the locals had such a reputation. What sort of scams?"

Shanghai is famous throughout Asia for "cheaters," as we call them. I heard of a neighbor who went there on business. A girl picked him up outside of his hotel and took him to what she said was her home. If the guy hadn't been so horny he night have noticed that there was no furniture or clothes, just a bed and a nightstand from what I understand, and a table by the door and a curtain. She got naked, undressed him, piled his things on the table by the door, got him over to the bed and pulled the curtain. Apparently he heard a noise before they even started making love and, when he pulled the curtain open, the door was open and his pants and backpack were gone... along with his wallet, his camera and his phone! He ran out to look for the thief and that's when she locked the door behind him! Of course when he finally got back there with the police, she was long gone. What a dumb ass! What kind of girl has a room without clothes, makeup, etc. OK, maybe he thought she just used the room for sex, but who the hell has a curtain in the middle of the room? Sex really makes you guys stupid sometimes!!

"Guilty," I said, "maybe it's because all the blood leaving the brain to make our dicks hard! Also quite an amazing story... what nerve! I wish we could add her to the list! What other scams have you heard of?"

Oh, ones where girls invite foreigners to a restaurant where the owner is in on it, order expensive dishes while promising sex later, then run out or stiff the guy with the bill, go to the bathroom while he's paying and disappear. I heard of another one where the girl took a guy to her "room," which only had a bunk bed and there were big, cardboard boxes on the top bed. The girls gets the guy's pants off, puts them on the top bed, then gets the buy to make out with her on the bottom bed. Of course she has an assistant or two in the boxes, who empty the guy's wallet and then ring her phone, giving her an excuse to end the date before any sex happens..."my mom was in a car accident" or something like that so she runs out and the guy only misses his money later on. And then there are the more ordinary scams, such as charging foreigners ten times the local price... they even do this to Taiwanese because they can tell they are foreigners by their accents and the clothes they wear, even though they speak Chinese. Now that I think about it, even the price for admission to museums was different for locals and foreigners... more expensive for the foreigners, of course!

"How do they live with themselves?" I wondered aloud.
    "Oh, they justify it by telling themselves that there are too many people and not enough resources and that, if people let themselves be cheated than they are being clever and the other people are just stupid. Not all Chinese are this way, of course, but enough of them are that they have a terrible reputation among other Asians."
    "Of course my old boss, Napoleon, invaded Italy at least twice just so they'd pay him off and then he used the money and whatever he'd looted to finance his other wars and of course Hitler and some of his generals were

famous for stealing art, so this type of behavior isn't exclusive just to China. Anyway, this is interesting. Keep going."

"On my trip to China, I was standing there one day, waiting for a bus. I was in Nanjing. I was the only person at the bus stop. As soon as the bus pulled up, suddenly there was a crowd of people who come from nowhere and mobbed the bus in front of me. I watched while people pushed themselves onto the bus to get a seat without even letting the people getting off to get off first. I was shocked to see some young guy, maybe around 20 or so, actually crawl between the legs of an old woman so he could get on and get a seat. When I was growing up, we were taught to respect older people. Apparently he didn't get that education."

"Incredible!"

"The same thing happened about a week later. I was the only person, standing in the hot sun, when the bus pulled up and a mob appeared from nowhere. This time was a little different, however. A young guy was 'swimming' his way through the crowd to the door of the bus when a handsome, blond foreigner, American I think, grabbed the guy by the collar of his shirt and threw him to the back of the line. I felt like cheering! At the same time, I was afraid the 'queue jumper' might pick up a rock or something."

"Did he?"

No, I think he was too stunned to figure out what happened, he just stood there looking around with a confused look on his face. I noticed the American guy seemed to be watching his reflection in the window, just in case the rude asshole went after him. Interesting thing is, about 2 weeks later, I saw the same American guy on the subway. I mentioned he was handsome... not too big but obviously he was pretty strong. I wanted to go talk to him, that was back in the days when there weren't as many foreigners in China and I find most Chinese guys to be short and unattractive, not to mention having poor hygiene and generally treating women like crap, which seems to be true for most Asian men, but anyway I was too shy and my English wasn't very good back then. Anyway, when the train stopped, a crowd of about 50 people tried to push their way onto the train. Of course the people trying to get off were pushing back, but they were losing. This American guy actually picked up a short Chinese guy who was standing in front of him... I remember the man was wearing one-piece workers clothes, coveralls I think you call them. The American turned the guy sideways, used him to push the entire crowd of people BACKWARDS so he and the other people could get out of the car, then he put the Chinese guy down and gave him a pat on the shoulder. I mean he actually picked a guy up and pushed at least 50 people backwards! Obviously this was someone who found a way to deal with the rude behavior of people in Shanghai.

I admit I really admired his approach, I'd never seen anything like it! I had this same situation happen to me at least twice during my trip there and I ended up stuck in the car and unable to get off until the next station, then I had to catch the next subway train going back in the other direction, all of which wasted about 20 to 30 minutes and the second time it gave the dickhead next to me a chance to fondle my ass in the press of the crowd—which of course happens all the time in Tokyo, but that was my first time getting groped on public transportation in China, but it certainly wasn't the last...

"Didn't the Chinese guy get angry? I mean the one that ended up being used as a battering ram?"

No, that was the funny thing... I guess he was so happy to get out of the train he thought the whole thing was amusing. He gave the American guy a big smile and just walked away. I was really going to follow the American then and hope he'd notice me but I was too slow and ended up having to fight my way through the crowd and by the time I got to the escalator he was most of the way up and when I got to the top he was gone. That was one of only a couple times in my life I felt really attracted to a guy I didn't even know. Of course you have to realize that, in Asia, EVERYBODY has dark hair. Foreigners with blond hair are a real novelty and usually very popular. Of course a lot of people nowadays, even guys, dye their hair, but it still isn't the same thing.

"And of course," she added with a sly smile as she sat up and trailed a finger down along the underside of my penis, making me jump with a small jolt of pleasure as she reached the tip, "everybody knows that westerners have bigger dicks than Asian guys, on average, and although I may not be that experienced, personally, all the articles on sex in ladies magazines say that size really DOES matter!"   Seeing my favorite muscle starting to stiffen again, she leaned forward and took it in her mouth and pretended it was a lollipop. After the prolonged lovemaking session we'd just had, I really didn't think I'd be able to cum again. Fortunately, that turned out to be wrong.

All the sex left me drained, and definitely in need of some life-sustaining (unlife-sustaining?) blood. Normally I'd just nip out to the pasture and help myself to some "boeuf au jus," so to speak, but my little minx deserved a reward, or so I reasoned, even though I had previously determined not to draw additional attention to ourselves after killing the three rednecks.

"So, my dear," I queried, "whom are we going to kill tonight?"

Chapter 24
It's a Fair Cop...or not...

Scott Foster was having a really shitty night... again! As usual, he was unhappy about his rank on the police force and his pay grade. After 8 years, he felt he should be a sergeant by now, instead of still a lowly patrolman. Of course he blamed Cheryl... the little colored girl he used to hit on back when she was fresh out of the academy. Now, however, after finishing her master's degree and earning several service citations and getting promoted ahead of other people because she was both black *and* female, she was a captain. She'd never gone out with him, but no doubt had only pretended to like him but she hadn't actually appreciated his advances and now was punishing him and making sure HE didn't advance in the ranks. Probably a dyke as well as being a cock-tease, he thought to himself.

"Nigger bitch!" Foster exclaimed to himself while opening his next can of Miller Genuine Draft. Of course, to be honest, he hadn't been seeking any sort of relationship, certainly not with a minority chick, but he wanted to have sex with at least one female from each race, just to compare the differences. He'd had a couple Mexican chicks (one willing, one with threatening to have her deported as an illegal), a somewhat chubby Filipina, but so far no blacks, Arabs or Indians and Cynthia was cute, so he'd hoped to make her his "token black fuck" Of course Cynthia was also smart and no doubt had figured out he was only interested in sex—not that he was very subtle in his come-ons.

"Thinks she's better than everybody else!" he added, though more to comfort himself than he actually felt there was any truth to it. Thinking about it, he figured he probably needed to add a Chinese, Japanese or Korean bitch as well as Southeast Asia islanders were probably a different ethnic group; at least he thought he remembered reading that in an ancient issue of *Playboy*. More of a challenge, of course, but that also gave him something more to shoot for. Of course you had to be careful—he'd heard of a guy in Elkhart who'd brought back a beauty from China, who showed her gratitude by sleeping around with multiple lovers immediately after the wedding..probably beforehand as well... then had beat him, tried to hire a 'hit' on him and eventually had him arrested on bogus rape charges when he refused a $10,000 bribe to continue in a sham marriage long enough for her to get US residency; all bullshit, but it effectively ended the guys professional career.

He also knew of another guy in Elkhart who'd worked at one of the local motorcycle dealerships who'd brought a Russian babe over and had enough sense to back out of the wedding at the last minute—that bitch had tried to run him over with his own car! Come to think of it, he actually knew a doofus from California, who'd been on a softball team some time ago, who'd gone all the way to Chicago to meet-up with a girl he'd met on a singles site only when he got there it wasn't really a chick, it had a dick! The same guy (who apparently was a slow learner), had also been conned into sending $600 for a plane ticket for a Russian girl (or someone *posing* as a Russian girl) who of course then asked for more money for a visa application and of course never materialized. Foster had decided after hearing those tales that he wasn't going to try to meet anyone online who wasn't at least local. Man, if he'd spent an all-day round-trip driving to meet some girl and found some faggot instead he'd have beaten the motherfucker to death—and ex-cops have a really hard time in prison!

He wished the Asian massage parlor on Cassopolis Street in Elkhart hadn't been closed down for prostitution. He'd been a rookie on the force back when it was open and had been worried about possible repercussions if he'd been seen patronizing the establishment. Now he was older and wiser and knew he could have used his badge and bullied his way into having sex with one of the girls if cash alone hadn't been sufficient incentive. "Why can't these damn high school kids buy some decent beer?" he asked rhetorically.

The beer he was drinking was courtesy of some kids he'd found out at Oxbow park, up in the watch tower. The park was actually outside of his assigned patrol area, but that was where the kids liked to hang out, so he made a point of cruising by whenever possible. Last night he'd found four pimply-faced kids trying to hide from him at the top of the wooden ranger tower. Dumb kids should have just run into the brush and come back for the car later, but he doubted any other officer in the county would have bothered to climb the tower, so their instinct to hide probably would have worked most of the time. They hadn't had any weed, unfortunately, but there was a broken tail-light in the car they'd come in, which had netted him $20 by reducing the ticket down to a 'warning'. He'd told the kids he was doing them a favor by collecting the fine in person, thus saving them the court costs associated with having to appear in traffic court. He didn't know if they'd believed him and didn't really care—it's not as though they were likely to run home and tell mom and dad they'd been out drinking, underage as it were, and had their beer confiscated by a cop who then let them go instead of taking them to jail. The little bastards were lucky to get off so lightly and they knew it!

Like most nights, sitting at home alone, he was feeling frustratingly bored. He'd seen every movie that was on TV tonight except some stupid chick-flick and one of those awful, almost-always-the-same 'B' movies with Dolph Lundgren. He'd played all his video games until they held no interest anymore and he'd seen all his porn 1000 times. What he really needed was a blow-job, but his most recent live-in girlfriend had left after an argument during which he'd thrown a glass ashtray at her. He'd missed her head (fortunately or unfortunately he hadn't yet decided) and it had merely shattered on the wall, but instead of just getting her and her fat ass to shut-the-hell-up, he'd come home from work the next day and she was gone, along with all her stuff, leaving only a "fuck you, asshole!" scrawled on the refrigerator in permanent magic marker. He'd thought about trying to have charges filed for criminal mischief, but decided the less the department knew about the ashtray incident, the better.

His temper, with only a hint of mingled curiosity, surged to a rage when the doorbell rang. "Who the fuck can that be?", he asked aloud, stubbing out his cigarette in the soap dish he was using for an ashtray, "if that fat bitch forgot something she's going to have to show some real gratitude for disturbing me this late!"

Half-stumbling to the door, he unlocked it and threw it open, ready to pour out a torrent of verbal abuse at whatever unlucky bastard had disturbed him in his self-pity. What he beheld there rendered him instantly speechless.

The girl was beautiful... and Asian. She was obviously in some distress as her shirt was torn, revealing a black bra-strap and there appeared to be dried blood spattered liberally over the once-white shirt. "Please help me," she gasped. Stammering for a moment while he tried to deal with the unreality of the beauty on his doorstep, the alcohol coursing through his system and the fact half the blood had apparently left his brain and was now giving him an instant erection, he just stood there for a moment, helpless, while he tried to form a coherent thought. Finally, he managed enough coherence to sputter, "please, come in".

"Thank you, oh thank you," the girl sobbed, collapsing against his chest for a moment, which only made his erection harder. Her hair smelled really good and she was trembling. Looking up at him with a hesitant smile, she repeated "thank you" and released him, walking past him into the small duplex he called home. Turning, he quickly let his gaze drop to her ass; a nice, trim ass, not like that fat bitch he'd been fucking only because it was the only pussy available at the time.

Now grinning evilly, he turned to follow her inside.

The sound behind him was almost imagined, but not the impact that drove the wind from his lungs and knocked him flat and stunned on the worn-out carpeting in front of the door. He was vaguely aware of a black shape entering and the sound of the door closing and then pain exploded in his gut as someone kicked him... very hard... with a pair of what his subconscious told him were motorcycle boots. He tried getting up when the pain exploded again... and a third time as he vomited, beer shooting out of his nose as well as his mouth. For a long moment all he could do was lie there, gagging. Dimly he was aware of two people grabbing his arms and dragging him across the floor.

The thought took awhile to form; then he remembered the girl at the door and became aware that one of the people wrestling with him was the girl. All thoughts of holding her down and fucking her long and hard had disappeared and his hard-on had vanished as quickly as it had arrived. While most of his brain was frozen in panic, he couldn't help contemplating, if only at a subconscious animal-survival level, what was happening to him and wondering about the "why" of the assault. He'd never seen these people before; what grudge did they have against him? Also, why did the girl have a knife in her mouth, held like a pirate in a Captain Blood movie? As his vision cleared slightly, he recognized it as one of his own kitchen knives.

As he was dropped unceremoniously into his bathtub, breathlessly and totally confused, he tried to voice "I'm a cop," expecting that revelation to halt whatever was going on; try as he might, however, no sound emerged. He was gasping for breath and just couldn't make a sound. A booted foot to his stomach held him down while the girl, suddenly no longer as lovely as he'd thought, stabbed him in the wrist, drawing the blade towards her to make a deep cut which burned with enough pain to momentarily turn him stone-cold sober. He tried again to speak, but the boot held him down while the girl... the girl was actually sucking on his wrist, sucking his blood into her mouth. With dawning horror he looked at the man standing above him: pale skin, black clothing and... oh God yes, his assailant actually had fangs! He started thrashing violently, trying to defend himself from what he'd suddenly realized were honest-to-goodness VAMPIRES! Whatever this was, he would wrestle with the realities of it later—right now the adrenaline was pumping as he realized he was in a fight for his life!

He gave a mighty heavy, again and again, but without success: the force behind the boot planted in his abdomen was beyond his ability to move, especially with one arm pinned. With his free, left arm, he balled his fist and hammered at the girl. He managed to dislodge her for a moment then, hissing, she grabbed his free hand, holding it extended above him, where the man in black grabbed it, holding it in an iron vise. She then pinned his right arm again on the side of the bathtub and returned to feeding at his severed wrist. In a wild panic, Scott tried pushing with his feet... but his socks refused to find purchase on the slippery tub and the man had him in a very effective hold: pulling up on his arm while keeping his boot planted in his stomach. Scott realized there was no escape, at least none he might affect by himself, and tried to scream, desperately hoping some neighbor might hear him.

Instead of hearing the scream he'd hoped for, all he heard from his own throat was a muted, pathetic gasp. He tried again to draw breath and yell. Instead, adding to his terror, he heard the man say "hand me the knife". He watched, helplessly, as the girl handed his paring knife to the man. In an instant the boot was replaced by a knee and he felt a new, blinding pain as his other wrist was sliced and then the man was sucking on his left wrist while the girl resumed doing the same to his right. Still struggling, the erstwhile dirty-cop slowly felt the vitality leaving his body and his consciousness fading. He made one last, mighty effort to free himself, then gave in to the inevitable and let the blackness wash over him. His final thought was of a girl he'd dated in high school, one of the first of many failed relationships. As he faded, he tried to recall her name... but it never came.

On the way home we'd driven past Theresa's old apartment. The light of a television showed that her former roommate was indeed at home, so I'd made half-hearted promises about going back another time for her photo album and the other, personal items she wanted. I was certainly that removing items with no cash value, just that of nostalgia, would be a very BAD idea as she'd undoubtedly been officially missing for several weeks...but:

   1) I could understand the sentimental attachment, and
   2) I wanted to keep her from doing anything stupid that might attract the attention of the authorities...

So, if empty promises helped her deal with her impatience, I was doing us both a favor. Theresa could sense that the vampire was deep in thought and, while she could not read his thoughts, exactly, she was able to gain a small Impression of his mood and what might be disturbing him. Clearly he was questioning the wisdom of the night's activities. She'd goaded him into killing someone—a cop, no less—when his entire existence was based on keeping a very low profile and not attracting any attention to himself. She'd made him put all of that at risk, simply because she wanted the thrill of the hunt, that and the satisfaction of making a kill. She could also tell that he was annoyed at her insistence on going back for personal items of sentimental value—little things, unimportant to anyone but herself, that would arouse suspicion if they went missing. She knew he liked her, but she also knew that, were she to present too great a risk, he was certainly capable of killing her to protect himself. So, what was she to do? Certainly she had to get back in his good graces, the sooner the better. But how? Obviously the best thing would be to get him to stop brooding and shift his thoughts to another topic. So, what could she do to change the subject? She needed to get him talking, but about what?

"You said something the other day that had me curious", she began, "you said the Biden administration didn't care about the environment, but didn't both the Obama and Biden campaigns focus a lot more on the environment, promoting the Paris Climate Accords and the Green New Deal and such and didn't Biden shut down the Keystone Pipeline and work to get the USA away from coal power and gas-powered vehicles?"

> Does 'the big con' translate into Japanese? Are you familiar with the concept? This is just another scam being perpetrated by the leftist administrations, just like 'Obamacare'. It's all about the money! For starters, the Trump administration did more to protect the environment than Obama ever did! Trump passed the National Resources Management Act, which expanded the amount of Federally-protected land and banned logging and mining and, if I remember correctly, even road construction in those areas and also added protections for other national parks. Among other things, I think they stopped people from uprooting hundred-year-old cacti to use in landscaping, but you'd have to fact-check me on that. Of course you won't see Trump get much credit—the internet is all full of hate towards anything that Trump accomplished, facts notwithstanding. I can look some of it up for you later.

As for the Paris Climate Accords, this was... or is... I'm not sure if the Biden administration has resurrected this like they did with the awful Iranian Nuclear Deal, but as it's bad for the USA and good for our enemies, they probably have. This pretended to be an international agreement to protect the environment but all it really was... is?... is a scam designed to tax the USA and transfer more of its wealth to other countries. The heart of it was/is a supposed 'carbon tax'. Now to begin with, carbon is the basic building block of all life on this planet, which you should know from Star Trek and other science fiction... and non-fiction... movies and literature. What these idiots claim is threatening the planet is, primarily, nothing more than carbon dioxide, CO_2, which is what trees breathe to give us oxygen.

You probably already know this, as I've read that Japan is an environmentally-conscious democracy with much cleaner cities than most other nations in Asia, yes? Okay, well you said you've been to China so you probably also know that socialist/communist countries, and military dictatorships, are the dirtiest and most environmentally-destructive governments because the people don't have the same type of political power as those in republican and democratic countries. Did you know that China produces so much pollution, particularly from the Bao Steel plants around Shanghai, that it pushes up the air pollution indexes on the west coast of the United States, thousands and thousands of miles away, on the other side of the Pacific Ocean? Well it does, and these supposed 'climate accords' didn't include China—which was probably funding the whole thing in the first place—on the list of countries they wanted to take responsibility for paying to limit carbon dioxide emissions. Stupid for one thing, ridiculous to think money was somehow going to fix the problem, not that CO_2 is actually a toxic gas or anything, and they didn't propose to make China reduce the sulphur or other crap they dump into the atmosphere.

Now there are other gasses in that magical term 'greenhouse gasses' that they use to scare everyone that actually are harmful, such as nitrous oxide, which decomposes into nitric acid and, as I just mentioned, sulfur dioxide, which combines with hydrogen in the atmosphere to produce sulfuric acid.

This is what leads to acid rain. You're too young to remember it, but this was a big deal back in the 1980's and early 1990's in Europe, when the forests were suffering from acid rain. It's not like they ever found a cure for it, either, but as more and more steel production shifted to first Japan and then to South Korea and China, the acid rain diminished. Go figure! The pollution didn't go away, it just moved to the magical land of 'somewhere else' and people stopped worrying about it. This is how managed to brainwash an entire generation of ecologists by getting them worked-up about the wrong issue and then sending them charging off in the wrong direction!

If they really cared about the environment, they'd be doing more to reduce the *pollution*, those toxic gasses that are causing damage to the environment—instead, they focus on CO_2, which is a key part of a healthy ecosystem. Needless to say, this subject wasn't part of the curriculum in Germany back in the 1790's, but Germans then, like Germans now, liked to relax by taking a nice walk in the woods or mountains or swimming in a lake, so after the internet was invented and I learned how to use a computer, I started reading of the acid rain harming the forests in Germany and studied up on the environment, etcetera. You have to wonder what they're teaching kids these days—so many of them seem to be completely ignorant!

Do you know some folks went around to college campuses with a petition to demand the government do something about H_2O and all the people it killed every year? They actually got dozens of people to sign this petition, just to show how completely oblivious these students were. Yes, I did say H_2O... water! And of course the information provided was true, H_2O *does* kill many people every year... from *drowning*! So, if these kids somehow managed to get through middle school and high school without knowing the basic chemical symbol for *water*, and are willing to sign a petition against it, what does that say about the intellectual level of today's college students? Anyway, feel free to check it out online—I think they did this on several different college campuses.

Getting back to your original question, yes, Biden has been bad for coal. I read recently that West Virginia has been losing a higher percentage of its population recently than even

California and New York, where people have been fleeing high taxes and ridiculous government policies. West Virginia's main export, of course, is coal. Now coal is not the cleanest fuel, it releases nitrous oxide and contains sulfur, although the amount released into the atmosphere depends on the type of coal—bituminous coal contains more sulphur while anthracite coal is much cleaner-burning, although naturally rarer and more expensive.

Humans have been using coal for a long time—I know, I have been around more than 200 years now. Want to know what people used before coal? Wood. Care to know why coal was considered a better fuel than wood? Coal is basically wood that's been compressed underground for millions of years: call it concentrated wood. You need less coal to produce heat than wood; it also produces more heat, allowing hotter temperatures for things like making steel.

Recently, they've converted some coal-burning power plants to natural gas. This is great because it is a cleaner-burning alternative and we have lots of natural gas, at least for now. Unfortunately—and here's where the BIG LIE comes in—they've converted other plants to burn what they're calling 'BIOMASS'. What does that mean? It means they're burning WOOD! Yes, they've built new power plants that burn wood chips, which has been great for the logging industry and the billionaires who've invested in the new power plants, but its driven-up the price of wood for housing, they've increased the number of trucks needed to transport the wood as it requires a lot more wood than coal to produce the same energy, which means a lot more oil for those trucks and they are destroying entire forests to get all the wood they need!

Isn't the idea, according to these climate charlatans at least, to reduce the amount of carbon dioxide in the atmosphere? Yet what is actually happening is they are using a less efficient, dirtier fuel than coal and cutting down hundreds of thousands of trees that would otherwise be turning that carbon dioxide into oxygen! At the same time, they are destroying the habitat of those animals that live in the forests, which hypocritical groups like the Sierra Club claim to want to protect, then they take millions of dollars in contributions from these organization that are destroying the forests!

Unfortunately, it's an even larger problem. The USA is exporting container ships of wood pellets to the UK to feed their power plants that have been converted to burn wood instead of coal—because the Brits have cut down all the forests they could spare and are running out of wood to burn, so they're now importing it from the USA and Canada! Certainly, trees are a renewable resource but do you know how many years it takes for trees to grow back? Pines grow pretty quickly but hardwoods take *decades*! How long will it be before they run out of trees to burn? And what about the poor animals that lost their habitats? They probably starve or get killed by automobiles or domestic dogs and cats and may never come back! And all the while this environmental devastation is occurring, the idiots out there are cheering because they have stopped the burning of 'dirty old coal' and never bothered to ask themselves what this 'biomass' is that's being burned in its place.

And some of the other proposed 'alternative fuels' are even more ridiculous. Apparently one company is using animal fat. Okay, great, that's something we used to use back in the 18th and 19th centuries. I know the Japanese still hunt whales; we used to use whale oil in lamps. I can even remember the smell—it was quite pleasant. In fact, a derivative of whale oil called ambergris was used quite extensively in perfume. In fact, I think it's still used in some very expensive perfumes to this day. The problem is, there aren't nearly enough whales left to use for electrical power, aside from the obvious desire to preserve whales from extinction—a given among true environmentalists, anyway.

So what will they use instead? Cows? Weren't the enviro-idiots blaming 'global-warming' on cow farts a few years back when they were still sounding alarms about warming until it because obvious the earth was actually in a long-term cooling period and then they changed the narrative to 'climate-change'. So what are we to do now, raise a thousand times as many cows so they can be used to fuel power generators? I'm not a scientist, but I hardly think that would be terribly efficient, although it might be a boon to the leather industry, not that I think there's any shortage of cow hides available these days.

Ever heard of Michael Moore? He is a guy who does documentaries and was really loved by the leftists because he looks like your basic conservative redneck yet he champions left-wing causes. He became famous with an anti-gun documentary that was full of historical inaccuracies, shoddy research, lies and distortions; they loved him for it! I always kind of figured he was a 'good old boy' who sold his soul to the devil in order to become a highly-paid monkey, dancing to whatever tune the Marxists/Globalists churned out on their organ-grinder. Then he came out with one called "Planet of Humans" that was factually accurate, as far as I could tell, and pointed out how these 'renewable energy' schemes *sound* great, but generally use *more* fossil fuels than they save. Suddenly the leftwing media and the libertards turned on him! They were okay when he was telling lies, as long as they conformed to their very narrow political views, but when he exposed the truth behind their climate scams, they were incensed.

As I recall from his video, there are scientists that spent time and research dollars to develop a way to use kelp as a fuel— when there's not nearly enough kelp available and pollution is killing the kelp forests—and even one who developed a fuel from alligators. For real? We're going to power cities burning alligator fat? I also recall a scene where machinery is destroying 500-year-old yucca plants to make room for a solar plant out in the desert that depends on natural gas to operate and will kill birds and other wildlife that accidentally wanders into the 'kill zone'. These yucca plants and Joshua Trees were probably the same types of vegetation that Trump had protected in Death Valley or wherever it was, yet the media kisses Creepy Joe's and Bath-House Barry's asses while "Orange Man Bad!" I don't know if the news media was ever really unbiased—Dan Rather certainly spread communist propaganda back during the Vietnam War—but it's certainly become much more biased these days, particularly with so much Chinese investment and something like 86% of all news media owned by something like 6 corporations. Again, it's all about the money—and if they can use Obamacare to limit people to using just a couple insurance companies by lying and saying it will lower people's insurance, when it does the opposite, or lie to people and say they will achieve 100% renewable energy, when they not only know it's impossible but that they are harming the environment in ways they aren't telling people about, they do it. Again, they *don't care* if they lie to people or if people pay more money for health care or if they ruin the planet as long as they make more money.

This is how some of these Millionaires and Billionaires operate. For some people, all they really care about is sex and how many people they can score with. Some just love to walk in and commune with nature. Some folks are rock-concert junkies and travel vast distances to hear their favorite bands. For others, it's love of family and/or country that drives their decision-making process. For others still, its getting their next 'fix' and staying high on drugs as much as possible. For the super-rich, money is like their drug. They don't care what the consequences are to others, or to the environment, as long as they keep amassing wealth. It's a game to them, along with buying-off members of the government and duping the public—that's what I was talking about before.

So, they enlist well-meaning fools to pressure members of government to go along with 'green' policies that actually aren't good for the environment. Wind and solar power not only depend on favorable weather to work—and kill a lot of birds in the process—they require batteries to store the power. Do you have any idea how much environmental impact is necessitated by the mining involved in making the turbines, solar panels and batteries? I can't tell you the exact numbers, but it's a lot! And these turbines and solar panels have a limited life and then need to be replaced. Those old wind turbines are actually toxic and non-recyclable and are an environmental threat in and of themselves. And, of course, since all of this less-efficient stuff is more expensive, the current scam is to use the government to force people into paying for it with their tax dollars. We're talking about trillions of dollars! Remember when you told me about these families in Japan that have to take out 100-year mortgages because the price of land is so high and their grandchildren end up paying off the mortgage? Well that's what the Biden government is doing with these idiotic policies, just pissing money away right and left on stupid shit! They're amassing generational debt; and, of course, paying some of those tax dollars out as bribes in the way of 'stimulus checks' and 'bailouts to bankrupt, Democrat-run state and local governments' to buy votes while they're at it—so people don't take to the streets in protest over $4 a gallon gasoline and double-digit inflation!

Theresa couldn't help feeling a little smug and awarded herself some mental 'brownie points' as her erstwhile roommate would have said. With just one question she'd not only distracted him and gotten him thinking of something else, she'd hit on something he obviously cared deeply about and now he was on a rant! This was something she'd noticed about him recently. When she'd first met him, he was unaccustomed to long conversations and made occasional errors in English with slips into French and German. Now, after daily conversations with her, he was far more eloquent in English and obviously relished the chance to espouse on subjects on which he was knowledgeable. Of course he was highly intelligent and had over 200 years of memories to draw upon, so he was highly informed and might even be the most knowledgeable individual on the planet! He also apparently liked to hear himself talk and show-off his wisdom. That was fine with her; anything that kept him talking kept him thinking about other things. She was determined to keep him interested enough in her to value keeping her around, but it was possible he might tire of sex with her someday, so being a fantastic audience-of-one was yet another way to stay in his good graces. Maybe someday she would be ready to strike off on her own, but with no car, no place of her own and no money, she really had nowhere to go and no way to get there. So, at least for the time being, the best strategy was to keep him interested.

"What about electric cars?" she interjected, "aren't the batteries for them and the solar power plants rechargeable?"

> For a time, but eventually they lose their ability to hold a
> charge and need to be replaced, just like any batteries.
> There is an automobile boneyard outside of Paris that I read
> an article about where they have this exact problem. Paris
> decided to 'go green' and purchased a fleet of electric cars.
> After so a few years the battery cells wore out and needed
> to be replaced. The problem is, the cost of the battery cells
> have increased and cost much more than a new vehicle.
> Also, there apparently aren't any recycling centers or

landfills that will accept them, so these hundreds of cars are just sitting there, rusting away, with toxic chemicals leaking out of them and leaching into the soil. Does this sound like 'saving the planet' or is this causing more pollution? But people are okay with it as long as their tiny corner of the world is cleaner and the additional pollution is happening somewhere else. People think electric cars are a great thing because the air is cleaner; the air in the immediate area surrounding the electric car, anyway. Those cars have to be charged. Where does the power come from to charge the cars? Again, it comes from that magical place of 'somewhere else', usually coal or nuclear power plants, or those plants I mentioned that are putting forests up the smokestacks and using natural gas to burn them! Even worse, there is a power loss during transmission: if that power has to travel hundreds of miles over copper wires, you lose power along with way. It's much less efficient than a gasoline engine—a gasoline engine that doesn't require hundreds of pounds of lithium and other rare-earth metals for the battery that will have to be replaced a few years down the road.

Come to think of it, I actually had a battery-powered lawnmower back in the 1970's. It came with 2 batteries so if one ran down while you were cutting the grass, the other one could finish the job while the first one was charging, which took awhile, as I recall. Of course my lawn out front is not huge; it took the Amish kid I hired maybe 30 or 40 minutes to cut it... again, maintaining appearances—I keep the place looking like someone lives here and maintains it during the daytime. Anyway, point is that after maybe 5 years or so the batteries didn't hold enough of a charge anymore so I threw the damn thing away and bought a gas-powered Toro that ran for a good 25 years or so before it needed to be replaced. That was when things were still made in this country, before everything was short-lived junk made in China!

"When I was in Shanghai", Theresa interrupted, "I was standing on a bridge once and watched as the entire river turned red. Some company must have been pouring paint or dye into the river and on out into the

ocean. An older couple I talked to there told me the city used to be relatively clean—after they rebuilt after the Japanese, who did a lot of damage in Shanghai as well as the terrible things they did in Nanjing".
"Like the rape and murder of hundreds of thousands of people in Nanking?"
"Yes, like that. As someone half-Japanese I'm really sad about that and feel...guilty, even though I didn't have anything to do with it. Anyway, this older couple told me about how, when they lived in Nanjing back in the 1980's, then Shanghai in the 1990's, the air was clean, the water was safe to drink, and pollution wasn't anything they worried about."

"Of course just about everyone rode bicycles back then, right?"

True. Even in the 1990's, people took trains or buses or rode bicycles—lots of bicycles! There were taxis, but otherwise few private cars and very few motorcycles—only the very few rich people back then could afford them and there weren't as many roads back then. Nowadays, with China getting rich from so much manufacturing moving to China from other countries, especially some of the dirtier, heavy industry, and people buying probably millions of cars and motorcycles, the air and water is dirty, cases of cancer have increased, respiratory illnesses have increased greatly—so yes, the environment is probably cleaner in the west than it was when there was more manufacturing here, but the pollution was just moved to China and other countries and the total pollution is probably worse, world-wide, but I doubt anyone has measured it to let us know. So, what was it you were saying about the pipeline? How was Biden canceling it bad for the environment?

Just because the Keystone Pipeline was canceled, do you think people in the USA stopped using any less oil? Of course not, especially coming out of both winter and the Covid lockdowns, there were a lot more people driving and using gasoline! So, where do you think the oil is coming from that would otherwise have been coming through the pipeline? Since Biden also used executive orders to cancel oil leases in southwestern states, that means more oil coming in oil tankers. Tankers tend to leak into the ocean, with the occasional environmental disaster like the Exxon Valdez. Once the oil arrives, it has to be moved, either by truck or rail. Either way it usually ends up being hauled by truck for at least part of the distance, and trucks burn gas. One truck tanker only carried so much oil, whereas a pipeline can move an almost infinite about of oil once it's in place. So, a pipeline is much more efficient and creates much less pollution.

Anyway, that's my big gripe with these modern-day environmentalists: they have been brainwashed into focusing on the wrong problems! Instead of worrying about carbon dioxide, they should be focused on pollution: chemicals that are actually dangerous, harming the environment and causing health issues for humans and animal life. If there's actually too much CO_2, which I doubt, all we need is more trees—trees love CO_2, which they 'breathe' to give us oxygen! Instead, companies are now clear-cutting entire forests to burn, inefficiently, which means fewer trees to convert CO_2 into O_2! This is especially worrisome in places like Brazil, because rain forests produce most of the oxygen on the planet, yet they're destroying the forests there at a truly horrific rate! So, all things considered, don't you think we'd be better off with coal? Or at least using natural gas instead of 'biomass'?

"I'm convinced", Theresa said in her most sincere and convincing voice, "you should write an article to the WSJ or something!" Snuggling up to him, she added, "So what would you like to do tonight?"

Chapter 25
Armed for Battle...

“I can't believe you'd never seen *Saving Private Ryan* before. How did you like it?" Theresa lay sprawled on the bed, wearing a tiny black négligée with clean lines, no lace (she'd learned her benefactor wasn't a fan... and, after all it was he who had purchased it online).

"Wow," was all she could think of at first, "war is so terrible...and yet sometimes so heroic, and then there's also cowardice and compassion".

"Fair enough, all so true, but I was actually asking what you thought about the movie as a production. What did they do right; what did they do wrong? Some things about this movie are so well done it's astonishing: realism that Hollywood usually just never gets right. On the other hand, there are mistakes that are so fucking enormous they piss the hell out of me every time I watch it!"

"Um, I really don't know," she admitted, "after all, you've been in wars, my grandfather was in World War II, but it's nothing I really know anything about other than from movies".

OK, first let's talk about things they did right. One of the huge mistakes made by the D-Day planners is that they outfitted soldiers with 90 lb packs, everything they'd need for several days of continued action, and then expected them to run a couple hundred meters up to the sea wall. They showed this at the beginning of the movie... some poor bastard trudging along with this heavy pack, making himself a perfect target for a German machine gun. Maybe you noticed that the men who made it to the high-water line had already dropped their packs and one guy had even dropped his BAR, which was a type of nearly-obsolete and very heavy 'light' machine gun. They also showed a guy drowning because he couldn't get his heavy pack off. All this was historically accurate.

They also showed a guy stop and pick up his severed arm and then run for cover. Even in a major hospital, they probably wouldn't have been able to reattach it. On a beach under heavy fire—impossible! However, wounded soldiers go into shock and that's exactly the type of thing people do! They say, "hey, I need that" and pick up body parts that will never go back on. What really pisses me off about that beach scene is how close they were to actually getting every detail correct and then how stupidly they fucked it all up!

Remember the scene when the captain stands in the open to draw the machine-gun fire so he can help the sniper get into position? All that was well and good until the sniper fires his Springfield rifle... firing a tiny little bullet... and the entire sandbag position explodes outward, spilling sandbags and machine-gunners all over the place! Fucking ridiculous! Even if he'd fired a rifle grenade it probably would have had little effect, but they didn't show one, his rifle didn't have a grenade-firing adaptor on the barrel, and if he'd fired one from the shoulder, in the position he was shown in taking the shot, he'd have dislocated his shoulder from the recoil! Do you know what happens when you shoot a sandbag with a rifle? You get a tiny hole in the sandbag and maybe some sand leaks out; you DO NOT blow up the entire fortification! That would have been bad enough, but then they REALLY fuck things up!

Pausing for a moment, I decided to really make my point. "Wait here," I commanded. Entering the adjoining room, I pushed the door closed behind me as I flipped on the light switch, revealing a very narrow room. Unlike most of the rest of the house, which was adorned with seasoned hardwoods and antique but tasteful wallpaper, this room was lined with cheap wood paneling. A threadbare sofa butted-up against the wall separating it from my bedroom/office/library, a low, well-used rectangular coffee table stood in front of it, festooned with a smattering of old magazines, mostly '70's and '80's vintage PLAYBOYs, and a couple of ashtrays. Completing the furnishings were a pair of equally hard-worn armchairs and a small but sturdy end table with a lamp upon it. In all respects, the room looked ordinary, uninteresting, and even boring, just as was intended. Lifting the lamp and placing it on the floor, I carried the end table over to the barren, unadorned wall opposite the sofa, and placed it on the floor.

Standing on it, I lifted a panel of the false ceiling, sliding it back to reveal a mere 4 inches of space between the top of the wall and the main floor above it. Reaching over the wall nearly as far as my arm could reach, I located the bent top of the piece of iron bar-stock I had fashioned so many years prior. Twisting it 90 degrees and pulling up on it, I unlocked the secret door. Pulling it towards me, the previously solid-looking paneling parted and revealed an opening. It took considerable effort to hold it up so it wouldn't scratch the floor, as it was rather heavy. Behind the sheet of paneling was a frame of 2x4s, which I'd painstakingly cemented into what was essentially a brick wall in a wooden frame—if it anyone rapped on it, it would seem quite solid and not at all hollow. Stepping down from the table and pushing the door open into the secret room, I flipped on the dim, overhead light.

Occupying much of the hidden room was a large, glass-enclosed structure. I'd built this to house my most precious works of art. It was climate-controlled and, as it was never exposed to bright lighting, it kept my treasures in perfect condition. The rest of the room was surrounded with racks and shelves on which rested and hung hundreds of rifles, pistols, shotguns, machine guns, knives, swords and even a few medieval weapons. I even had an original Viking chain-mail tunic. About the only thing I lacked was a suit of plate armor. My father had had one of our ancestor's armor and weapons displayed in the family manor house (not quite a castle, but close enough). There was one for jousting, with a helmet with a solid front and only a small slit for seeing through, and another, more practical suit for actual warfare. I'd always hoped to be able to purchase those someday, but for now they were in a private collection and "not for sale," although their solicitor had my name and address on file, should they ever consider selling off their assets.

In any case, my attention was focused on the end of the room to my right, wherein lay 2 wooden pallets on the floor and on them were stacked case upon case of ammunition, bottles and kegs of gunpowder, and even some century-old artillery shells. After only a moment's search, I found what I was looking for. Moving the case of Wolf 12 gauge buckshot off of it, I picked it up and carried it back to the bedroom, making sure to pull the door closed behind me (some secrets I wasn't yet ready to share with my companion, however dear to me she was becoming).

"This is a .50 cal ammo can, holding 880 rounds of 30.06 ammunition in Garand clips," I explained to my somewhat-uncomprehending piece of Asian pussy, "this is about half of a case of standard ammunition for the US army during World War II and most likely almost exactly the same thing a lot of the soldiers would have carried onto the beach on D-Day. Come here!" With a supple, smooth movement I could never have managed when I was a teenager, she swung herself out of bed, giving me a momentary "beaver shot" as she did so. Straightening in order to walk over to me, I again congratulated myself for guessing the correct length of garment... it was just long enough to conceal her pubes, but short enough to reveal her bush almost every time she moved. It's not that I had grown tired of seeing her naked—far from it—but sex is mostly mental, at least sensuality is, at any rate, and getting a quick flash was more exciting than having the same, unchanging view all the time. I think it was Larry Flint who criticized the older Playboy Magazines of being "bare and square". Of course I preferred those to the newer ones where they shaved off the entire bush for their "pedophile audience." After all, Hugh Heffner had had a point: sometimes leaving things to the imagination was more arousing... like the suspenseful build-up in a Hitchcock movie. Having erogenous zones partially concealed just made it that much more enjoyable when the anticipation was finally greeting with revelation.

Now she was standing in front of me and I was able to enjoy her moderate cleavage while searching for an elusive nipple. Again, it was the anticipation that made it more interesting.

Shifting my hands to the sides of the can, so she could grasp the handle, I held it out in front of me. "Take it; hold it with both hands". As she did so, I let go. Knowing what would happen next, I was already moving as I released it and was able to catch it a few inches off the ground, just before it would have smashed into her bare feet and probably caused injury.

She jumped back out of harm's way, shaking one wrist in pain. "Damn that's heavy!"

"Quite so!" Picking up the remote, I restarted the movie, skipping through chapters until 20 minutes in, then quickly fast-forwarded to the "That's quite a view" scene. "Now," I said, "watch this and tell me what's wrong". As expected, my clever little minx figured it out at once.

"The boxes and cans are floating on the water! That can't be possible!"

> Precisely! You just felt how heavy ammo cans and crates are when full. Obviously they wouldn't be floating, or even moving at all in the waves, unless they were empty. Are we supposed to believe that, while under heavy fire, some soldiers opened the ammo cans, emptied them, then paused long enough to close the lids, replaced the empty cans and then nailed the tops back on the wooden crates!? This is totally bullshit! They spent a ton of time and millions of dollars staging this elaborate beach scene, totally realistic in almost every respect, and then ruin it with the stupid sniper scene and obviously unopened ammo cans floating on the fucking tide! Couldn't they have hired some beachcomber at minimum wage to spend an hour shoveling sand into the cans and crates? This blatant disregard for the laws of physics ruins so many movies by turning scenes into unbelievable horseshit. Do Hollywood writers and directors really think their audiences are that stupid or is it just that *they* are that stupid?

"Maybe it's both. I saw a video on YouTube of a guy interviewing US college students. They knew all about celebrities, but couldn't answer basic questions like 'who fought in the Civil War'. I grew up on the other side of the planet and even I know it was the Confederate States of America versus the United States aka The Union!"

I'm not at all surprised! I read an article recently where a researcher looked into the reasons why the modern generation graduates high school knowing less than 7th graders did 100 years ago. He blamed most of it on how liberalism has destroyed academic standards, but also added a good measure of disrespect for video games and cell-phone app usage. Want to know what he called them? Vampire phones! As the phones get smarter they suck the intelligence out of their users, making them more stupid. I liked the analogy so much I have used it myself, as you know. You're one of these young college students with a smart-phone, or at least you were a student recently, do you agree with his assessment?

"Vampire phones...obviously not in a literal sense, like us, but I can really see his point. I can't believe some of these idiots running cash registers who can't do simple math, like when the bill is $16 and you had them a twenty and a one because you want a five back and they try to give you the $1 bill back, thinking it was a mistake and you have to explain it to them three times!" Smiling sweetly, she deftly changed the subject, "after all that love-making, I need a shower!"

Sensing it was already twilight, I dismissed her to deal with her personal hygiene, while I replaced the ammo and checked on the humidity and temperature of my art 'humidor' (after all, with a value I estimated to be at least $10 million USD, it didn't hurt to check on them from time-to-time!). I also checked to be sure the small (and very quiet) freezer was still running. In it were stored about 50 bags of whole blood I'd stolen from a company that supplied hospitals. I had no idea what freezing would do to the blood—but I figured it would tide me by in the case of an emergency. After all, a few years ago we'd had about 5 feet of snow, which made getting out to the cattle barn somewhat hard to explain for a supposedly feeble old man in a wheelchair. I also checked the dates I'd scribbled with a felt-tip marker on my small supply of canned food.

The food wasn't for myself, of course, it was for the occasional female guest as well as for appearances sake, just in case. Expiration dates on canned food were always on the conservative side—often they were good for many years beyond their printed shelf life, but I pulled out a couple that were past their prime. I intentionally purchased things the dogs liked, such as double-meat ravioli, so that they didn't go to waste. Of course they filled another particularly useful purpose as well—making my trash appear more "ordinary".

Sure, I always had beer and wine bottles in the recyclables, but the occasional empty food gave an appearance of normality. Given the garden and the chickens, it could be assumed I produced a lot of my own food, but I didn't want Miguel or anyone else becoming suspicious. Heck, at Thanksgiving I even purchased a turkey or goose, froze most of it after cooking it, and fed most of it to the cat and the dogs in stages while also sending some "leftovers" home with Miguel. I usually did the same with a ham at Christmas. Once in a great while I even fed the animals a chicken (usually one of my own that was getting on in age) and maybe every 3 years or so I'd order a pizza. The pizza went to the dogs (sometimes the cat would lick some of the sauce and he liked the ground beef topping) and the box went in the recyclable bin.

Why not? I could afford it, and keeping up appearances helped me maintain my anonymity. I even went so far as to occasionally lift empty food containers—particularly things I had no use for, such as orange juice cartons—from nearby neighbors when I went prowling at night and then deposited them in my own recycling bin... all to keep up appearances that I was an ordinary person eating ordinary food. After all, I'd worked long and hard to create a persona that would not elicit any untoward interest from anyone in the community; attention to detail never hurt!

Chapter 26
Far Away Eyes...

Sheriff Gene Miller knew something was up the moment he walked into the office; the tension was almost palpable. "OK, what's the poop?"

"A city patrolman was found dead of an apparent suicide"

"Anyone we know?"

"A mister Scott Foster... apparently he wasn't that popular; he didn't show for work and it took three days for someone to send a unit around to check on him."

"How'd he do it?"

"It looks like he slit his wrists in the bathtub with a kitchen knife. Apparently he'd had a bad breakup with a girlfriend recently, but the guys who knew him best said he hadn't seemed particularly torn-up about it. The detective on the scene apparently thought something was out of the ordinary as she called in the crime unit; they're going-over the place now. The girlfriend has already been ruled-out as a suspect as she was out-of-state the entire week, although there hasn't been any suggestion yet of any 'foul play'. That's all I know so far."

Scott Foster... Gene seemed to recall he'd heard scuttlebutt that Foster had been investigated for improper conduct on at least one occasion. As he had relatively little contact with city cops other than the police chief and some of the more senior officers, he couldn't even put a face to the name.

"Well," Gene added unnecessarily, "keep me posted"

"Will do!"

Chapter 27
Kill one man, you're a Murderer...

Theresa had grabbed fresh undergarments and of course a fresh shirt (the blouse she'd worn last was soaking in water with some bleach in a laundry tub; she hoped the cop's blood wouldn't leave a stain) but was wearing the same black jeans she'd worn the night of her first murder... not counting the calf, of course. She'd practically flown up the stairs, not knowing how much time she could count on for privacy, and fished out of the back pocket of the pants the one thing she'd stolen, unobtrusively, from the cop's coffee table—his smart phone! Scanning quickly through the menu, she found the icon that let her select Wi-Fi providers. There was only one that appeared and, naturally, it had a password! "Damn!"

She checked to be sure it was still on silent mode—a ringing phone would have been a dead-giveaway—after all, her vampire-lover had been adamant about his rule of "no calls, letters or emails!" Still, she really had to find a way to let her mom know she was OK. Slipping the phone back in her pocket, she brushed her teeth, clipped a few split-ends, and had barely begun her shower when she had company. At first he just stood there, watching, which always made her feel a little embarrassed and as if she were being naughty somehow. After several long moments, he joined her. This time he wasn't seeking sex... after all, they'd just finished a long session of daytime lovemaking; Theresa discovering that his having fed on a human gave his dick a lot more power and he'd almost worn her out as he'd fucked her again and again. No, at the moment he was only interested in getting clean, particularly removing the peculiar-smelling 'joy jelly' (in this case, Crisco) he'd heated and used to make them both feel more like they were having sex with a live person rather than an undead one. Well, maybe he was *mostly* interested in getting clean—he certainly took advantage of the opportunity to 'scope her out' and 'feel her up' as her American classmates might have said.

Showered and dried, he'd smiled in the mirror over her shoulder as she was studying her eyebrows and lashes and offered, "Can I take you to dinner?" Once again, Theresa was glad of his sense of humor. "Certainly, kind sir, what shall we have tonight, French cuisine?"

"Sorry to disappoint, but I think all my cattle are of English and Scottish ancestry." Theresa dressed quickly and told him with her most endearing smile, "I'm hungry, um, thirsty, uh famished! I guess British bovine blood will have to do!"

They made the familiar trip out to the pasture. Theresa fretted with impatience as he stopped to feed the dogs and cat first—she'd have preferred some extra time alone in the house, but it was well past dark and the animals had no doubt been waiting some time for their dinner. The dogs were much more tolerant of her these days, but she wasn't about to try to pet one while they were eating; she'd heard some dogs didn't like to be bothered and might bite. She contented herself with scratching Caesar behind the ears while he crunched his dried cat food. He rumbled a satisfied purr, but didn't move from his food.

The animals taken care of, they went to the back for the needle and medical tubing, as well as a halter, which they often used to secure a cow's head while feeding; some of them resented being pricked with the needle. There was a chill in the air and gray clouds shrouded the moon. A distant smell of burning leaves, somewhere off in the distance, lay like a pall over the normal, farm smells of straw, hay, mud, grass—and of course cow shit! She wished she'd worn a jacket. While the cold didn't bother her as much as it used to when she was a mere mortal, she still felt the cold. It was obvious winter was approaching earlier this year. Thinking about it, she realized Halloween was just 2 days off. She wondered what sort of things vampires did to celebrate 'ghost night'. She'd have to remember to ask later.

Glad that she was given the chance to drink first, she did so with relish, enjoying the warmth of the fresh blood trickling down her throat, even though she still didn't really care for the taste. As she reached the point where her thirst was sated, she intentionally allowed some blood to splash on her white T-shirt. "Oh my! I had better soak this right away or it will stain! Why don't you finish without me?

Hardly waiting for the reply, she turned and made for the gate, then decided to take the more direct route. She hurdled the barbed-wire fence like an Olympic high-jumper and walked rapidly towards the house, breaking into a sprint once she was around the corner of the barn and out of sight. Her shirt was in her hand before she had even reached the porch and she dashed down the stairs to the laundry/storage room. It only took a moment to toss it in a plastic tub her other shirt and add some detergent and enough water to submerge it entirely. Entering the main room in the basement, she hurried went over to the computer desk. As she remembered, there was a post-it note on the modem that provided the Wi-Fi connection for the computer as well as the cable for the TV. The smart phone already in her hand, she entered the number in the password field. She had to do it twice because she was so nervous about being caught. Success!

She'd guessed correctly that Stanislaus, or 'Stan' as she'd begun calling him, might have written down the password in case of tech issues, just so he wouldn't forget. The next thing was to install the LINE application. It wasn't commonly used in the USA, but it was the big thing in Japan and Taiwan; and it was a free download. Fortunately, her stolen phone had internet search options on the screen, so she didn't have to search through the menus. Standing next to the stairs, so she could hear if Stan came in, she stamped her foot with impatience as the LINE App slowly installed.

Finally! She knew the vampire would drink from a different steer, or maybe one of the bulls, so as not to take too much blood from a single animal, and then he'd clean the equipment and usually took a walk around the property just to check on things, but she didn't really know how much time she was going to have. She also wasn't sure how long the battery was going to last, and once it died, she'd be locked out by the cop's password even if she were able to charge it later, somehow. Entering her user name, she congratulated herself on picking a user name easy enough to remember. She was in! She used the LINE app for communications with most of her friends and family in Asia, for those in the USA she was quickly able to log in and access her emails (re-installing her other 'chat' applications would have to wait until later).

Damn! She had tons of messages! Quickly, she clicked on her mom's last message and tapped out an apology, saying she'd found a job and hadn't had internet access while she was moving to a new place and someone had stolen her phone and she hadn't been able to buy a new one until she'd had a few paychecks because she also had to find money for rent, the deposit on her new apartment, etc. And, of course, she was OK and she was enjoying her new job and she'd say more later on.

She copied the message to a couple friends in Japan—in English, of course, as that's what the default language was set for, hoping they'd understand, then scrolled pretty much the same things to send to her friends in the USA, twitching impatiently the entire time. Again, she had a real *shitload* of messages! Not bothering to read any of them, she quickly copied and pasted the message to everyone that was important to her, not that there were that many, unfortunately. To her friends she still kept in touch with who still played vampire role-playing games, such as

Masquerade and Requiem, she added a quick 'you'll never guess what happened to me! Really, just try and guess!'.

She'd started reading some of the seemingly endless string of messages when she realized she had another problem—battery life! The phone was showing about a 50% charge and was undoubtedly passworded, meaning that once the battery died, she would never be able to use it again. She didn't dare turn it off and she only had a day or two to figure out how to charge it and she didn't have any cables! While she was trying to puzzle out a solution, she heard the vampire close the kitchen door. Swiftly dashing to the bedroom, she concealed the phone under the mattress and grabbed a shirt from the one drawer that was now hers, pulling it on hastily and then took a deep breath, trying to calm herself down.

Hearing the sound of boot heels on the wooden steps, she went out to try to put phase two of her plan into action. Throwing a big hug around her lover/captor, she dangled from him with her arms around his neck and gave him a mischievous smile. "It's almost Halloween. What are we going to do to celebrate?"

"Nothing. We're out in the country, we don't get trick-or-treaters and we certainly aren't going to throw a party"

"Well, can't we have our own party? Can I borrow one of your cars and some cash so I can go buy some decorations and a couple bottles of nice wine? I can get some things to make costumes too, if you'll join me. Maybe we can even go to a bar and pick someone up for dinner!"

Actually, before you came along, Halloween was the one night for certain every year I used to go out hunting. After all, you can wear a disguise, even gloves, and nobody thinks anything of it. Of course these days I try very hard *not* to do anything to draw attention to myself. As for you going shopping, you're still a 'missing person', what if someone recognizes you? That and stores nowadays all have security cameras; it's just not worth the risk. Tell you what, I'll go to the store for you and get whatever you want, how's that?

But how can I know what I want until I get there and see what they have? Tell you what, I'll wear a hat and scarf and sunglasses so nobody can see my face. I can wear some of your clothes and nobody will recognize me. Come on, I have been stuck in this house for weeks! Besides, you said we could break into my apartment so I could get my passport and photos and some of my clothes... what better time to do it than on Halloween when we can be all dressed-up in masquerade, if that's the right way to say it!

She hung there, doing her best impish act, smiling up at him while wishing she could do a Jedi Mind-Trick. Clearly he was at least thinking about it. After several long moments, finally she got her wish as he smiled down at her and said, "OK, let's go shopping"

She'd made herself up, putting some color on her face to help her look more 'western', but had been told the scarf wrapped around her face was "too weird for Indiana" Eventually they'd settled on a medical mask to go with her nurse's outfit. Of course even medical personnel usually didn't wear them outside of the OR, unlike Taiwan where people frequently wore then on the street on public transportation and particularly when riding a scooter or motorcycle, because of the smog, but they'd decided if she coughed frequently people would conclude she had a cold and was being considerate by not sharing her germs; which was another common practice in both Japan and Taiwan and something Theresa felt should eventually catch on in the USA, especially with all the exciting new diseases being brought in by unscreened immigrants from third-world countries. After all, they were still dealing with a typhus outbreak or something like that in California, and she remembered hearing about a new SARS outbreak somewhere, maybe in Minnesota.

As she'd hoped, 'Stan', always the gentleman, had dropped her at the door and then driven off to find a place in the crowded parking lot. Trying to move swiftly but not so much as to draw attention to herself, Theresa had grabbed a shopping basket and headed directly to the electronics department. It took a few minutes, but she quickly located what she was seeking—a standard USB cord to charge her stolen smart phone. Dropping it in the basket, she wandered over to the nearby bath and shower department and pretended to look at the sample shower curtains that were hanging there. Sliding the basket up her arm, so that both her hands were free, she slipped the small item behind one of the curtains and deftly peeled the sturdy plastic packaging from off the USB cable, which she then dropped into the top of her open handbag, dropping the empty husk of plastic (and any security device it might contain) behind the curtain, where it was likely to remain undiscovered for some time. She hoped she'd done it in such a way as to conceal her movements from any store security who might be watching her courtesy of overhead surveillance cameras.

Theresa had never stolen anything in her life, no matter how poor or desperate she had been, and it haunted her conscience even now that she was a murderer, but she knew she had to keep the existence of the phone a secret if she wanted to continue using it. Finding enough time to keep it charged using the one PC in the house, which was of course in the basement where both of them spent most of their time was going to be tricky, but at least now it was an option. At least she felt she had a decent chance of getting away with it. After all, how often do people look *behind* their computer towers when they're located beneath their desks (as the vampire's was)? She could have also attempted to steal a DC adaptor and plug the phone into a wall outlet, but that would have been even more obvious, so she felt she had chosen the plan with the least amount of risk.

Making her way to the Halloween section, she arrived just before her companion and managed to appear as though she'd been there already, browsing. After opting for some cute LED ghost and pumpkin lights, some paper bats and a DIY giant spider-web complete with an accordion-style fold-out giant spider, she'd assembled a costume for her and a cape for him, along with a bottle of fake blood, just in case. "I'll do the makeup for both of us—I just need some foundation, blush and lipstick...oh, and a long, black skirt for me."

Her holiday shopping complete, they'd picked out several bottles of wine and some hard cider... and a bag of candy for Miguel's kids—and just to have some on hand in the very unlikely event of 'Trick-or-Treaters', which was not a rural past-time. Those parents with small children out in farm country drove them to well-to-do subdivisions in the suburbs and followed them around for an hour or so as they got the better candy in the wealthier neighborhoods. Walking hundreds of yards if not miles between homes out in the countryside would have been a very disappointing way to collect free candy!

Theresa felt happier than she had in some time. She hadn't left the farm more than a couple of times since her arrival, so just getting out was a cause for celebration. She was looking forward to decorating the house and then playing dress-up: COSPLAY, as it was called nowadays. She was going to enjoy her little, inside joke: 2 real vampires dressing up as phony vampires for Halloween. At least she was finally finding ways to have fun in her 'unlife'!

Chapter 28
Deathly Hallows Eve?

Miguel had finished his daily chores and, as was his custom, picked up the mail from the box down by the street, then carried it up the 200 foot or so sloping driveway to the old, brick farmhouse. As was often the case since the nurse's arrival, the front door was both unlocked and ajar. He had only set his first, cowboy-booted foot on the steps up to the porch when a hearty, female voice from deep in the house called, "come on in, I'm in the parlor".

It had been weeks since he'd last seen her out in the garden, with her bonnet, sunglasses, work gloves and sometimes a scarf tied around her face. Of course that had been summer and now it was autumn, so less tending was required and Miguel had been tasked with the "dirty" work of harvesting the onions, potatoes, pumpkins and other gourds and tubers. There were still a few die-hard tomatoes, but the lettuce had all gone to seed long ago and the herbs had all been cut and hung for drying.

Of course he didn't mind the work—much of what he harvested either went home to his family, or to a little roadside co-op vegetable stand he'd built and his wife operated seasonally, from which they kept any and all profits. He didn't take advantage of the old man—not much, anyway. The old man treated him quite generously and he knew it. Just last week, he'd been told to stop by after dinner, just before dark, and had been given several bushels full of corn, beans and pumpkins and told there would be more soon, along with some potatoes. With the price of food these days, the value of these handouts often exceeded a day's pay. Yes, he knew he was more fortunate than most people in his situation, especially as he wasn't even required to pay rent for the mobile home he lived in on the corner of the property, not even utilities!

Leaving the mail on the kitchen table, he walked through and on into the parlor. Always darkened, to protect the antique furniture, fabrics and paintings, the old man had once told him in this very room. Now, however, a multi-hued glow was emanating from the doorway. Curious! Even before entering, he'd encountered a strange, heavy odor. It was somewhat smoky, somewhat musky, yet unlike any scent with which he was familiar. After a long pause, a word came to mind: incense. The girl was burning incense in a room full of antique furniture and oil paintings. While Miguel was certainly no expert in such things, he questioned the wisdom of such...not to mention the fact she was hanging light strings and Halloween decorations across picture frames he was certain were around 100 years old or more. Well, it was none of his business. "Anything you want me to tell Mr. Miller," the nurse asked, obviously enjoying herself with her party decorating, although Miguel was skeptical the old man actually had any friends whom he might invite to a party. Maybe he was allowing the girl to invite some of her friends over to the house? Again, it was none of his business.

"No, miss", was his reply.

"I have to take Stan... um... that is... um... Mr. Miller, to a hospital in Chicago for some tests. We may be gone a couple of days. He asked me to ask you to watch over the place while we're gone. There is some food for the animals on the porch, he'd leave you the key but he plans to set the alarm system while we're away. Oh, I almost forgot..." Theresa turned around, looking quite nice from behind in her white nurses outfit and white stockings, he observed, then presented him with a softball-sized, orange, plastic pumpkin, stuffed with candy. "This is for your kids: Happy Halloween!"

"Many thanks to you...and Mr. Miller," Miguel bowed and rapidly made an exit. He wasn't sure why exactly, but recently the girl made him feel— nervous! It also seemed a bit strange that she'd be decorating for Halloween when they were going out of town. Did the Japanese even celebrate Halloween? He doubted it. The old man had never decorated for ANY holidays, EVER! Strange... Another thing: she'd called him 'Stan'. Miguel had brought the old man's mail to the house for years: he'd seen "William" on most of them, with the occasional 'Will' or 'Bill' and even a 'Wilhelm', but 'Stan'? This was peculiar to say the least.

Maybe she'd spoken a Japanese word? Yes, that was probably it, like maybe the word for 'boss' or 'employer'. The extent of his Japanese was limited to Sapporo, Nippon and Ichi Ban. He'd learned that Nippon meant Japan and Ichi Ban meant Number One and he was proud that he'd figured this out himself while sharing a six pack with one of his friends who worked at one of the local factories that welded vehicle frames and chassis together. Also, he realized he was angry with himself that he hadn't even asked what kind of tests; did his employer have cancer? An even worse thought hit him: was his employer going to die? Miguel had no illusions regarding being able to find a better job at his age, with his lack of education and inadequate language skills. His English was much better than it had been, but the only thing that had allowed him to get this job in the first place was that his boss spoke perfect French, which was similar enough to Spanish that they'd managed to communicate after a fashion...with a fair amount of body language and note-scribbling thrown in.

Miguel decided on the spot that, this weekend, he'd set-up his old VHS player to record any football or soccer games he'd usually have stayed home to watch. It was time to join the family and attend Mass and say a few prayers for the man who'd given him and his family a place to live and food on their table for many years. Certainly, God blessed generous people like old man Miller and would at least help him to hang-on until the last of Miguel's kids had finished high school...wouldn't He? Anyway, he'd light a candle and make a donation...maybe $10? He wanted to be sure his prayer was heard. While he'd sent enough American dollars home over the years that his brother had purchased him a small bit of land with a small house for him back in Mexico, his kids were still making their way through school in the USA and if he moved back to Mexico he'd have to kick his brother out of said house he was currently living in (for a very modest rent).

No, it was better if things went on as they were for at least another few years, at least until his kids became "legal" in the USA somehow. Maybe he'd offer up $20 with the candle and go to confession; God alone knew when his last time to confession had been. At least he had little to confess—hopefully that would help make up for the fact that he usually avoided going to church whenever there was a conflict with televised sporting events!

I'd considered taking Theresa to Chicago for Halloween. After all, I owned a safe-house there: one of my other pieces of real estate. It was a small, 3-story, 30-unit limestone apartment building on the southwest side of downtown. A property-management agency rented out the aboveground floors for a small sum...which was reduced to only a modest income after management fees, upkeep and taxes. Much of the surrounding area was severely run-down, which kept rents to a minimum despite the fact it was a decent enough structure for its age, having had several renovations, including modern lighting and heating.

What I kept for my own use was a drive-in, underground parking area and basement. One of the things that had attracted me to the property in the first place was that it had originally had a coal cellar, consisting of a large furnace room, which originally had adjoined a large area with bins for coal storage and a boiler for the old-fashioned steam-radiator heating. Few other buildings that had been in my price range at the time had had basements with concrete ramps leading in that you could drive up and down with a motorcycle or small car. The original, angled cellar doors were long-gone; in their place were a set of vertical, solid-steel doors, with both key and hasp-style locks. It was a "just-in-case" investment, more for the security it offered as a potential retreat than as a financial investment.

Filling about 1/3 of the basement area was a small, 10-foot shipping container, containing a very comfortable sofa, some books, a battery operated lamp, etc., which could be securely bolted from the inside. I'd had my personal space walled-off from the newer and much smaller gas furnace, leaving myself with a small, windowless safe-zone. There was no emergency blood supply, but with a city the size of Chicago, sustenance wouldn't be a problem. So far I'd never needed it as a hide-out, but it had proved handy several times in the past when bovine blood became too boring and I'd needed the thrill of the hunt and hadn't had sufficient time to safely return to my domain in Indiana before daybreak. Also, I enjoyed the occasional opera or rock concert and the Rosemont Horizon on the west side of Chicago was a bit of a drive from Goshen, although I'd managed the drive before, as well as to the Memorial Coliseum in Fort Wayne. I'd even been to one once in Hamilton County, just north of Indianapolis, but that had been so long ago I didn't recall the name of the venue and just then didn't feel like expensing the mental energy to make myself remember: it wasn't important.

The key word in this mental self-discourse regarding Theresa and Chicago was "considered". Yes, I'd thought about it—and then rejected the idea. There was still the chance the police might someday stumble across Theresa somehow—and they'd no doubt have a lot of questions for her regarding any information she had regarding the Hillenburg deaths...or the cop...or the high school girl, or any one of the hundreds of other people I'd consumed (i.e. murdered) since or even before coming to Indiana...or the literally thousands of people in New York and Pennsylvania going back to the time I'd arrived in the USA with a wave of refugees from war-ravaged Europe (or, more accurately, in a packing crate stowed as part of a vast cargo of luggage on it's way from the old world to the new). No, the whole purpose of having a secret bolthole that nobody knows about is...to keep it secret!

No, it would have to be Indianapolis. The 3-hour drive made it possible to get there well before midnight and to get back before dawn. Also, if some emergency arose, it would be possible to find a taxi or hijack a car or even find someplace to spend the night—it wouldn't be the first time I'd had to hide out in an abandoned house or warehouse or even under a derelict railroad bridge once when the roads had iced over during a freezing rainstorm and travel had become impossible.

Although the weather forecast called for cold weather, it wasn't quite winter yet, and it was only when the sky was completely overcast and the clouds were thickest that a vampire could risk walking about in full daylight (scarved and hooded against the cold, of course). No doubt there would be people milling around downtown at the circle, around the war monument, but that area is awfully open and there was a possibility of trouble with teenage gang-bangers. Maybe Broad Ripple would be a better bet, with the small bars and Microbreweries. To be honest, for a big town and a state capitol, Indianapolis was pretty boring.

"Hey, whatcha doin?" came Theresa's interruption of my reverie which, before I could reply, she followed up with, "can I use your computer?" Before I could even ask her why she wanted to use it, she continued on with her freight train of thought:

"I want to do an internet search to see if there are any Halloween parties. Obviously we won't be going over to Goshen College, but there's Bethel...and we're not too far from IUSB and Notre Dame, or even Valpo."

I wasn't sure whether or not to be impressed that she'd had such a good idea or upset with myself that I hadn't thought of it first. Of course I tended to avoid universities when I went hunting: an old man following young girls around on a college campus was likely to attract attention, as that was probably the stereotypical destination for would-be rapists.

I still wasn't sure this was a good idea. While it was highly unlikely any of her former classmates would be there, and she'd be in costume and makeup, making it even less likely anyone would recognize her, there was still a possibility. However, I had agreed to it in a moment of weakness and had no really good reason to back out. Also, I had to admit I was somewhat curious. After all, I'd never actually been to a Halloween party. The custom of "trick-or-treating" wasn't new—children of poor families had gone around begging for "soul cakes" and people had worn masks or dressed as saints in order to avoid being attacked by vengeful spirits even back in my time as a living, breathing human being. In France, in those days, people had believed the dead rose from churchyards on that one day of the year to perform the danse macabre and in some villages people even dressed up as corpses, somewhat like the modern-day "zombie parades" one saw on YouTube, enacting in the flesh what the ghosts were imagined to be performing in the spirit. Candles or "soul lights" were lit in homes to assist the spirits of dead relatives wishing to pay a visit, and of course Jack-o-

Lanterns were hardly a new invention. Modern-day traditions, however, appeared to be somewhat different, at least from what I'd seen in movies.

After entering my password, taking care that Theresa wasn't able to learn the combination of keystrokes, I stood behind her, bending over so I could slowly stroke her bare thighs while she performed a quick, internet search. I covertly stole inhaled breaths, savoring the scent of her hair (and also enjoyed the tickling sensation of her hair cascading across my bare genitals). Watching her searching for information on student parties, I couldn't help feelings of trepidation; after all, I studiously avoided large, public gatherings, holding them in the same regard as Morpheus had had of the notion of travel on the highway in *The Matrix Reloaded*. Cat person that I was, I wondered if I might later regret that I hadn't heeded the cautions associated with curiosity.

"This looks cool," she exclaimed after a few minutes, "a big party at Heartland... that's a restaurant with a huge auditorium behind it where they have rock concerts all the time, sometimes headliners like Ted Nugent...live band, open bar, costume contest; there should be a lot of high school and university students. If we can't find someone there, Notre Dame students always have off-campus parties we should be able to crash" (I chose not to belabor the point and tell her I'd been to Heartland on any number of occasions. What can I say? I enjoyed music and hated rap and hip hop, so the symphony and rock cover bands had been my usual weekend entertainment until she charmed her way into my life).

"I'm so tired of cow's blood and getting their shit on my shoes when we go out to feed," she continued, "I really hope we can pick someone up on Halloween. I don't know why, I just really feel like biting hard on someone's dick! Hmm... why wait?"

Turning away from the computer, her hands were already at the right altitude, so she had my favorite organ in her hands in an instant. The unexpected caress brought me to an instant erection.

OK, to be honest, it was a partial erection at first... we'd already had our normal "morning sex" after waking (which for us was usually about the time humans were sitting down to dinner). In fact, once hadn't been enough, and I'd jumped on her a second time for a 'deuce'. As she began tracing a circle around the tip of it with her tongue, I wondered if I really had enough power left, without a recent infusion of blood, to make it a third time in as many hours. I didn't have to wonder for long as she took me all the way in, deep-throating me, then started rocking back and forth. I felt her gag a few times, but she kept at it, hands gently caressing the "family jewels" at the same time. Then, in a new twist, she began humming. I didn't recognize the tune, but the vibrations of her vocal cords sent ripples of pleasure shooting up my spine. Clenching the top of the chair in my hands, I held on with an iron grip while the most sublime of sensations continued, finally coming to a bittersweet climax—one I certainly enjoyed but, at the same time, would have delayed for quite a lengthy pause, had I been able to do so.

She had no difficulty swallowing, as the volume of ejaculation was of course reduced by our recent lovemaking. Leaning back, still holding my erection in her hands, she smiled up at me. "What would you do if I bit it?"

"Like in The *Lair of the White Worm*? Tell you what, let's not find out; we can find you some teenage nerd with no diseases other than acne and you can bite it all the way off if you wish!"

"*Lair of the White Worm*?" she inquired. "A classic film," I explained, "it's so old I think it's on VHS, but the quality is pretty good, as I recall". "Go make us some popcorn and I'll find it for you."

"Popcorn?"

"Just kidding."

Chapter 29
La Masquerade Infernale

All Hallow's Eve arrived with the scent of burning leaves in the air, a gentle breeze with just a hint of winter's chill, and low-hanging clouds that lit with fire in a rare, red and orange-tinged sunset. As had become a habit, they'd emerged onto the porch as soon as the sun had dipped below the horizon, enjoying a few brief moments of indirect daylight. Probably this was the basis for the title of *Twilight*. Theresa regretted that she'd never had time to read it; she'd been too busy with college entrance exams, assigned reading, research, writing papers, waiting tables... pleasure reading just hadn't been a priority. She remembered enjoying the Nancy Collins novels, back in high school, prior to entering university, after which she'd scarcely had time to see a movie or go for a bike ride. Now, of course, with life as a vampiress fact rather than fiction, she doubted the story would have the same appeal now that it would have when she was... unchanged. After all, fantasy was not nearly as fun when reality came in the same shapes and sizes!

Spending nearly all her waking moments in the old farmhouse had really started to become frustrating; she was accustomed to always being on the go, burning the candle at both ends, going to classes during the day then waiting tables at night then studying for final exams and trying to grab a few hours of sleep before doing it all again. At first, of course, her physical changes and the corresponding mental and psychological adjustments had kept her occupied. Since then, however, she had begun to chafe at the inactivity.

She couldn't even do any online shopping, not really. She had to ask for help even to purchase cosmetics as he had cut up her credit card at the outset, as any activity on her card would alert the authorities to her presence and there was the small matter of three dead bodies. Even though she'd had no culpability in their deaths, she had no illusions about what would happen to her if she were discovered as a real, live, undead individual— she'd end up in a lab somewhere having experiments performed on her, like the aliens at Area 51, if there really was such a place.

So, wheeling her 'patient' out onto the porch to catch the final light of day had been her idea—it got her out of the house while there was still a little light left to see by. They were mostly in shadow under the roof, so there was little to fear in the way of injury from the fading light, but they took the precaution of sun block and UV-blocking sunglasses, nevertheless. They'd made a point of having Miguel come by a few times to pick up some vegetables or eggs after his work-day had ended, just so he could observe them out of doors when it was still technically daytime.

Tonight, however, they were supposed to be out-of-town, so Theresa grabbed a quick smoke and then they went back into the house to prepare for the party. She had rather enjoyed explaining the modern fascination with COSPLAY, while dressing them up and plastering on the heavy, white, foundation makeup with red and black highlights. She was quite pleased with herself when she viewed the final results and hoped the effect was really as scary as she hoped. Scary and sexy... she had nixed the idea of a long skirt and was wearing a very, very short skirt and fishnets with a few intentionally-inflicted rips, army-style boots and a ruffled tuxedo shirt. Both of them had black, vampire capes with a scarlet lining that had been overnighted from an online costume company, and the vampire was wearing a vintage Tuxedo that "The Count" as she was going to refer to him tonight, brought with him from France, so it was at least 100 years old. It was beautiful! (aside from a few moth chews, which she'd dutifully, helped repair with some black, silk thread he'd produced from somewhere.

His boots were black, Italian, and very expensive. She could tell from the way he'd looked at himself in the mirror that he'd been both surprised and pleased at the look she'd created. Laughing to herself, she remembered that, in some vampire legends, vampires were unable to see themselves in mirrors. Wouldn't that have taken all the fun out of it!

As 'The Count' turned from side to side, admiring himself in the mirror, he passed his hands up and down the tuxedo and a shadow of distant memory passed over his face. Not knowing how she knew, Theresa could tell, had a feeling of absolute certainty, that all he wanted to do was take the Tuxedo off.

"What is it?" she asked, "you don't like the white rose I pinned to the lapel?"

"No," he sighed, his voice a million miles away, "I just remembered whose suit of clothing this was. Did I ever tell you the story of how I left France to come here to the USA? How I transformed myself from a soulless... that means penniless... a sou was a small coin in old France, like a nickel here in the USA... vagabond, sleeping in crypts, abandoned cellars and derelict barges, always in fear of detection, knowing that discovery practically guaranteed destruction?" Without allowing Theresa the time to respond, he continued his narrative without pause.

I was being sought by the police in connection with a number of suspicious deaths. I tried to be careful, of course, but apparently I had been observed with some of my victims and my description had been tendered to the local constabulary. Gendarmes had already visited my small house once before, just part of a routine questioning of everyone who lived in the vicinity. As it had been daytime, I had hidden in the attic, successfully avoiding detection, but I knew they would be back. As I only went out at night, I realized the more they learned of my routine, the more inquisitive they might become. I was still living in the same house I'd purchased in 1815, only now it was 1919. I had legal documentation for the property transfer and ID showing me to be a person who would never be found to dispute the identity theft, but I still feared discovery.

Fortunately, at just that time, a wealthy nobleman was arranging transport of one of his households to New York City. This was the post-war era when there was a mass migration of Europeans to the USA, so I decided to pay him and his family a visit.

I tied them up and killed the man's wife in front of him and threatened to do the same to his daughter, after raping her first. Needless to say, he was willing to agree to anything. I filled a sack with jewelry, banknotes and other precious items. I also had him execute several letters of accréditation... letters of credit... basically these were bank checks I could present for payment or assign. Most importantly, I had him execute a contract giving me tenancy for a term of years of his property in New York. I'd have had him deed the property to me, but that required witnesses and the notary of the court, so I settled for a 2 year tenancy and a letter to his attorney in New York with a small stipend for management fees, to make it appear legitimate, all of which dated two weeks prior to my visit, to make it seem less suspicious.

I don't feel all that bad about taking his money—the guy inherited most of his wealth, the rest of it he reputedly got through illegal means, primarily business dealings with crooked politicians. All right, he wasn't exactly running the Clinton Foundation or selling heroin, but the guy was a crook. No, what I felt bad about was lying to him; I promised he and his daughter would be safe if he simply did as I demanded, that I would just leave them in peace. I forget who once said, 'When you lie, you kill a piece of your soul'. No, that wasn't it. Hmm... "Hard truths can be dealt with, triumphed over, but lies will destroy your soul" That was it... from a book about werewolves I haven't gotten around to reading yet, I think the name is *Moon Called*. I just remember the quote because someone used it when Hillary Clinton was running for president and all her scandals were piling up and the stress was obviously destroying her... it just seemed so incredibly appropriate.

Of course in the classic literature, the old stuff with priests and holy water and crucifixes, vampires didn't have souls: we were the damned, the unholy, the accursed... I don't know about all that, but I do know that it doesn't bother me as much to kill someone as it does to lie, I mean a REAL lie, like breaking a vow, lying under oath, intentionally misleading someone to his or her detriment; there's just something inherently evil about it. Killing... that's just a part of life. If a farmer raises a pig, feeding it every day and caring for its needs, the pig probably feels some affection for the farmer; after all, pigs are intelligent creatures. When the blade slices its throat, I have no doubt that pig feels betrayal as it bleeds out its life on its way to becoming bacon... but nobody will blame the farmer—that's why he fed and cared for the pig in the first place, to turn it into food. Joe Everyman who eats his hamburger doesn't spare a thought for the cow... with us it's the same as every creature who's higher on the food chain—it is just and right and natural to consume the creatures below us. There is, of course one colossal difference. Unlike probably all other predators, we USED TO BE THE SAME AS OUR PREY and have the intelligence and morality to feel remorse. I suppose that's another reason for my cows and goats; I hide myself from the prying-eyes of my fellow man, but I also feel no guilt when all I do is borrow a little blood without having to take a life. Anyway... where was I?

"You were telling me about the rich man and his family"
Ah, yes. Of course, I couldn't leave them to make a report to the police. So, naturally, I killed them. As I already related, I killed the wife first, so the old man would do everything I needed of him. The old man was next, so he wouldn't have to watch his daughter suffer. I broke his neck. It was quick. I doubt he felt very much and he didn't see it coming, so he died as well as could be managed. I'd already fed on the wife, after all, and had no need of his blood.

"And the girl?" she asked.

Well, I was going to kill her anyway, so I still raped her first. 'Waste not, want not', as they say. I see you don't look surprised...   As you're already realized, vampires need sex like every living creature... and you're the first female vampire I've had as a sex partner in over 200 years! Yes, I suppose I could have created others like I made you, but my goal has always been to stay hidden... I'm already breaking that rule tonight by going out with you in public—I hope that's a decision I don't end up regretting! Anyway, needless to say, she was rather distraught after seeing her father killed before her eyes; oh, those eyes! She was gagged, but I can still remember the hurt, fear and accusation in those eyes. I choked her into unconsciousness from behind her, so I wouldn't have to endure the stare of those lovely, tragic, terrified eyes. She was a virgin, so at least I spared her that pain and indignity by knocking her out first.

"Did you also feed on the girl?"

Yes. In true vampiric tradition, I slashed her throat with my dagger and drained her lifeblood as I fucked her. The more blood I drank, the more lust I felt, so after awhile I forgot my guilt and really enjoyed the power of thrusting myself into her innocent flesh, hands on her firm, teenage breasts, the perfumed smell of her skin and hair—she was so much more pleasurable than the whores who had usually provided my sexual release. I think I actually toyed with the idea of turning her and having a companion, not to mention being able to enjoy her body whenever I wished, but time was against me; against us, perhaps. Of course I felt guilty afterwards: guilty and ashamed. This and many other, similar incidents is why I live as I do now—dining on my cattle and only taking life when I feel an overwhelming need to do so and, even then, trying to only kill those individuals that the world is better off without!

A shipment of the man's furniture was would sail in a few days. I had many preparations to make and little time in which to make them. My 'coming to America' was managed in the cabinet of a piano. I don't mean a spinet, like you're probably most familiar with, but one of the older Querpianos that looked like a large, writing desk. I believe they called them 'square pianos' in English. These were truly horrible things as musical instruments go: poor sound quality, impossible to keep in tune...but there was sufficient room for myself and some bedding in the packing crate, along with some rolled-up paintings and some of my more valuable treasures, the rest of which I inserted into some of the other crates.

As I said, I've hated myself for this for untold years. Not the fucking and killing her part of it—that's just what we do! No, it is the lie that stains and damns my soul! The entire episode has to be the greatest act of deceit and cruelty I ever performed. Still, I did so because I wished to go on living, to survive.

I was able to provide myself with tools so as to permit myself egress from within the crate, an awl, for drilling peepholes, tar and cloth for sealing any holes to keep any daylight out. I also stashed a few extra boards, clamps, nails and what other tools I imagined I might need to be sure I could not only escape from the crate, if necessary, but also to be able to re-assemble it again in a sturdy fashion. As you will soon know: a vampire's greatest fear is being caught out in daylight with nowhere to run and nowhere to hide. Being caught in a cage of some sort, with sunlight leaking in to provide a slow, agonizing death...that's the one thing I can think of that might even be worse! And of course this was only 8 years after the Titanic, so I had the fear of a disaster at sea to consider as well.

I spent one entire night creeping in and out of the warehouse, masquerading as one of the other graveyard-shift dockworkers, surreptitiously tossing clothing and furniture into the harbor and replacing the contents of some of the crates with my books, paintings and other treasures. So, with a stroke of luck, I left France with my mementos of my past as well as a stolen future.   I also had a brief opportunity to engage in some tourism. When the ship stopped in London for 2 days to transship cargo, I went sightseeing, taking in as many sights of that historic city as were possible at night, The Tower, Parliament, Temple Church of the Knights Templar, even attending evensong at St. Paul's Cathedral.

In case you ever wondered, yes, we vampires can enter so-called consecrated ground; that again is a difference between vampire fiction and vampire fact. Religious icons have no more effect on us than Vogon poetry—less, maybe. I'll explain the reference later, just remind me to show you the *Hitch-hiker's Guide to the Galaxy*.

In any case, back in France I would often go to mass and make offerings and light candles for the souls I'd sacrificed for my continued existence. I did the same for my unwilling benefactor and his family prior to leaving for my new existence in the Americas. Not that I think God is likely to listen to *my* prayers, but just the acts of contrition help me assuage my guilt for my own sins.

Anyway, getting back to my adventures: For a scant two nights I sampled and learned to love British beers and ales and of course I sampled several English girls. The Great War had left many war widows; there were literally tens of thousands of prostitutes in London at the time, women forced into that life to support themselves and/or their children, like Fantine in *Les Misérables*. I even packed a lunch, so to speak—I filled several wine bottles with blood from girls I'd released from that cruel fate, which I stowed in a small cask with chunks of ice I'd stolen from a Thames icehouse. I managed to make it last the first week of the voyage. The second week I simply gritted-it-out. We can, after all, go a very long time without feeding—months at least, years maybe, I somehow doubt anyone has ever researched the topic.

Anyway, that's the story of how I came to the USA: as a thief, rapist and murderer. I never made it to Moscow, I was no longer in army service when Napoleon marched in for his empty triumph, but during my travels I visited many of the great cities of Europe: London, Paris, Toulon, Berlin, Ulm, Augsburg, Freiburg, Mainz, Wiesbaden, Augsburg, Potsdam, Vienna, Budapest, Florence, Rome, Milan, Odessa, Warsaw... I wish I'd been with Bony for the Egyptian campaign so I could have seen Alexandria and the pyramids... in any case, I came to the great American city of New York and have also been to Boston, Philadelphia, Chicago..and here I am now in the pastoral hinterland, surrounded by my fields, my small woods, a pond, my animals—not much to offer distraction to one who used to be a man of action! I have the internet, which helps, but again, I find my thoughts have wandered.

So, at long last, this brings me to the point I was trying to make, aside from the fact that I still feel guilt after killing innocents, the ones who don't deserve to die. Anyway, the MAIN point I was trying to make is that going out with you tonight goes against my self-imposed rules, the rules that have kept me alive all these years. Just having you here, living with me, and going into a very public place to hunt goes against EVERY rule that has kept me safe and undiscovered. I supposed I agreed to it because I'm as bored as you claim to be—and the last real party I can recall attending was the ball that was held when Napoleon was crowned King of Italy in Milan in 1805! So, after more than 200 years, I guess I'm ready to get out and do some people-watching. Now, let's go before I change my mind!

Theresa was certainly not going to argue: after just a few weeks, she felt bored and in need of some distraction, a change of scenery. How many years had it been since he'd moved to this farm, only leaving for occasional runs to nearby cities? Theresa both admired his patience and feared that she would find herself in the same situation, hiding from the world and never getting out to do anything interesting. It's not like she was a big-time party-girl before, but at least she had friends she would go out and do things with, she loved to travel to new places, she was a big fan of museums and art galleries (the older stuff that took talent to create, not the crap known as 'modern art'). Did being 'undead' necessarily mean not having a life? Did that even make any sense? Or, was that part of being undead? In any case, she was determined not to spend the rest of her life sitting in a basement.

She was going to out tonight, she was going to have a good time... and she
was going to kill somebody!

Chapter 30
Allegedly Intellectual Idiots

Heartland is a long, narrow restaurant in front with a cavernous room in the back, smelling of stale, spilled beer, sweat and vomit. A reasonably decent cover-band blasted excessively loud 1980's rock. Halloween decorations festooned the walls and ceiling and strings of colored, LED lights shaped like pumpkins, ghosts, mummies, bats and skulls circled the dimly-lit room, not so much providing illumination as adding ambiance. The sticky, concrete floor was alive with a crowd of heaving, gesticulating, costume-clad celebrators. I and my Guinness were proverbial wallflowers while I contemplated my feelings of empathy for Sean Connery's character in *Finding Forrester* when he suffers an anxiety attack in a sports stadium and ends up hiding in a broom closet. Claustrophobia had never been an issue for me. Actually, when one contemplated the very nature of existence as a vampire, fated to sleep in coffins and crypts, being claustrophobic was somewhat antithetical. Of course there was an old 'artsy' movie, *Body Double*, in which an actor portraying a vampire in a film suffered from claustrophobia and couldn't climb out of a coffin—but that was Hollywood, not reality.

Now, in my reality, I found myself in the unfamiliar setting of being in a moving mass of humanity, pressing against me in torrents. I'd been to concerts but only in reserved seating, where I didn't have people bumping into me. I felt... uncomfortable. It wasn't actually claustrophobia, per se, but the last time I had been in such close proximity to hundreds of bodies, with my senses being hammered by penetrating smells, blinding lights and crashing percussions had been in the trenches of World War I!

Yes, that was it, the loud music, strobing stage lights, frantic motions, smells of sweat and excitement, all of this was having an effect on my subconscious, dredging up memories of a century past, when I experienced the horrors of a war that had passed from living memory that my recent revelations to Theresa had dredged back up to the surface. Make that the 'most horrible' war of human (and undead) experience. How ironic that it was deemed 'The Great War', great in the sense of 'big', of course. A better label would have been to have called it "The Great and Terrible War," like something from the *Wizard of Oz* but not nearly as pleasant!

No wonder I was so jumpy—part of me was remembering the roar of the guns and the concussion of exploding artillery shells. After all, I had been a soldier of the Confederation of the Rhine, fighting in Napoleon's Grande Armée, and later a camp-follower during the Franco-Prussian War and World War I, pretending to be a stretcher-bearer in order to feed on injured and dying soldiers, an endeavor that kept me at the front lines of three military conflicts.

Now, this close-quarters rock concert in a room lacking proper acoustics, where the floor vibrated and the sound reflected from the flat walls with the force of hammer-blows and the smoke from some flash-pots they'd set off to create smoke in front of the stage was bringing it all back to me—the sharp crack of rifles, the smell of cordite and gunpowder, human waste and unburied corpses, and the screams of wounded horses. Yes, that was a memory I wished had stayed forgotten; amid all the horrors of the three wars I'd experienced, the screams of wounded horses had been the worst among a plethora of truly unimaginable horrors. What word meant something *worse* than horror? Was there such a word in the English language? If so, I couldn't think of it, but I'd lived it... or whatever it was that undead do—I'd stopped trying to figure out the proper expression for it.

Theresa, on the other hand, was certainly enjoying herself. At present, she was encircled by a collection of young men and girls she'd attracted to herself. Somehow she was spinning in a circle on the balls of her feet, one leg at a time, lifting and planting alternating feet in a maniacal grace, while gyrating at the waist as if spinning a hula-hoop whilst her head flew about in an elliptical orbit, thrashing her hair about her head in a great, black circle.

Even while all this was going on, she was pumping her arms up and down and rotating her hands around her wrists in something reminiscent of Thai dancing, only sped up like a 33 1/3 rpm record played on a 78 rpm turntable! I couldn't see how she could possibly keep her balance, not to mention maintain the syncopated rhythm of all those different movements, but she maintained it until "Sweet Child of Mine" finally crashed to a halt. As the last chord banged out, she kicked to an end, right leg bent under her, left leg stretched-out straight and long behind her, arms out at right angles, back bent at a painful angle and her head pulled back almost like a cobra ready to strike, hair hanging across her eyes. As the echoes faded, she held this pose, like a gymnast sticking a landing at an Olympic event.

The crowd around her went wild with applause; I clasped my now-empty beer glass in the crook of my elbow and joined-in; after all, it had been a truly impressive and inspired performance. "Please remember to appear out-of-breath," I whispered to myself, unheard.

The band announced a recess and I went off in search of a refill. Although I was enjoying the music, I felt a bit of a sense of relief as I began to put the ghosts of centuries-past back into whatever Pandora's Box they'd escaped from.

This was my first time listening to a live band in quite some time and, for a local cover band, they were quite good. By the time they started the second set I'd totally forgotten about the horrors of war as well as our declared mission to find someone to suck and fuck and was really just enjoying the Guiness and electric guitars. After about an hour, the set ended and Theresa appeared at my elbow. "Come on, we're leaving," she announced, "I managed to swing us an invite to a party at a big apartment complex just off the Notre Dame campus...lots of university students."

It took longer to find a place to park than it did to drive there (I could have parked in one of the university lots, but I felt to better to avoid any place that had 24-hour camera surveillance...in case I had to lie about my whereabouts later on). Theresa hadn't exaggerated...there were numerous apartment buildings and what I supposed you'd call a 'clubhouse', which was obviously where the party was being held. I say 'obviously' because it was impossible to miss the Halloween lights, decorations, loud music and literally hundreds of people milling about both inside and outside the building (what, in another life, I'd have referred to as the 'commons').

As you entered, there was a large, galvanized-steel tub full of ice, which would have looked right at home as a watering trough on my 'farm'...in fact, it may well have been a newer model of the ones I had in 2 of my pastures. A "$2 a brew" sign was taped to the front of it and dozens of long-necked bottles could be seen, jutting out from the ice chips.

They didn't have anything I considered to be 'real' beer, just Corona and Miller Lite, so I congratulated myself on having had the foresight to have brought a flask of brandy. A very cute hostess, dressed as a mermaid, caught sight of me taking a sip and gave me a wry glance askance. From the slight smile, I guess she secretly shared a similar opinion of the beer selection, so I corked the flask and wandered over to make conversation.

"Corona, Sir? Only $2!"

"Thanks," I demurred, "but anything you have to add lime to for it to taste good isn't beer in my book. Would you care for a taste of hundred-year-old French brandy? It's very precious—I only break it out on special occasions" From the way her eyes flared, I could tell she was intrigued, even as she made her apologies. "I'm working... I'd love to but I'm not allowed to drink alcohol here, especially as I'm only 19 and there's a strict policy against underage drinking in public. The university turns a blind-eye to it if you keep it in the dorm or off campus, but when it's a public event with outsiders coming in, which could include the ATF, they get serious about it. That's a really beautiful container, by the way!"

"Thanks, it's an antique". I inverted it and glanced at the maker's mark, etched into the bottom so many years even before it came into my possession, one of the treasures I'd liberated from the marquis.

I passed it across the tub of ice and inferior, bottled beverages so she could enjoy a closer inspection. "1757, that makes it older than the country we are standing in" The scene worked into the silver was one from antiquity or perhaps mythology: a battle scene with bare-chested soldiers in skirts with long spears and Greek helmets set versus a charge of chariots decorated one side. On the other side was a partially-clad female figure reclining beneath a tree alongside a riverbank. There appeared to be a creature lurking in the foliage, observing her, perhaps a faun or satyr. No doubt it harbored ill intent for the unsuspecting female! Other figures could be seen in the background, bathing in the river. I hadn't polished it for many years, but occasional use had kept the raised surfaces shiny, while the patina of the decades had left a darker tarnish in the recesses, accentuating the 3D effect. It was truly a museum-quality piece and the young lady was visibly impressed. As she returned the flask I noticed she also gave the ruby broach tied around my neck, another acquisition from my involuntary benefactor, a long, less-than-casual look. I could see the mental gears in motion as she wondered if it was indeed a genuine ruby and was probably trying to calculate its worth.

Of course it was indeed genuine, the centerpiece of the jewels of the family I had obliterated from history in one fell evening. I had other pieces of jewelry, including a signet ring with a large emerald and a tiara breathtakingly-encrusted in diamonds and sapphires, but the ruby was undoubtedly my favorite. A psychiatrist would probably claim it had something to do with vampires and blood and might have even been correct. Whatever—I just knew I liked the bloody thing! I wasn't alone: a smaller one, much like it, had sold in 2019 for $30.3 million.

I'd never had it appraised, but I'm sure it was worth more than the famous ND football stadium just a couple blocks away from the building we were standing in and I'm fairly certain the pretty bit of fluff standing in front of me, push-up bra trying to make the most of her limited cleavage in her salmon and aquamarine fish-scale bra had reached the conclusion it much simply be costume jewelry. After all, who would walk around wearing a gem like that to a college party if it were the real McCoy?

The flask, however, was undisputedly the genuine article and many young girls were very impressionable where rich, older men were concerned and the 'vibes' I was beginning to get from her made it clear to this old predator that proper exploitation of these first impressions could yield the sacrificial victim we'd set out to find. However, it was much too early in the evening and she was busy working.

I didn't want to scare off our potential prey by 'coming on too strong', in case nothing else presented itself throughout the course of the evening, so I decided to 'play it coy' and circulate for awhile, and took my leave of her, although I made a point of stopping by later to flirt a little and try to set myself for a potential meeting with her later for a little of my favorite pastime, la mort d'amour (in French, loosely 'death during the act of lovemaking' which, to a vampire, meant 'getting your rocks off' while draining someone—preferably a sweet, young thing—of her lifeblood). Goodness, the colloquialisms were playing on my thoughts tonight, like lines from some cheap dime store novel! Yeah, "dime store"... there I was, showing my age again, fortunately only in my own mind. No doubt it was the alcohol. I must have had about 8 beers by that point and the brandy was quite strong; I decided to put it away and return to something softer.

It was just then that Theresa appeared from out of the crowd, handed me an Oberon Ale she'd acquired somewhere, blew me a kiss, and disappeared as quickly as she'd arrived. "Good girl," I thought, once again glad I hadn't killed her. After all, you really had to appreciate a girl who not only swallows, but also brings you a new beer when you needed one!

A young, presumably student who was done up in a very good imitation of Elvis...Costello, not the first one...was apparently lecturing several other students on a point of interest. I sidled up to listen in...

"The Electoral College is obviously outdated and should be abolished. I mean look at what happened in 2016... Hillary won the popular vote but Trump was put into office because a few political appointees voted for him, against the will of the people. Now I grant that Trump wasn't quite as bad as expected, some of the things he's done have been good for the country but still—he's a racist misogynist elected against the will of the people so therefore it was not a legitimate election and therefore he was legally elected president, isn't that right, professor?"

> I was a bit surprised to be put-on-the-spot. I wasn't sure if
> he'd mistaken me for a member of the Notre Dame faculty or

just assumed an obviously older gentleman at a university party must be a professor. Anyway, I was happy to put the little shit in his place.

Actually...no! Trump won the electoral vote, the popular vote has no say in electing a president, that's how the system was designed. Even so: watchdog groups investigating voter fraud after the election identified at least 7 million fraudulent votes in California alone: 4 million illegals and 3 million votes cast by dead people—or perhaps it was the other way around; I honestly don't recall. In any case, people in New York and Philadelphia actually admitted voting multiple times. They were driven around from location to location and voted with fake names in states where you don't need to show an ID. They found another eighty-five to ninety-five thousand fraudulent votes in Austin, Texas, as I recall, and so on all across the country.

There was an office—again I think it was Philadelphia—where a worker-slash-whistleblower reported people copying absentee ballots by hand and changing the name of the candidate. The prosecutions are still making their way through the various court systems. I remember reading back in 2017, I think it was from PEW Research, that it was estimated that as many as 20 MILLION illegal votes were cast for Hitlery... I mean Hillary. So, even if you figure this is an exaggerated number and you subtract out half of these... leaving 10 million votes that shouldn't have been counted... then Trump clearly won the popular vote as well.

I don't recall the exact numbers, but if you look at all the individual counties and voting districts, Trump won over 3000 out of about 3200... even more than Ronald Reagan! Here's one number I DO recall: Clinton won 57 counties. Think about that for a moment: Clinton carried 57 counties to Trump's over 3000! He also won a much higher percentage of the black vote than Clinton. Trump was filling entire football stadiums, often 15,000 people at a time, while the Clinton campaign had to hire people on Craig's list just to get 200 or so to stand behind her on stages in high school auditoriums to make it appear as though she had a crowd, meanwhile Trump was filling football stadiums. Is it logical to think he did all that but lost the popular vote? Anyway, why are people still arguing about this? It's ancient history—and a perfect example of why the Founding Fathers created the electoral college in the first place!

A better thing to consider is the widespread claims that Trump won again in 2020 and that is was only voter fraud on a massive scale that put Biden & Harris in the White House. Again, Trump was filling stadiums at his rallies while 'Sleepy Joe' was doing what? Hiding in his basement? We're supposed to believe that Biden got more votes from women than Hitlery did, more votes from 'people of color' than Obama—and that's with Biden's long history of voting against legislation favoring minorities and hanging out with avowed racists and Klansmen like David Duke and Strom Thurmond! Thousands of individuals reported election 'irregularities' while audits of voting machines in Arizona and other states have shown the machines were hacked and votes were switched, most likely by agents in Mainland China! The media and Congress have seemed less-than-interested in getting to the truth of it, but isn't this a matter of National Security? If, in fact, CHINA stole the 2020 election, isn't this at least as grave an assault on the USA as the Japanese attack on Pearl Harbor? Why so little interest in finding-out the truth?

The "intellectual, yet idiot" (I forget who coined that phrase-I wish I could take credit for it) started to sputter, so I didn't give him time to riposte and I kept up the attack.

What's the source of your information... the Mainstream Media? The same folks who ran poll after poll showing Hillary was going to win? Did they even *mention* the extensive voter fraud? Did you do your due diligence and research the political fact-checking organizations to see how much voter fraud may have occurred or do you just turn on the TV news and accept everything they say as fact without question? You also claimed that Trump is a racist but I'd be willing to bet you $1000, cash, right here and right now, that you are unable to cite one single, verifiable example of him committing a single, racist act. Am I correct? Or are you interested in taking my wager? No? I didn't think so. How

about a secondary wager that I can find at least one instance
of blatant racism on the part of Joe Biden? What was it he
called urban blacks that one time—Super Predators?   I'm
sure I can find that on YouTube for you...
     Was Trump perfect? No! Was he born with a silver spoon
in his mouth? Yes! Still, the facts are that Trump won, the evil
Harpy lost, just accept it and get on with your life!

The little twerp's face had one pale with shock and, judging by the angry look in his eyes, he longed to devolve into name-calling, the 'strategy' the leftists usually resorted to when losing an argument. No doubt my imagined status as a 'professor' kept him in check. Glancing furtively around, he jerked like he'd been tapered when a linebacker-looking dude blurted out 'awesome' to a chorus of nodding heads and muttered agreements. Apparently not all university students are brain-dead 'snowflakes. I thought, or perhaps this university has fewer progressive (i.e. leftist radical) professors. Being the Midwest, attitudes did tend to be more conservative than in, say, California or New York. I hadn't forgotten the purpose of our little expedition, of course, so I decided to continue role-playing in the role of professor, as the first speaker's assumption had apparently been accepted by the entire group, and I decided to swiftly change the subject to anything other than politics and swiftly took stock of the group gathered around me.

The cutest girl in the crowd had a somewhat bulbous nose, sunken cheeks, and long lackluster dirty-blonde hair and was so pale I wondered if she were completely healthy. Still, she had a square-shaped jaw I found attractive and she was tall and slender (meaning she had long, luscious legs). Her costume, clearly hand-made, was that of a turn-of-the-century cigarette girl. Betty Boop! Excepting, of course, that Betty was a brunette.

In any case, she was wearing dark nylons, complete with garter belts, under a very short, ruffled skirt. The tray of fake cigars and cigarette packs—also obvious fakes—had amusing names such as "Fool," Camel-lot," "Pell Mell" and "Marco Polo" The packs were illustrated or had cutouts pasted to them. Fool, I could see, had a picture of a Court Jester. Marco Polo had the classic Marlboro red and white design, but instead of a cowboy there was a picture of a Venetian Nobleman that might have been scanned off the cover of Machiavelli's, *The Prince*. The creativity that had gone into making them was impressive; the King Arthur on the "Camel-lot" pack she'd probably painted herself. Two of them I had to think about for a bit. The one with '666' had a picture I recognized from the old "Dragula" video...Rob Zombie and 3 Halloween devils with plastic pitchforks, driving around in a dragster. The other was named 'Minnesota Fats' and pictured 15 billiard balls in a triangular rack. After a moment's consternation, I recalled that '555' was a foreign brand, possibly English, and while Minnesota Fats had been a billiards champion and trick shooter, there was a cigarette brand called 'Virginia Slims'. The leap from genuine brands to pseudonyms I found to be quite impressive. This girl apparently had a very sharp mind.

Turning to her and stabbing at her with my beer bottle, I asked "why did the Founding Fathers invent the electoral college in the first place?"

Without missing a beat, she replied, "for the same reason there are 2 houses in the legislature: to keep the more populous states from dominating the government to the detriment of less-populous states".

"Bravo... brilliant... a perfect answer!" As the Trump-hater, finding himself outnumbered, beat a hasty exit, I seized upon the opportunity to change the subject and followed up immediately with a one-liner: "what do you call a vampire dressed in drag?"

"What?" she gasped, blinking, clearly disoriented by the sudden deflection. "What do you call a vampire drag-queen? Class?" Looking around the small, momentarily-speechless group, I tarried a moment longer and then dropped the punch-line:

"A Transylvestite!" I heard a few groans but more laughs, so I felt I'd 'counted coup' on political correctness. I was about to continue trying to woo the cigarette girl but, at that moment, up walked a genuine transvestite, who sidled up to the cigarette girl and handed her a drink. He was in a long, white evening dress, close fitting, with a curly-haired wig, long dangle earrings and—the most striking feature of the costume—a large microphone was suspended on a hoop around his neck: a double hoop, actually, which kept the microphone sticking out, thrusting forward like an intensely erect phallus. After a moment I made the connection: he was supposed to be a nightclub singer, she was the cigarette girl. In any case, as they were clearly at the party together, it was time to move along and look for some pussy elsewhere.

"I need a refill," I lied to the small collection of students around me, "enjoy the party... and Happy Halloween!" Extricating myself from that group, I turned around and, due to the press of the crowd, found myself in the middle of another conversation. A very tall, emaciated-looking individual, who was aptly made-up as a zombie, was postulating on the nature of same.

Why is it that zombies only eat the living? In a lot of movies you're a zombie for like 5 minutes and the other zombies won't eat you. It's like you join a club or something and then, once you're on their team, they leave you alone. I can understand maybe not wanting to eat rotten meat, or preferring something alive, but do you really think a zombie would be so picky they wouldn't want to eat someone who'd only been dead for only a very short while? Sure, there are lots of animals that prefer live prey but, if they're hungry enough, they will still eat dead meat. Sure, maybe they can sense that the person is infected with the zombie virus, as he pointed out (gesturing towards a guy dressed as an X-Box, with a joystick mounted in a distressingly appropriate location), but if the zombie were also already infected... why would it care?

"Good point," I thought, easing my way around a pudgy belly-dancer and heading back towards the impromptu bar, "if the zombies ate each other there wouldn't be so many of them and *The Walking Dead* would have ended after season 3". I was somewhat surprised at how much I was enjoying this. "I really should get out more."

The next group of students was debating whether or not some group of popular musicians had 'sold out' or not. Having no interest, I kept moving, finally ending up back at the entrance, where I found a home for my empty in a plastic tub of similar 'dead soldiers'. A group of Frat-types were busy wrestling a large, aluminum beer keg into position in a sawed-off blue plastic drum, full of ice. "Reinforcements," said one of them, smiling at me, "$3 a glass...Heineken". The 'glasses' turned out to be incredibly flimsy plastic tumblers and Heineken wasn't my favorite beer—they had spent a fortune on advertising to achieve their fame, when there were far better European beers on the market: Carlsberg, Tuborg, Hacker-Pschorr, Beck's, Chimay... and pretty much everything from the UK. Not that Heineken beer was bad—it was passable. After all, all the advertising in the world won't work if people don't like the product. For no particular reason, the jingle from one of the old Drewry's TV ads popped, unbidden into my head—no mean feat with the party music loudly thrumming and pulsating...

"Here's to the man who drinks beer cold, he likes the taste of Drewry's." It had been a Canadian beer brewed for many years right here in South Bend, Indiana. The beer had been produced for nearly 100 years but had still vanished into history through some sort of merger or acquisition. I could also recall the Kamm's brewery as well as the Studebaker auto plant. At one time there'd been quite a bit of manufacturing in South Bend, but then the UAW had killed Studebaker and firms had been reluctant to locate there ever since. Why was I thinking about old, dead factories when I was supposed to be looking for some young, living entertainment?

I handed over my $5, took the 20 ounce cup of beer that had taken an interminably long time (they'd had to tap the keg and get the air and initial foam out of the line). While waiting I'd scanned the crowd, looking for Theresa and sizing-up the females on display. I'd finally settled on a very long pair of legs, scantily-clad in fishnet stockings and button-hook, lace-up, high-heeled boots. The legs belonged to a brunette with an adequate amount of cleavage thrusting its way out of a black and lavender lace-up corset. Her 'do' was what I would refer to as a 'pompadour', named after a mistress of king Louis XV, although it was used more recently by the Gibson Girls and rockers such as Elvis and The Stray Cats. I wasn't quite sure what she was supposed to be: frontier whore, riverboat gambler hostess, a character from Bonanza... ? After brushing aside a few intellectual cobwebs, a name finally presented itself: Lilly Langtry, wife and courtesan to royalty, actress, whore, horse-racing aficionado... a 'parson's daughter' who'd used her looks, charm, wit and skills in the bedroom to become one of history's real rags-to-riches stories. I'd expected little more than witches, zombies and skeletons, but I was being treated to quite the masquerade (the Cleopatra in the corner bore watching as well. I'm sure it was a wig she was wearing, but I'd still like to see if the carpeting matched those thick, black drapes!).

I had only made it about halfway over to those legs I very much wanted to meet, when I spotted Theresa in a small group sitting on the stairs leading up to the 2d floor. She caught my eye and beckoned me over, so I changed direction and went over to join her. "This is Dr. Miller," she declared, introducing me to the group and keeping to the subterfuge we'd planned earlier, "he used to teach history; now he's semi-retired and just serves on the board of trustees. Dr. Miller, this is Betsy, Leticia, Jasmine, Ivy, Roy, Dilbert and Fiona. They are all students in the English Department, mostly in Applied Linguistics" She'd said Fiona with just a touch of emphasis, so as I mumbled introductory pleasantries, I gave her a quick once-over. She was dressed as a zombie-cheerleader: cute, but not exactly original (probably 1/4 of the costumes I'd seen tonight had been zombies). Slightly built, she seemed to be a natural redhead with bright green eyes (although, of course, those may have just been contact lenses—these days anything was possible... I'd already seen a pair of yellow stars on one student's eyes tonight and red skull-and-bones on another). Those eyes also seemed a bit glassy. Upon closer examination, Fiona seemed to be a bit tipsy. Perhaps that was what Theresa was indicating to me.

"We've been discussing diversity. I'm sure you know that Japan is the most homogenous, modern country in the world."

"Yeah," spoke up the one she'd identified as Roy, "and we've been asking her what they intend to do about it!"

"Do about it?" I inquired, "why should thy have to DO anything about it?" There was almost a collective intake of breath; it seemed that, once again, I was breaking some sort of new age, social taboo by not kowtowing to the social narrative of the day.

"This is the era of multi-culturalism, don't you know?" This was Betsy talking, a fat bespectacled girl dressed in a tight, black body stocking with a large, felt Jack-o-Lantern around her midsection. I took an instant dislike to this woman. The pushy girlfriend in *Bachelor Party*, the obnoxious girlfriend in *1941*, the student-torturing, temporary headmistress in one of the Harry Potter movies... she just seemed like a stereotype of the classic, universally-hated, overweight and obnoxious movie character. "Certainly Japan should do more to become more multi-cultural!"

"That has worked ***so well*** for Sweden, Germany and Italy," I couldn't help the sarcasm, "tell me, have you ever visited Europe?" I got a few affirmative nods—and a blank stare from the girl I was starting to think of as "Nurse Ratched"

"What was the best thing about traveling around Europe? Back in the old days, that is, when it was still safe to visit there?" Ignoring the now icy glares I was getting from Roy and Betsy, I encouraged the others to add their input.

"the architecture"

"the museums"

"all the different kinds of food"

"the different music, folk dancing and festivals, like Oktoberfest in Munich"

> In other words, you were enjoying the ethnic and cultural ***diversity*** of visiting places having their own, unique ethnicity: something that is only possible when you have completely DIFFERENT cultures! I was born in Germany, traveled all over Europe, and have lived in the USA for many years. You folks are too young to remember, but cities in the USA used to look different. Nowadays, you get off the highway and the strips near the exits around big cities all look the same: McDonald's, KFC, Holiday Inn, Taco Bell, Day's Inn, Red Roof Inn, Wal-Mart, Long John Silver's, some banks and gas

stations. Okay, maybe you don't ALWAYS have Cracker Barrel, Perkins, Waffle House, Arby's or Hardee's, but still the landscape is dominated by all the big chains, and usually an independent Chinese restaurant or two, am I right?

Seeing understanding dawning across their faces and getting nods in agreement, I continued:

When you go on vacation in the USA, it's probably to some natural park, as the USA is blessed with so many. If you go to a city, it's because of something that is DIFFERENT there, such as a theme park, historical sites, local festivals, etc. If every place were the same, would you ever bother to leave your own town? DIVERSITY is what makes the world such a fun place—you can go somewhere else and experience an entirely new culture, try new foods and meet people different from yourself. Look at yourselves. I can tell from your accents that most of you are from other countries. Why study in the USA? Don't they have language programs at universities in your own countries? Or could it be that you're here for the *cultural experience* of living abroad as well as the education? Yes, I agree that DIVERSITY is a wonderful thing, but what they're trying to sell you these days isn't really diversity, they are trying to sell you UNIFORMITY. You're drinking Corona, I have a Heineken for lack of anything better, she's drinking a Smirnoff Ice... all different. Now, if I pour some of my drink into yours and you pour some of yours into hers and we go around a few more times, we no longer have different drinks, what we end up with is something probably not all that good-tasting and more-or-less the same... that's not diversity, that's the DEATH of DIVERSITY!

Surely you guys are smart enough to figure out that this Political Correctness bullshit is one way they're trying to control you these days. not to mention restricting your right to free speech. If you wanted to see Mrs. Clinton indicted for her peddling of influence and lying under oath and national security violations with her illegal server and spoke out about it, you were a MYSOGYNIST. If you didn't like Obama or his policies, such as having to pay higher rates for health insurance so you could subsidize healthcare for low-income, pro-Democrat voters, you were obviously a RACIST. If you didn't like the fact he had a transvestite... what you probably call a 'girlie-boy' pretending to be a woman as First Lady for 8 years, that makes you HOMOPHOBIC and SEXIST. If you object to illegal Mexicans invading your country and living off *billions* of your tax dollars and Syrian 'refugees' being flown in at your expense who might or might not later commit terrorist attacks, again, you're a RACIST and ISLAMOPHOBIC.

Has anybody here read George Orwell's *1984* or Aldous Huxley's *Brave New World* or seen the movie *Brazil*? (a few nods). This is not much different than referring to the propaganda ministry as the "Ministry of Truth". Remember Hitlery... Hillary... Clinton blaming her loss in the election on 'Fake News' after months of polls that showed her way out in the lead—well, if she was so much more popular than Donald Trump, as the polls showed, how come she won fewer than 10% of the counties and voting districts in the USA? If Biden were really so much more popular than Trump, how is it that Trump got tens-of-thousands of people to attend his rallies while Biden—when he did appear in public—only managed to gather a dozen or so? Even his online events only attracted audiences in the triple—or even double—digits! Don't you think that maybe there's something wrong with the polls?

Seeing the obvious Fabian-feminist drawing a lungful and realizing that this was about to become an argument I really had no interest in pursuing, knowing that anyone still willing to defend the Clinton career-criminal-cunt was not going to listen to reason or keep an open mind, I decided to keep ranting with a quick change of subject.

Trump tried to stop the wholesale importation of Muslim 'refugees' that originated under Obama, the liberals accused him of racism, and what happened almost immediately afterwards? Biden opened the border which immediately led to record numbers of people from Central and South America illegally pouring into the country. What did we get? More terror attacks in the USA, including shootings, knifings, rapes and thefts, people run over with vehicles...now how is trying to protect your own people by keeping people with NO RIGHT to enter the country out, knowing there are probably terrorists among them, being racist? To me, that's just showing good sense.

When my ancestors came here about 100 years ago (yeah, I was one and the same, but that wasn't a conversation I wanted to have, either!), they hardly knew a single word of English...but they studied and embraced their new culture. However, if I object to Mexicans coming here and being coddled and not having to learn English in a country they intend to live in, people will call me a racist, won't they?

Oh, speaking of English, here's something—all of you are in the Applied Linguistics Department, right? (again, realizing I was just setting myself up for a protracted argument, I decided to switch gears). Most of you...Okay, tell me this: how was the language we are communicating in...English...derived? Where did it come from?

"Latin"

"French"

"Anglo-Saxon"

"Good...what else? No? Can any of you tell me WHY Latin influenced English? Or French? Or what Anglo-Saxon actually means?"

Dilbert, who by his accent and appearance was probably from Korea and had no doubt borrowed the name from the comic strip, chimed in with: "The Romans used Latin and they were the big trading partner and political force in the old world for centuries, so there are elements of Latin found in French, Italian, Spanish, even a little in German".

"Don't forget Romania," I added, "just the name of the country indicates how much of an influence the Romans had on everything, including their language".

Still, that doesn't explain why words with Latin roots are more common in English than Norwegian or Swedish or Danish or Russian. Anyone? Dilbert at least can probably tell us what Anglo-Saxon means...?

"Yes, this was German-speaking people."

Good, and where were they from? No idea? Anybody else? Okay, brief history lesson. In ancient Briton, you had various tribes of illiterate, stone-age people running around: the Picts, Jutes, Brigantes, Celts, Scots, Welsh and Caledonians. They gave English some words, particularly nouns, especially those without plural forms, such as 'sheep'. Then, about 1000 years ago, the Romans invaded and spent hundreds of years occupying what is more or less England of today. Many Latin nouns and verbs and verb structure exists in English today. After then left, folks who'd come over with them from Brittany in France tried to continue their language, laws and culture. This is where the word 'British' comes from; King Arthur was a Romano-British king, who fought against invading Saxons, from Saxony in what is now Germany, and the Danes. Later, there were invasions by the Irish, the Norse...usually known as Vikings, later on the Angles—which is where the word "Anglish' or 'English' originated from, who came from the same Germanic area on the Jutland Peninsula the Jutes had migrated from earlier. Finally, the Norman French invaded and that ended hundreds of years of England being repeatedly invaded by its neighbors. The Normans brought a version of French that is now commonly referred to as 'old English'.

A couple hundred years later, after all this constant moving about of armies and people following after them or running away from them plus some trading and migrations due to drought and disease and so on and we now have modern English, which incorporates many German words, usually spelled differently; French words with the pronunciation changed; Danish words that are spelled with paired-vowels to create new vowel sounds that didn't exist in the original alphabet; and words from other languages as DIVERSE as 'bungalow' from India or 'Kung Fu' from Chinese or 'Wampum' from indigenous North Americans who probably came over from Mongolia during the Ice Age.

This DIVERSITY everyone seems to be excited about these days has been going on for thousands of years. Armies and individuals have been moving all around the world ever since the first tribes left Africa. Why is it suddenly such a big deal? Could it be because it is *unwanted*, just like other invading armies of the past, so the people organizing it are trying to *sell* it to you, by inventing a new, nice-sounding name, like making 'sanitation engineer' a better sounding job title than 'garbage man' or referring to criminal aliens who've entered the country illegally as 'undocumented migrants'.

You may be unaware of this, but the Japanese did the same kind of thing in Asia last century, announcing 'co-prosperity spheres' and trying to convince other Asian countries that Japanese education and technology was a good deal in exchange for exploiting their people and resources. Of course the Germans and Soviets had similar propaganda campaigns to try to convince people that the bad things they were doing were actually good things. Fast-forward to today and folks like Angela Merkel insist that letting in million of Muslim barbarians to rape and rob and murder—all while receiving free food and housing paid for with the taxes of the people they are terrorizing—is something wholesome and wonderful because those poor people from 3d-world slums are being welcomed into the civilization of modern Europe—never mind the fact they are destroying it in the process!

I wonder if the public relations campaigns would sound any different if it were millions of unarmed Vikings raping and plundering across Scandinavia and Western Europe instead of Muslims and Africans? Of course the Vikings were Caucasian, so they couldn't accuse people of racism based on skin color if they objected to their women and children being raped and their property stolen. Can you imagine the same propaganda being used to accuse people of being Azgard-a-phobic instead of Islamophobic—prejudice against the Norse gods instead of Islam—or of accusing people of being prejudiced against white guys with long beards? Of course it sounds ridiculous, because it is, but how is it any different from the bullshit being told to the people of Europe who object to being taxed to provide food and housing for these invading foreigners who are destroying their lives and their cultures?

"That's why we don't allow Muslims to immigrate to Japan—and the government limits the number of foreigners allowed in every year—and they try to maintain an optimum population size." So said Jasmine, a very serious-appearing little Oriental girl dressed only in blue jeans and a black t-shirt that announced, in very large letters, 'LEAVE ME ALONE'. Apparently she wasn't into the Halloween spirit! Still, I liked her attitude.

"Isn't there pressure on Japan to be more diverse?"

Theresa, Jasmine and I chuckled almost in unison. "The entire history of Japan has been one of isolationism," Theresa explained, "While we were happy to take new technology from foreign countries, we rejected most philosophies or other influences that clashed with Japanese culture, values and traditions."

> Our education system hasn't been taken-over by leftists teaching liberal ideas. In Taiwan, on the other hand, the educational system is being slowly destroyed by liberals—for example, we have a lot more gays than before and where Taiwan used to rank in the top 10 in the world in education in 2000, now they aren't even in the top 50. I also seem to recall that there's something like 100,000 Muslims working in Taiwan, mostly domestic workers from Indonesia and factory workers from the Philippines, and they've started having

problems with rapes and stabbings, although nothing like
Europe, probably because most of the Southeast-Asian guest
workers are women!

Ivy, an extremely flat-chested Asian girl with nice legs dressed as a French
Maid (a low-budget French Maid...her 'apron' was nothing more than a
paper towel attached with black, electric tape, wrapped around her waist)
nodded in agreement, "the Muslims in Taiwan are mostly women, taking
care of old people or babies and are very peaceful. I don't know of any
terrorist attacks by Muslims in Taiwan."

"No," added Theresa, "just a few rapes and other 'normal' crimes—and if
there were, you can bet the government would be very quick to deport
every Muslim in the country!"

Fiona, weaving a little, added: "see, not all Muslims are bad people!"

"True, said Dilbert, "but I had a cousin who was killed in the nightclub
bombing back around 2002, in Bali, *Indonesia*!"

"And I had a classmate who was gang-raped and murdered by Africans
in Italy around Christmas in 2016," added Ivy, "her friend was talking to
her on her cell phone when she started screaming. I watched the poor girl
running around with her phone, trying to figure out what she could do to let
the police in Italy know that her friend was being attacked!"

"Why don't we find something happier to talk about?" I suggested.
"Who needs another drink? Anyone? I'm buying..."

Chapter 31
Shreck Sex?

Fiona, it turns out, was of Spanish-Irish ancestry, with a generous helping of Scottish added in. Having lived in that era, I was well aware of the informal alliance that had had the Irish and Spanish colluding against the English. I seemed to recall reading somewhere that there'd even been an Irish Brigade fighting for Franco's forces during the Spanish Civil War. Of course just then I had other things on my mind—namely finding out if this little girl I was partially supporting, propping her up with one hand on her right elbow while Theresa assisted with her left—was in fact a natural redhead. She was probably around Theresa's age—meaning she hadn't developed enough of an alcohol tolerance yet to be able to 'hold her liquor' (i.e. "Every Young Man's Dream," to quote the title of a song from the Scottish rock group Nazareth).

"Shanks for walking me home," Fiona mumbled, "Oh no..."

She managed to stumble over to a short evergreen before throwing up noisily once, then again. We helped her to her feet once she was finished, and held her from falling as she languidly wiped her mouth with the back of her hand. "Urp," I shink I'm a widduw drunk"

"Yes, I can see that. Tic Tac?" asked Theresa.

"Which house is yours?" I asked. "That way," was the only response.

"Okay," was mine, "how about a horsie ride?"

Dark though it was, I admired her firm, slender thighs while I bent down behind her, placed my hands just above her knees, in front, and pushed my head between her thighs. Standing up, while holding firmly to her legs, I held her slight figure on my shoulders as easily as a father would balance a child. "Off we go!" I set off at a brisk walk and, within a few minutes, with her pointing the way, we'd arrived at the small, one-story house she rented with a pair of other students. If she'd noticed the way I felt-up her thighs with my thumbs on the way, she didn't say anything.

The house was blue or gray or some combination thereof, with a white, wooden fence around the side yard. It was difficult to tell the exact color in the dark, for that's what the house was—dark. There was a single yard lamp on a poll, and a dim front-porch light on, the rest of the house was dark. "Good," I thought. On the front porch was a half-full basket full of candy...the cheap stuff...bubble gum and sour candies that were mostly paper and small paper boxes with a few pieces of candy in each. Hanging off the handle of the basket was a small, hand-written sign saying, "help yourself but leave some for the next kids." Clearly, whoever left the basket understood the first part of trick-or-treat...the implied threat...no treat and you're likely to be the recipient of a trick...toilet paper in the trees or soap on the windows being the preferred mediums.

"She told me her roommates went to Chicago for the weekend," volunteered Theresa, somewhat belatedly, while the zombie cheerleader fumbled for her keys with her feet back on the ground. Of course I'd taken advantage, slowly sliding my hands up her thighs and under her skirt after I'd placed her back on the ground. Nice and firm: I really did prefer young girls, teenagers and those in their early 20's...their skin was usually nice and tight and smooth. I could feel a hard-on beginning already, anticipating what was about to follow.

Fiona had finally unlocked the door (having dropped her keys twice in the process), and turned to face us, clearly intending to thank us for helping her home and say 'goodnight'. Theresa preempted the 'goodbye' by placing both hands on the back of the girl's neck and kissing her on the mouth. French-kissing, apparently, and I found my erection growing as the kiss lingered...and continued as the little redhead apparently was not only not objecting, but seemed to be enjoying it after the initial surprise.

"Let me help," I said, picking her up, this time in front of me, as if cradling an infant. "Which way to your bedroom? Theresa, get the door."

I carried her across the threshold in mimicry of the tradition of carrying the bride across the threshold. The meaning has been somewhat lost in modern times, but in my days it was thought to symbolize that the girl wasn't too eager to lose her "chastity" and that there was an element of force prevailing over her resistance, much like a captive being carried off to be taken against her will. How this tradition started, even I didn't know, despite the benefit of an additional 200 years of knowledge, but I planned to continue the part of the tradition involving carrying the woman away and ravishing her (skipping the nuptials, of course).

Theresa found a light switch, revealing that the main room, in which we were standing, was about 10 by 20 feet, fairly good sized for the size of the house. The furnishings were start, to say the least: 1 sofa, a couple folding chairs, an old CRT-style TV on top of a 1960's style TV cabinet, only the interior, which would originally have held the TV workings, instead had a shelf on top of 1 cinder blocks, containing a DVD player, DVD's and a pair of remote controls. Putting the TV on top, I thought actually put it at a more comfortable height for viewing, I could see that the kitchen was ahead and to the left, so I headed down the hall to the right. To my left was a very small bathroom with a combination shower/bath with a sliding plastic curtain to keep water from soaking the room while one showered, a commode and a sink with a cabinet underneath and a mirror/cabinet above. I didn't even see a closet, just a shelf above the commode with extra toilet paper and cleaning supplies, and bars on the walls on which were hung 3 bath towels.

"Which room is yours?" was the question...to which there was no response. I looked at the limp form in my arms; she was passed-out, quite unconscious. Not knowing if I should just choose a room at random, I decided the bathroom floor would do just fine—easier to clean up any spilled blood, at any rate.

Gently laying her down, I proceeded to run my hands up her things, under her pleated, blue-and-white cheerleader skirt, slowly enjoying the warm smoothness of her living skin. Theresa, with seeming impatience, unzipped and pulled off her letter jacket, the sweater underneath with a large, embroidered megaphone patch affixed to the front with 'cheerleader' on it in cursive lettering, unbuttoned and removed the blouse beneath the sweater, the undershirt and, finally, the brassiere. Her breasts were small but nicely shaped, with small areolas and very small nipples. Frowning at her hurry—I quoted Little Nell from *The Rocky Horror Picture Show*, the quintessential Halloween Movie for those engaging in non-monogamous, unnatural sex acts, "some things are too good to rush!" I certainly felt that way when it came to exploring a new female's secrets.

"I want to watch you fuck her!"

I started to explain to Theresa that I had already decided it was an unnecessary risk. I didn't need the outlet for sex—after all, I now had a live-in girlfriend for the first time in my life/unlife. She was unconscious, so we could just borrow a little blood and leave and she'd probably be none-the-wiser and there would be no evidence of any *mauvais*, or evil on our part: the perfect crime! Before I could begin to protest, however, Theresa had unzipped my fly and reached into my trousers, massaging my privates, while at the same time nuzzling my neck. I couldn't help reaching out and gently squeezing the pert, warm breasts that a moment ago I had been merely ogling. Between the sight and touch of a new pair of tits and the ministrations to my neck and groin, I was 'standing at attention' almost immediately.

"Fuck Her," Theresa demanded, "I want to watch you doing it!" My loins were certainly ready to comply with her request, so with a silent sigh,

I located the zipper on the side of the skirt, slid it down, then did the same with the skirt, down her legs, not bothering to remove her shoes. Her panties were black—with a large, yellow 'smiley face' looking up at me. Cute!

I slid them down, expecting a patch of the curlies, only to find, with pleasure, short, straight hairs, not unlike what Theresa sported in her nether region, only these were strawberry-blonde in color. While both experiencing a nearly painful increase in the size of my hard-on and a mild sense of bewilderment: girls of European stock ALWAYS had curly pubes, unlike Asian girls. After a moment, logic reasserted itself: she'd either shaved recently and they'd only grown back in about half-an-inch in length, or she had done a masterful job of grooming herself with a pair of scissors. Either way, I enjoyed the effect and the very unique coloration of her hair against skin that, in the harsh light of the unshaded, naked light bulb, was almost the color of cream—and looked nearly as delicious. Easing my restrictive garments and sliding them down released me from the discomfort caused by the restraint. I engaged in about 90-seconds of foreplay, tasting her inner thing and sliding my tongue rapidly up her soft, smooth skin until my nose was resting on those very short little hairs and my tongue was probing the warm, wet holy-of-holies beneath. "Why is it they so often smell almost exactly like my armpit?" I couldn't help wondering as I shifted position, lifting her legs with my elbows beneath her knees, then (at this point I was fully 'into it', so to speak) greedily plunged in with no additional hesitation.

Theresa had her face resting against the underside of the girl's thigh, watching as I entered over and over, deeper and deeper with each thrust until I achieved maximum possible depth. From the movement I sensed with the small part of my consciousness that wasn't focused on the young woman I was violating, I surmised that Theresa was masturbating herself in accompaniment to my molestation. Yes, I confirmed with a quick glance, there was a flurry of motion going on beside her pussy. She was definitely massaging her clit while I pumped away with one hand while she had at least one finger from her other hand inside of her.

I don't know if it was the heightened arousal or the tight fit and friction, but I came almost immediately, gushing again and again, with electrical discharges firing in my brain as I rode the wave of ecstasy, momentarily losing myself, surrendering to the rush of sensation. It had been quite some time since I had either enjoyed such an intense feeling, similar to a drug-induced high, but not lasting for more than a few moments-the best of all natural highs, except it was over too soon, likewise it was a long time since

I had ejaculated so quickly; fortunately, I could feel that I still had sufficient stamina left to 'soldier on' for some time. To quote another line from *Rocky Horror*, 'I wasn't spent, yet'. I studied her face to see if my rude entry and explosion had intruded upon her consciousness; good, she was still out cold. Always better if you could violate your dinner and leave her completely ignorant of the fact and without the accompanying psychological baggage—there it was again, that pesky conscience of mine!

"Are you finished already?" inquired Theresa in a near-giggle, her head a mere 6 inches from where I was joined to the evening's entertainment, where she could best view the ins-and-outs.

"Just getting started," I explained, "here, want a taste?" She accepted the offering, cupping me with her hands and taking me into her mouth, sucking off the slimy residue and reversing the receding process, which had already begun, giving me renewed strength. After only a few minutes of her...ministrations...I was ready to resume my felonious assault on the sleeping girl. I re-entered her and, at first slowly Theresa, quite eagerly, bearing witness to the assault, chiming in with "oh yah, oh yah," egging me on. After a time, from the sound of her faint moans, it became obvious that she was doing more than just engaging in voyeurism, but that she was vicariously participating in the rape.

The first fuck had ended almost before it had begun, although with some tremendous mental fireworks at the crescendo. This second time I was slow, tender, as with a familiar lover, then with increasing power and authority, I drove deep into our unsuspecting host while my gaze devoured her in detail...breasts, slender stomach and navel, slender legs, delightful short hairs and then I retraced my path, again and again as I pumped away, with long, steady strokes, like an old Otto reciprocating engine, the type I had so admired at the 1867 World's Fair in Paris, a pair of large wheels, going around and around and, with each revolution, a large piston in between them, thrusting forward...and back...and forward, over and over, a sexual metaphor, stones and a pillar, pumping and pumping without cessation, as the earth revolves around the sun, on and on...timeless, insurmountable.

Okay, with my twig and berries it wasn't nearly as long as all that, but I was enjoying myself, taking my time, and the little girl I was taking advantage of was completely oblivious that I was raping her, which was totally fine by me. "And say hello, to oblivion," another *Rocky Horror* line came to mind, albeit unbidden and totally out of synch with the enraptured mood I was in. When my brain took hold of a line of thought, sometimes it just did it's own thing; yes, sometimes my mine had a mine of it's own.

I hadn't noticed when Theresa had left, but I certainly noticed as she came back into view; she knelt down, thighs on either side of the comatose play-toy, her straight black pubes a sudden contrast to the reddish-orange I'd been scoping-out and, eyes back centered on those small yet perky little breasts, I finally shuddered to a second climax. Panting a little, I raised my head up to my partner in crime, preparing to make some witty remark, such as "was it good for you, too?" but instead, I heard myself exclaiming, "what the fuck!"

I don't know how I moved so fast, but I caught her wrists...off balance...falling...I managed to arrest our downward progress with my elbows, stopping the kitchen knife she was holding just inches...no, a fraction of an inch...before it would have plunged into Fiona's chest.

"Just what in the name of Hades do you think you're doing?"

"You're done, right?"

"Yes, but... "

"So I want to cut out her heart and hold it while it stops beating; and, I'm thirsty, I'm ready for some blood. Anyway, it's as you said: we're vampires, this is what we do, we fuck the living for sport and then they're our dinner...right?"

"Yes, but... ," I repeated, sounding stupid even to myself. Twisting the knife out of her grasp and setting it on the floor beside me, while changing position, disengaging from the little twat and getting my legs under me, I took her hands in mine, clasped over the still beating heart that had nearly been forever stilled. Taking a deep breath and calming myself, I made myself give her a patient lecture, rather than screaming at her as I had nearly done.

> We only kill if we have to. Dead bodies attract police detectives and forensic scientists and then people go around asking questions and getting descriptions of people seen with the victim and they look at traffic camera recordings and examine the occupants of cars looking for people that match said descriptions and then they run license plate numbers. How many people might remember seeing whom she left with? There can't have been that many cars with 2 people both dressed as vampires. Why do you think I parked so far off campus so we had a long ways to walk to get to the party? Now, it was dark, I think we only passed under that one traffic camera on the way in and it's probably it didn't get a very good image, but why take the risk?

"I thought this is what we came here to do! Have a little fun, drink a little human blood for a change, instead of drinking from those smelly animals, and then kill them: dead men—and college girls—tell no tales and all that!"

Yes, but now we don't need to, do we? I just fucked her for a good 20 minutes or so and she hasn't moved—tomorrow she won't remember a thing and what she doesn't know won't hurt her. She'll be hung-over, a little weak from loss of blood—yes, we are going to feed on her—but she probably won't remember much after leaving the party, so there's no need to kill her. Besides, disposing of a body is a tricky business, or making it look like a suicide, or packing up all her stuff and making it so it look like she 'up and left town'. Missing persons get a lot less attention than dead bodies. People who wake up with a hangover and don't remember anything from the night before and don't mention a thing to anyone attract ZERO attention, which is much better for those of us who want to stay completely under the radar!

Taking the knife, I make two slight incisions, one on either side of her neck. The girl stirred slightly at the second cut, and I froze for a moment, until the shallow, steady breathing resumed. "Drink," I commanded.

I hadn't cut *too* deeply, so it took some time for us to drink enough. Theresa clearly wasn't satisfied when I insisted it was time to stop and I bandaged the cuts with a couple band-aids I found in the medicine cabinet.

What was this new attitude I was seeing? I'd seen Theresa pouting before, particularly during the first few weeks when I wouldn't let her go into public or get her things or use the internet—all of which had been perfectly understandable. This, this...*sullenness* she was exhibiting, as she grudgingly helped me to gently dress the girl again...this was new...and disturbing!

I picked up the girl, again using care to be as gentle as possible so as not to awaken her and spoil all our good work (dinner AND a show and the only mystery she would have is the cuts on her neck), and placed her on the sofa, covering her with the sweater and jacket, which would have been difficult to put back on her, while Theresa follow my directions to clean and replace the knife, wiping any prints off it and anything else she may have touched. I did the same in the bathroom, using a bit of toilet paper to dab up the few stray drops of blood that had fallen on the cheap, vinyl flooring, and wiping it thoroughly to remove any palm prints or hair or fibers that might have originated with myself or Theresa, then flushed the evidence, careful to use my knuckle, not a finger, on the flushing mechanism.

Flipping out the light and pulling the door shut behind us, again careful not to use a finger-tip, I heaved a silent sigh of relief as we re-emerged into the brisk, October air, with the faint smell of burning leaves lingering on the air and tickling the back of one's throat. Faintly, in the distance, were the sounds of party revelers still enjoying themselves. I felt for the chain and pulled my pocket watch from out of its pocket in my vest, glancing at it in the dim light afforded by the yard lamp. Midnight...or thereabouts—my watch no longer kept perfect time—in fact it was probably time to send it away for cleaning and oiling. There weren't many craftsmen around any more who worked on old watches such as the gold, 1916 trench watch I held in my hand. It was a very rare piece, which I'd found on a dead, English colonel during my days as a litter-bearer/ghoul during the Great War. As pocket watches were not exactly practical in combat, this was a transitional piece, a step in the evolution of wristwatches. Instead of the normal, glass front, it had hinged front and back metal covers. Instead of the normal, rounded metal loop for a chain, there were lugs, top and bottom, for a strap.

"Let's go back to the party," I suggested, "you said you wanted to find some young thing to dance with for awhile and I wouldn't mind another beer." Theresa visibly brightened at the suggestion; of course what I had in mind was something quite different, I intended to stay a couple hours and establish an alibi and be seen leaving with Theresa...and only her...when we finally departed for home. We'd just drained a petite person of maybe 2 pints of blood...probably not fatal, but it was possible she could go into shock and die. If so, I would like to be able to place us elsewhere. Actually, I had enjoyed the band at Heartland and they would probably be playing for awhile yet...maybe the thing to do was mingle a little while at the party, flirt with the mermaid—she'd been interested in the flask, maybe I could show her the watch and she might recall the time we'd spoken. We could let Fiona's friends know she'd arrived home safely, if anyone asked, and then go create another alibi downtown. I could use my credit card at Heartland, sure, that would show we'd been there at a particular time. What it would not explain, of course, is what a supposedly feeble old man was doing at a bar late at night, but explaining a sudden need to get out and about 'one last time' was better than having to explain where you were when the girl you'd escorted home suddenly expired from blood loss. Of course I'd deliberately not locked the door when we left; even if somehow we were placed with her at her house, having walked her home, it was always possible someone else could have wandered in off the street—after all, we'd gone right back to the party and from there, back to Heartland. When you'd been at this game as long as I have, you try to consider all the angles.

Walking back into the party, we split up and mingled, thus maximizing our exposure to potential alibi witnesses. Not that we could ever allow ourselves to be dragged into court, but if she died and there were an investigation, the fact people might remember us at the party until long after the time of death should eliminate us as potential witnesses: better if nobody even tried to determine who we were in the first place.

I soon found myself in a conversation concerning *Game of Thrones*, one of my favorite series of all time, following *Battlestar Galactica*. Probably I'd rank it second, closely followed by *Rome* and *The Walking Dead*. A tall, seemingly-black guy dressed as The Joker from *Batman* was speaking. I say 'seemingly' because his make-up was so thick you could only see skin at his neckline and around his ears. "A black guy in white-face," I thought to myself, "I wonder if the irony was intentional." Being that these were among the better-educated university students, rather than the dumbed-down libertards occupying many campuses these days, it could well be...or perhaps he was mocking Obama. T-shirts had, in years passed, pictured Obama in similar fashion. I casually wondered where he'd found the purple jacked and bright-green vest. They didn't look particularly well made, perhaps they were a costume-shop rental or something he'd purchased on the internet. I'd almost forgotten that Halloween was big business: they were probably mass-produced in China.

"The *Game of Thrones* is a modern-day morality play," said The Joker, having to speak loudly over the din of the crowd and the (in my opinion) tasteless rap music thumping away somewhere in the background.

> Think about it. While lots of people in the series die, the good ones die quick, relatively clean deaths, while the evil ones die in much less pleasant ways. Ned Stark, the 'star' of the series who dies in a real shocker in season one, has a quick, clean beheading. His wife has her throat cut. Three of his sons are either stabbed or killed with arrows: an acceptable death to warriors and less terrible than some other ways of dying. Joffrey, on the other hand, the little sadistic psychopath that everyone came in hate over several years, dies a terrible death from poisoning. Oberon Martel, who is a bully and an arrogant jerk, has his eyeballs driven back into their sockets

and his skull ripped apart by Gregor Clegane, aka The Mountain, no doubt for the crime of being a philandering faggot! I think it's a given that this was a rather unpleasant way to die! Renly Baratheon is killed by a demon. He wasn't a particularly evil person, but he was a homosexual, so he had to die in a less pleasant way than other, more righteous people like the Starks.

The most evil persona, of course, is Ramsay Bolton. He's a true sociopath who enjoys torturing people, particularly Theon Greyjoy, torments Sansa, his innocent, virgin wife, kills his own men, one of his lovers, his mother-in-law and her baby: basically he's the personification of evil. Being eaten alive by his dogs is a terribly unpleasant way to die...and probably was longer lasting and more painful a death than even Joffrey's poisoning.

"But what about Margaery Tyrell?" asked a little nymphette dressed as Cleopatra, wearing a gold-painted tiara that had probably been cut out of heavy paper or thin plastic, "she was a kind woman who gave money to orphans, why was she burned to death in an explosion? Certainly that's a more painful way to die than getting your throat cut?"

Perhaps, although it was probably much faster—the people who died in the explosion might not have had time to feel much; their nerve endings were probably burned away so quickly they only had one, intense blast of pain and then nothingness. Also, remember she wasn't engaging in charitable endeavors because she actually liked the orphans or had sincere empathy for them: she admits when she's held captive by The Sparrow that she was doing it for political 'brownie points'. Of course she could have been just telling him what he wanted to hear, but Cersei knew what she was up to, so it's pretty obvious she was a fake. She pretended to be nice and sweet, but it was mostly an act. She was less evil than many of them, so she, The Sparrow, who was another fake, using religion to gain power, and her brother who was another sodomite who'd had a homosexual relationship with Renly Baratheon, among others, die when wildfire consumes the Sept of Baelor...again, in my opinion it was not as terrible a death as poisoning, because it was quicker, but still probably a very painful way to die.

"What about Myrcella," questioned a very obese demon, complete with horns and a plastic trident, clearly enjoying the opportunity to play 'devil's advocate', "she was poisoned, just like Joffrey, and died in the arms of her father Jamie, and Rob Stark gets pin-cushioned, so it wasn't exactly a quick death, was it?"

Ah, but it wasn't nearly as painful a death as Joffrey's, was it? You could tell that it was more like being drugged, after all, both Elia Martell and Bronn take the same poison and are cured by an anti-dote whereas Joffrey was obviously in a great deal of pain and even ended up bleeding out of his eyes, as I recall. I even seem to recall a conversation involving Varys, where they mention that some poisons were more painful that others. As for Rob, don't forget that he'd sworn to marry one of Walder Frey's daughters, then broke his solemn oath and married the woman he loved instead. Less serious of an offense than torturing whores and so on, but still, he broke a sacred oath which is a crime and/or a sin, depending on the moral code being applied, so of course his death had to be somewhat more painful than those of his parents.

"What about Stannis?" this from a petite little thing dressed in a black-and-white, tight-fitting Harlequin outfit, with a jester's-style cap with bells on the ends of long points, a star painted over her left eye, but, unlike Ace Frehley of KISS, she had an elongated diamond painted over the right one—an effect I could to be quite eye-catching (pun intended), "he used black-magic to have a demon kill his brother...the crime of fratricide...and let his daughter be burned alive, but he suffers an honorable death in combat!"

Ah, yes, but he really didn't order the assassination, did he? That was the plan of The Red Woman, Melisandre, and Stannis didn't really find out about it until afterwards. Stannis was completely without personality and friends, according to the story, but he WAS the rightful heir to the throne. Of course, as you point out, he DOES allow his daughter to be burned alive...one of the worst crimes in the entire story, but the death you mention is considerably less honorable because he was slain by a woman! In some cultures, particularly Islamic ones, being killed by a woman is probably the most dishonorable death possible. In fact, it is believed in some cultures that this is enough to keep that individual from going to heaven. So, depending on his belief system, this may have been a particularly unnerving or at least a very embarrassing way to die.

"Why did the little girl get burned alive? What was her crime? Also, why do you call it a 'morality play?'" asked a zombie football player (clearly an actual member of the football team who was either short on funds or imagination or both, who'd merely donned his football uniform and done a bit of make-up for the zombie look). '

The Onion Knight's daughter wasn't a major character. She was like the 'expendable crew members' in the first Star Trek series. After awhile, every time they introduced a new bridge officer you knew that person was going to die so they didn't have to kill off one of the major characters. Do you remember when Brienne is escorting Jamie Lannister back to King's Landing and they find 3 dead girls hanging from a tree? Breinne asks if they were giving a quick death. She's told TWO of them were given quick deaths...meaning the third one was the pretty one, so the three men gang-raped her before killing her. Brienne says to him 'three quick deaths' before she shoves her sword into his guy...slowly. Again, it's a morality tale: she intentionally makes his death take longer as a punishment for him and his comrades raping the girl before killing her.

Morality plays were popular in the late Middle Ages. The actors personified moral attributes such as good and evil or charity versus vice or one of the deadly sins and so forth. Even the evil people who aren't killed are forced to suffer a LOT more than the good people in the story. Theon, who has 2 innocent, orphan boys burned alive and kills defenseless prisoners after betraying his friend he'd sworn to support 'now and always', ends up being tortured and brainwashed and has his...manhood...cut off. This is the moral lesson: bad things happen to bad people. The worse a person is, the worse their punishment.

Tyrian is put on trial, made a slave, imprisoned again and sentenced to death by his father, escapes by spending days stuck inside a wooden crate, but his fate is MUCH better than his siblings. Jamie is beaten, locked in a cage for weeks in mud and his own bodily wastes, then has his hand chopped off and has his daughter die in his arms. But, he isn't completely evil, he has his good points as well, so his death is better than many of the other characters.

Cersei, the most evil character so far, aside from her Satan-spawn Joffrey and Ramsay 'the bastard' Bolton, is imprisoned and tormented and then forced to walk through the streets naked while having abuse heaped upon her by the entire population of King's Landing! The Nun or whatever who torments her gets hers in the end, as well, tied up for The Mountain-turned-Frankenstein's Monster to torment. And we know from his rape and murder of the Martell princess before he became undead or whatever, that he was probably raping the wicked sister who was a sadistic bitch who enjoyed tormenting prisoners rather than showing them mercy. Irony, for sure, but did you feel any sympathy for the nun or did you feel she was getting what she deserved? If you've seen...

I chose this point to disengage myself from the group, taking advantage of the press of the crowd to slide my hand along the thigh and buttocks of the Harlequin...the thin fabric of her tight-fitting tights (was that a homonym?) allowed me to cop a really nice feel—enough to give me a partial boner—while making it seen incidental (she may have suspected otherwise, but I didn't stop to ask). Whatever else The Joker had to say about morality plays was probably nothing I didn't already know and mention of the 'undead' and 'rape' reminded me that we were here on a mission; one which I felt we'd accomplished.

Finding Theresa engaged in a conversation about the annual massacre of dolphins by Japanese islanders, I loudly complained about the rap music they insisted on playing (and to think I'd hated disco music back in the 1970's...shit, I'd happily listen to the Bee Gees or Earth, Wind & Fire all night rather than have to listen to this rap crap!), and insisted on going back to Heartland...all part of the alibi strategy, of course...offering to take anyone with us who might want to go, knowing that there would be no takers.

"Oh, I almost forgot," we were now on a particularly dark patch of street, so I sensed rather than saw the questioning look on her face, "happy Halloween!"

Chapter 32
A Momentary Lapse of Reason

Teddy McPhee was a fourth-generation police officer. His great-grandfather and grandfather had been part of an American stereotype—police officers in the city of Boston. His father, the first one in the family to ever graduate from college, had left what he referred to as the "People's Republic of Massachusetts" after graduation and had worked in the other, traditional enclave for police officers of Irish ethnicity: Chicago. Decades of Democrat mis-leadership, along with drugs and gangs, and Chicago was a mess. Equipped with a master's in the sciences from U of I and a medical degree from IUPUI, Theodore (he hated that name) had stayed on in Indianapolis, and now was a senior, forensic pathologist at the Indiana State Crime Lab. Ted, as he was known at work (Teddy to his friends, wife and kids), wasn't sure what he was looking at. The microscope and imaging system he was using were state of the art, was the sample perhaps corrupted or tainted? Whatever it was, he had a feeling it was going to provide some distraction from a job that was feeling more routine with each passing year. After all, how exciting could staring at tissue samples under a microscope really be, anyway?

"Morning! Hey Hector, where did this swab sample come from?"

"Notre Dame girl. I was just skimming over the file...seemed pretty routine. I'm going for some coffee, want some?"

Teddy walked over to the monitor Hector had been using. It seems the girl had fainted while standing in line at an ATM in the campus post office. She'd been taken to the medical facility where a nurse had become suspicious, suspecting a roofie when the girl explained she'd been escorted home after a party by 2 strangers, she'd passed out, and had awakened partially undressed and with her t-shirt on inside-out. A blood test had revealed an absence of any drugs, but the nurse had suggested a rape-swab before the results of the drug test had come in and revealed...what?

"Here you go, one cream, one sugar. So, what's your boggle?"

"The sperm in this sample...they're just...weird! Take a look and tell me what you think."

"Hey, you're the expert, I only work here," demurred Hector, but he took a look all the same. "I'm not sure what it is, but yeah, they do look strange...are you sure these are human? Could they be from some form of primate or other animal?”

“I'm not really sure. I guess the thing to do is shoot a file over to the FBI guys and see if they have anything on their database that matches.”

Five hours later, when gentlemen from the Federal Government appeared, waving ID's and seizing his samples and having everyone who knew anything sign confidentiality agreements, it confirmed the feeling he'd had. He'd really like to learn more about the nature of the strange sample he'd examined...but he was pretty confident he never would.

Chapter 33
The Hangover

Several hours of drinking and dancing had left my playmate in a good mood...until the next morning, of course, when she awoke to a good old-fashioned hangover (yes, vampires get them too). I was in better shape, but then again I had had less to drink and I had developed a very good tolerance to alcohol over the years. Well, perhaps 'good' isn't the best word...it took several drinks to just give me a slight buzz and I drank expensive hooch!

So, we spent the entire next day in bed, sometimes sleeping, sometimes watching movies, other times just sitting in the dark, listening to music. I had a great deal of music she'd never heard before, so I was choosing things that had to be listened to, like Alan Parsons, Rush, Pink Floyd, Genesis...none of the modern, popular tripe they usually played on the radio these days.

The dark—that really was a vampire's world. Artificial lighting didn't bother us, and we could travel on days when it was heavily overcast, with the proper precautions. But the light of the sun was death, if one of our kind were to be exposed for too long.

"Is that really how war is? How dreadful! I mean I've seen war movies before but never ones that seemed so real!"

We were having a Brad Pitt day and I'd just shown her *Meet Joe Black, Inglorious Basterds* and *FURY*.

"There was that other one you showed me, where the guy stops on the beach to pick up his arm...and this is what you used to do for your job!"

"Warfare was different in my day, of course, but a lot of the things were the same: the fear, the smells, the noise, the death—it's not all the 'ride of the noble 600' or 300 Spartans holding off 80,000 Persians or little David with a sling killing a really big dude armed with a sword! Unfortunately, as good as this movie was in many ways, you still had the inevitable, unnecessary, Hollywood *stupidity* that detracts from the pleasure of watching the movie. Can you tell me if you spotted any of the mistakes right there at the end?"

"Um...I wasn't really watching it for mistakes, can you play that part again?"

"But of course...that's what the extra buttons on the remote control are for—just a moment..."

"Okay, I see; Brad Pitt is on the back of the tank when he's shot the first two times but somehow he is magically inside the...door...the last time he is shot."

> It's called a hatch and yes, that's one of the problems, although he could have theoretically climbed over while the camera was on the German soldier. The thing is...why didn't they dog the hatch...lock it from inside...so the Germans couldn't toss in the grenades? They had enough time. Even if the sergeant was too badly wounded to move, the hull gunner had plenty of time. Also, when the machine gun suffers a ruptured casing, which could really happen, by the way, the gunner decides he's going to replace it with the .30 caliber machine gun from the roof. Really? It would have been much easier to extract the broken case. For one thing, the gun on the roof had a barrel shroud. To remove the machine gun, take the barrel shroud off the replacement machine gun, then put it in the hole would have taken a long time, if it were even possible...tanks in my day were not very sophisticated, but I have occasionally looked at technical specs and designs of modern tanks and I seem to recall that those gun barrels are threaded, so they screw into the gun mantle, so they don't just slide around loosely in the hole. If I remember correctly, the one on the roof could be taken apart and could use the barrel from the tank gun after it's receiver was removed...again, why not just pry out the broken cartridge casing!?

Just then came the buzzing of the intercom. "That must be Miguel. You look like shit! Just stay in bed, keep quiet, and I'll go see what he wants." I was still in my boxers and an old sweatshirt I'd worn to sleep in—while it wasn't winter yet, it was chilly enough at night that I'd begun wearing clothes to bed. My hair was a mess, I hadn't shaved—basically I looked exactly what an old, single guy on his own would be expected to look like.
I raced up the stairs and then made a show of slowly walking across the kitchen to the door, glad it was late enough in the day that the front of the house was in shadow. Sure enough, it was Miguel, with a certified letter he'd signed for on my behalf. I explained that I'd given Theresa a few days off and lied, claiming that I was about to make dinner for myself and asked

him if he wanted to join me. Naturally he declined, preferring his wife's cooking to whatever the old German guy was likely to whip up. We chatted for a bit about the livestock and the weather, and he complimented me on how much better I was looking and that having a private nurse seemed to be doing good things for me. Panzer and Brutus came in off the porch for a couple of rawhide treats and a little TLC, then all three of them went back outside and I went downstairs with my mystery letter.

"I have an idea," announced Theresa as I re-entered the basement bedroom, "that Shanghai girl with the poodle? Let's go pay her a visit—you can fuck her, we can drink her dry and then I can cut out her heart! With all the guys she's tricked into buying her a meal and then running off on them, the police will have tons of suspects. How's that for a plan? So, whatcha got there?"

A letter from an attorney. I own a building in a run-down part of Chicago. It seems the city is finally making good on the promises Trump made years ago to fix the ghettos and they plan to renovate several old neighborhoods and I have an offer to sell my building. The lawyer thinks it's a very limited time offer and that the city will be using eminent domain on anyone that doesn't sell—basically, that's a legal mechanism to *force* you to sell...basically the government takes your land and gives you whatever they feel like for it. It's as Unconstitutional as hell, but the Courts have been letting them get away with it for forever as it's all for the 'common good'...in theory, anyway. Of course usually developers, realtors and lawyers and assorted buddies of the legislators making the decisions make money off of these 'public good' transactions while the landowner gets fucked, but it beats the old days. There was a time when, if you owned the land, you also owned the people *on* the land! If you were a tenant farmer and the landowner kicked you off the land, you'd likely starve unless you could find some other line of work—and there weren't factories or convenience stores back then or unemployment compensation. These idiots out protesting because their 'stimulus checks' ran out or they don't get free 'Obamaphones' anymore or because their free food has been reduced and they might actually have to go out and get a job must be the most spoiled, worthless assholes in the history of civilization!

Anyway, I am going to take the offer, but it also means putting my renters on notice that they're going to have to move, which the property management can do—I've never actually met any of them, anyway, but it was a place I kept primarily as a bolt-hole...call it a 'safe house'. I use it occasionally if I go to Chicago to hunt and sometimes it gets late enough I worry about getting home in time, and also it's there in case I ever had a need to leave here in a hurry and 'lay low' for awhile. There's a very small income from the tenants, but maintenance fees eat up most of that. I do get a tax credit, I think—I leave all that up to my accountant.

I guess I need to go up there on Monday and stay for a few days. I'll think up some lie to tell Miguel...medical procedure of some kind...probably best if I have him take care of feeding the dogs and you just stay quiet and keep the lights off except here in the basement—it might look odd if you were here while I was away. I can trust you for a couple of days NOT to go kill anyone without me, right? I also recommend you feed late at night, just to be sure Miguel and his family are asleep and not out wandering-around where they might happen to see you moving around, as unlikely as that would be. Now, if you'll excuse me, I need to draft a couple letters to the attorney and my management company. Remember, I gave you a couple days off, at least that's what I told Miguel, so don't go outside. It is dark enough you can play piano in the parlor, if you wish—it's Miguel's dinner time, so I don't think you have to worry about him looking in the windows!

Chapter 34
While the Cat's Away...

Theresa couldn't believe her luck! While she was grateful to Stanislaus for saving her from being gang-raped and murdered by the rednecks, not to mention allowing her to live, surrounded by all these beautiful works of art, no material wants (except she still missed her cigarettes)...and he was both an excellent teacher and lover, with a great collection of movies, music and knowledge of history and language—much better than the professors at school, one of whom (a liberal nutbag) had apparently made international headlines a few years ago by declaring that "all men who stare at women are committing rape!" (It was before her matriculation, so she'd only learned of it afterwards, via campus gossip. followed by an internet search for the details. Still, it was mostly a good school, despite a few nutball-loony professors). She missed her friends, she missed going out, shopping...feeling free.

Since the night she'd stolen the phone, she'd broken one of the cardinal rules, one that would get her in real trouble if she were found out: she had contacted people she knew to let them know she was OK, after all. After they'd gone shopping, and she'd stolen the USB cord to charge her stolen smart phone, she'd plugged the phone into one of the USB ports in the back of the computer, with the volume set to mute, where it had received a full charge without any real danger of discovery. While it was sometimes difficult to be sure she'd be alone and uninterrupted, she'd managed to find time to let her mom know she was OK and contact her few, close friends, telling them of the momentous change in her life and, of course, cautioning them to keep it all a deep secret and not tell anyone they'd heard from her at all. So far, she hadn't said anything to anyone about where she was staying or whom she was living with—the lectures on maintaining secrecy and anonymity and done that much, not to mention the fact she might be a suspect in the murders of the 3 would-be rapists (that all seemed so long ago she sometimes almost forgot she might be a wanted person in a murder investigation!).

But now, she had a small window of opportunity—she had to make the most of it. Sure enough, it was twilight outside...dark enough for her to retreat to the 2d floor bedroom that was "hers" She kept most of her personal items there, not *too* well organized, to make it appear lived-in, as though that was where she was staying, per her benefactor's instructions...*just in case*... Personally, she thought the vampire's obsession with details and appearances bordered on paranoia, but it was his house, his rules (except for the few she chose to break, of course).

The cat, Caesar, was sacked-out on her bed. Seeing her, he yawned, stretching out one paw, exposing his extended claws, then curled back up to resume his nap. As all cats did, he apparently felt he owned the entire house. She didn't begrudge him the use of the bed—she didn't use it! "Now," she said to herself, "whom do I contact first?"

I left just after dark, driving the old, red MG convertible. I'd fed first, from a somewhat uncooperative beast that I was going to have turned into hamburger sooner rather than later, left a note for Miguel, telling him we'd gone to the Mayo clinic for a few days for tests for an undiagnosed ailment, asking him to feed and water the dogs while I was gone. I'd said my goodbyes to Theresa and the animals and again cautioned her—no lights, no noise, only go out late at night if at all. No, the old British roadster wasn't the best car for late fall weather—I kept the drafty top up—but it was the only car I owned that would fit down the ramp to the basement, through an entrance that had once been a coal chute.

Fortunately, it was late enough I'd missed 'rush-hour'. I hated driving during rush-hour traffic: really rush 2 or more hours, if one were honest about it, particularly if one were driving past Elkhart or Nappanee, where many factories let out around 3:30, then you had the office workers getting out at 5, so traffic tended to be heavier from 3:30 to 6:00 if one were driving north out of Goshen. My biggest fear was being in an accident when the crazies were out in force—referring of course to late-night drunks. It was a crime to leave a property-damage accident, and the plates and title were in my name. I hadn't had to experience one to realize it would take longer to resolve a traffic accident long after business hours. This is one reason I made it a firm rule to be off the road at least 2 hours before dawn; in my part of Indiana, hitting a deer at night was a genuine road-hazard. The prudent vampire made sure there was enough time to deal with the police or sheriff's department, get a vehicle towed, and call a cab for home prior to dawn!

Being a Monday night, traffic was merely terrible by the time I reached the toll road and turned West towards Chicago. Governor Pence, prior to him becoming Vice President, had invested a lot of money in improving the roads in Indiana to make it more attractive to potential investors/developers. Instead of having to muck-about in South Bend or take 6 all the way past

Valparaiso, I merely headed due north and got on I-90 at the new interchange just east of Elkhart. Easy peasy!

If we'd had roads like this, we'd have never lost the army retreating from Russia when Alexander refused to surrender after the capture of Moscow. Correction: Napoleon wouldn't have lost the army: by that time, I was no longer with the army, I was permanently AWOL. Of course it was Nappy's own fault—he spent a month sitting in Moscow, waiting for an envoy that never came; and playing footsie with a Polish princess who, by accounts, had used all of her feminine wiles to try and persuade him to promise a return of Polish independent sovereignty.

The army had crossed the Niemen River into Russia at the end of June and arrived in Moscow in mid-September. Anticipating the return trip would take the same amount of time, had they left at the end of September, it would have taken until mid-December just to retrace their steps as far as Poland! Hadn't the experiences of the Teutonic Knights and Charles XII of Sweden fighting the Russians in the winter taught him anything?

When le Petit Emperor finally realized that no surrender was forthcoming and he ordered the long march back to France, his next fatal decision was the abandonment of the attempt to break through the roadblock the Russians had thrown up in the French rear (from what veterans had told me in Paris, after the war, they could feel the Russians breaking at the end of the 2d day of battle and, to a man, they were sure one more day would have cleared the road to Minsk and the supply depot the Russians had recently captured there). By turning aside and taking the longer, more northerly road back through Vilnius instead of the more direct road, he compounded the problems of logistics (most importantly the delivery of food supplies) and lost more time before the weather turned foul. He made another, critical blunder, ordering the burning of his pontoon bridges, thinking to speed up the pace to the frozen Berezina River and cross the ice, only to discover a thaw had made the ice too thin, causing another delay as 2 entire villages were dismantled for wood with which to build a bridge (which cost the lives of hundreds of engineers, including 160 Dutchmen). Finally, what really doomed his army was his wasting additional time romancing some piece of Polish princess pussy in Warsaw, which resulted in the Grande Armée being caught in an early snowstorm as they belatedly made their way out of Poland. 400,000 dead—many of whom might have made it back had Bony shown a little more haste in returning home, and that didn't include the artillery, horses, wagons and captured treasure that were abandoned along the way.

Why was it so many men were laid low by women? Not wanting to continue this particular line of thought, I decided I needed something louder to listen to. I had a box of cassette tapes on the seat next to me (I'd upgraded from 8-track to cassette back in the 1980's and left it at that; I didn't drive the car that often-red sports cars tended to attract too much of the wrong kind of attention-just a few times from April to September, to keep the tires and valve seals good, the oil from sitting and separating, the battery charged, etc.).

The sound system wasn't the newest, but I'd put serious money into it back when, and it still sounded pretty good. I pulled out a tape I'd dubbed from LP's years ago, when everything was analog. AC-DC "Highway to Hell" on side 1 and Van Halen 1 on the other. "Perfect," I told myself. Keeping the speed to just over the limit (not easy with the heavy bass beat and drums speeding up my heart-rate and the car drove better at speeds above 80 mph as well), The building was near the Hyde Park area. I took the University of Chicago exit, wondering if there were any young, college girls wandering around alone and night and quickly discounted the idea— they took security at that university very seriously, considering shootings and other gang activity occurred frequently within just a few blocks of campus. Driving down mostly-deserted streets (it was Monday night, after all), I reached my property just moments after midnight and pulled around to the back, where my private entrance awaited.

Putting the car in park, with the only the running lights on for illumination, I walked down the steep incline to the large, windowless, steel-reinforced hardwood doors. The heavy, Diebolt padlock was still in place, although the hasp was slightly bent and there were scratches around the hinge where it appeared someone had tried to beat a pry-par underneath it. Either the noise had attracted attention and scared them off or the perp(s) had decided there was likely to be nothing of value in an old basement and had given up when it turned out to be too much work. Probably they were just looking for a place to shoot-up and crash, or perhaps they just wanted access to the building to rob and rape some of the tenants; Chicago in 2016 had finally passed Detroit for the greatest number of homicides in one year. So much the success of Democrat-party policies and the anti-gun laws in Cook County (where there were plenty of guns, but it generally only criminals who had them!).

So far, this year, they were about tied. I'd never been to Detroit but I'd seen photos—all indications are it was even worse than Chicago, which at least had a magnificent downtown area. Ruined buildings, dilapidated schools, abandoned shopping malls, vacant dwellings...and tons of vandalism. Of course this was nothing new: I'd seen magnificent statues from the time of the Roman Republic that had had initials scratched onto them. The very name 'vandalism' had come from a Gothic tribe of near-savages who'd delighted in breaking apart any piece of artwork or infrastructure that couldn't be stolen. Even a group of drunken artillerymen in the French army had shot a piece off the nose off the Sphinx in Egypt. If their officer hadn't come along to and put a stop to it, they probably would have shot the entire thing to pieces.

It is a sad reality that it has always been easier to destroy something than to create something magnificent. Sadly, there were individuals in the world who took a perverse satisfaction in destroying things of beauty. Okay, maybe as children most of us do things we would never do later in life, carving our initials into a picnic table in a park, for example, but it was something most of us grow out of. I had just never understood those people who never learn to appreciate beauty and delight in its destruction. In that way I guess I was the personification of Hannibal Lector in Silence of the Lambs: I felt that there was really only one good use for people of that ilk: they should all be killed and eaten (or, as was the vampire way, drunk and then killed).

Of course, most humans would probably consider me far more of a monster; after all, I didn't spray graffiti on buildings—I murdered people and often raped the women I killed! Of course, to me, there was nothing significantly different in my killing a human than a human killing and eating a chicken, or a cat killing a mouse. I killed, of course, but I did it to survive (mostly). Also, I was probably different from most other vampires (were there other vampires?) in that I cultivated my own herd in order to keep my depredations against humans to a minimum.

I avoided children and innocent people living simple lives—at least, to the extent it was possible. All of this, of course, is why I'd set myself up in a terribly boring part of the USA, without the attractions of a major city or the scenery of mountains, forests or oceans, just so I could feed on smelly, stupid cattle, in order to avoid having to kill humans (aside from the occasional individual whose removal made the world a better place and gave me a little thrill in the process). Likewise, sex was something that all manner of life feels compelled to engage in—but I didn't rape for the fun of it; in fact, I never engaged in involuntary sex unless I was going to kill the girl anyway, so ultimately it didn't really make any difference—she was still going to die; if she provided a little entertainment value as well as nourishment, so much the better for me, and the inevitable end for her was the same. If the USA hadn't had such puritanical laws concerning prostitution, I would have been able to satisfy those needs in other ways and wouldn't need to kill as often as I did, as infrequent though that may be. At least now I had Theresa. And, I also had things to do. There would be plenty of time for ruminating later.

Traffic was heavy, being as it was a Friday night, so it took a little over three-and-a-half hours to arrive in downtown Chicago. Still, the night was plenty young; some of the bars would only just now be filling with patrons. I had dressed for the occasion and had a couple thousand dollars in my pockets, along with an assortment of knives concealed about my person (the Socialist Republic of Chicago was not a place for someone from out-of-state to carry without a permit!)

Rush Street turned out to be a serious disappointment. Named for one of the signers of the Declaration of Independence, it had once been one of the 'truly happening' places in the USA. Basically a bar and entertainment district back in the day, I had spent many nights searching for prey while also enjoying the music and party atmosphere to be found in the nightclubs, restaurants and dance clubs from the 1950's to the 1990's. I'd enjoyed some incredible blues bands, some good rock and roll and, although not my preferred genre, some excellent jazz. Eventually, many clubs were replaced with tall office and residential buildings. Also, the quality of entertainment declined and improvements in video surveillance and electronic security in the face of growing gang violence had made it more difficult for me to feed safely led me to cease my visitations (the last thing I wanted to do was drink alcohol or drug-laced blood from some wino in an alley).

Tonight I had visited out of nostalgia, as I was in town, anyway. For starters, the music was generally crap: rap and hip-hop were more prevalent than rock or blues. I did find a decent jazz band for awhile, but after only 20 minutes or so it was time for them to take a break and the live music was replaced by cop-hating gangster-rap, so it was time to pay for my beer and go.

Within a block I was bothered by two bums 'panhandling' for change, as well as a group of teenage hoodlums who obviously felt that an old, white man walking down the sidewalk simply demanded harassment as a means of entertainment. Eventually they decided I had nothing worth taking and left in search of other diversions before I was forced to kill them; not that I would have minded doing so, but I was of course doing my best not to draw attention to myself.

I tried several other locations that had once been my 'haunts'. One place that had always had good, live bands was now an Indian/Mediterranean restaurant. Another place had been torn down and replaced with a pay-by-the-hour parking garage (I drove around the block three times, thinking I'd forgotten the location, before I recognized the building across the street and realized I was in the right place after all). A third place was still a club, but they'd removed the stage where the bands used to perform and had some moron of a DJ, bare-chested under a denim vest and sporting a rainbow-striped wig and, again, the music was total shit.

I ended up at the Hard Rock Café, but they had a private hip-hop party going on and the entire establishment had been reserved. Now thoroughly discouraged, I spent 20 minutes systematically driving around the downtown area looking for action but didn't find anything that looked interesting. Belatedly, I tried and internet search on my phone to see if I could find a Blues club or something with a Rock n Roll cover band, but anything that looked good was out in the suburbs. I thought about having a drink at the 96th floor of the Hancock Building but a quick inquiry of my phone revealed they had closed at midnight! So much for my plan of spending three nights enjoying big city nightlife! It had only been about two years since my last visit, but it seemed as though nearly everything had changed in that time.

Chicago had once been one of the great cities of the world. In many ways it still was, of course, but when there were 10 shootings a night (more like 20 during the hot, sweltering summer nights), drug dealers everywhere, areas in which the police were afraid to go, and the average career of a public school teacher lasted less than a year even when starting salaries were something like $100,000 a year just to get bodies in classrooms, it was truly saddening. While not all the problems could be blamed on the decades of government by the Democrat party, the fiscal-mismanagement and overly-liberal justice system they were responsible for were certainly to blame for much of the societal rot and decay the city was suffering.

I feared Chicago would go the way of Detroit. While I had never visited, I did have access to the internet. Photos of abandoned schools, shopping malls, parks and office buildings told a grim story—it reminded me much of my corner of Europe after the Spanish Flu, except the desolation was the result of social failures rather than a plague-like contagion. I recall reading once that a box had been discovered in a warehouse in Detroit containing 14,000 unprocessed rape kits. Were these all from cases for which a suspect had never been identified or, like Gaius Baltar deciding it would simply take too long to test everyone for Cylon DNA, had some hospital workers simply decided removing bullets and sewing up trauma victims held a higher priority so they simply ceased doing the tests? Whatever the cause, it was a damning indictment of a failed society.

During the brief drive to my building I witnessed two arrests, a woman with her underwear around her ankles urinating in a darkened doorway, an obviously very high, shirtless male wandering through traffic playing an air guitar and no fewer than four 'dumpster-divers' (homeless people who would search through trash cans and dumpsters for recyclable containers they could sell for a few pennies), I decided it was time to go.

I also decided to give up any thoughts of feeding tonight. Never mind, it would not be the first time in my unlife I had been unable to feed—I have gone for several weeks on more than one occasion, as a matter of fact. Instead, I focused on the task that had brought me to Chicago in the first place as I pulled around to the back of the building that I had purchased more to have a 'safe house' in case I had to flee my farm, although it had also allowed me to visit the city on numerous occasions. Although I would have to find another bolthole, so to speak, after tonight's experience I did not think I was going to miss my infrequent trips to Chicago!

Despite the late hour and the chill temperature, there was a block party going on one block over. Most of the buildings in the neighborhood seemed abandoned, so maybe there weren't that many people to call and complain to the police; or perhaps the police were too busy dealing with shootings and other serious crimes to respond to a noise complaint. Either way, there were people making noise. Or, I thought, perhaps they were providing a useful distraction.

The building was old—meaning it was built rather solidly—and would no doubt do a good job of muffling my hammering from the few tenants living on the ground floor. What I feared was the sound escaping through the wooden cellar doors. A curious passer-by might call the police who while likely too busy with robberies, rapes and murders to respond directly, might yet do so—it was a risk I wished to avoid. Another tap with the hammer resulted in slight depression. I could see it was going to be a long night!

Oiling first the padlock and then the inset lock with the 3-in-1 oil I'd brought for this purpose, I unlocked the locks and pushed the doors inwards, smelling the dusty, stale odor of air long undisturbed. Flipping on the overhead light, I returned to the MG and backed it carefully down the ramp. I had a good 2 meters of clearance on either side, as put it in park and killed the engine. Before I had an opportunity to forget to do so, I hung the padlock for safekeeping on the hook I had mounted on the inside of the left door for just that purpose.

Returning to the car, I pulled out the letters I'd prepared for the tenants, then exited the building, pulling both doors to and locking the deadbolt. I reasoned just the one lock would be sufficient for the time being. Pulling my collar up against the chill in the air, I walked around to the front of the building, sliding one page into the slot at the top of each mailbox. I wondered briefly at the fact that each of them had a pair of locks, then concluded that one of them was for each tenant and the other must be a lock using a generic USPS key, allowing the postal carrier to place larger items in the boxes. One of the advantages to living out in the countryside, as I did, was that parcels were still left on people's front porches in relative safety— and mailboxes didn't need to be locked!

Next, I decided to take a walk around the neighborhood; I hadn't been around for a while and chances were I wouldn't be back again. There were other, reasonably well-maintained buildings such as mine, invariably with bars on the ground-floor windows and security cameras mounted over the entranceways. They were, sadly, outnumbered by dilapidated and sometimes simply abandoned buildings. No doubt some of these were crack houses. With no potential buyers, landlords had simply ceased paying either the mortgage payments and/or the property taxes, forcing the banks or the government to take title to the properties, some of which were inhabited by the dregs of society. They didn't pay rent. On the other hand, they didn't have utilities, either. Living for free, but without light, heat or running water: I'd lived that life for enough years to know that it was better to spend half your life working for someone else, so the other half you spent working for yourself could be spent in some degree of comfort.

What was with all this philosophizing tonight? I guess I was bored; no luck finding some good music or a bar where I might pick up a young lady looking for a little excitement... or cash. I'd forgotten to bring a novel and I'd become accustomed to having someone to chat with. I had better be alert—I was walking through a dangerous neighborhood, particularly for an older white guy who was wearing expensive clothes. Reflexively, I felt to make sure my Colt .45 was under my left arm, where it was supposed to be. Of course I didn't have a carry permit, but I carried a gun everywhere I went; it would have been foolish not to. Of course a strict interpretation of the 2d Amendment made such carry permits an illegal usurpation of Federal law by the states, along with waiting periods, limitations on barrel lengths, rate of fire, magazine capacity or banning ownership to entire classes of people.

Originally, the Federal government was limited in its powers and the states held most of the power. Those limited areas of Federal authority...which of course have grown leap-over-bound since the war between the states, with Congressional excess and bad court decisions...supersede state and local laws and ordinances. "Shall not be infringed" is pretty clear. The legislators and judges who thought otherwise were either completely ignorant and must not have been paying attention during school, or didn't give a damn about their oaths of office or—even worse—were closet-communists, working from within to destroy the USA: the Bill Ayres and Howard Zinn disciples, most of them completely ignorant of the fact they were working to slit their own throats. I'd never been to a communist country—Russia was Imperialist when I was there—but I knew what authoritarian government looked like.

As a young boy I'd watched as a group of peasants had been escorted through town, hands tied in front of them, heads two-at a time locked in wooden yokes, the type usually used on oxen for plowing, all of whom were connected by one long rope, with men on horses with guns leading them and bringing up the rear. I couldn't recall if the land they worked had been sold and they were being forcibly relocated or if they had failed to meet their tax obligations and were off to debtor's prison, but the result was the same: their homes and possessions had been taken from them and their fates were being determined by the men who had wealth, land and guns. They were little more than slaves, lacking any real liberty, like most people who had passed through the centuries of history since the concepts of kings, government and land ownership had been created. Slavery had existed from ancient times. The Chinese and Egyptians, for example, had enslaved entire civilizations for their building projects. It had been part of the culture and religion of the Incas, Aztecs and Mayans, providing labor for their construction as well. In more modern times, it was practiced by the Romans throughout their empire. Later on, the British 'impressed' (i.e. enslaved) American sailors on British ships and purchased African slaves from Arab slavers (who usually purchased them from other African who had captured them during tribal warfare) for agricultural work in the new world and, of course, it enjoyed a brief existence in the early history of the United States, becoming one of the causes of a long and bloody civil war.

While not usually called 'slavery' per se, it was practiced in one form or another by the National Socialist Germans (most famously Jewish factory workers, as portrayed in Shindler's List and Imperialist Japanese (notably Chinese & Manchurian miners and farmers) during World War 2 and imposed in all but name upon the Jews and millions of subjects of soviet Russia and communist China. Africans and Arabs still practiced slavery, apparently many of the women working in the sex trade in Thailand were sex-slaves to some degree or other, and I'd even read about Vietnamese boat people who had been enslaved in China, not to mention the worst of the worst, which was the Khmer Rouge of Cambodia who had killed something like 1/3 of their population while trying to eliminate anyone who disagreed with their hard-line communist philosophy. The Barbary Pirates, Islamic slavers, had sailed as far as Britain and the Americans to steal white women and children to rape and sell in their slave bazaars. The Marine Corps Anthem's line "... to the shores of Tripoli" had come about through efforts to combat this slave trade... odd that the governments of Europe had failed to predict the epidemic of gang-rapes that had occurred as the inevitable result of allowing in millions of 3d-world barbarians from "shit-hole" countries (okay, maybe Trump hadn't actually said it—but if he had, one can't deny the accuracy of the label!). Where the Moors were concerned, their religion taught them it was acceptable to steal property, including women, from members of other religions. Their crimes, however, were generally on a smaller, more personal scale. The crimes committed by nation states generally dwarfed those of other groups, even the adherents of Islam.

Collectively, the socialist and communist governments of the past century, plus the Imperialist Japanese, had murdered upwards of 50 million people, many if not most through slow starvation, which was happening again at this very moment in Socialist-ruled Venezuela. Why was it that so many Americans, particularly those in education (who should know better!) seemed to hate the freedoms they were so lucky to have and which most of the rest of the world envied? In the USA you could own a gun; there was enough land everyone could own their own small piece; automobiles, while increasingly expensive, were still affordable by nearly everyone; common-folk had no fear of being carried off or raped or imprisoned or executed, yet the weird little socialist Bernie Sanders had nearly won the nomination for the Democratic party in 2016—had won it, if there was truth to the reports that the Clinton machine had stolen the nomination for the unpopular, arrogant, thoroughly-corrupt, scheming opportunist Hillary. Obama had trebled the debt with his version of socialism that was like a schoolboy playing at being FDR, creating a financial nightmare that would haunt future generations. I remember reading that, during his 8 years of playing golf, vacationing and reading the teleprompter, the economy grew at a sluggish 1.5 percent, just half of the historical average. In comparison, 6 years of Ronald Reagan's economy, from 1983 to 1988, had known a robust 4.42% growth. Under Trump, growth was nearly equal to that enjoyed under Reagan and might soon surpass it. Obviously the economics of Milton Friedman work and those of that nutbag Keynes don't. I may have been born in an age that predated credit cards by a couple of hundred years, but we had money-lending even back then; when people chose to kick-the-can-down-the-road, as in Keynesian economics, the end result was usually lost of home, poverty, sometimes starvation or prison. Mozart was a great example: his lavish largesse and practice of having friends sign as his surety to Jewish money-lenders ended up with a number of his former backers bankrupted.

Of course Bernie Sanders had vowed to make it far worse with 'free' this and 'free' that—but what good is a free college degree when there are no jobs available? What happens to quality when something is free? Already there are thousands of millennials defaulting on their student loans after discovering that degrees in Gender Studies and Art History are worthless! And, of course, many members of the Democrat leadership are all about banning guns and shouting down free speech when it was in conflict with their own narrative—in some cases quite literally as public speakers were verbally assaulted and harassed off the stage at Town Hall meetings and campus lectures. I remember reading of similar events in other countries and it usually led to the government disarming their citizens and then slaughtering and imprisoning them by the millions.

For a while it seemed the ironically-named ANTIFA hooligans in the USA were trying to follow the same path, but of course they only represented the fringe element of society and, without popular support, their movement quickly faded into virtual obscurity. If never ceased to amaze me that a group could call itself "anti-fascists" while employing literally the same intimidation, violence, and free-speech-suppression tactics as typically employed by socialist and fascist governments. They reminded me greatly of Hitler's Sturmabteilung or "Brownshirts," but the SA had at least had the distinction of being much better dressed. These so-called Anti-Fascists had no style or class whatsoever!

Then, of course, you had the NFL players who were fortunate enough to be earning millions of dollars to play a kids' game who refused to honor the country and the flag to the point at which fans turned them off and revenues plummeted until the league belatedly took actions to put a halt to the self-destructive behavior. It just didn't make any sense to me. People from all around the world were trying to emigrate to the USA, millions of them illegally, unable or unwilling to do so legally (some to commit crimes and run away back to Mexico but others just looking for a better life), yet it seemed many of the younger generation in the USA would willingly exchange their freedoms and opportunities in a capitalist society to be members of the unprivileged classes of a system in which oppression was normal, rights few and the means to effect peaceful change for the better almost nonexistent. Idiots, I grumbled, shaking off my reverie and getting back to the task at hand.

Retracing my steps, I walked around the exterior of the building, calculating relative locations in my mind. Directly above the basement where my MG now resided was a laundry room and, from the lack of curtains or blinds in the windows, what was obviously an unoccupied apartment. This meant that I could make a decent amount of noise with nobody directly about to hear me.

I had originally planned to place a phony WORK PERMIT on the front of the building and do my work during the day, when noise would be less likely to draw attention, but now I had a new plan: I would uncover my stash *now*, while the party revelers provided some cover.

I re-entered the basement, grabbed a flashlight from the car and slipped it into my pocket, then pushed the heavy doors closed. I picked up the heavy, oaken 4x4 and dropped it into place over the angle-irons that had been welded to the backs of the doors, two to each, and then swung the two, steel locking arms through their 270 degree arcs, one at the top, one at the bottom, locking them into the protruding lugs. Using the small hand light, I retrieved the larger, battery-powered work light I had brought for this occasion, flipped it on, and went to work.

I moved the old, rickety workbench from its spot next to the wall where it had stood for so many years, then retrieved my sledgehammer from the trunk of the little roadster. It took a surprisingly short time for me to smash through the half inch of cement that covered the hollow-out hiding place I had dug so long ago I could not remember the year or season. Tossing aside the shattered chunks of cement, I revealed an old, metal World War I era ammunition can. Grabbing hold of the handles on both sides, I pulled the large, stamped-steel, dark green chest from the cavity. It was quite heavy and required no small amount of exertion on my part. Chest heaving, I carried it over and set it in the trunk of the MG. I couldn't imagine one man having carried such a large container when it had been full of ammunition. No doubt this explained the large handles on each side: it had been intended to be carried by two men.

Next I went over to the door, placed my ear against the tiny gap where the two heavy, hardwood doors met and stood there listening for several long minutes. I could faintly hear the sounds of music and loud voices from the party, along with someone revving an automobile engine over and over. "Assholes," I said to myself then, satisfied that my labors had not attracted any unwanted attention, I hung the light from it's hook from the underside of the trunk lid, where it cast its light down into the trunk, then opened the clasps on the front of the large ammo can and raised the lid.

Everything was as I remembered. Two well-oiled pistols wrapped in oilcloth, boxes of ammunition sealed in rubber to keep out the damp, ten thousand dollars packed in vintage, depression-era plastic bags, and several rolls of gold eagles and double-eagles, plus some loose in two small, cloth bags. At the current price of gold, I was looking at a small fortune, probably in excess of two million dollars. This, of course, was why I had had to take the risk of leaving Theresa unattended while I retrieved it. The paper money was so old it would raise serious questions if anyone tried to pass it or exchange it at a bank, what with the recent quest to make the US dollar forgery-proof, with security tapes, then watermarks, colored printing and seals. Fortunately, they had come from a bank in uncirculated condition, so if I ever felt the need I could always list them on Ebay and sell them to collectors.

I made sure everything was ready to go, just in case, although at this point I did not expect to be disturbed and. even if the police had received a call, all was quiet now and they wouldn't go about breaking in without a damned good reason! That was one good thing about this country: personal and property rights were generally well respected. Other than guns, of course—those rights were under attack from those who wanted to see the little people disarmed so they could be ruled just as those people who wanted control over everyone and everything had always wanted to be the only ones with power. The currently leading Democrat candidate was even talking about outlawing semi-automatic rifles by executing order and the House majority was talking about holding a Constitutional Convention to write the 2d Amendment out of the Constitution. "Good luck with that," I thought to myself.

With my mission accomplished and nothing else to do for a while, I pulled the sleeping bag and pillow from the trunk of the MG, along with the foam pad I'd prepared. Spreading out on the dank concrete with my pistol by my side, I settled down to sleep through the day. I considered calling Theresa on my landline, then remembered I had disconnected it in order to make sure she didn't make any phone calls. No matter, it would be fun to surprise her with my early return.

Chapter 35
An Unwelcome Reckoning

C C What the fuck? Who? What the hell?"

I had left Chicago just after dusk, around 7pm, and had made good time, arriving back home before 10:00. I was both surprised and alarmed to find a strange vehicle parked in the yard. Not merely strange, but incongruous! It was a Honda Accord that must have been at least 30 years old, with the rust that came with the salt they put on the roads in this northern climate, with a smattering of stickers on the back including, of all things, a Biden/Harris sticker (most of those had been scraped off long ago once those who had actually voted for those losers suffered 'buyers remorse' after it became clear they were intent upon wrecking the economy, raising taxes, and generally ruining the country) along with what I guessed were non-mainstream rock bands, a 'Save the Planet' sticker, one proclaiming 'No Person is Illegal' and some other, similar counter-culture-type messages. Clearly whoever came in this particular vehicle did not belong here!

Grabbing the .45 from the fishing tackle box I had stored it in during the trip (in case of a traffic stop), I slowly made my way into the house. Faintly, I heard voices coming from the basement. In the small smoking room off the bedroom, the one with the false door and secret room, I discovered Theresa sitting on a chair, animatedly talking to four young people, two of each gender, who appeared to be college students, most likely friends of hers. There were a number of beverage containers on the old, stained coffee table, along with a couple of pizza boxes. Clearly they had been here for a while. What did they know? I could only assume that they knew too much. Even if she hadn't told them anything—which I doubted very much—could I afford to take the risk?

The color drained from her face as she saw me standing in the doorway (sliding the pistol into the small of my back under my shirt—I didn't want to send the surprise visitors running) and her eyes grew quite wide indeed. The pregnant pause stretched on for several long moments, while the four individuals on the sofa merely blinked and looked back and forth between Theresa and myself like spectators at a tennis match.

Throttling down my anger as much as I was able, I tried to ask in a level voice: "Theresa, I need to speak with you...now!" To her apparent 'guests', I added, not wanting to alarm them unnecessarily, "please excuse us, I wasn't expecting company. Just relax for a moment and I will be back with some fresh drinks for you." I turned and marched off through the bedroom, knowing she would be right behind me.

Theresa was talking as she followed me through the library/art gallery, past the priceless masterpieces and antiques she had now placed in jeopardy. I wasn't listening. At least I wasn't listening to whatever she had to say. Instead, my thoughts were whirling, synapses firing far faster than possible for a mere human, drawing upon the memories and experiences of my two-and-a-quarter centuries walking the early, trying to find an easy way out of this dilemma, any way out, really. I didn't find one.

By the time we reached the laundry room, I was committed to the only course of action I could see. Unlocking the door to the tool room/armory, I flipped on the light and stepped across the room to the bamboo sword rack. With no fanfare, wishing this to be over quickly for a multitude of reasons, I went down my mental checklist of options one last time.

In my current state of extreme, mental arousal, it was as though I was outside of myself, watching myself moving in slow motion. A part of me remembered building this rack by hand, cutting the holes to insert the upright poles in the base pieces, lashing on the long, skinny cross-pieces (merely because I thought it looked cooler with the lashings) and carefully drilling the angled holes for the hollow, bamboo pegs upon which the swords rested. The Shinto katana was about chest-height with the handle facing to the right: perfect and appropriate. Lost in whatever excuse or explanation she was espousing, Theresa had dutifully followed me into the room, nattering away, while I reached out to the veteran Japanese blade that was even older than I was, placing my right hand upon the handle and my left on the sheath, just beyond the sageo cord. With one abrupt, violent move, I pushed my hands in opposite directions, simultaneously pulling the blade out with my right and pushing the sheath off with my left, clearing the blade action. In the same motion, I cut a curve through the air, turning to locate my target even as the accelerating edge began to whistle and hum just at the edge of my enhanced hearing. Theresa's eyes had barely had a chance to go wide when the Japanese steel finished its arc, coming to rest in my outstretched, quivering arm as I battled a sudden urge to vomit.

Mouth still open, half in interrupted speech, half in astonishment, Theresa looked me in the eye, nodded...and then her head was falling at my feet as the blood began to fountain from the severed stump of her neck.

Blood! And I was wasting it! Almost by reflex, I dropped the sword and grabbed the headless torso, pulling it up so I could drink deeply.

This was my first ever taste of vampire blood. I suddenly realized it might not be a wise thing to do, but then I felt a surge of energy and power that I had never before known. I drank my fill, then dropped her now totally lifeless husk, pulled my Colt from my belt, and went off to tie-off the loose ends.

The kids were still where I'd left them, although one somewhat pimply lad was standing in front of the wall, doing something on his phone. His phone! "Drop it," I commanded. He looked at me in astonishment, at the gun in my hand, then back down at the phone in his. His thumb began moving across the touch screen but what he didn't do was drop the device. The first two rounds took him in the chest, a third hit him in the neck, passing through and into the wall, and a fourth missed him completely, putting a hole in the paneling behind him. Blood fountained from the wound in his neck as I turned to finish the other three, left hand already searching in my jacket pocket for a spare magazine. More blood! And here I was wasting it again!

Anyone who has ever been to an indoor range knows that a gun, while loud to begin with, is much louder in a confined space. Needless to say, I had the full and undivided attention of the survivors of their little get-together. "PHONES ON THE TABLE, NOW!"

This time there was no hesitation. "STAND UP! EMPTY YOUR POCKETS ON THE TABLE! NOW STRIP DOWN TO YOUR UNDERWEAR. MOVE! NOW!" There was a slight hesitation to this last but, seeing their friend gasping his last on the cement floor and the still-smoking gun in my hand, they only hesitated a moment before complying.

I marched them into the laundry room and then into the tool room, had them lie in a pile near Theresa's corpse, with the smallest girl on top and then locked the door. I had control over the berserker rage that had filled me at first, but my head was still swimming with the aftereffects of drinking Theresa's blood, and I had no idea how long the present turbo-charged euphoria would last so, working quickly, I grabbed handcuffs from the drawer, then chains and padlocks, and soon had them secured to the pipe that ran the length of the ceiling. Duct tape ensured any protests that ensued would be muffled. I then located some plastic laundry tubs, which I had them stand in prior to taping their ankles together (my previous experience with the captive, Mexican girl had taught me something about dealing with bodily wastes). Using a craft knife, I cut off the girls' panties and dropped them in the tubs. The male I ignored for the time being—if he wanted to crap his pants, I could care less. In fact, I was rather surprised none of them had, so far. I left the bras in place for now; after all, sex was the farthest thing from my mind at the moment.

Once I had my uninvited guests properly restrained and silenced, I went to the front porch and gazed in the direction of Miguel's trailer, straining my ears for any evidence that he might have heard the shots. Trying to calm myself somewhat, I realized that the sounds probably would have been muffled by all the brick and earth, as the room where I had shot the lad didn't have a window, so I had probably dodged a bullet there (even in my current mental state I was making puns... or perhaps because of it, who knows). I set about the unwelcome task of cleaning up the mess. Going through their pockets and bags, I collected several sets of keys. A brief trip to the barn and I returned equipped with a heavy sledge hammer and several over-sized, heavyweight trash bags, and a roll of duct tape and another of binder twine.

Not yet ready to face what remained of Theresa, I started with the corpse of the kid I'd perforated with the pistol. Three solid blows with the hammer shattered his spine just about his pelvis, allowing me to fold him roughly in thirds. It wasn't easy, as body and floor were both slick with blood and the plastic was, by nature, both slippery and stubborn to work with, but eventually I got most of him inside a trash-bag and taped it to him, so it would stay in place, then did the same with the bits of him that were protruding from the first bag, so that he was mostly covered. Cutting about a 20 foot length of twine, I wrapped it around and around the bundle, periodically pulling it tight, then tied it off, hoping the arrangement would be enough to keep him from sliding out of the plastic during transport.

The Rottweiler held an old gardening glove between his massive paws, slowly pulling it to shreds with his teeth. The cotton glove had many smells: good, clean dirt, earthworm, straw, various plants...even the master's new bitch, who had worn them a few weeks ago when last she was mucking-about in the garden. He wasn't doing it to be destructive, of course—the wise master had given each of his canine companions a glove or an old sock. The master was wise because he knew that, by ripping the clothing items to bits, the dogs were actually cleaning their teeth. So many humans brushed and flossed every day (not that the dog knew the words for such things), without giving a thought to their pets' dental health.

This particular canine, however, had had enough dealing with normal two-legs to know his master was special. This was perhaps why his loyalty and devotion transcended what most dogs felt for their owners. The master didn't just provide food and shelter and the occasional scratch behind the ears—as a fellow hunter-killer, the master understood about 4-legs needs! The master was wise!

Pausing a moment from shredding the glove, he studied the other dogs' faces. Humans are aware, to some extent, that dogs communicate quite a lot using body language. Tail-wagging, running in circles, jumping up and getting dirt on one's clean clothing...every dog owner is familiar with canine ways of expressing joy when reunited with their human(s). Some humans are familiar with some of the ways that dogs communicate with each other, particularly the tail between the legs, rolling over on one's back to show submission, or growls and bared teeth to give a warning or show hostility. What very few people are aware of is the variety and subtlety of communication animals in general and dogs and monkeys in particular are capable of, using (to humans) almost imperceptible facial movements.

He could see the other 4-legs were troubled as well. Something was upsetting the master and his mood had been very dark recently. He was also much busier than usual, and something unnatural had clearly happened and was continuing to the other humans. Panzer, as he was called, was worried about his master and he could sense the other dogs were as well. Apparently the master could sense their distress, for once as he went rushing past, he stopped and gave each of them some comforting pats. Surely theirs was a wise and thoughtful master!

I paused for a moment, trying again to think ahead and consider all eventualities. From a hook off the pegboard wall, I took a Ruger .357 in a shoulder holster and a pair of speed loaders. I still had the Colt model 1911 stuck into my belt. From a drawer in the old, steel office desk came an inside-the-pants holster and half a dozen loaded magazines of .45 ammo that I had loaded years ago while wearing gloves, to make sure there were no fingerprints. Next, I grabbed a t-shirt I used for oiling my guns and was careful to wipe any blood off of my shoes. Making a brief detour, I grabbed one of the kids' mobile phones—I couldn't imagine a need to make a call, but just in case—then grabbed a BDU jacket (it was cold at night these days, with winter approaching, and a coat also helped to hide the pistols and the large pockets provided a nice repository for the magazines and speed loaders).

I poured some bleach I'd brought from the laundry over the blood that was still all over the tiled-floor—I'd have liked to have cleaned it up now, before the blood had a chance to dry, but I was under time constraints to remove the bodies and return home before dawn. Picking up the plastic bag with the head in it, lifted and balanced the curtain-wrapped bundle with the rest of what had been my companion and entertainment for the last couple of months, now just the most recent and painful of many, many memories, and somehow managed to lock the door behind me.

Leaving the barn, I grabbed one of the 1 quart motor-oil bottles that was used to keep gas for the weed-wacker (sure, state law said that gas had to be dispensed from the pump into approved containers, but that didn't mean people didn't have other means of storing it at home in defiance of the law), a book of matches AND a disposable lighter, just in case I needed to torch the car. Tossing a shovel and a hank of rope on top of the load, I closed the boot... trunk... started up the engine and headed off without a glance back.

Sticking to just a mile or two per hour over the speed limit, I took state road 15 (the 'back road', so to speak) through the small town of Bristol (until about 10 years ago or so there had been just one stop light in the entire town!) all the way to the even smaller town of Mottville, Michigan. Taking a left onto US 12, I had no alternative but to use a major road, but only for about 5 minutes, so the danger of being 'stop-and-copped' by local law enforcement was fairly minimal. Turning right onto M-40, I drove for another 15 minutes, past another tiny town, Jones, and started looking for the pig farms I remembered.

I was still experiencing the 'high' from drinking Theresa's blood, so my high vision was enhanced even more than usual—but it was still not easy trying to find a pig farm at night. After all, the beasties weren't nocturnal and all they usually had to mark a farm was tiny, open-ended 'Quonset huts' to give them shelter from the elements while out in the field. I wasted a good 45 minutes circling around, driving down back roads in need of some significant maintenance (decades of Democrat administrations had ruined the state socially and financially; a populist backlash had given the governorship and a majority in the legislature to the GOP, but fixing things, such as the roads, wasn't happening overnight).

Finally, I caught a glint of moonlight on something vaguely metallic-looking. I pulled over, shutting off the lights, but left the engine running. Walking across the cracked, paved surface, to the gravel on the edge of the road, a sickening feeling building in my stomach. I had found what I'd been looking for, a number of pig shelters in the form of a concave sheet of galvanized, corrugated steel. Even in the dark, however, I could see that the shelters were dirty and/or rusty and didn't appear to have been occupied in some time. Where there should have been large areas of dirt or mud (depending on recent precipitation), I was looking at a field of tall grass. Weeds were growing tall against the barbed-wire fence, and around the shelters. The slight was blowing directly across the enclosure towards me and I could smell...absolutely nothing to indicate any large animals were in residence.

Cursing myself, I remembered reading something, maybe about 10 years ago, about how the state of Michigan had decided to outlaw domestic husbandry of so-called 'wild hogs'. Clearly these pig farmers were out of business! Damn!

Standing there, cold air blowing through my air, the rustle of dried leaves foretelling the coming winter, I tried to decide what to do for 'plan B'. The unfortunate thing was, I hadn't planned for this eventuality; I didn't have a fucking clue what to do! I could leave the bodies in the car and set it on fire, destroying any evidence linking them to me, but a fire would attract attention and there was the small problem of traveling the 30 miles or so back home, on foot, before sunrise.

I allowed myself the luxury of a brief moment of time to curse myself. Why hadn't I brought a shovel? I had been in a hurry, true, but I should have planned this better. Getting back into the car, I retraced my path to a large copse of trees I'd seen earlier. Daring to shut off the engine—no need in drawing excessive attention in case a roving sheriff's deputy happened to pass by, I opened the trunk and quickly tossed both bound bundles over the barbed-wire fence that ran alongside the road. Leaping the fence as the deer in the area likely did frequently, I grabbed Theresa's body (I could tell it was hers as it was lighter...and shorter by a head), tossed it over my right shoulder, and grabbed the smaller, soccer ball-sized parcel in my left hand. The trees were a good hundred feet from the road, so I pushed myself into an irregular jog over the broken ground.

One again thanking whichever gods had gifted vampires with superior night vision, I still made much slower progress than I would have wished. The ground was soft and strewn with the remnants of the corn stalks that inevitably remained after the harvest. A cold, late-Autumn breeze was blowing, carrying the promise of approaching winter, yet I felt no chill, my exertions keeping me quite warm.

Clambering over fallen branches and drifted piles of leaves, I quickly found a depression in the ground. Gladly tossing the burden that had become increasingly heavy into the depression, I paused for just a moment, breathing heavily, then turned and headed back to repeat the process. The second trip was more arduous—the body was heavier, the plastic bags, already slippery, had torn and threatened to come completely apart.

Upon reaching the copse, I momentarily lost my sense of direction and had to wander in a circle until I found the desired depression, my defilade of the deceased. As I gratefully dropped the second corpse next to the first, the breeze suddenly picked up, rattling dead leaves that still clung to half-naked branches and causing the drier leaves on the ground to skip and titter. I could almost imagine it was the ghosts of my victims, taking umbrage at the disrespectful manner in which I was disposing of their remains. Truthfully, I felt quite distressed about it—but I had work to do, I would mourn later. In truth, interring them in the earth was a better end than having them end up in the bellies of swine, which had been my original plan!

The fabric of the curtains wasn't a problem, but the smooth surface of the trash bags and duct tape might easily hold my fingerprints, so I pulled out my knife and cut the tattered remnants free, stuffing them inside both jacket and shirt, where they would remain secure, as I swept leaves over the bodies with a fallen branch. When I was satisfied they were reasonably well concealed, I heaped as many dead branches as I could find on the pile, even breaking a few branches off a nearby pine tree to complete the camouflage. Winter was rapidly approaching, which tended to keep people indoors, but there would be deer hunters in December and this was just the type of wooded area that might attract them..and the mushroom hunters in the spring as well after the snows had melted, so I suffered no delusions that the bodies would probably be discovered eventually.

My hope was that it would be some time and that the elements and scavenging critters would render them unidentifiable. Damn! Again, my lack of planning came to light as I realized I should have brought a hammer with which to knock their teeth out. I had my pistols—I could shoot them out, but making that degree of noise would be counter-productive to my need for stealth and secrecy.

The celestial clock that was the earth was ticking, rolling resolutely in its orbit, rotating resolutely towards the dawn. The most easily-recognized constellation, Orion, was already rising—and I didn't want to be stopped on the road, so it was time to get going; "Time for me to fly," in the words of the classic REO Speedwagon song. Marching tiredly back to the old Toyota, I was glad when it started with no hesitation. Say what you want about the Japanese and their porn-rape culture, the way they compete unfairly in trade and economics, such as when they flooded the market with counterfeit 16-bit computer chips back in the 1980's, and the way the previous generation had raped and murdered their way across China and Southeast Asia like the hordes of Genghis Khan—they did make good electronics and automobiles!

On the return trip, I took the risk of driving quite a bit faster than usual, constantly scanning the road ahead for any hint of law enforcement. My brief bit of solo brainstorming had tripped an old memory. One night, years ago, I'd been prowling in Elkhart and had a bad experience with a car that refused to start (the next morning I'd called and had it towed and discovered a bad alternator and dead battery were to blame). In any case, I'd been forced to find an alternative method to return home to Goshen. Hopefully, this would work for me tonight as well; make that THIS MORNING! Time was passing rapidly!

Crossing over the 6-span bridge, I briefly regretted not simply weighting down the bodies and tossing them in the river. All the bridges had far too much traffic, however, and the risk of being observed would have been too great. Turning onto 120, paralleling the river, I was glad the speed limit was fairly high, as I did not drive too fast now that I was approaching the city limits: the city of Elkhart had a LOT more police that rural, southern Michigan! At the first intersection with a traffic light, I turned south in the direction of the small industrial park. I am sure there were factories with trash dumpsters in the parking lot, or maybe behind the UAW hall, but I didn't want to waste the time—or be seen on a security camera. As I crossed the single rail line, I lowered the window and tossed the assorted bits of plastic burial shroud and used tape out the window. I'm sure that, at that location, nobody would think twice about a little bit of plastic trash, particularly as the wind would probably deposit it in a bush or leaf pile. Turning around, I headed back to 120 (aka East Jackson Blvd at this point) and drove the rest of the way to downtown as another 10 minutes ticked off the clock.

Chafing at the delay at the Main Street traffic light while I sat there without another car at the intersection, I impatiently rushed ahead on the green, turning left on Second Street. The four blocks to the railroad underpass only took a few moments, but at 39 mph, it seemed interminable! Passing under the railroad tracks took me into the bad part of town. Elkhart was one of those places where the expression 'the other side of the tracks' had real meaning, although there were some nasty neighborhoods of older, wooden buildings and drugs and gangs and poverty on the north side of the tracks as well.

It was for one of the worst parts of town I was now headed. From the section 8 housing at the corner of Benham Avenue and Dr. Martin Luther King Drive to the deserted storefronts a few blocks away on South Main Street was an area that was featured on an almost daily basis in the ARRESTS section of the local newspaper. I took my first left on St. Joseph St. and, after a brief search, found a parking place along the side of the street. Ideally, I'd have left a window down to attract attention to the fact I was leaving the keys in the ignition, but this late in the year, it would have looked TOO unusual and I didn't want the police taking an interest in the vehicle, particularly as it had out-of-state license plates.

Taking the bandana/kerchief I'd brought for just that purpose, I wiped down every part of the interior I might have touched. Opening the door, I paused long enough to pull several one dollar bills from my wallet and drop them on the front seat, then I closed the door and proceeded to wipe my prints from the exterior of the vehicle as well, not forgetting the trunk lid. I could count on someone passing by, looking in the window and then helping themselves to the money I'd left on the seat, probably sooner rather than later. With any luck, they'd also at the very least open the trunk, looking for additional valuables, and get fingerprints all over the place. If I were very lucky, someone (or ones) would steal the car and be caught using it in a crime.

I wasted a few precious seconds just standing there, staring at the car, and wondering if I'd forgotten anything. Not thinking of anything, I spun and started jogging the half-a-block over to South Main St. Passing the grand-sounding New York Central Railroad Museum (which I'd never visited but which appeared to be nothing more than a couple old engines and a dozen or so freight and dining cars), I quickly came to the curve where two railroad tracks ran past the diminutive Amtrak station then made a gentle right turn, paralleling Middlebury Street for a block, then turned southeast towards Goshen.

This is where my plan would either prove to be genius or folly. The Robert Young Yard on the west side of town was one of the largest and busiest railroad switching operations in the entire country, probably in the entire world. Trains ran out of there day and night—the longer freight trains particularly ran at night in order to avoid blocking automobile traffic more than necessary during daylight hours. Trains passing through downtown areas always slowed down, particularly on curves, so jumping the train would be a simple matter—IF the fates smiled on me enough to send a train in my direction. If not, my backup plan was to hijack a car at gunpoint. I didn't like that option, so I muttered a brief prayer to the train gods to send transportation in my direction.

Walking down the tracks about 100 feet in the direction of Prairie St., I found a wide tree not far off the tracks, a few feet from a signal of some sort, comprised of a framework of metal tubes, arching out over the tracks, with large black ovals mounted on top that presumably contained switching lights that could be viewed by train engineers. Leaning against the bole of the tree, I pulled back the sleeve of my black, leather biker's jacket and pushed the illumination button on my wristwatch. Damn! I hoped a train would be along presently. Dressed as I was, standing behind a large tree in the dark, I was fairly confident I could wait until a train passed by without being seen by the engineer, as long as I kept my face and hands out of the light that would be cast by the headlight. Once passed, as the train rounded the curve, there was next to zero chance I'd be seen boarding the train; assuming I got the opportunity to do so!

The minutes slowly ticked away from 3:30 to 4:00 a.m. and I became increasingly impatient. I thought about perhaps stealing a bicycle and riding home. It was less than half an hour from here to home by car—less at this time of morning when there was hardly any traffic. Certainly I could travel the distance in an hour or so by bicycle, going straight down South Main Street and finessing red lights where there was no traffic (a cop seeing a motor vehicle running a red light would react like a hound after a rabbit; a cyclist coasting a bicycle against the light, one foot on a pedal and one pushing off the pavement, was likely to be ignored and, in either case, there wouldn't be the same danger of arrest and/or search on a stolen bicycle as in a car!).

Then, finally, my hyper-sensitive ears picked up the faint sound of wheels click-clacking in the distance, a repetitive, metallic percussion, faint, fading in and out, but clearly drawing closer. A moment later, the alternating, school-bell chime of a crossing signal joined the symphonic movement. Next came the brass section, adding a long, low, blaring horn to the score. A single note, but it was an entire melody to my ears.

This did not, however, mean I was about to be rescued from my self-stranding. To be sure, the train was heading in my direction and would be arriving in a matter of moments. Once it arrived, however, it had options after passing the post office. The train might bear to the right, passing alongside my perch in this stupid tree, taking me home to safety. Or, if it were of a contrary mind, it might bear to the left, going straight towards the high school and then passing on one side or the other, bearing either East or North, depending on its whim.

I could tell that the signals both above and on the ground beside the tracks were now lighted, tiny electric lanterns giving a faint illumination. The crossing gates came alive, lights flashing and bells ringing. The steady beat of the tympani section was quite loud now, beating in a steady rhythm to accompany the bells and chimes. The strings and woodwinds were noticeably absent, this was to be a percussion-section symphony, but the melody of the approaching train was music to my ears, regardless.

The long, humming serpent hurtled across Main and then (*YES!*) it veered slowly in a southerly direction. I doubted the engineer would be fully alert at this time of morning, but I shifted so the tree sheltered my face and hands: even in the bright beam of the spotlight, I doubted my black, leather jacket and boots or black denim pants would stand out against the deep shadows, but the headlight on a train is brighter than daylight, so the solidity of the old Maple tree gave me the security of knowing that the engineer wouldn't have suspicions as to why someone might be hanging out on the railroad right-of-way after midnight. I was probably being unnecessarily paranoid, but I'd read the FBI patrol the nearby Robert Young rail yard (the largest switching yard between Chicago/Kansas City and the east coast) and it was probably in the engineer's job description to call in and report any train-jumpers.

With a whoosh and a roar, the engine was there and then it was past. I opened my eyes, which I'd screwed-shut and covered with my hand to preserve my night-vision, and then I started searching for a freight car with an open door. Naturally, with the luck I'd been having since I pulled into my drive and found invaders in my home, the first set of cars were auto transports, cages on wheels of steel with walls of steel slats that afforded no concealment or any visible entry. The next few dozen cars were even worse: flatbeds, probably used for transporting rolled steel. After them came shipping containers on other flatbeds; instead of sliding doors along the sides, as I'd hoped, these opened from the ends. Even if I'd wanted to take the risk of being locked in a container and having my desiccated corpse discovered months later in some port in China or Taiwan, there wasn't enough room between cars to open the doors. Following along...predictably, at this point...was tanker car after tanker car, no doubt full of the corn syrup or ethanol that were two of the major agricultural products of the area. Staring into the darkness from which the mechanical monster was extruding itself, I could hardly see beyond the tankers to what were probably coal cars!

"Fuck it," I said aloud (eavesdroppers were hardly a danger at the moment). The train was curving at this point and the engineer wouldn't have been able to see me now even if he'd had his head out the window with a spotlight aimed backwards and a pair of binoculars. I rushed over to the framework, something like metal scaffolding, upon which the signals were mounted. Grasping the sides of what was somewhat like a ladder, although the cross pieces were at the diagonal instead of horizontal. Pushing my boots into the angles where the pipes were joined together, I climbed my way up the vertical framework, then pulled myself up to where

I could balance, albeit precariously, on the top of the framework. Moving across to where I was above the final cars, as they passed beneath me, I aimed at the small platform in the middle of one of the last tanker cars, where the capped pipe was that I assumed was opened to fill the tanks. There was a small platform around it with a small safety railing that looked like a good place to land. Naturally, with the way things had been going tonight...I missed!

Landing on the top of a rounded cylinder traveling at 25 or 30 miles per hour and trying to find something to grab onto in the dark is not an experience I would recommend to anyone not named Bush, Clinton, Biden, or Obama! (Okay, I could easily add to the list: Harris, Pelosi, AOC... why was I thinking along these lines at a time like this!?). I slid own the side of the car, vainly searching for a handhold, until my booted toes smacked hard against a railing that ran the length of the car. Bending at the knees, I was able to push up and to the side and was just able to grasp the ladder that extended down the side of the railcar from the platform I had unsuccessfully tried to land on.

Swinging myself to the side, so my feet were now underneath me—and bending at the knee to avoid catching my feet on the ground which might have threatened to pull me loose from my precarious hand-hold—I pulled myself high enough on the ladder to get my toes onto the bottom rung. In no particular hurry, I scaled the car to the top where the hatch was set into the top of the cylinder, which, I was now certain, had to be used to fill the container. Around it, as I had earlier observed, was a skeletal railing, a fence, of sorts. I could have simply stood on the small platform there, but I was concerned a line or signal pole extending over the car might have a mind to joust with me and unseat me from the iron horse that had almost thrown me to the dirt just moments ago, so I decided instead to take a seat on the narrow grating, leaning back against the railing.

I could imagine I was on the deck of a U-boat, conning tower at my feet, wind and spray in my face...except the wind was dry and had the acrid odor of diesel exhaust as an aftertaste. I gave quiet thanks that I wasn't sitting right behind the engine! A random thought came to me as I wished for a cigarette. Considering I'd never been a habitual smoker, this was a bizarre thought to have at any time, but particularly just then. Maybe I was cracking up!

"Fuck the cigarette," I said to myself, "I need a drink!"

Unzipping my jacket, I reached in and felt for the inner pocket...and heaved a sigh of relief as I touched the cold metal of my flask. A moment later I was sipping vintage brandy, tapping out a beat on the metal railing, trying to remember the words to "Train, Train" by Blackfoot. After a moment it came to me: "Train, Train, take me out of this town...that woman I'm in love with, she's got to go!"

How appropriate, I thought!

One thing about trains, of course, is they don't stop for traffic lights...or much of anything, really. In just a matter of minutes we were passing the old Concord Mall on the right, then Oxbow Park on the left. The train had slowly begun accelerating once it had completely rounded the corner back in Elkhart and was picking up speed. New, very expensive underpasses in Elkhart and Goshen had both reduced the threat to traffic and the problems with wear-and-tear on the tracks due to constant traffic. This train was long, so acceleration was slow, but I needed to stop thinking about the two young girls I'd once discovered passed-out from drinking beer in the ranger tower in the park (they'd been tasty in more ways than one—and I'm sure they'd had serious hangovers the next morning!) and start thinking about the best place to jump ship, er, train.

My property was southwest of town, so I should disembark at County Road 17 which was...just there! Not quite believing how quickly I'd arrived, I clambered down the ladder on the other side of the car this time, lowering my feet to the ground and tried to run, attempting to match the forward speed of my ride before I let go. I wasn't entirely successful and ended up sprawled in the ditch behind what I remembered was some type of kindergarten. I'd overshot by a couple of blocks, but that wasn't a big deal, unlike the shuttle crew in Independence Day overshooting their landing zone! There I was again with these random, unhelpful thoughts!

I brushed off the dirt and loose grass and sucked briefly on an abrasion on my left hand, then sneaked a quick look at the time. Damn! Had it been high summer, false dawn would have already been breaking. With the winter solstice only a few weeks away, however, I still had time. A man dressed all in black, feet clad in motorcycle boots, *jogging* in the early morning hours looks suspicious as hell, but it really couldn't be helped. I stuck to Old County Road 17, not the new one, figuring there would be less traffic, including the type that came equipped with roof-mounted bars of flashing lights.

Many of the houses I passed now had lights on in the windows, as this was a working-class neighborhood, mostly farmhouses and the occasional duplex, or single-story house, usually older, wood construction but sometimes even modern, modular slapped-together pre-fab houses, the occupants no doubt getting ready for their early morning shifts in the mobile home, trailer and RV factories in Nappanee and Elkhart. While they'd had hard times economically in recent years, the boom Trump had brought to the economy had trickled-down and Am General had recalled laid-off workers and the other factories had seen their orders pick up once again.

Surroundings began to look increasingly familiar as the sky started to lighten in the east. It was nearly 6 a.m. and I was shaking with fatigue when I finally clambered slowly over the front gate and into the yard (usually I could leap the fence but this had been a night of Herculean efforts). There was already enough of a glow in the sky that my old rooster broke the relative silence with his morning greeting. Stupid bird—the sun came up every day, why was he always surprised?

Speaking of surprise, a small, black shadow emerged from the shadow of the old oak tree, giving my right boot a solid 'whack' as it passed by, disappearing into the long grass near the fence. Even in my fatigue I smiled as the cat disappeared from view. "Well done, you little bastard, I should have named you 'Cato' like in the Pink Panther movies." I wondered where the dogs were, then I remembered: the basement.

At last, with scarcely a margin of safety before the hateful orb rose in the sky, I trudged over to the porch and entered the house. MY house! My experiment with sharing my residence had come to an unpleasant end and given rise to this most unpleasant of evenings. The dogs were happy to see me and equally happy to be turned loose out-of-doors to pee on anything that caught their fancy. I locked the door behind them—no need for Miguel to wander in and see...or hear...anything out of the ordinary.

I'd looked in on my 'guests' when I let the dogs out of the room, but now I went back to check on them again...and have a little breakfast. All the handcuffs, chains and gags were secure except for the little blonde girl, who'd managed to get the duct tape partially loose. "A strong tongue, I like that in a girl," I told her, as I pulled off the old tape—fast. Before the echo of her surprised yelp had faded in my ears, I had shoved on her chin, closing her mouth with a clack of teeth, and applied a new piece of duct tape. I then went to the workbench, found a roll of electric tape, and wrapped it half-a-dozen times around her head, securing her mouth more effectively.

Despite the fact I had a lot to do before dawn, I couldn't pass up the opportunity to appreciate the feel of a naked female for at least a few moments. I ran my hands up and down the thighs and buttocks of each girl in turn, feeling the familiar rush of electric energy up the back of my neck and into my brain. I reveled in the moment for only a short while; after all I had work to do. Previously, I had been in too much of a rush to remove their brassieres, an omission I now corrected, cutting them off with my pocket knife and dropping the remnants in a pool of urine the heavier of the two and left in and around her impromptu toilet. As with the young man, they made feeble and futile protestations. Having to stand on tiptoe for hours, however, had left them in a weakened condition. Taking a few moments to admire—and squeeze—their young, pert breasts, I looked them both in the eye and assured them, "whichever of you makes me happier gets to live longer!"

Knowing that there was precious little dark left before dawn, I forced myself to delay gratification—there would be time later—and headed off in search of the leftover paneling I'd stored somewhere, decades ago, just in case I ever needed to replace any of the panelings in the 'smoking lounge'. After all, with a fortune in art and an arsenal of weapons hidden behind the false wall in said room, I'd kept the leftovers, after paneling the cement walls beneath, in anticipation of flood, fire, rot, rodent, warping, termites or any other calamity.

I found them in the first place I looked—leaning in the corner between a rack of old rifles and shotguns and several oil paintings in their climate-controlled cases (I never said I was particularly neat or tidy, but I was organized enough I was usually able to find things I had stashed away somewhere). Good—I was afraid they might have been stored in the rafters of the barn, where time and damp might have damaged them.

Now—to work. First, I laid down more plastic, to be sure I wasn't walking in blood or spreading it around. Next, I piled the pieces of paneling on the coffee table—the same table upon which their cell phones had been left and which I had just now transferred to a Ziploc bag, careful not to get my fingerprints on them—one more thing to dispose of—and went back to the tool room for a crowbar and claw hammer, fondling the girls' bare thighs again in passing.

Two panels had bullet holes and at least one more had blood-splash. After measuring and making sure the replacement panels would fit and weren't too badly warped, I moved replacement panels, table, sofas, lamps... everything... out into the main room of the basement, then returned and proceeded to pull the old panels from the 2x4" studs underneath, exposing the brick behind them (the secret room was at the other end—I may have been half out-of-my-mind with anger and grief, but I wasn't going to unload a magazine of .45 slugs in the direction of priceless art, cases of ammunition, and some cordite and other explosives I'd brought with me from World War I!).

Pulling the 3 obviously damaged panels free, along with a 4th panel I suspected might have caught some blood spray (if only I had one of those UV "black" lights the CSI investigator used), I made sure the blood was dried/absorbed before stacking them—bloody sides inwards—up the stairs and out of the barnyard. Like many ordinary farms, there was a rusty, old oil drum used for burning trash. Quickly breaking them in half and arranging the plywood panels in a teepee shape in the barrel, I hurried to the barn, came back with an old plastic oil bottle full of gasoline and an Ohio Blue Tip match I hoped would still light. Quickly I poured the gas liberally all over the slender, varnished boards, tossed the empty bottle into the barrel, scratched the match tip against a bit of rust on the exterior of the drum, and was gratefully rewarded with a flame.

As the first rays of true dawn began to creep over the horizon, I tossed the match into the decrepit barrel, being rewarded with an instantaneous WHOOSH of sound and flame. Tarrying just long enough to assure myself that there was no need to fear the fire might somehow escape from the cylinder and set either barn or house alight, I hurried indoors before the sun could wreak its awful vengeance upon me.

It had been a night of some exceptional expenditure of energy, a great deal of driving, an emotional roller-coaster ride and no small amount of stress. Even I was tired after all of that! I grabbed a Black & Tan from the fridge, twisted off the cap and took a deep swallow. I briefly considered leaving a note for Miguel and then remembered I'd left one before my trip to Chicago and the disaster that had resulted in, claiming we'd be out of town for a few days. With the sun starting to rise, I didn't really care to adventure back out onto the porch anyway, so I grabbed a couple more beers for future reference and made my way downstairs, closing the basement door behind me, slamming the deadbolt into battery and hooking a spare finger under the seat of a stool in the corner, balancing it just well enough to bring it along with me.

Placing the stool in a position to have a good vantage point and leaving the extra beers on the workbench, I took a seat where I could ogle the two young, naked females at my leisure and consider my next move. Information was what I needed next. A brief visit to my tool bench produced a pair of bolt cutters, an antique upholsterers or cobblers needle— I'd had it so long I had forgotten even where it came from, it might have even come with the house when I purchased it—in any case it was so old it had been hand-made, and a Zippo lighter.

Checking to see that my knife was readily accessible, I proceeded to the male. Opening the bolt cutters, I centered his miniscule penis between the cutting blades and slowly squeezed down on the handles, bringing the jaws closer together until they began to bit flesh. Needless to say, I had his full attention at this point (and he was protesting and pleading as enthusiastically as he was able to do in his bound and gagged condition).

"I am going to remove the tape and ask you some questions. You will not scream or shout. You will answer me quickly and honestly. If I feel you are not being completely honest with me you will get the John Bobbit treatment. Understood?"

He nodded like a bobblehead doll on the dashboard of a vehicle speeding down a Detroit roadway.   Setting the cutting tool aside, I pulled out the knife and cut away the tape from beside his left ear, then slowly... intentionally and agonizingly slowly... pulled the tape around until his mouth was clear of the tape.

"Can I have some water?" he rasped out. "Sure," I said, "but questions first: who knew you were coming here?"

"What?" he mumbled. "Great," I thought to myself, "I'm doing the scene from *Pulp Fiction.*"

Very slowly and distinctly, I asked again, "Who...did...you... tell... you... were... coming... here?" Realizing I'd just switched movies and was now doing "Did you make the Vide-o Tape" from *Enemy of the State*, and not wanting to elicit another "what?" and slip back to Tarentino, I prompted him a little. "Your mom? Other friends of Theresa? The guy at the gas station where you stopped to ask for directions (damn, now I was doing Roger Rabbit!)—who knew?"

"Nobody," he stammered, "Didn't tell nobody... anybody!" I picked up the bolt cutters from the stool on which I'd placed them and gave him a skeptical expression.

"No, really," he insisted, "Ninja... I mean Theresa... made us promise we wouldn't tell anyone before she gave us the GPS coordinates" Eying the heavy cutters I was still holding, he added, "I swear—I kept my promise to her and didn't tell anyone, not a soul!"

"GPS? How the heck did she get GPS coordinates?" I wondered. "Ninja?" I also couldn't help wondering at her nickname, but no doubt it resulted from her Japanese heritage. In any case, I had more pressing issues. Replacing the duct tape temporarily, I hurried over to the cabinet over the sink next to the washing machine. Finding an old, yellow plastic cup with a cartoon alligator on it that I believe was from the old POGO comic strip, I rinsed out the dirt and dust that had accumulated over the decades during which the cub had been disused, I filled it up with water and, in keeping with my promise, gave the pimple-faced nerd a drink before securing him with fresh tape.

Next, I interrogated the girls, although I took a bit more time doing so. Taking my lighter and the old needle, I heated the tip of it in the blue flame of the light that, old as it was, had taken several attempts to fire it up (reminding me of another Tarentino movie with Bruce Willis in a cameo role). I didn't heat the tip to sterilize it; I was doing so just so it would hurt more.

Starting with the slightly plump girl (she had the bigger titties), I slowly pierced both nipples with the needle, horizontally, then allowed myself the luxury of squeezing her breasts while sucking the blood from the fresh puncture wounds I had inflicted. I could see where she had worn a naval ring, if not at the moment, and she had tattoos, so she was no stranger to piercings; heck, under other circumstances she probably would have enjoyed this!

After a few minutes of play, I repeated the process on the skinnier girl with the smaller breasts. I'd already decided she'd be the one I killed last— I was most definitely a 'leg man' and she was better looking in the face as well. Most Germans felt the same way about breasts as most Americans seemed to—the bigger the better—but I preferred them firm and aesthetically pleasing. Big, shapeless mounds of droopy skin-encased fat just really didn't excite me!

"You wondered about the lifestyle of vampires; this is the fun part!" Retrieving the bolt cutters, I positioned myself in front of the two captive females, more-or-less centered between them. "Of course it's hard to drink much from just a pin-hole in a nipple. If I were to cut a nipple off entirely, however," gesturing with the cutters, "I could get a lot more blood a lot more quickly; do you get my meaning?" Like does caught in headlights, the wide-eyed former vampire-wannabes nodded their understanding. Repeating the questioning process, I was greeted with the same denials: they had promised not to say anything to anyone. At least Theresa had been good for something, I thought; although I was certain her own self-preservation had been first and foremost in her mind when she insisted upon promises of secrecy from her friends. Of course she had been a fool to think anything as gossip-worthy as the existence of an actual, in-the-flesh vampire would have remained secret for longer than the time it took to need a refill on your morning cup of coffee!

The fondling and sucking of two pairs of titties had, unsurprisingly, made me horny, so after watering and re-taping the girls, I stripped from the waist down. Staring at my growing erection, the skinny girl's eyes looked fearful, the fat one, angry. Being careful to keep my feet wide of the puddle underneath her (I was going to have to clean that up), I took the heavier girl from behind. Even standing on tiptoe as she was, she wasn't quite tall enough and, when I'd go to grab her breasts, inevitably I'd slip out of her. Changing strategy, I walked around to the front, grabbed her by the ankles, pulled her up until I could get her knees up to about shoulder level, and re-inserted myself. She was shaven and had pubic stubble, which was rather unsightly, but her jugs were quite nice so I kept my gaze on them, occasionally licking off drops of blood that were still leaking from her nipples.

Without lubrication, it was tough going at first, but it got easier as I went along, particularly after I climaxed the first time... and again a second time after a slight pause during which I'd played with her toys some more. Once I was finally satisfied, I let her legs drop to the cement floor; or her toes, rather, as the steel handcuffs attaching her to the long, steel pipe and the chains attaching the pipe to the eye-bolts in the heavy, wooden timbers of the ceiling were hardly flexible and she merely returned to her previous position—hard, thanks to gravity doing it's normal thing. The bar swayed slightly with the impact of her toes on the cement, then came to a halt.

> So ladies, this is what life is *really* like as a vampire. There is no one who loves you and no family and no friends. You have no one who cares about you or whom you care about (I was omitting my animals and the fact that, for a time, I'd had some companionship with Theresa, but those were exceptions rather than the rule).
>
> Pretty much any sex you have is either like this—non-consensual—or in your cases your feminine wiles would probably be used to trick a male victim into a situation in which you'd then drink his blood and kill him, which rather takes the romance out of it, I would think. It is an inconvenient life, as there are certain things in modern life that have to be done during daylight hours. It is a life where you always have to fear being discovered. You never get to go to the beach or do any of a million other things that people do for fun. Now that you've seen it without all the glamorizing from Hollywood, are you still interested in membership?

Of course that was a rhetorical question: with their mouths taped shut, they were hardly in any position to respond. I did notice the slender girl was crying—and I hadn't even raped her yet! Women!

Usually I preferred to drink from the necks of my female food only, using wrists on the males. No doubt it was the French eroticism I'd carried with me all these years, but the throat was too sensual, too much of an erogenous zone, for me to feel comfortable feeding from a male victim, particularly as he was still naked from the waist down, as the last thing I'd done before embarking on my quest to dispose of the corpses was that I'd removed all of their underwear and placed old, empty coffee cans between their legs, in case they needed to 'go' while I was out. In any case, as his wrists were strung up out of reach, I simply stabbed him near the collarbone, placed my mouth over the wound, and fed, slapping a piece of duct tape on the wound once I was sated.

While I had certainly exerted myself a great deal over the past few hours, it hadn't been that long since I had fed, on Theresa, which had given me sort of a Superman rush of energy, so I didn't need to drain him of too much—not yet, anyway.

After rummaging through my tool chest, I returned with an upholstery-mending kit I had acquired I remembered not where and, albeit with some difficulty as his skin was slick with blood, I put enough stitches in the wound to close it up, then slapped a piece of duct tape over the whole thing to help it hold together. Needless to say, it was obvious through his writhings and whimperings and feeble attempts to kick me that he was not enjoying himself. It was also needless to say that I cared not. If anything, the petite girl's crying made me feel worse than the physical harm I'd inflicted on the other two—or it would have if I allowed myself to feel that type of sympathy for others.

I remember, as a young man of 12 or 13, going on a hunt with my father, brother, and some visiting nobility. I felt both thrilled by my kill of a doe that was flushed out of a thicket by the hounds and, at the same time, saddened that I had brought about the death of such a lovely creature. At any rate, she'd tasted good as one of the featured courses that night and I certainly ate my share. When your survival depends on killing another creature, it becomes much easier to lay your regrets aside. It was much the same with the pretty, tear-dripping brunette in my 'pantry' or any of the other people I had fed on and often killed over the years—they are/were my food. Obviously I still felt some remorse, or I wouldn't have put so much effort into building my cattle ranch, but it doesn't matter if you're a dog or a human or a vampire—the same diet becomes boring after awhile; so, when some little bits of fluff invade my home, I might as well enjoy myself.

At the moment, however, I had work to do. In the bottom of one of the old, battered school lockers I'd purchased from a newspaper ad decades ago (delivery was included), I found a can half-full of medium, gray paint and an old brush that wasn't too hard. While searching for a can opener, or at least a standard screw driver, I continued the train of thought I'd embarked upon moments ago; after all, when you spend much of two plus centuries by yourself, you end up talking to yourself, either actually or mentally.

Yes, back in the 1700's, when life expectancy was half of what it is now... or less...and education, for those who were able to afford it, proceeded at a much more rapid pace than in so-called 'modern' schools with their social-justice propagandizing, people were expected to have adult responsibilities at a much earlier age. Many heads-of-households were in their twenties, girls were often married as soon as they could bleed—it was a much different time.

First, I had to finish replacing the torn-out paneling, which took several hours. Then, because the colors didn't quite match, I ended up returning to the locker to dig out a can of light stain, pulled the baseboards, stained the paneling then, while the baseboards were off, I first poured out some bleach on the floor and wiped it down, then put the mop head in a plastic bag for future incineration, along with the old sneakers I was wearing that I was careful to remind myself not to wear outside of that room for fear of tracking trace amounts of blood—and the DNA therein—throughout the house.

By this time I was feeling a bit tired—I could tell the sun was high in the sky and it was long past time for vampires to be in their coffins (or, as in my case, a bed), so without further ado, I stripped down, turned on the lava lamps near my bed, put *I Robot* on the turntable (the Alan Parsons Project LP, not the movie) and set the amp to a low volume, pulled down the bedding (black top sheet over a scarlet-red bottom sheet—my way of paying lip service to what the upholstery of coffins looked like in the old movies), and gratefully laid my head on the pillow. I was asleep in moments.

Chapter 36
The Truth Will Out

The X-Flies was, of course, pure fiction. As many have observed, however, fiction is often rooted in fact. Thus it was that an actual department in the Washington DC office of the CDC (Center for Disease Control) was tasked with researching certain, highly classified matters. It was their agents who, having received samples from a swab taken from a particular date-rape victim, had gone in, waved their badges and ID's around, and confiscated all the genetic material and forced anyone with and knowledge of anything related to sign non-disclosure agreements. It's not as though this was an uncommon practice nowadays; after all, in the aftermath of the Pulse nightclub shooting in Florida, hospital workers had been forced to sign such documents relating to medical treatment of the victims (if there actually were any—such repressive actions by government agents caused many to question whether this had been an actual shooting or another bit of theater like the widely questioned Sandy Hook incident). The sample was downright odd, like nothing anyone had ever seen before, which is why it had been forwarded to their lab. Unable to conclude anything, they had set it aside in refrigerated storage.

Now, a couple months later, they had received similar samples from a different agency in a neighboring state, from the bodies of two girls found dumped in an empty coal car. Fearing a possible contagion, they had called in a genetics expert and made inquiries of the officers/agencies who had found the victims in the first place. The first girl had been a Notre Dame student, while the others, along with a male victim who had been discovered with them, had attended nearby Goshen College, both in Indiana. A car belonging to one of them had been found in one of the seedier neighborhoods in Elkhart, while a car belonging to another had been found in a grocery store parking lot in Goshen. Security camera footage had been located, showing both cars in the lot, where the students had met-up, prior to all leaving in the car that later was discovered in Elkhart. Interviews of friends and relatives hadn't turned-up any clues as to where they had gone or who they might have met, but what might have been a dead-end for the local police was a different matter for the CDC.

A request to the NSA had, after some weeks, resulted in a transcript of all of the phone messages they had sent or received during the month leading up to their disappearance. These revealed that each had been in contact with a former Goshen College student named Theresa Hasegawa, who had herself disappeared some months earlier. More importantly, an address and GPS coordinates had been sent, directing them to a rendezvous on the outskirts of Goshen. What really got the small number of people allowed to see the communications going, and had also caught the attention of the NSA agent who had forwarded the transcripts, and the attention of his superior and her superior, was the claim made by the formerly missing person, in text messages to the newly-deceased individuals, that she had, in fact, become a vampire!

Given the odd circumstance and even odder samples, what would normally have been dismissed as adolescent fantasy was suddenly investigated with renewed interest. Specialists were brought in and orders came in from the highest levels of government that local law enforcement was to be kept out-of-the-loop. The scientists were required to sign confidentiality papers upon submission of their findings, but the story was too good to entirely stop the inter-office gossip that was quietly circulating. Were vampires, in fact, real?

Chapter 37
Judgment Day

The days following my betrayal by Theresa had been anything but pleasant. I was nervous... frightened, actually...that the police might come around asking questions. Even worse, they might want to take me in for questioning—during daylight! Ordinarily, I could have fed off three humans for weeks, not taking enough blood to kill them, but I was racing against a silent clock of paranoia that was ticking in the back of my mind. I had sex with the skinny girl as often as possible, while completing the repair and repainting of my 'smoking room' and cleaning up the floor where Theresa had bled-out. I had to paint that floor as well, and also remove the living evidence. The boy went first of course, followed by the heavy-set girl. As I had done before, I broke them in half and packaged them in multiple layers of heavy trash-bags and duct tape.

I would have preferred to do this outside of the presence of the smaller girl (I could have learned her name, but that would have made what I had to do all the more difficult). Hanging from the pipe, hearing me dispose of her friends had reduced her to a terrified, quivering wreck. I say hearing, because I put a blindfold on her to spare her the shock—but it was impossible to hide what I was doing, or for her not to guess what the plastic-wrapped bundles in the corner of the room contained.

Not being entirely heartless (strange as that sounds), I occasionally removed the gag to give her a drink of water. I didn't feed her though, as I didn't want to add to the solid waste problems I had been dealing with. It was as King Robert had alluded to in *Game of Thrones*: when an animal dies, human or otherwise, their muscles relax and they invariably piss and/or shit on themselves. Of course every time I removed the gag, she begged me not to kill her, promised she would never tell anyone, even swore to serve me if I would turn her into a vampire. "I am sorry," I had explained,

You're cute, seem like a really nice person and I would enjoy having you around for sex and stimulating conversation; I recently found I had quite missed both of those things when your friend Theresa was staying with me. However, I allowed her to stay here against my better judgment and things did not end well: she broke the rules and invited you folks to visit—and even told you she'd become a vampire! What do you think would happen if anyone ever found out about me? I don't know if they'd prosecute me for murder, dissect me in a lab, or just march me out into the sunshine to put me in a patrol car. In either event, I would die. Yes, they call us the 'undead', but I quite like my existence, lonely as it is. I have my pets, my art, my music, my books... I know it is no consolation to you, but I wish there were another way, but that's the cold, hard reality of the situation and I have to protect myself.

Her turn came much too soon for either of our liking. I took her down (leaving the handcuffs in place even though she was already weak from blood loss from my having fed on her that morning), fed her some leftover pizza (I'd put the remains of the pizza they had brought in the fridge—it was a little dried-out, but probably tasted wonderful to someone who'd been without food for several days. I had made a Long Island Iced Tea for her, which I encouraged her to drink a large volume of, until she was quite intoxicated. Then made love to her one last time, with only a plastic sheet between us and the cold, cement floor. As part of her efforts to endear herself enough to me that I might consider sparing her, she had become an active (if not exactly believable) participant in the sex. Even now, intoxicated, she clasped her legs around me, urging me deeper into her, moaning in pleasure and saying "yes, yes, yes" and "oh God, oh God" as she gyrated beneath me. She hardly flinched when I stabbed her in the carotid artery with a craft knife, and proceeded to drain her of her life, allowing what I could not finish to drain onto a pile of paper towels I had prepared for the purpose.

As her life ebbed away, I admired again her gentle, youthful curves, enjoyed the fragrance of her hair and, as her heart finally stopped, a single tear traced its way down my cheek. Wiping it away, I went about the unpleasant task of packaging her for disposal, like her erstwhile companions.

This time I was unburdened by a motor vehicle that could have been traced to one of the students, so I placed the burdens in the trunk of one of my older vehicles, having first lined it with additional plastic, just in case anything leaked out, and then parked on country road near a railroad overpass. The first train that came along was nothing but tanker cars for ethanol, similar to the one I had ridden on that fateful night, so I went back and waited, I had better luck the second time: a long line of freight cars followed by some empty coal cars. I laboriously tossed them in, one-at-a-time, then shook out the bag containing the broken bits of their cell phones and their car keys. Their ID's I had already disposed of by burning them and scattering the ashes in the pond. Even though fleeing the scene seemed like the best course of action, I paused for a moment to rest and stretch my back. Why was it that people always seemed to weigh more dead than alive?

I removed my gloves and lit up one of Theresa's remaining cigarettes and slowly made my way home. The dogs needed feeding, Miguel had left my mail and newspapers on the porch and the floor needed cleaning and the chains and handcuffs needed to be oiled and buried, along with the other items in my chest of gold. I left the other contents in it as well, as I had no immediate need of the cash or any additional firearms—I had enough guns and ammunition to have altered the outcome of the battle of Gettysburg if I had a time machine. Okay, maybe not that many, but I had more than I could possibly use in my lifetime, especially as target shooting at night really wasn't an option! I placed an old piece of farm equipment over the spot where I buried the old ammo can (like me, another old relic of a forgotten war) and scattered pine needles and leaves over the fresh dirt to try to hide any evidence of the digging.

With at least an hour left until dawn, I decided to relax. After all, the fresh paint needed to dry before I moved the contents of the room back in, so for the first time in days I had nothing to do. Sipping a glass of fine, old brandy, the entire weight of the last few days came crashing down on me. Without warning I was sobbing: deep, wracking sobs, while the tears streamed down my face. Why had I been cursed like this and why did you hate me so? I asked the starlit sky above me. If there were a God, as I was sure there must be, why had he made me this way? I had never wanted to kill anyone, not even when I was a soldier. The cat, which had joined me on the bench, spared one disgusted glance as I fell to my knees, then jumped down, walking between the dogs on his way to hunt something. The dogs merely lay there, watching me curiously as I bawled out my regret for all the people I had killed, asking forgiveness for a life of evil I had never chosen, but had been thrust upon me. Better that I had died in that field hospital in Russia than have to have endured. This life... unlife... whatever.

I briefly considered just sitting there until the sun rose and ending it all, but my instinctive sense of self-preservation kicked in and I made my way back inside, put the Mozart Requiem on and lay down, exhausted. It wasn't as though this was the first time I had begged God to save me from this cursed affliction. As always, my prayers failed to bring any change or relief. Of course at other times I had cursed God for my condition: with the same result, of course: nothing but silence.

Over the next few days I put the house back in order, got the guns back out of hiding that I had put away after Theresa came to stay, put out some trash including one of the pizza boxes and an empty egg carton to indicate someone was doing human-type things (I kept the other pizza box for future reference) left Miguel a note that I'd returned and that I'd been giving medication that made me very drowsy, so I would prefer to be left alone for the next week or so, and that my "nurse" had taken another job and would not be returning. Of course the first snows would be coming soon so, other than taking care of the farm animals, there was little for him to do and he would spend most of the next several months doing whatever it was he did, probably watching TV and surfing the internet and drinking beer, like everybody else. He didn't even need to feed the dogs. With winter coming on they would be staying in the house with me and only going outside to do their business. Of course the cat did as he pleased.

Weeks went by without anything more eventful than an evening run to the liquor store one night when I needed to restock, along with a brief stop for pet food and some of the human variety just to keep up appearances. Walking from the barn to the house, I had the strange feeling I was being watched. Looking around, I didn't see anything, so I let the dogs out and was relieved when they came back in, apparently not sensing anything out of the ordinary.

That all changed at sometime around 3 a.m. when first Brutus, then the other two dogs suddenly raised their heads and cocked their ears. I didn't hear anything, but of course my hearing wasn't nearly as good as theirs. I quickly slipped on a pair of blue jeans, grabbed my .45 pistol, which I kept with me constantly these days, and went upstairs to the second floor and make a circuit around the darkened house, peering out each window in turn. The road in front of the house appeared quiet and empty and I failed to see anything moving in the yard or the pasture. Still, something was making the dogs nervous, so I went back to the basement, just the old soldier in me taking precautions.

As usual, I had a candle burning (like a cat, I could see very well in low light but not in total darkness) so I flipped the switch which turned on a small, LED light, giving me just a small amount of steady light—just in case. I took the Garand down that I had begun keeping on two hooks above one of the book cases, ever since I had had to dispose of my unwanted guests. I pulled the bolt partway to confirm that there was a round in the chamber and visually confirmed that I had several additional 8-round 'n block' clips on the leather sling, readily available if reloading became necessary. Next, I grabbed the Mossberg 870 shotgun from beneath the bed, and likewise checked to see that it had a round 'in the pipe'. The shotgun was the more powerful of the two and loaded with buckshot containing nine 32-caliber balls, which, if they all hit, would be like hitting a target with 9 pistol bullets at the same time with the resultant trauma that should kill anything smaller than a rhinoceros. The Garand, on the other hand, was loaded with World War 2 vintage black-tip armor-piercing ammunition that would go through about anything short of an armored car.

I was just putting extra magazines for the .45 into my pockets when nearly simultaneous loud crashes indicated both my front and back doors had all been forced open. As the sound of boots came from the upstairs, the dogs charged for the stairs to the kitchen, not barking, all business. Picking the Garand back up, I reached the bottom of the stairs just as the sound of a hail of machine-gun fire and a couple yelps from my faithful hounds erupted overhead. Through the emotional like I shared with them, I knew my companions of many years were lying dead or dying on the kitchen floor. I flipped off the safety on the Garand and took position to the side of the stairway as the old, once-familiar battle-lust came over me. I was trapped like a rat but that really didn't matter to me now—all I wanted was revenge for my canine friends against whoever these trespassers were.

I didn't have long to wait. Seconds later, I heard the sound of booted feet descending the stairs, swiftly yet cautiously. Waiting just long enough for them to start down, creating a choke point for however many there might be behind the point men, I swung around the corner and opened fire.

The men were dressed all in black, wearing ballistic vests and helmets with night vision goggles attached. I shot the first three straight through their body armor, dead center of mass. At point-blank range, the projectiles pierced the steel plates inside their vests, passing through their bodies, and straight out through their back plates. Their armor would have protected them from the 12 gauge or the .45, but was completely incapable of stopping the high-powered, armor-piercing 30.06 ammo I had in the Garand. The three tumbled down the stairs to lie in a heap. The fact they were not alone was soon evident as a small, baseball sized object came clattering down the stairway. GRENADE! I thought and turned and ran for the nearest cover, which turned out to be much too far away.

The flash-bang was designed not to kill, but to incapacitate, and it did its job. I found myself on the floor, head spinning and ears unable to hear anything over a loud ringing, trying to turn around and bring the rifle to bear when a pair of boots came into view, stepping over the bodies at the foot of the stairs through the blur that was preventing me from completely focusing. My hands were sluggish as I brought the heavy, old World War II rifle to bear. Too slow, too slow! As I raised my line of sight I saw another black-suited figure pointing what seemed to be an impossibly large weapon at me, something that looked like a short, fat bazooka! I couldn't hear the report, but clearly he fired the weapon because I had a brief impression of a large projectile that for some reason seemed surrounded by a spider's web and found myself being struck in the head with a hammer-blow (like I really needed anything else to disturb my coordination!) and, when I attempted to rise again, I discovered I could hardly move. After some very long moments, trying to puzzle out my thoughts, I realized I was covered by something... a NET! After some additional moments of confused thought I realize that that strange weapon had fired a net at me and I was now ensnared by it. I never saw what hit me in the head next, probably a boot, but I went down again. I must have again been stunned into unconsciousness because the next thing I knew I was being dragged up the steps with my hands, arms and feet bound and something in my mouth that I later discovered was a ball-gag.

The men who had carried me up the stairs were apparently worn-out from the effort, for I was unceremoniously dumped on the kitchen floor while they stood there, hands on knees, gasping for breath (at least that's what it looked like what they were doing—I still couldn't hear anything but a loud ringing in my ears). It was from this upside-down vantage point that I saw another one of these men (Soldiers? Troopers? Agents? Hired thugs?) come stumbling into my line of sight, bleeding from the face and holding a hand to his eye. I was having trouble focusing—my vision kept blurring—but in moments of clarity I observed four men standing, watching me with clubs in their hands that looking like they were electrified while someone who must have been a medic applied something to a line of four, narrow, parallel scratches that traversed the injured man's face and applied a gauze patch over his eye.

CAESAR!? Had that little furry bastard had tried to claw his eyes out!? My thoughts were coming only slowly, but I suddenly realized that, with the dogs gone, the cat was the only friend I had left in the world and thus the only possible cause of this man's injury, despite how implausible it might be. Had they shot him too? After watching an exchange between the wounded man and someone who was apparently his senior office (although none of them had any rank insignia I could see), I could tell from his body language that he wanted to take his MP-5 and go back into the house, but the officer was ordering him outside. I heaved a small sigh of relief—that meant Caesar much have escaped and the man he'd wounded wanted to go looking for him. "I hope you're okay, little buddy," I thought, "I hope you can make it on your own." It had just occurred to me that I wasn't going to be around to take care of him. In fact, it was unlikely I would ever see him again. I tested my bonds and confirmed that I was securely bound and was no longer capable of offering any resistance. "Game over", I thought, as a wave of regret washed over me. With consciousness no longer as appealing, I allowed myself to slip towards the awaiting darkness, just hoping I would die quickly and get it all over with.

With the officer waving his hands around, presumably giving orders, I was jolted back to semi-wakefulness as I found myself being lifted onto a stretcher. Memories of my days as a stretcher-bearer in World War I came flooding back and for a moment I almost forgot where I was. My vision cleared for a moment, enough for me to see a holstered pistol on someone's belt, just within my reach. My hands were bound in front of me—if I could grasp it I should be able to flick the safety off with my thumb and maybe have a chance to shoot my way free! I reached for it—faster than your average human but still much slower than I normally would have—it was as though I was moving through pea soup—and there was a cracking sound of lightning just behind my ear and the world went dark once more.

The next thing I became aware of was an unfamiliar vibration. I opened my eyes and tried to move my head and almost passed-out again in a jolt of pain—or maybe I did, I am not sure. I tried to assess my situation and remember where I was and what had happened. I was having difficulty remembering, but I knew something was seriously wrong and I needed to shrug off this malaise and get my shit together! Problem was, I could hardly move and I had a terrible headache, and could hardly think. One thing at a time: I opened my eyes and forced my eyes to focus on what was in front of me. I wasn't sure what I was looking at. A small lip of folded metal, painted gray, with a rounded, irregular line of something under the paint that seemed to have been put there to join two pieces of metal where they came together. A weld. That was it. Thoughts came together successfully and confirmed my initial hypothesis: I was lying on a vibrating floor, staring at a weld. Experimentally, I tried moving my arms, then my legs, and discovered I remained securely bound. A brief test moving my hands and fingers confirmed that my hands were now handcuffed behind my back. I felt the beginnings of panic somewhere in the distance where my consciousness was trying to find it's way back to me. What time was it? How long until dawn? A thought came bubbling up to the surface of my consciousness. I must be on a helicopter. But why? Who was taking me and where was I going?

I risked another wave of dizziness by raising my head slightly so I could see above the floor. My vision blurred and cleared again as I attempted, surreptitiously, to take a look around. My eyes slipped in and out of focus while slowly registering some details: first the back of the pilot's seats, then a sliding door with a window mounted in it, then at the men in suits sitting in seats a few feet to my right, armed with what a memory in some distant park of my mind identified as UZI's and an MP-5, plus what my brain finally identified as stun batons. One of them leaned forward and spoke to me. He appeared to be shouting over the noise of the engine, not that it made any difference with my present deafness. I must have been wearing a look of incomprehension, that or he realized I was temporarily deafened by the stun grenade, so he paused and began again, his lips moving slowly enough I was able to understand or at least guess at what he said.

"Hello Mr. Vampire, there are some people who are very anxious to meet you!"

END OF BOOK ONE

About the Author

Ian O'Brien was educated in the UK and USA. The author spent 20 years as a university professor, editor and technical writer in Taiwan and China. Having traveled extensively, he is able to use his extensive knowledge of foreign cultures to add flavor to his writing. His interests are likewise diverse. Long before "participation trophies" were invented, he won awards in archery, riflery, violin & viola performance; played on an undefeated soccer team; and was a National Merit Scholar (yes, a high school nerd, he also played Dungeons and Dragons, among other things). Hobbies in his later years have included: alpine skiing, paragliding and wreck diving. He's climbed the Great Wall (twice), ridden out a tsunami in a small dive boat, been scuba diving with sharks, drove his motorcycle around a locked-down city during the height of a typhoon, and has also published a poem and a cookie recipe.

Always eager for a new challenge, he decided to write a novel even while working two jobs and cycling hundreds of kilometers every month. He plans to write at least two more novels in the series and hopes to retire to Taiwan a decade from how, along with his wife and feral cat, depending on the political situation there in the future.

9 781737 492009